T0157087

FOR THE

Love

— OF —

Jade

Diamond Drake

iUniverse, Inc.
Bloomington

For the Love of Jade

iUniverse books may be ordered through booksellers or by contacting:

iUniverse
1663 Liberty Drive
Bloomington, IN 47403
www.iuniverse.com
1-800-Authors (1-800-288-4677)

Because of the dynamic nature of the Internet, any Web addresses or links contained in
this book may have changed since publication and may no longer be valid. The views
expressed in this work are solely those of the author and do not necessarily reflect the
views of the publisher, and the publisher hereby disclaims any responsibility for them.

Any people depicted in stock imagery provided by Thinkstock are models,
and such images are being used for illustrative purposes only.

Certain stock imagery © Thinkstock.

ISBN: 978-1-4697-4671-5 (sc)
ISBN: 978-1-4697-4672-2 (e)

Printed in the United States of America

iUniverse rev. date: 1/24/2012

For Marviel, Bria, and Kaila. Still the true loves of my life.

Acknowledgments

Once again I'd like to thank my husband of fifteen years, Marviel Thomas. I love you so much and I thank you from the bottom of my heart for all your love and support. Thank you for taking me to my favorite restaurant every week and listening patiently as I described what the characters were up to. Thank you for participating and understanding that, to me, these characters are real. Thanks for being my biggest cheerleader and sacrificing what ever you had to, to see my dreams come true. Thank you for loving me unconditionally.

To my girls, Bria and Kaila, thank you for your excitement and encouragement and for being proud of me no matter whether my accomplishments are big or small. I love you both very much and I appreciate you. I'm proud of you and I love you dearly.

To Marlena Williams, somehow thank you just doesn't seem like enough to express my sincere gratitude. Your input has been invaluable in helping me write the best book I possibly could. I thank you for your honesty and for challenging me to push harder when I wanted to give up. Thank you for loving these characters as much as I do (one in particular) and talking for countless hours about them and what they were going to do next. I love you so much and I'm grateful to call you my best friend. Thank you.

Finally, to all of you who supported me with Imagined Love. Thank you so much for your love and encouragement. I truly appreciate it. And a special thanks goes to my parents, Franklin Campbell and Wanda Brooks-Miller for sharing your memories of our hometown and helping me paint a more vivid picture of it. Thanks for your support.

Chapter
ONE

January 27, 1998

PIERCE WAS STANDING AT the kitchen counter eating the last of his wife's homemade chocolate cake when she walked in and began putting away the leftovers from dinner.

"Look, Jade, if you didn't want me to go to the game tonight all you had to do was say so. You don't have to try to manipulate me into staying here with you."

"*What?*" Jade frowned, as she turned from the refrigerator to face him. "What are you talking about?"

"Don't try to play innocent. You know what you're doing ... strutting up in here looking all hot and sexy like you're trying to seduce me or something!"

"Oh, stop," she laughed, waving her hand at him. Jade didn't find anything hot or sexy about the Snoopy pajamas and robe she'd thrown on after her shower. Though, she could have come in wearing a potato sack and Pierce would've found her attractive. There was no denying Jade was a beautiful Black woman—like beauty queen beautiful, and he was enamored of her. At 5'8" and a perfect size six, she looked more like someone who spent her days walking the runway than at home cooking and cleaning. And her flawless, honey-colored skin and almond shaped hazel eyes made Jade irresistible, most of all to Pierce.

"Alright, dude, you better quit playing," Jade warned when he took her into his arms and planted a soft, sweet kiss on her lips. She all but melted

1

when Pierce kissed her neck and ran his hands around her waist. Jade could never resist him, but he found it amusing when she tried.

Pierce DeJuan Jamison was definitely a pretty boy but his 6'4" muscular frame was all man, and his wife enjoyed him tremendously! The running joke amongst their family and friends was that Pierce and Jade made love whenever and *wherever* the opportunity presented itself. It explained how they'd managed to add two new members to the family in the short amount of time they'd been married.

"Seriously, babe," Jade giggled when Pierce kept kissing her. "The kids are in back. Plus, Landon's on his way over because he needs to talk …"

"Oh here we go. What the hell is he coming over here for this time?" Pierce asked, as the anger he'd feigned just moments earlier suddenly became very real.

"Oh my god, Pierce, don't start," Jade huffed, as she snatched the refrigerator door open and resumed putting the leftovers away. "You treat Landon all stank even though you can never tell me what he's done to deserve it when who you *need* to put in check is your boy!"

"*Who?*" Pierce frowned.

"Marcus! Now *that's* who's disrespectful. He says and does the most inappropriate things but you always laugh it off and say, 'oh, that's just Marcus being Marcus', but if Landon even breathes around me you're ready to fight him! That's ridiculous, Pierce, and it's getting really old."

Before he had the chance to respond, the doorbell rang and Jade hurried out of the kitchen to answer it.

"Hey, baby girl," Landon smiled, looking like he'd just walked off the pages of Ebony Man! "What's up, Pierce, how are you?"

"Hey," he replied, coolly.

"What's wrong with y'all?" Landon asked, as he looked from Pierce back to Jade. He could feel the tension between them and had a sneaky suspicion he was the cause of it--again.

"Hey, Uncle Landon," six-year-old Dane beamed as he came running out of the bedroom with his little sister in tow.

Landon gave him a big hug then lifted eighteen-month-old Pooh into his arms and planted kisses all over her face. Pooh's laughter made Jade smile as she made her way to the girls' bedroom to get her six-month-old daughter who'd just awakened.

"There's my Sugar, Sugar," Landon smiled brightly as the infant nearly bucked out of her mother's arms to get to him. Landon was definitely one of her favorite people and Sugar loved when he came around.

Jade had a huge smile on her face until she looked over at Pierce who was growing more enraged by the moment! For the life of her she couldn't understand why he was still so jealous of Landon. True, he was a very attractive man. At 6'5" with milk chocolate skin and a magnetic smile, Landon was the very definition of tall, dark, and handsome and women adored him. However, all Jade had ever seen him as was her obnoxious, overprotective older brother. And that's all he'd ever behaved as.

"Are you hungry, Landon? I can heat you up a plate if you want," Jade offered.

"Shoot, yeah, you know I'm always down for some of your cooking," Landon said then followed her to the kitchen.

While she tended to Landon, Pierce got the kids bathed and put into pajamas. Once they were settled, he sat next to Jade at the table to find out what was so important that Landon had to come rushing over.

"Before I start," Landon stated after he'd taken the last bite of the rib roast dinner Jade had prepared, "I just want to ask you both to keep an open mind. Just hear me out, okay?"

Pierce and Jade passed a look between them wondering what he was going to say.

"Well, as you both know these past few years haven't exactly been great for me. After my divorce and once Jade and I decided to close up the wedding planning business I didn't really have a clue what to do with myself. There I was alone in that big house without a career or a wife or any kind of future. And in a weird way I had started getting used to my humdrum life. But then when we almost lost you," Landon trailed off. He didn't want to get emotional and took a moment to compose himself. "Anyway, I was cleaning out your old office thinking I would turn it into a home gym or something when I came across our next business venture. I knew I would need to go back to school, so that's what I did. I just finished my last course a few weeks ago."

"So why did that need to be a secret?" Jade frowned.

"Well, I thought if you knew what I was going for you might try to talk me out of it."

Pierce and Jade passed another look to each other then stared at Landon waiting for him to explain.

He took a deep breath. "I went back to school to become a literary agent."

"Oookay," Jade said still not getting why that needed to be a big secret.

"See, the thing I found when I was cleaning out your office was that Halloween story you wrote for Dane's class a few years ago and it got me to thinking."

Pierce was seething! He knew exactly what Landon was thinking and he didn't like it one bit.

"Do you remember Desiree? We did her wedding in San Diego at the Hyatt."

"Yeah I remember Desiree. What about her?"

"Of course you do because she was crazy, but if you'll recall, her fiancé worked at a publishing house in L.A. So, I flew down there to meet him. And I read him your story. And he *loved* it, baby girl! Aw, man, you should've heard him. He went crazy talking about all the ways they could market it and how they could ..."

"So wait a minute," Jade said shaking her head. "You gave Dexter my story?"

"I *read* it to him. But even if I had given it to him it wouldn't have mattered. Your story is copyrighted."

"Since when?"

"Since I had it copyrighted like six months ago," Landon said hoping she wasn't too angry with him.

"How you just gone walk up in here ..." Pierce began until Jade gently touched his arm.

"We said we'd hear him out, okay? Please," she pled, hoping Pierce wouldn't lash out at Landon like she knew he wanted to. "So you went to school to become an agent. You had my story copyrighted. Then you took it to a publishing house for Dexter to read. Now what?"

"Well, after Dexter finished raving about it he told me how much it would be for him to take on the project. So I started thinking why should we hand over all that cash to him when we could keep it for ourselves, if *we* publish and market the book."

Pierce was furious! How arrogant and presumptuous of Landon to decide on his own what he and Jade were going to do. Though, the worst part was that Pierce knew she would jump on board with whatever plan the man had devised.

"So exactly how are we supposed to publish and market the book?" Jade asked, growing more intrigued.

"I found a reputable and affordable publisher that would print the books for us and you know I'll sell the *crap* out of those bad boys! And the best thing about it is that you've already done the hard part. Shoot, baby girl, you sitting on a goldmine with all those stories you've written for the kids. All we'd have to do is get them copyrighted and then it's on. So what do y'all think?" Landon asked, excitedly.

"It sounds good to me. What do you think, babe?" Jade asked Pierce with a sparkle in her eyes and a huge smile on her face, despite the scowl on his.

"Well, maybe y'all can talk about it and get back to me," Landon said. He knew Pierce was having a hard time with the idea, although he wasn't sure why. "But just think about it, what do you have to lose? I'll put up the money to get the books published. And who can market you better than me, baby girl? I've known you since you were ten years old. And you already know we make a great team from how successful our wedding planning business was. This could be a great opportunity for us."

"Ooh, what about Laila J.?"

"What?" Pierce and Landon frowned.

"For a pen name," Jade smiled.

"No, there will be no pen names," Landon replied. "In fact, I was thinking it might be a good idea for you to use your maiden name. That way we can hit up all our former clients who told us to call them if there was ever anything they could do for us."

"Humph. You still trying to get rid of me, huh?" Pierce asked, as he squinted at Landon.

"Come on, brother, you know it's not like that. You're a businessman yourself so you know what I'm saying makes sense. People last remember Jade as Caldwell. Jade Jamison and Laila J. are virtually the same nightmare from a marketing standpoint. Don't you see that?" Landon frowned at him.

"Whatever," Pierce mumbled, knowing full well he had a point.

After a few awkward moments of silence Landon asked them to give it some thought then he left.

"So what do you think, babe?"

"Well, I can see you're all fired up about it. You already got a pen name and everything so I don't think it really matters what I think."

"I wouldn't be asking if it …"

The doorbell rang again and that time Pierce left the kitchen to answer it. His best friends Marcus Moala and Anthony Davis had arrived to take him to San Jose for the hockey game. Just like Landon had, they noticed the tension between Pierce and Jade immediately.

"Alright, don't make me bring down the law up in here. Now that I'm all buffed and everything I'll put these guns on y'all if need be," Tony said, as he attempted to make a muscle.

Jade laughed so hard that she nearly choked! Even in his oversized San Jose Sharks sweatshirt she could still see how incredibly skinny Tony was. According to Pierce and Marcus, he'd been that way since the three of them met in first grade. No matter how much he ate or worked out he could never add any bulk to his 6'1", 155 pound frame. The fact that his two best friends grew up to be big jocks only made it worse for Tony. He always seemed like the lanky little brother compared to them. And it didn't help that Pierce and Marcus had always jumped in to protect him from getting beat up in school.

In junior high, when it became cool to have a group name, the three of them started calling themselves The Clique. Unfortunately some of their meaner classmates had another name for them, The Half Breeds, since all of them were bi-racial. Each had a Black father but Marcus's mother was Tongan, Tony's White, and Pierce's Puerto Rican. Though, it was Tony who was most sensitive to the teasing and he would talk himself into fights that Marcus and Pierce had to get him out of.

"*I'll* bring down the law," Marcus said, as he flexed his massive, tattooed arms. At 6'6" and 300 pounds with hoop earrings in both ears and a cigarette always wedged behind his ear, he looked menacing and unapproachable. However, Marcus was cute and charming enough to have women tripping over themselves to get to him. "Now let's roll out, dawgs. I'm ready to see these hockey players do some damage."

Pierce told Jade he loved her before caressing her face and kissing her goodbye. Then he put Marcus in a playful headlock when he tried to kiss her too!

"My fault, dude, I thought she was kissing all of us night, night," Marcus teased.

Jade shot Pierce a look and he understood that that was a perfect example of what she was saying earlier. If Landon had tried to put his lips on her Pierce's headlock would not have been playful.

After Jade read stories to the kids and put them down for the night, she sat on her bed wondering what to do about publishing the book. She was impressed by all the work Landon had done and felt excited to see what could come from it. Though, she couldn't imagine doing something her husband was against. And then there was the agreement to consider. Before they were even married Pierce and Jade decided that when they had kids of their own, she would stay home with the baby and take care of their home. Pooh came a little earlier than either of them was planning but as agreed, Jade gave up her business to be at home. Sugar, just as unexpectedly, came soon after. And as much as Jade loved being a wife and mother there was a part of her that missed having a career. What Landon was proposing would give her the chance to have a small piece of her life that didn't revolve around Pierce and the kids-- and she wanted that.

"Ugh," Jade moaned, trying desperately to get her mother's voice out of her head. Every chance Willa got she warned her daughter not to be completely dependant upon a man. And it was nothing personal against Pierce. Willa adored him and believed he truly loved Jade. She just knew love didn't always last and didn't want her daughter to go through what she'd gone through with Miles. When they divorced, Willa had nothing and struggled to care for herself and Jade. It was that experience and others like it that made her decide to keep a bank account her husband Daniel Wade knew nothing about—just in case he decided being married to her was no longer what he wanted.

Pierce returned at eleven thirty to find Jade waiting in bed to talk to him.

"Did you have a good time?" she asked.

"No," Pierce replied, as he changed into his pajamas. "You know I can't stand when you're mad at me."

Jade smiled when he gave her his best puppy dog eyes. Then Pierce climbed in bed and wrapped his arms around her waist as he laid his head on her chest.

"I'm sorry for overreacting earlier," he said, as Jade ran her fingers through his silky jet black hair. "If there's one thing I know about you it's that you're a woman of your word. So I shouldn't have assumed you'd toss our family to the side to go back to work with Landon. I'm sorry."

Jade was stunned. She assumed having time to think about it would make Pierce agreeable to the idea when he clearly thought having time to think would make her turn down the opportunity.

"What's wrong?" Pierce asked once he looked up and saw the expression on her face. "You were seriously thinking about doing it?" he frowned.

"Well, yeah … I mean, I thought it was something we could at least discuss. It's not like I'm putting the kids in daycare to work full-time. It would be more like a hobby."

Pierce sat up and let out a deep breath before he faced Jade. "Well, here's something else I know about you. You don't do anything half way. You're either all in or all out. So telling me that publishing this book will be a hobby isn't gonna fly, Jade. In order for the book to do well, which I'm guessing you and Landon would want, you'd have to go on tours and do events and really dedicate time and energy to it. So while you're off doing all of that, what happens to me and the kids?"

"Wow," Jade said, as she fluffed her pillow then lay down. "Wow."

"So the conversation is over now?"

"There doesn't seem to be much to discuss. We made an agreement and you're holding me to it."

"Aw, come on, babe, don't be like that," Pierce whined when she pulled the covers up around her neck.

"Goodnight."

"So it's like that? I don't even get a kiss?"

Jade sat up and kissed him way more passionately than he was expecting.

"That was *nice*. Can I get another one of those?"

"Of course you can, Mr. Jamison. That's part of the agreement," Jade sneered then lay back down.

"Wow," Pierce uttered. "So it's like that, huh?"

Jade didn't answer. She was trying desperately to silence the sound of her mother's warnings.

Chapter TWO

THE NEXT EVENING PIERCE returned home to his usual greeting. Dane and Pooh hugged and kissed him before he picked Sugar up from the playpen to smoother her with kisses. Then he made his way into the kitchen to greet his beautiful wife.

Pierce stood behind Jade and wrapped his arm around her waist. "Oooh, you smell *so* good, he said, planting a kiss on her neck. Sugar smiled as if she understood what was going on. "We'll have to put the kids down early tonight."

"Yes sir," she said then called out for Dane and Pooh to wash their hands for dinner.

"Yes sir?" Pierce asked, as he cocked his head and looked at Jade strangely. She smiled at him but he didn't get the sense she was kidding. Before he could inquire further, Dane and Pooh came trotting into the kitchen and took their seats at the table. Pierce put Sugar in her high chair and helped Pooh adjust her booster seat. During dinner Jade interacted and laughed with the kids but didn't have much to say to Pierce.

"So what's the occasion, babe?" he asked, once Dane took his sisters to the den. She'd cooked one of his favorite meals and was dressed up a little more than usual.

"What do you mean?" Jade frowned. "I'm just trying to do a good job. Apparently cooking, cleaning, and taking care of you is all I'm good for so I want to make sure I'm doing it to the best of my ability. I wouldn't want to go back on our agreement," Jade commented, as she removed his plate from the table and headed for the sink.

"Hey, hey, come here," Pierce said, as he grabbed Jade and pulled her into his lap. He took the plate out of her hand and sat it back on the table. "Why you doing me like this, Jade? Come on, babe, just talk to me," he said, staring at her with those intense eyes. "I'm assuming this is about you publishing the book with Landon. So tell me why I'm wrong for wanting to stick to what we decided as a couple. Why is that wrong?"

Jade stared at Pierce momentarily. "I don't think you'd be responding this way if anyone other than Landon had come up with this plan."

"What?"

"When Dane's preschool teacher tried to convince me to publish my stories you were all for it. And I truly believe if one of your sisters, or Marcus, or *anybody* besides Landon had come up with this you'd be behind me a hundred percent. But you've made yourself hate him so much that you'll do anything to keep us apart, even hurt me. And I swear I don't understand it, Pierce. Landon's a good guy and if you'd ever take the time to get to know him you'd see that."

"So you honestly don't see anything wrong with this dude going to school and basing his whole career around you without even bothering to ask you?"

"To be honest, it did annoy me a little at first but I know why Landon did it that way. He knows me, babe, and he was right when he said I would've tried to talk him out of it. But Landon has done all the things I would have been fearful about so I don't think there's a reason not to at least try. If it doesn't work then it doesn't work but at least we would've tried it. But you've already got your mind made up so ..." Jade said in response to the look on Pierce's face.

She got up to take his plate to the sink. Then she went to get the kids bathed and spent time reading and playing with them before bedtime. Pierce joined them but his mind was on what Jade had said to him. He wanted to refute her statement but he knew there was some truth to it.

"Babe, can we talk?" Pierce asked, as he lay beside her in their enormous bed. "First of all, let me just say that I do *not* think all you're good for is cooking and taking care of me. You're a talented woman who could do whatever you wanted. I just like things the way they are," he admitted. "I like coming home to a happy family and a wonderful meal everyday. You make me feel like a king, babe, and I don't want that to change. But I love you and all I want is for you to be happy. So if publishing the book will do that then *I'll* put up the money to get you started. You're my wife and I'll get you whatever you want. I just need some ground rules to be established. I don't want our lives to be turned upside down because of this. And I'd also appreciate a schedule so everybody knows which days or hours will be spent towards the book. I don't want Landon dropping by at all times of the day or night. And I don't want him here when I get home from work. Is that cool?"

"Yeah, that's cool," Jade smiled. She knew Pierce loved her and was putting his personal feelings aside to please her. "Thank you."

"And don't worry. You can be my Laila J.," he smiled and planted a kiss on her lips. "So are you gonna stop being mad at me now? You know I can't take it," Pierce said, as he rubbed his warm hand up her thigh. "Ooh, I've never wanted to be a pair of panties so bad in my life," he said once he got a glimpse of Jade's black lace panties.

"You say some crazy stuff sometimes, you know that?" she burst out laughing.

Not surprising, they made love. The only things that ever seemed to stop them were Jade's painful periods which they called The Menace and Sugar. Even being angry wasn't enough to keep them from being all over each other as was the case last night. Jade used to think it was ridiculous for couples to be furious with each other and still have sex. Then Pierce got his hands on her and she finally understood how that could happen.

They spent hours making up. Then after a quick shower, Pierce and Jade cuddled up in bed together where she fell asleep in his arms. Unfortunately sleep didn't find Pierce so easily. He couldn't get rid of the nagging feeling that he'd just made a huge mistake. If there was one thing Pierce was sure of it was that Landon was in love with Jade. And he couldn't help wondering what kind of fool would give the man more access to the very thing he desired!

The next morning, after dropping Dane off at school, Jade and her girls stopped by Landon's house. She was trying to think of a delicate way to tell him about her conversation with Pierce. No matter how she put it Jade knew Landon would have a fit. And there was a part of her that couldn't blame him.

They'd been close for nearly seventeen years and Jade hated feeling like she had to exclude Landon from her life because of Pierce's unwarranted suspicions. It wasn't all that surprising, though, since every boyfriend she'd had was jealous of Landon. He cared deeply for her and Jade often felt that men confused his brotherly love for something else.

None of them, including Pierce, knew about the abusive upbringing Landon endured. His mother beat, belittled, and sometimes even starved him. When Landon met Willa and Jade they were like angels to him and he attached himself to them very quickly. They were the only real family he had so it was only natural for Landon to want to be close to them, particularly Jade.

"So are we gonna publish this book or what?" Landon asked, as he sat cuddled on the couch with Pooh and Sugar.

"Yes," Jade smiled. "I'm so excited!"

Landon filled her in on all the details of getting the book published and his plan for marketing it. He also told her about the people he'd been in contact with to set up book signings and other promotional events.

"I chose the picture I thought looked best for the cover and posters but you can choose another one if you'd prefer ... what's wrong, baby girl? Why do you look upset?"

"Oh, nothing's wrong. I was just thinking it probably would be a good idea to come up with a schedule for us to work by. If we have certain days or hours that we work then I can plan my week around it, you know?"

Landon just stared at her. "And you came up with that all by yourself, huh?" The look on her face was answer enough. "So what was the deal, you can publish the book as long as I'm not around too much? I've gotta be on a *schedule* now to come over?" Landon snapped. "This jealous husband act is getting old, Jade! I mean what does Pierce think I'm gonna do anyway? I've been with you since you were a little girl. We've worked together, *lived* together, so if I wanted to ... "

Landon stopped when he saw the pitiful look on Jade's face. She looked close to tears and he couldn't take it. So he gave in and helped her devise a schedule. Landon had no intention of following it but to keep the peace he played along. He also had no intention of letting Pierce put up the money to get the books published. His pride wouldn't let him. So Jade called Pierce at the Quik Stop he owned to suggest they each put up half the money needed. Neither wanted to back down but to appease her, they both agreed.

"Oooh, y'all driving me *crazy*," Jade said before gathering the girls to go home.

Later that evening, Jade was in the kitchen getting ready to cook dinner when the doorbell rang. Dane and Pooh instantly came running from his room to see who was at the door. As Jade made her way across the living room she peeked at Sugar who was in her playpen perfectly content playing with her feet.

"Who is it?"

"It's your fairy godparents," Alejandra and Roland replied.

"What in the world?" Jade asked, allowing her sister-in-law and brother-in-law inside. "What are you two doing here?"

"Your man sent us over here to help you get ready for your anniversary dinner," Alejandra, whose nickname was Hawn, said as she handed Jade a garment bag.

Their anniversary wasn't until next Thursday. And they agreed not to do anything big on the actual day since they were going to Vegas next weekend to celebrate.

"Things change, Chicka," Hawn said after Jade reminded her of those things. "Now come on so I can help you get ready. Roland is gonna take care of dinner while I pack your overnight bag."

"What?" Jade frowned.

"Me and Roland are staying with the kids so you and Juan can get your freak on at the spot where he taking you. It's pretty too. Me and Eva decorated it earlier. That's where I was when you called. But anyway don't worry about the kids because we got it all under control. I'll help Dane with his homework tonight and take him to school in the morning. And the girls will chill with me all day because I'm sure you gone need time to recuperate from the festivities we know will be taking place tonight. So let's get moving, Chicka. Juan will be here in about an hour."

Jade couldn't believe her husband and his sisters had fooled her but she was excited all the same. She hurried to shower and dabbed herself with Skin Musk Oil. It was a perfume she'd been wearing since she was a teenager and it always got Pierce a little hot and bothered. He said it was the most sensual thing he'd ever smelled.

"Alejandra, what's wrong with you?" Jade fussed when she saw tears in the woman's eyes. "Don't start that junk, girl, I just put this mascara on."

"I'm sorry, Chicka. You just look *so* beautiful. I feel like I'm helping you get ready for your wedding," Hawn said, dabbing at her eyes. "I'm just glad you okay. When that doctor said you would die I couldn't bear it and ..."

"I'm okay, Alejandra. I'm as good as new, okay?" she said, hugging her sister-in-law tight. Five months ago Jade had been in the hospital and her family and friends feared the pancreatitis that nearly killed her would return and take her from them. "I'm all better. So stop being all dramatic and help me finish getting ready." A few minutes later Hawn started crying again. "What's wrong with you now? Look, girl, stop this mess before I have to beat you!"

"Well, if your ass hadn't ran off and eloped I wouldn't be going through this every anniversary!"

"Shut up," Jade laughed as they both cleaned their tear-streaked faces. "This dress is *amazing*. Thank you so much, Alejandra," Jade said, as she stared at herself in the floor length mirror. The gold necklace and four inch heels went perfectly with the strapless chocolate and gold dress Hawn had designed.

"Chicka, why you always gotta say my whole name? You sound like Mama or my siblings when they pissed off at me," Hawn laughed, as she smoothed a flyaway strand of hair on Jade's romantic up do. "Just let me hear you say

Hawn one time. Come on, Chicka, say ... ooh, it sounds like your man is here."

Jade rushed out of the bedroom to greet her husband. Whenever Pierce took her out on special dates he rang the doorbell instead of coming in through the garage.

"You look beautiful, Mommy," Dane said.

Pooh smiled and clapped like she did for everything.

"Thank you, sweetheart."

Hawn took Sugar to the back for a diaper change and Dane and Pooh went to the kitchen to see what Roland was cooking. All Jade saw when she opened the front door was the biggest arrangement of yellow roses she'd ever seen in her life! Pierce slowly lowered them so he could get a good look at his wife.

"Wow!" They both said.

"Pierce DeJuan Jamison, you look *incredible*," Jade cooed, as that magical smile of his melted her heart.

No one could tell her he wasn't the finest man in the world! His smooth caramel skin, jet black hair and neatly trimmed goatee still made Jade swoon. Though, it was his intense eyes, the ones so dark they almost looked black that got Pierce whatever he wanted from her.

She was attracted to him no matter what he was wearing but the chocolate brown suit he had on made Pierce even more desirable. The ivory silk shirt and brown tie with hints of gold in the design made it obvious Hawn had made his outfit too.

"Umm, you are *so* fine," she purred. "How did I ever get so lucky?"

"Girl, please, I'm the lucky one," Pierce smiled before giving his wife of nearly two years a kiss. "Oooh, you smell delicious. We might not make it to dinner," he said then kissed her again. "Shoot, let me stop before I get in trouble. Alright, let me see you. Turn around ... oh yeah, that's *nice*. Look at that booty," he moaned, admiring Jade in her curve hugging dress.

Pierce came inside to put Jade's flowers on the dining room table and kiss his kids and sister goodnight. Roland took a few pictures of them then Pierce pulled a beautiful fur coat Jade had never seen before out of the closet. The winters of Union City, California were usually rainy but thankfully that night was dry and crisp. It was forty-five degrees and the perfect time for Mrs. Jamison to sport her new coat.

Jade grabbed her gold clutch and made sure there were plenty of Hawn's business cards inside to hand out to anyone who asked about what she was wearing. It was something Jade did often to send customers to Hawn's and her other sister-n-law Tamika's boutique. The sisters recognized just how many clients Jade brought to the store and dressed her as often as she'd let them.

They told her often that she was the best advertisement they could ask for but in Jade's opinion, Pierce's five older sisters were the most naturally gorgeous women she'd ever met and Jade knew they brought in *way* more business than she did.

During the twenty minute drive to San Jose all The Jamisons did was laugh. Jade had a great sense of humor and kept Pierce laughing everyday. Her friends often said it wasn't so much what Jade said as it was the way she said it that they all found hilarious.

Pierce and Jade devoured their delicious steak and lobster meals and enjoyed the ambience of the restaurant Marcus had recommended. More than anything, they enjoyed each other's company.

"Thank you so much, babe. This was wonderful," Jade smiled sweetly, as she reached across the table for two to squeeze Pierce's hand. "I love you so much."

Pierce planted a kiss on Jade's hand then caressed it in both of his. His eyes began to water as he stared lovingly at her. "You're such a beautiful woman, Jade, and I'm *so* in love with you. I can't believe how fortunate I am to have you," he smiled and melted her heart. "I'm the happiest I've ever been and I want to spend the rest of my life showing you my gratitude for making me that way," Pierce said, as he reached into his coat pocket and pulled out a long, black velvet box.

"Pierce," Jade cooed with her sensual sounding voice. "We promised we weren't exchanging gifts this time."

"You should've known better than that. I love showering you with beautiful things," he said, lifting the lid of the box. "It's not like you ever buy anything for yourself so I *have* to do it." Pierce removed the gold charm bracelet and put it in Jade's hands. "Do you like it?"

"Oh, this is incredible, babe. It's got all my babies on it," she began to cry.

The first charm was of a knight in shining armor which obviously represented Pierce. Then there were three gold circular charms with each of their kids' birthstone in the middle and their dates of birth inscribed on the back.

"We'll go back to the jeweler so you can choose the rest of the charms you want. And we're going back, so don't try to come up with some reason that we shouldn't buy them. You hear me?"

Jade smiled at him sweetly. "Yes, I hear you. Thank you so much, babe. This is beautiful," she said as he put it on her wrist. "I just wish I had something special for you. Oh my, what do we have here?" Jade asked, as she removed a little white box from her clutch. "I wonder what this is."

"Why you so hard headed, girl?" Pierce laughed then opened the box. He laughed even harder once he saw what was inside. "This is almost the best gift you could've given me. Thank you."

"It's *almost* the best gift?"

"Well, I'm gonna get that one once we get back to our honeymoon suite," Pierce said, giving her that sly grin she adored. "But this is amazing, babe. I can't believe you remembered this."

When they were dating, Pierce told her about his, Marcus's, and Tony's obsession with dog tags. When the three of them were in high school they thought tags were the coolest things and even considered joining the Army just to get an official pair! Pierce removed the set of silver dog tags and read the back of both pieces. One read "Pierce D. Jamison" and the other read "Property of Jade E. Jamison". That tickled him and he laughed loudly.

"I *am* yours, baby … all and only," he said.

"Umm huh, we'll see back at the hotel. But right now I need to go clean this mascara off my face. Between you and your sister I can't keep it on my eyes."

"Well, we can go now if you want. I've got dessert for you back at the suite."

"I bet you do," Jade smiled, as Pierce escorted her out of the restaurant. Neither of them had a clue the drama they were about to stumble upon.

Chapter

THREE

ON SATURDAY, JANUARY 31ST, like she did every morning before a big party, Jade awoke wondering what on earth she was thinking to have Dane's in their home. Every year she swore she would have the kids' parties somewhere else. And every year she ended up doing it at home because it seemed most convenient. That was until their residence was swarming with kids running, screaming, and spilling things all over the place. No matter how hard Jade tried, it was impossible to keep everyone contained in the area she'd designated for the party. More than anything, though, she wanted their guests to be comfortable. And Jade realized there was no need for them to be piled on top of each other when there was more than enough space in their home for everyone to spread out.

Shortly after they learned Jade was pregnant, she and Pierce found and fell in love with the five-bedroom, three bath house at 32576 Monterey Court. Before they moved in, however, some major renovations were made. One of the bedrooms was enlarged and transformed into Pierce's "man cave". A sunroom was built and a wall knocked out to give Jade the dining room she'd always dreamed of having. She also wanted a nice, big kitchen since she'd be spending a great deal of time in it. And it was important to Pierce and Jade to have a great living space and den area where their family and guests could be comfortable and at ease. Neither of them wanted a living room that no one could set foot in because it was so fancy and unapproachable.

The backyard was Pierce's domain and he made sure his kids had a nice, safe place to play. He, his father Jackie, stepfather Miguel, Marcus, and Roland set up a playground equipped with a swing set, sliding board, monkey bars, and a big tubular structure for them to climb through. They also built a tree house similar to the one Pierce and his sisters had growing up. The other side of the backyard was considered the grown ups' area. Pierce had the patio and barbecue grill set up across from the 16'x32' rectangle pool. His and Jade's place was definitely the party house and they enjoyed entertaining their family and friends. Sometimes it just got a little overwhelming.

Jade was still in the process of wondering why she hadn't just rented a place for Dane's seventh birthday party when she walked into the sunroom. It looked great and she knew the expression on Dane's face when he came in and saw everything would totally be worth a few hours of stress. Jade was just hoping, for once, she didn't have to be stressed out *before* the party started. No such luck.

"Look, can you take them somewhere for a few hours so I can finish what I need to do?"

Jade said that as if Pooh and Sugar were getting on her nerves when it was actually Pierce! She didn't know what it was about those moments, when she had a million things to do, that made him want to aggravate her. He always did, though. Pierce thought it was hilarious to move things around and watch Jade come unglued putting them back or to constantly keep lifting the lids on her pots and opening the oven when he knew that drove her nuts. Each time Jade swore she was going to ignore Pierce and not give him the satisfaction of seeing her upset. It never worked out that way, though.

"I'm gonna knock you unconscious if you don't get out of here! I don't know why you always do this mess when you see I'm busy! You play too damn much," Jade snapped.

"Why so violent, Mrs. Jamison?" Pierce teased, as he tried to kiss her.

"Gone somewhere, Pierce," she groaned, attempting to push him away. He didn't budge. "Move!"

"Oooh, you so sexy when you mad," he moaned and lifted her up on the counter. Pierce planted kisses on her neck and started tugging at her robe. "You still mad?"

"*Yeah*," she lied.

"Get down!" Pooh demanded after she climbed out of the playpen with Sugar.

Jade burst out laughing. Pooh was mimicking the way her mother sounded when she told Dane to get down off the counter. He was notorious for climbing up on it to get his dad's favorite Archway lemon cookies from the cabinet.

"Who you talking to, little girl? You not the boss of me," Pierce laughed, as he helped Jade down. Then he went to pick up his daughter and tickled her mercilessly. "Get down," he repeated then tickled her some more.

Thankfully, Pierce got the girls bathed and dressed and took them to his mother's for a while so Jade could finish cooking and putting the finishing touches on everything. She only had an hour of peace before the phone calls started. People who'd waited to the last second to buy Dane a gift called asking what he'd like and others needed to be reminded what time the party started or what their address was even though they'd been at Pierce and Jade's plenty of times.

By eleven o'clock Pierce and the girls were back and his mother Luisa and her husband Miguel came in carrying a ton of gifts. Jade hugged her in-laws then ran off to get dressed. There was no point in even saying anything to them about all the toys and clothes they'd bought. Miguel and Luisa spoiled all their grandkids that way.

At a quarter to twelve there were nearly sixty people in the Jamisons' home. The closet by the front door filled up quickly and Jade had to start taking coats and purses to the guest room closet. Thankfully it wasn't raining or else she would've had a mess on her hands.

Right at noon Dane's biological mother Tina and her husband Myron arrived with the birthday boy. And as Jade had hoped, Dane went *crazy* when he walked into the house! He was so happy and excited that he screamed and jumped in to Jade's arms.

"Thank you *so* much, Mom, this is great!" Dane said, as he held tightly to her. "I feel like I just walked into Captain America's house!"

The crowd erupted into thunderous cheers and applauds to welcome Dane to his party.

"Okay, okay, everyone, may I have your attention please," Jade said to quiet the crowd. "We have a very special guest for a *very* special seven-year-old and I'd like you all to help me welcome him."

Dane's eyes were as wide as saucers in anticipation. The other twenty eight kids were equally eager to see the special visitor. Jade changed the song playing on the stereo to something you'd expect to hear if two gladiators were going to battle. Then she made the big introduction.

"Ladies and gentlemen, boys and girls please put your hands together and give a warm welcome to … *Captain America!*" Jade yelled over the music.

"Oh my *goodness!*" Dane screamed, as he jumped up and down. "This is *so* cool! Look at my dad, guys," he said with pride to some of his cousins and classmates. Then Dane looked up at Jade with the sweetest smile on his face. "Thanks, Mom."

"You're welcome, baby," she said and hugged him. Sometimes it still tickled Jade how much Dane looked like her. He definitely had his father's eyes, but his skin tone and the color and texture of his hair was like hers.

The crowd went nuts! And the kids marveled at Pierce as if he really was a superhero. Pooh was clapping and smiling up at Pierce and Sugar almost leapt out of Landon's arms to get to her dad. He seemed larger than life to the kids as they stared at him in awe. Pierce looked spectacular in the dead-on costume Hawn made for him. Jade couldn't take her eyes off him and was eager to play superhero and damsel in distress! Some of the women couldn't wipe the huge grins off their faces as they were definitely impressed with Captain America.

As expected, Pierce's boys gave him a hard time for being at the party in tights. Once they finished with all the jokes, however, they admitted it was a really cool thing for him to do for his son.

"You buffed bastard," Tony teased, making Marcus and Pierce laugh.

Captain America sat next to Dane in the sunroom as they ate. Then he took pictures with the kids, played a few of the games with them before announcing his departure. Jade was hoping he'd keep it on for the duration of the party but they agreed on just the first hour. Jade was tempted to abandon her hostess duties and go play with Captain America but she was called to the sunroom to get the next game started. She played and danced with the kids until it was time to open gifts. Halfway through, Jade left Tina and Myron to finish while she went to get Dane's cake.

"First, let me just say *damn*!" Jade's best friend Tamara Addison whispered, once she and Jade were alone in the kitchen. "I know you can't wait for our asses to get out of here so you can get your hands on Captain America."

Jade smiled, devilishly. Then they high fived and snickered conspiratorially like two devious little kids. Something completely inappropriate was on the tip of Tamara's tongue when Pierce and some of his relatives came into the kitchen in search of leftovers. The guests had devoured the food and there was barely anything left. It was always that way as Pierce and Jade's family and friends loved her cooking.

"Aw, thank you sweet baby. You brought this for Daddy?" Pierce asked when Pooh handed him a goody bag that she'd swiped from the table. He was planting kisses on his little twin's face when he noticed tears in Jade's eyes. "What's wrong with you?"

"Pooh's just the sweetest little thing. Every time I lay eyes on her I think, look what our love made."

"Awww," Pierce's family cooed.

"That's such a sweet thought, babe. I like that," Pierce said then kissed her.

"Yeah, well from the way Jade was looking at you in that Captain America costume y'all might have a few more little ones running around here," Luisa said.

They all laughed, everyone except Jade. She didn't find the thought of having more kids amusing at all.

"Please don't wish that on me. Three is plenty."

"You say that now because Sugar is still small but you might change your mind when she gets a little older," Luisa persisted.

"That's what I said but Jade wants to fix it so we *never* have kids again," Pierce chimed in. "At first she was talking about me getting snipped but since that's out of the question she wants to get her tubes tied. I'm still not down with that, though."

If looks could kill Pierce would have been dead! Jade could not believe he shared something so personal in front of his overly opinionated family.

"Oh now see, I don't believe in that kind of stuff. You don't alter your body to keep from having the kids God has planned for you to have," Luisa said. "Uh, uh, don't do that, baby. They could go in there and mess up stuff."

The hypocrisy of that statement was not lost on Jade. Fifteen minutes earlier Luisa was enraged to find out her broke daughter Veronica was pregnant with the fifth child "God has planned for you to have" but the idea of her daughter-in-law getting sterilized to prevent unwanted pregnancies was a problem.

"I honestly don't know why this was even brought up," Jade said, cutting her eyes at Pierce, "but it's not anything that needs to be discussed. I'll decide what's best for me to do, so let's just sing happy birthday to Dane and forget about it."

"So you don't give a damn what we have to say about it?" Pierce's second oldest sister Diana instigated. "We can take care of your kids but we can't say anything to you about them, right?"

"*Excuse* me?" Jade snapped.

"It's funny how you don't mind when Mama takes the kids for the weekend so you and Juan can have some time alone. Or when Hawn has them so you can go get your nails done or do lunch with your friends. We can be involved then but as soon as somebody say something your spoiled ass don't wanna hear then we need to mind our own business."

Pierce tried to step in to diffuse the situation but Jade pushed past him to address his belligerent, alcoholic sister. He was silently praying she wouldn't say anything about the discovery they'd made at the hotel after their anniversary dinner. Jade was very sweet and loving but when she got mad she could be cruel and vicious.

"First of all I don't know where all this *we* stuff is coming from since you don't do anything with or for the kids! You're too involved with your own mess of a life to give a damn. So no, your opinion doesn't matter at all as far as I'm concerned," Jade snapped, as she rolled her eyes and started walking towards the refrigerator to get the cake.

Pierce breathed a sigh of relief. Unfortunately, Diana couldn't just leave well enough alone. She kept pushing the issue until Jade let loose on her.

"Oh, so you think the family should be involved in all decisions, huh?" Jade asked, as she slammed the refrigerator shut. "Well, let's talk then, Diana. Let's discuss why you and Drew have been divorced for months and nobody in the family knew anything about it!"

Loud gasps filled the air as all eyes were on Diana.

"What the … is that true?" Hawn asked.

Diana looked close to passing out. Her heart was racing and tears poured down her face. "Yeah," she uttered.

Pierce's family looked one to the other not believing what they'd just heard. They wanted to know why Diana hadn't told them and how long Pierce and Jade had known about it. In true Hawn fashion, she was more concerned with whether Jade had confided in Tamara or not. She was jealous of their relationship and always wanted to be closer to Jade than her best friend was. Pierce put a stop to all the chatter and said they'd discuss things later.

"I guess some things *should* remain private, huh?" Jade sneered at Diana. Then she grabbed the cake and rolled her eyes at Pierce before heading back to the sunroom.

"Looks like you in trouble, boy," his father Jackie teased.

"Yeah, and not the good kind either," Pierce uttered. He sincerely regretted mentioning anything about Jade having her tubes tied.

After the party, Pierce apologized and acknowledged that it was a personal decision his family didn't need to be involved in. However, he still believed it was a mistake for her to do something so drastic.

"I'm sorry you feel that way but I don't want to be pregnant again and I think that's the best way to keep it from happening. You made it known that you wouldn't be getting snipped so it leaves me with the responsibility."

"So does that mean you're gonna do it anyway regardless of how I feel?"

"I want us to be in agreement but it doesn't seem like that's gonna happen. You just don't understand what it's like, Pierce. I love our kids to death and you know that, but it's not easy constantly having to meet their needs all day long."

Jade gave a drawn out list of all the things she has to do on a daily basis and why adding another child to that would be unbearable.

"Damn, Jade, you make it sound like I don't do anything with the kids, like you're doing everything on your own!"

"Come on, Pierce, you know that's not what I'm saying. You're a wonderful, devoted, hands-on father and I appreciate you for that. But who do you think is here day after day taking care of our kids' *every* need while you're at the store or the gym or out with the boys? It's me. And if I'm telling you I don't want the responsibility of not only carrying another child but having to care for it everyday then it shouldn't be an argument. Three kids are enough. We have both a boy and girls so what's the issue? Why do you need more kids?"

"It's not that I need more. And I'm not even saying I want more. I just don't wanna remove the possibility completely. What if three years down the road we decide we want another one?"

"Or what if three days from now my birth control fails again and we end up with another unplanned pregnancy? I just don't want that to worry about every time we have sex. And we have sex a *lot*. So why can't you understand that, Pierce? I don't want to be pregnant ever again."

"I hear you, babe. I do. But I think you might regret doing something so permanent a few years from now. Can we just hold off for a while and then decide?"

"You just don't get what it's really like, Pierce."

"How you figure that when I was a single dad for four years?" he frowned at her.

"So you think caring for three children and a spouse is the same as taking care of one kid?"

"Yeah, for the most part."

Jade couldn't hide her frustration.

"You act like I've never taken care of all three of our kids on my own. Remember your girls-only trip when you and my sisters left us for the weekend? I took care of the kids by myself."

"I basically did everything for you, though, babe. I rearranged the girls' doctor's appointments so you didn't have to deal with how they act after getting shots. I cooked all the meals so all you had to do was take them out the refrigerator and heat them up. All the laundry was done and the kids' clothes were laid out for each day. Everything was taken care of for you, Pierce."

"Wow! So I guess you think I'm some kind of chump that can't take care of my own kids, huh?" he chuckled. "I'll tell you what. Tomorrow we'll switch places. You'll run Quik Stop and I'll run the house."

"Yeah, right," Jade uttered, waving him off.

"I'm serious. For the whole week you'll work at the store from nine to five and I'll be here with the kids. And I'll do everything-- all the errands, cooking, laundry, the whole bit."

"And you're serious?" she asked, skeptically.

"I'm dead serious. Starting tomorrow morning we'll switch. Deal?"

"Wait, I just wanna be clear. You're gonna do all the grocery shopping, bill paying, helping out in Dane's class, and the ..."

"I've got all of it, Jade. You'll see."

"Oookay," she said then shook his outstretched hand. "But make sure at the end of the day when you're ready to collapse because the kids ran you ragged that you turn over and look pretty while you sex me crazy, alright?" Jade laughed, slapping him across his butt.

"Shoot, that's gonna be the best part," he smiled.

Tuesday morning, an hour after she'd left the house, Pierce called Quik Stop begging Jade to come home. She hoped seeing how challenging it was to take care of the kids would be enough to change his mind about the sterilization. Pierce still thought it was a mistake and refused to give his support. Jade was so frustrated that she planned not to have sex with him in protest. It didn't work out, though. She couldn't resist him no matter how hard she tried.

Chapter
FOUR

On Monday, February 9th, after dropping Dane off at school and the girls with Luisa for the day, Jade stopped by Landon's to see what his problem was. He'd left a few angry messages the night before and she was annoyed by it.

"What is your problem, dude?"

"My problem is that I've been out here busting my ass to get this book sold and I feel like you aren't doing your part. Every time I tell you we need to set up book signings or drive down to other cities to get you out there you have some stupid excuse for why you can't go. And I know it's because of Pierce but he needs to get over whatever his problem is and grow the hell up," Landon snapped.

"This isn't a hobby for me, Jade. This is my livelihood. I don't have a cushy little life where somebody else provides everything for me! Oh yeah, that's right just run away like you always do when somebody tries to talk to you," he said when Jade grabbed her purse and headed for the front door. "Baby girl, wait. I'm sorry, okay? I'm just frustrated. I really need your help to make this work. We get way more orders and support when you're present than when you're not. I need you to make some time for this. And I know you can't go everywhere with me but I need you to come to the book fair in L.A. and commit to doing some book signings and appearances. Please, baby girl. I realize Pierce and the kids need you at home but I need you too."

Jade felt so conflicted. She wanted to travel and do the events but she didn't want to rock the boat at home. Pierce had agreed to support the project as long as the interruptions to their daily lives were minimal. And she had agreed to honor that. What Landon was asking would make it necessary for

Jade to get sitters and rearrange her family's entire schedule. And she knew Pierce would have a fit.

"Look, Landon, I've got to go get Tamara right now but we'll figure something out, okay? But you can't be going off on me like that. I'm not the same single girl who built the wedding planning business with you. I'm a married woman with a family and they're my priority. I don't mean that to sound foul but it's how it is. I'm trying to make everybody happy but no matter what I do somebody's mad at me," she said and began to cry.

"Hey, hey, stop that mess," Landon said as he hugged Jade. "We'll figure it out, okay? You don't have to be in here crying. We'll figure it out," he said, hugging her tighter and kissing her cheek.

Jade left to pick Tamara up to do their grocery shopping together. They went to have breakfast first and spent over an hour gossiping about Tamara's in-laws. The two of them finished eating then continued the conversation on their way to Lucky's grocery store.

"Uh, beauty queen, what are you doing?"

Once they arrived at Lucky's Jade climbed in the back of her burgundy '98 Toyota Sienna minivan and lifted the spare tire to retrieve a pouch. It had all of her coupons in it.

"Girl, I have to find creative spots to put these to keep Pierce from throwing them away. You know how much he hates my coupons."

"That's a mess," Tamara laughed.

Pierce's family had always been well off so he didn't know what it meant to use candles because the lights had been shut off or to scrape change from the couch to buy a loaf of bread. Jade did. When her parents divorced and she went to live with her mother, things were tight and they struggled to eat sometimes. And it wasn't much different when Jade moved to California to live with Landon. There were a lot of tough times and she had to find creative ways to stretch what little they had. So being frugal was a part of who Jade was and she couldn't stop just because her husband was embarrassed by it.

Besides, she didn't see the point to paying more for something than was necessary. Pierce claimed she only saved a few pennies with the coupons when Jade actually took hundreds of dollars off their grocery bills by taking advantage of double coupon days or other specials and sales. It was an ongoing fight between them which was why Pierce and Jade rarely went grocery shopping together.

The best friends were still laughing and talking up and down the aisles when Tamara spotted the rep from Lay's Potato Chip Company.

"You oughtta walk over there and slap that hoe in her mouth!" Tamara shouted.

"Girl, shut up," Jade laughed, as she pushed her friend towards the check out line. "Take these coupons and quit starting trouble."

They stopped by Wal-Mart to get household goods then decided to check in on Pierce at work. When Jade pulled her minivan into the parking lot they spotted the Lay's rep getting out of her car and heading inside Quik Stop.

"Now tell me that hoe ain't up to no good," Tamara snapped, as she hopped out of the minivan.

Jade and Tamara walked through the double doors and stopped at the counter where a small line of customers were being waited on.

"Hey, Jade, how you doing? I was stopping by to see if, uh, it's me, Regina. Remember I met you …"

"I know who you are," Jade stated, dryly.

"Oh, well you were standing there looking confused so I thought maybe you didn't remember who I am."

"I'll tell you what I'm confused about," Jade said, as she removed her coat and placed it on top of the newspaper rack. "We just saw you at Lucky's a short while ago in your little gray pantsuit and silk blouse and you looked real professional. But less than an hour later you show up at my husband's store, in the dead of winter, in this micro mini skirt and blouse with your breasts hanging all out. So it makes me wonder what's going through a girl's mind to make her do something like that. And I also wonder if she realizes just how close she is to getting beat down."

Pierce's twenty-two-year-old store manager Tripp's eyes got wide with anticipation as he hurried to get rid of the customers. He couldn't *stand* Regina because he knew what she was up to and was hoping Jade would knock her silly!

"Well, Jade," Regina snickered.

"Mrs. Jamison," Jade corrected her.

"Whatever," she rolled her eyes. "I haven't been questioned about what I wear since I was fifteen years old. That was ten years ago, and I don't answer questions now."

"*Oooh*, girl, hit this hoe!" Tamara shouted, barely able to keep still. Jade had to wedge herself between the two women to keep Tamara from striking Regina. "You just a little too light in the ass to be talking smart, tramp!" she warned the very petite and dainty woman.

"Hey, what's going on in here?" Pierce asked.

He'd been out back taking a delivery and heard Tamara yelling when he walked into the storage room. To everyone's surprise Regina started crying, telling Pierce she didn't understand why Jade and Tamara had attacked her!

"Don't even try it," Tripp spoke out. "Boss, this chick been in here talking mess to your wife until Jade put her in check and now she wanna play the victim!"

"Well, that's easy enough to fix. I'll just have a different rep take my order from now on," Pierce stated.

"No, but, Pierce, please!"

"What are you even doing here, Regina? I'm not due for a re-order for at least another three weeks. So I don't know what kind of game you playing but it's not gonna work here. I'll put in the request for a new rep and you can go about your business."

Stunned and humiliated, Regina apologized to no one in particular and hurried to her car.

"Yeah, you better run," Tamara taunted, as she followed the woman out the door. "You lucky Jade is classy 'cause I woulda beat that ass!"

"And *you,* come here," Pierce snapped before snatching Jade's hand and leading her to the storage room.

"I'm sorry, babe, I didn't mean to cause a scene in the store but she ..."

Pierce grabbed Jade around the waist and backed her against the wall. "I'm so turned on right now I can barely control myself," he groaned, planting kisses on her neck. "I like seeing that territorial side of you. It's sexy as *hell,*" Pierce whispered then kissed her passionately.

"Babe, stop," Jade giggled and pushed his hands away when he started undoing the button on her pants. "We can't do this now," she protested weakly, knowing full well they would. And they did, to each other's complete pleasure.

"Alright now, stay out of trouble," Pierce said, after they'd cleaned up in the teeny tiny bathroom.

"I love trouble when it's with you. Can't you tell?"

They kissed each other goodbye before Pierce walked Jade out to the front of the store where Tamara was patiently waiting behind the counter with Tripp. The package of lemon Archway cookies she devoured helped pass the time.

"I guess Weight Watcher's went out the window, huh?" Jade asked Tamara who'd gone from a size twenty to a size fourteen in her eight months of attending meetings.

"Y'all been back there boning, haven't you?"

"No, now come on," Jade blushed, as she grabbed her coat and pushed Tamara out the door.

"No, huh, then how you get his cologne all over you? Hmm? How'd that happen? You went back there smelling like Skin Musk and then you come out ..."

"Okay, okay, I did it, alright? Now would you *shut up?*" Jade laughed as they climbed back into the minivan.

Tripp stared at Pierce with a huge smile on his face.

"Mind your business, boy," he smirked then walked past his employee to get to his office.

Like clockwork, at 4:45p.m. Pierce was heading to his work truck to go home. Only this time he had a visitor waiting outside the store to talk to him.

"Pierce, I'm *so* sorry. I just had to come back and apologize to you and Jade for the way I behaved. Please, I'm begging you to forgive me and reconsider taking me off the route. I've worked really, really hard at Lay's and something like this could hurt me, Pierce. Please, I promise I'll never be out of line like that again. Just please don't take me off the route," Regina cried.

Feeling sorry for the woman, Pierce decided to keep her on with the understanding that he was a happily married man who wouldn't tolerate his wife being disrespected in any way. Jade wasn't too keen on the idea but she accepted Pierce's explanation that Regina meant absolutely nothing to him and going through the effort of having her removed from the route would imply that she did.

"So we're good, Laila?"

Jade laughed then they spent the rest of the evening listening to their favorite songs and remembering back to when they first met. They had no idea how much of a mistake it would be keeping Regina on the route.

Chapter
————/————
FIVE

IT WAS THE DAY before Valentine's Day and Jade had just finished baking heart shaped cakes that she planned to give as gifts to all of her friends and family. Pooh was still napping but Sugar had awakened ready to eat. Jade prepared her baby's bottle and was sitting on the couch feeding her when she heard the garage door open. Fridays were one of Pierce's busiest days with back to back deliveries and meetings so Jade was surprised he was home. She knew instantly something was wrong the moment he walked in.

"What's the matter, babe?"

"I need to tell you something, Jade," Pierce said, looking close to tears. He sat next to Jade on the couch but had a hard time looking her in the eyes. "I know we have all these big plans to celebrate Valentine's Day tomorrow but I can't go through with it carrying this guilt."

Jade felt like her heart was going to beat right out of her chest! "Why are you guilty?" she asked, barely above a whisper. "What happened?"

Pierce nervously bounced his knee as he clasped and unclasped his hands. "I'm so sorry, Jade. I swear. It's just that one thing led to another and I got caught up in the moment."

Jade repositioned herself to be able to hold Sugar and the bottle with one hand while she wiped away tears with the other. "Tell me what happened."

"Okay," Pierce said then swallowed hard. "I slept with Laila last night," he burst out laughing.

"*Idiot!*" Jade shouted then punched Pierce in his chest! "Why would you do that? It's not funny, Pierce! You got me in here crying thinking you had really done something! *Move*," she yelled when he tried to hug her. Jade's raised voice startled Sugar and she began to cry. "I'm sorry, Sugar, Sugar," Jade cooed, as she rocked her little twin and kissed her cheek. "It's okay. Your daddy's just a jerk," she muttered, wiping the tears still falling down her face. "Stop, Pierce," she said, when he tried to kiss her, "just leave me alone."

"Come on, babe, I'm sorry, okay? I couldn't resist. I've been practicing all morning so I wouldn't laugh," he admitted. "Oh, stop being mad at me, girl. We joke around with each other all the time."

"Not like that, Pierce. That was cruel. And I'm willing to bet money if I'd played a joke using Landon like that you wouldn't have found it funny."

"*Landon?* What the hell does he have to do with anything?" Pierce scowled.

"He's a sensitive subject for you just like being cheated on is for me. It's heartbreaking to be betrayed," Jade whimpered, as more tears poured down her face.

Pierce took Sugar out of Jade's arms and laid her in the playpen. Then he pulled his wife to her feet and held her close to him. He apologized profusely as he squeezed and kissed her.

"It was supposed to be funny because I thought you knew I would *never* hurt you like that, Jade. I have every single thing I've ever dreamed of with you and I'm not ruining that for *nobody*, you hear me? Look at me," he said, lifting her chin. "You're it for me, baby. I don't even notice women like that anymore because I know what I have at home. And there's nothing on this good green earth worth losing you over. I barely made it when you got sick thinking I was gonna lose you forever. So I'm sure as *hell* not gone do no dumb junk like screwing around to end what we have," he said, caressing her face. "I need you to understand me, Jade. I love you, more than anything. And I'd rather be dead than hurt you that way. So I'm sorry for the stupid joke. I definitely wasn't trying to upset you like this. Just please stop crying because you know I can't take it. I'm sorry, okay?" Pierce whispered then planted a soft kiss on her lips. "You forgive me?" Jade nodded at him. "Hmm?"

"*Yes*, Pierce, geez," Jade said.

He hugged and kissed her again then ran out for the meeting he'd made himself late for.

By mid-march Jade's first published children's book, "Who's Baby Is That?" was selling remarkably well. That was due, in huge part, to Landon's tenacity. He spent twelve to fourteen hours a day selling books and researching new places to sell them. He and Jade had gone to L.A. for that book fair and sold all one thousand of the copies they had in his pickup truck. The fact that they always sold twice as much when Jade was present told him a lot of people bought it just because she was beautiful. She laughed him off but when

Landon arranged a book signing in New Park Mall, the line was wrapped around the store with nothing but men! He paid to have poster boards with Jade's picture and the time and date of the event at every entrance to the mall. Landon also ran ads in all three of their local newspapers being sure to include her photo.

"Now you know those dudes didn't have no kids. They just wanted a chance to talk and take a picture with you," Landon said, as he drove Jade home. "So you just keep on smiling, beauty queen, and we'll sell out again."

"What are you my pimp now?"

"Of course not, baby girl, I'm just working with what we have. I mean, let's be real. Your looks get people in the door. And then that sexy voice and laugh captivates them even more. But it's your talent that will keep them coming back. Folks genuinely love this book!"

Landon couldn't count the number of times he'd run into a customer who actually thanked him saying the book was incredibly helpful. A lot of parents didn't know how to deal with bringing a new baby home but Jade's book offered clever ways to deal with sibling rivalry and make all the kids in the family feel special and loved. The fact that it rhymed made it perfect and easy to keep kids interested.

"Here you go, Ms. Writer," Landon said, once he'd pulled in front of Jade's house. "It's your first official check as a published author."

"Are you *serious?*" Jade screamed, unable to believe her eyes. "Is this for real, Landon?"

"Yep! In a month's time we've sold six thousand books at eight dollars a pop," he grinned. "And that doesn't include what we just sold or whatever your husband and in-laws have done. I won't mention that it probably would've been twelve thousand if you'd gone with me to …"

"Yeah, thanks for not mentioning it," Jade rolled her eyes at him.

Landon and Jade had agreed they would split the money fifty-fifty. So they both had checks for eighteen thousand dollars which wasn't a bad return on the seven hundred dollar investment. Because Landon ordered the books in large quantities they were basically paying two dollars per copy to have them made. So that left him and Jade making a six dollar profit. However, Landon knew that same deal would not be in place with Jade's next book as the publisher, Lou Sparks, knew he was getting ripped off. The only reason he even put that eighty percent discount on orders over a thousand books was because he never dreamed Landon would ever order that many. He was just trying to entice him into signing the contract with Buy the Book, Inc. Next time would be different and they both knew it.

"Surprise!" a large crowd shouted when Jade entered Roland and Hawn's three-bedroom, two-bath house.

Jade, who thought she was coming to model Hawn's designs for a new client, was shocked and fought back tears as she looked around and saw the people she loved and cared for most there to support her. Hugs and kisses were in abundance as she made her way through the crowd to thank everyone for being there. Pierce and his sisters had the food catered by her favorite soul food restaurant and it was amazing. Then, as was the case every time they got together, Jade's family and friends wanted to see her dance. They were convinced she would've made it as a professional dancer if she'd chosen to. Jade, however, didn't give it much thought. She just loved to dance.

Landon made a copy of her first check and put it in a picture frame that was being passed around the party.

"Hey, Pierce, you better make sure you keep that jimmy going strong 'cause she ain't gone need you for nothing else making bank like this," Marcus teased.

Pierce had never wanted to hit his friend more than he did at that moment! Instead, he walked away, grateful that only a few people had heard Marcus's ridiculous comment.

During the toasts Pierce didn't say much. He busied himself with the kids rather than be with Jade. It hurt her feelings, but not nearly as much as his so called joke.

"Shoot, I think that's wonderful, baby girl, to be able to make that kind of money doing something you love," Willa said, as she held the framed check. She would talk to her daughter later about stashing some of that cash in a place Pierce was unaware of.

"Yeah, Jade's lucky. We all have to break our backs to see that kind of cash but she throws a few words on a page and folks just *give* her their money," Pierce laughed. He seemed oblivious to the fact that no one else found him amusing, least of all Jade.

"Excuse me," she said before making her way to the bathroom.

"Dumb ass," Tamika muttered then followed Tamara and Hawn to check on Jade.

Pierce saw his wife dabbing at her eyes when she opened the door to answer the women's knock. Jade told them she was okay and would be out soon.

"Jade, baby, it's me, open the door."

"I'll be out in a minute, Pierce," her voice quivered.

"Come on, babe, let me in. Please."

She unlocked the door but didn't open it for him.

Pierce entered the bathroom then pulled Jade through the connecting door which led to Roland and Hawn's master bedroom. "Tell me what's wrong."

Jade tried not to cry but burst into tears anyway. Pierce caressed her trying hard not to start bawling himself.

"From the way your girls were looking at me I'm assuming I'm responsible for this," Pierce said, wiping tears from her face. "I was only kidding, babe."

"I don't believe you were, but it's not just that. You seem so bitter and angry with me and I don't know what I did to make you feel that way. I thought you were proud of me but you act like you resent me," she sobbed.

"I *am* proud of you, Jade. I'm so, so proud. It's just that ..."

Hawn knocked on the door. A few more guests had arrived and it was time to cut the cake. Jade told her she'd be out in a second and went to the bathroom to clean her face. Pierce tried to convince her to stay so they could finish talking but she wanted to get back to the party. He had really hurt Jade's feelings and she wasn't in the mood to hear what he had to say.

"Do I need to change my sheets?" Hawn teased, as she linked arms with Jade and led her back to the party.

"Ugh, Alejandra, no," she whispered. "We didn't have sex in your bed."

"Well, you know y'all prone to stuff like that. Remember last New Year's Eve?" Hawn asked. "Ooh, Jade, baby, I'm about to go to the moon ..." she mimicked her brother.

"Girl, *shut up*," Jade cringed as she nudged her sister-in-law.

Pierce and his drama would just have to wait.

"Jade, I'm sorry, okay?" he said during the ride home.

"We'll talk later," she stated, fully aware that their nosey son was in the backseat listening.

Once the kids were tended to and put down for the night, Pierce joined Jade in their room. She was sitting on the edge of their bed brushing her hair when he took a seat next to her.

"Babe, I'm so sorry. I didn't mean to put a damper on your big night. Are you still mad at me?"

"I'm confused, Pierce. You said you supported me doing this and now you act like you resent me. Why?"

"I don't resent you, Jade. I'm really proud of you," Pierce said then took her hand in his. "The truth is I've been feeling insecure. I never thought of myself as the type of man that would flip out if my woman made more money than me but apparently I am. That's why I was about to buy that stupid location for the second store because I wanted to double my income. I wanted you to know Landon's not the only one hustling for you. But I guess you don't need me to do that. You made forty thousand dollars in a month on just *one* of your stories. And that's incredible, Jade, but it scares the hell out of me. I get confidence from being the main breadwinner. I like knowing that you're counting on me. But if y'all keep pulling down numbers like that it won't be long before you surpass me. Pretty soon you won't need me at all and I'm wondering how long before you won't want me either."

Jade stared at him with her mouth open. "Pierce DeJuan Jamison, are you serious right now? You honestly think I'm with you for your *money*?" she asked, still dumbfounded. "You can't actually believe that check or any amount of money can change how I feel about you. I love you, nut! And not because you pay the mortgage or my car note or shower me with gifts. I appreciate those things and everything else you do. But it's *you* that I'm in love with and not for your money, but for the way you love me and our kids. I love that you're loyal and devoted and you still look at me like I'm the most beautiful woman in the world. I'm the happiest I've ever been because I have you.

"Oh and for the record, Landon's not hustling for *me*, Pierce. This is his livelihood. When he works twelve hour days it's to put food on his own table, not mine. For me the books are just a way to be creative and express myself. I like doing it but I don't *need* it. You hear me? So put all that crazy junk out of your mind, alright?"

"Alright," Pierce said, staring at her with those intense eyes.

"Nope, don't even try it, dude. I know what that look means," Jade laughed.

Unfortunately, The Menace was rearing its ugly head. So Jade cuddled up in bed with Pierce hoping his insecurities were put to rest. Somehow she didn't think so.

Chapter
——/——
SIX

On Monday, March 16th at around 1a.m. Landon loaded the back of his black Ford pick-up with hundreds of books and took off for L.A. He'd made arrangements with a few libraries and independent bookstores to carry "Who's Baby Is That?" and wanted to be there first thing to deliver their copies. There were also a few places that told him no on the phone that Landon felt might be more agreeable in person. He figured all they could do was say no to his face.

It was a little after seven 7a.m. when Landon checked in at the Hilton Hotel. The smell of bacon and fried potatoes enticed him enough to get breakfast at the restaurant right off the lobby. The waitress sat Landon in a booth directly across from three women who seemed to be recovering from a night out on the town. He heard them laughing about some of the men they'd met and how the club scene was tired. Landon wondered if either of them had considered that Sunday might not have been the best night to go clubbing.

"Excuse me, sir, but are you laughing at us? You do know it's rude to eavesdrop on other people's conversations, don't you?" one of the women teased.

"Well, if y'all weren't over there laughing and talking all loud a brother might be able to enjoy his breakfast in peace," Landon laughed.

"Girl, he is *fine*," another of them groaned through gritted teeth. "Now if somebody looking like him had been at the club, I'd still be in that joint," she cackled.

Landon smiled brightly as he got up and approached their booth.

"Lord, have mercy! He got good teeth and he tall too," the woman who'd first spoken to Landon shouted. "Look, y'all might as well just go home 'cause he's got Chaundra's written all over him! Don't you see it?"

"Girl you better learn how to read. It says Victoria's in big, bold letters."

"I think there's room for all three of us!"

"Okay, shut it down, Sharonda! You always gotta take it to some whole other freak level! Sorry, sir, but I don't get down like that," Chaundra said. "You have to excuse my friend here. She's still a little hung over from last night. I'm the designated driver so I probably should take her home before she says something else crazy."

"It's all good," he smiled. "I'm Landon, by the way. Landon Campbell," he said, extending his hand to her.

"Chaundra Lane," she smiled, as they shook hands. "And these are my girls. This is Victoria Billingsley. And this freaky one here is Sharonda Pike."

"It's nice to meet you, ladies."

"Damn, Chaundra, slide over so he can sit down," Victoria scolded.

"Oh shoot, I'm sorry. Have a seat," she said, sliding around closer to Sharonda.

"Sooo, Mr. Landon Campbell, what are you doing at a hotel at this time of the morning?" Victoria inquired.

"Well, I'm a literary agent now so I drove down from the Bay Area to get my sister's books placed in a few bookstores and libraries out here."

"What do you mean you're a literary agent *now?*"

"I used to own my own business but …"

"Oh, lord, he ain't got a steady job! See, I knew you was just too good to be true, Landon Campbell. Come on y'all, let's get out of here."

"Victoria!" Chaundra shrieked.

"It's all right, let her keep jumping to the wrong conclusions. You were the one I came over here to meet," Landon smiled.

"Whatever," Victoria rolled her eyes then got up to leave. "You coming, girl?"

Sharonda slid out of the booth and they both stood there staring at Chaundra. She looked at Landon, up at her friends, then back at Landon.

"No, I'll catch up with you two later. I think I'll stay and have a cup of coffee with Mr. Landon Campbell here," she smiled and did a little wrinkle thing with her nose that turned him on.

Chaundra could hear her friends grumbling as they stomped out of the restaurant and through the lobby. They weren't too thrilled about having to catch a cab but both of them had ditched her plenty of times for a man so Chaundra didn't feel bad not one little bit.

"So what business did you own before you became a literary agent?" she asked, after they'd ordered coffee.

"My sister and I had a wedding planning business but it became necessary to close up shop."

"Hmm, so you used to plan weddings, huh?" Chaundra asked with that "look" on her face.

"Yes," Landon smiled. "And no, I'm not gay."

"I guess you get that a lot," Chaundra laughed. "So are you bi?"

"Girl, what kind of men have *you* been dating? No, I'm not bi-sexual. I'm strictly into women … always have been, always will be," he assured her. "So what about you? Are you into men, women, or both?"

"I only like men, although, I did kiss a girl in college on a dare once. But it was just a little peck on the lips. I swear it's true," Chaundra laughed loudly when he eyed her suspiciously. "I can't believe I just told you that."

Landon laughed too. Then, for the next few hours, he and Chaundra had the easiest conversation either of them had ever experienced. They had so much in common that it almost seemed too good to be true. And yet, Landon was convinced he'd met the woman he was going to marry!

Chaundra Unique Lane was a twenty-eight-year-old professional make up artist. For eight years she'd worked on movie sets, video shoots, as well as celebrity weddings, and red carpet events. She met her former husband, Eric Livingston, at an event where he was the featured piano player. It wasn't a love at first sight thing but through time they grew fond of each other and eventually fell in love.

"So what happened? Why'd you get divorced?"

Chaundra let out a long sigh as she stirred her glass of water with a straw. "Okay, I'm just gonna say it. I'd rather know now if it's a problem before I fall in love and then get left again."

The look on Landon's face was a cross between curiosity and flat out fear.

"The reason my husband and my last boyfriend left me is because I can't have children." Chaundra waited for an adverse reaction but Landon just smiled at her. "And the men that are cool with it usually have about eight kids already and don't want more. Being barren makes me a good catch in their eyes. So is that the reason you're smiling at me instead of flipping out?"

"No, that's not the reason I'm smiling. But I'm wondering if not being able to have kids is something that hurts you. I mean, do you feel like you can't be happy without them?"

"Actually, no it doesn't hurt me. Nobody's ever asked me that before," she smiled. "People automatically assume I'm miserable and willing to do anything to have a baby. But the truth is I was never really that thrilled about being a mother. So when I found out I wasn't able to conceive, I was okay with it. Well, I was sad initially just knowing I couldn't, you know? But soon after, I was ready to move on with my life. Eric seemed ready to move on too but as the year went by being a father was all he could talk about, and then he became one unbeknownst to me. His baby was three weeks old by the time I got wind of it and I was out of there. It still shocks me that Eric really thought he and I would raise his bastard child together! Can you believe that?"

"What I can't believe is how perfect you are for me. I think I might have to marry you, Ms. Chaundra Lane."

After his divorce Landon didn't think he'd ever want to date let alone get married again. However, there was just something about Chaundra that drew him in. He knew in his heart they were supposed to be together.

In his youth Landon dated all types of women but as he got older he seemed to be drawn to tiny but curvaceous, light skinned, extremely pretty women. Ones like Victoria Billingsley. Chaundra was the complete opposite. She was 5'10" and slender, dark skinned, and what most people would call cute in her own way. In Landon's eyes, however, she was the most beautiful woman in the world.

"I love your smile. You've got the prettiest, most perfect teeth I've ever seen," Landon declared.

"I can say the same about you, mister."

"Yeah, well I don't know about you but I paid big bucks for this smile. I used to get teased mercilessly when I was growing up for having a raggedy mouth. I can still hear those mean ass kids now. 'Mush mouth, mush mouth, Landon's got a mush mouth! Dang, Landon, your teeth don't know *which* way they wanna go!'"

Chaundra turned her face into her shoulder.

"I hope that's not your way of trying to hide your laughter. If it is then you're doing a pitiful job," Landon snickered. "What kind of person are you? I confide my deepest, darkest hurt and you just laugh in my face? That's it, the wedding's off!" he laughed.

"I'm sorry," Chaundra gasped, as she tried desperately to stop laughing. "I know that's not supposed to be funny but," she laughed even harder. "Okay, okay how about this? How about I tell you one of my own deep, dark hurts and you can laugh, okay?"

"No, don't try to bring me down with you. I have the decency not to laugh in somebody's face when he's bearing his soul. That's just wrong."

"Yeah we'll see. Anyway, when I was growing up the mean ass kids had a name for me too. Starting in second grade, every time I walked into class they would say it in unison."

Landon tried to control the tremble in his stomach because he knew he was about to laugh.

"Do you remember Gonzo the Great from the Muppet Show? Oh, so is this your idea of not laughing because you're doing a pitiful job," Chaundra giggled.

Landon fell over in the booth laughing so hard that tears poured down his face. As soon as she mentioned Gonzo he knew it had to be because of her bug eyes that sat pretty close together. Every time he looked at her his laughter increased.

"Look, I'm leaving!" Chaundra teased.

"Wooo, girl, I'm sorry," he said, dabbing his eyes with a napkin. "You got me with that one. So I guess we're even ... oh, shoot!" Landon shouted, when he got a glimpse of the clock on the wall. "I was supposed to be at the bookstore at nine o'clock. You're a bad influence on me, Chaundra."

"You're only forty minutes late. Just blame it on the traffic. It's always a nightmare so I'm sure they'll buy it. I need to get going anyway. I can't believe I'm still awake."

"So you're sleepy, huh? I was about to rearrange my appointments so we could hang out and you punking out on me? I'm just kidding, about the punking out part, I mean. I do want to hang out with you but I know you need your rest. Maybe we can meet up tonight."

"I would like that. Let me give you my number," she said, grabbing her purse for a pen and paper.

Landon wrote down his cell phone number as well as his home number. And for some reason he wrote down his address too. They swapped papers before walking out to the lobby. Landon placed his overnight bag in a chair and reached out to hug Chaundra. He normally had to bend all the way over to hug his women but she was a perfect fit.

"I'm so happy I met you, Chaundra Lane. You just don't know."

"I know," she whispered, still holding tightly to him. "Trust me, I know."

They finally let go of each other and Chaundra promised to call once she was rested. Landon walked her to her '97 Infiniti, they hugged again, and he watched her pull out of the parking lot. He was standing at the elevator when his cell phone rang.

"Hello?"

"I was thinking my place would be far more comfortable than your hotel room. What do you think?"

"I'll be right out," Landon grinned.

Back in Union City a visitor was ringing Landon's doorbell for the third time that day. Even though he'd come a long way, a part of him was relieved no one was home. He was nervous about how he would be received and wondered if he was making a mistake by being there. He decided to come back later that night. If no one answered, he'd drive back to Arizona and rethink the whole situation.

"The makeup artist business must be booming, Ms. Lane! This is *nice*," Landon said, as she led him through her home. "Wow! Although I do have to admit all these windows freak me out a bit."

"Really? That's what sold me on this house over the one I was looking at across town. I love the open space and all the natural light that pours through when I open the curtains. It's weird, I guess, because I love looking outside but I don't like being outside. Shoot, I'm dark enough so I don't need to be out in the sun," Chaundra laughed.

"Girl, stop it, I love your complexion. Your skin is beautiful."

Chaundra recognized that Landon wanted to say something else but stopped himself. "What were you gonna say? You can tell me," she prodded, noticing his reluctance.

"Don't get mad, but I don't think you need that much makeup on. Your face is beautiful without it."

"Spoken like someone who has never seen me without it," Chaundra giggled. "Thank you, though. That was sweet of you to say."

Landon was impressed. Normally women got defensive when a man offered any type of criticism but Chaundra took it in stride. She seemed to appreciate his comment instead of resenting him for it. He liked feeling as though he could say anything to her without it being a problem. If only Landon knew how insecure his comment had made her feel.

After Landon made some phone calls to reschedule his appointments Chaundra showed him the rest of her house. The kitchen was phenomenal and Landon realized quickly that it wasn't just for show. Chaundra had top of the line cookware and cutlery as well as spices she'd collected from her travels. Everything was clean and orderly but well used. He could tell she liked entertaining from the curio filled with an assortment of wine glasses and plates. It was next to a large wine rack filled to capacity with some amazing wines. Most of all, the large open space was inviting and comfortable. It made him feel right at home.

Next on the tour was the bedroom Chaundra had transformed into a home office and work space. Landon had never seen so much makeup in his life! There were two work areas with large, lighted mirrors and stylist chairs. Dramatic before and after pictures covered one side of the room while the other was filled with Chaundra and her celebrity clients and all the awards she'd won. Landon was definitely impressed.

He'd already seen her huge living room with the fireplace and the oversized two-car garage as well as the guest bedroom and bathroom. Chaundra saved her master bed and bath for last.

"So this is as far as we can go?" Landon asked, when she stopped at the door and let him peer in. "No company allowed?"

"I want you to come in but …"

Landon kissed her and Chaundra lost all train of thought as they made their way towards her bed. They were kissing and tugging at each other's clothes when she told Landon she didn't have any protection. It had been over a year since Chaundra last had sex so she had no reason to keep condoms in the house.

"Don't worry I have some in my bag."

Chaundra pulled away and took a step back. The look on her face was enough for Landon to know he wouldn't be spending any more time in her bedroom. So he led her by the hand back to the living room and they sat on the couch.

"So tell me what just happened."

"I don't know. I guess it bothers me to know you brought condoms. It makes me feel like you came down here already planning to have sex with somebody and I just happened to be the one you ended up with. I thought this was going to be special."

"And now it's not simply because I brought protection with me?" Landon frowned. "I don't get that, Chaundra. I'm sorry, but I don't. I thought you would appreciate me being responsible but instead you're punishing me for it."

"I'm not punishing you, Landon. I'm just telling you how I feel. Maybe I *should* be grateful that you brought them with you but all that's going through my mind is that you'd be having sex with somebody else if we didn't just happen to meet. You can't see why that would bother me?"

"I guess I'm just dumb then because I still don't get it. I've spent the whole morning bearing my soul because I feel connected to you. I trusted you in a way I only trust Jade but none of that matters now because I have condoms in my bag. You're assuming I was going to do something that I didn't plan to do. Yes, I have condoms but I have them all the time. And that doesn't mean I have sex everywhere I go. It just means I know things can happen and I always want to be prepared. I'm not a teenage boy that can afford to get caught up in the moment and think about the consequences later. I'm a grown man who enjoys having sex and would rather be safe than sorry."

All of a sudden Chaundra felt like an idiot. How many times had guys been willing to sleep with her without using any type of protection and there he was caring enough about both of them to be safe. *Stupid girl,* she thought.

"I'm sorry, Landon. I must sound like a silly little girl who can't control her emotions," Chaundra said, bowing her head. "Meeting you has been wonderful. I, too, have shared things with you that I don't share with others so please don't think that doesn't matter to me. It does. It's just that I felt disposable in my previous relationships and I never want to feel like that again. I want to be special to a man, his one and only, you know? But I didn't mean to take out on you what are clearly my own issues. So I'm sorry, okay?"

"Okay," Landon said then planted a kiss on her hand. "So would it make you feel better if I ran out and bought some Chaundra condoms?"

They both laughed. Then she offered to make lunch. Landon enjoyed watching Chaundra in the kitchen. Her love for cooking was obvious as she made fresh pasta and bread. She unthawed one of her homemade spaghetti sauces and made delicious vinaigrette for their salads.

"So is there anything else you want to ask me?" Landon asked, after she said grace. He could sense something was on her mind.

Chaundra smiled nervously. "When was the last time you had sex?"

"Are you sure you want me to answer that?"

"Of course I do. You can be straight up with me, Landon. I'd prefer you to be. I don't wanna be bothered with lies and deceit. Just tell me the truth, okay?"

"Okay. I had sex a week and a half ago."

"With who?"

"A woman I met a week and a half ago."

Landon was expecting her to get mad since his confession seemed to prove her point about the condoms but it led to one of the most open conversations he'd ever had with anyone other than Jade. Chaundra was definitely curious about his experiences; far more curious than he was about hers. Landon listened because he could see how important it was for her to be able to talk to him about anything. Though, he couldn't help feeling like he'd moved from a potential love interest to a buddy.

"You're not mad are you?" Chaundra asked when she walked Landon to the door a few hours later.

"No, I'm not mad. I'm perfectly content just having been here with you. Now that I think about it, it probably would be best to wait. Once I put all this on you you'll be sprung and then I won't be able to get rid of you!" Landon laughed heartily.

Chaundra laughed too, playfully pushing him away. They hugged goodbye and promised to talk later that evening. Landon left to get Jade's books in the stores and libraries and Chaundra showered and went to sleep. They met for a late dinner, had a drink, and laughed for hours. The two of them were definitely flirty with one another and Landon thought for sure Chaundra would follow him back to his hotel room. Instead, she kissed him goodnight and wished him a safe return home.

"Landon wait," Chaundra called from her car. She got out and stood in front of him. "I hope this doesn't sound crazy but you're who I've been waiting my whole life to meet. You're the man I wanna love."

She kissed him then hopped back in her car and pulled off before he could say a word. Landon smiled as he stood in the middle of the parking lot watching her drive away convinced he'd met his future wife.

Chapter
SEVEN

FOR NEARLY TWO WEEKS Landon spent his days selling books and his nights on the phone with Chaundra. They talked until the wee hours of the morning about their pasts, their futures, and what they were going to do to each other when the time came. Landon and Chaundra were definitely falling in love and couldn't wait to see each other in a few weeks when both their schedules allowed.

Dane and Pooh's usual squeals when Pierce came home from work grew into ear-splitting shrills!

"What in the world is ..." Jade began, before seeing what had caused so much excitement with her kids. She was furious. "Pierce!"

"I couldn't resist, babe," he said, relinquishing the puppy to Dane. "One of my customers brought three of them in but this little one just stood out. It's like he was smiling at me. Oh, come on don't be mad. He manipulated me," Pierce chuckled. He kissed Jade on the lips then took Sugar from her arms. "Just look at him. He's a German shepherd, your favorite dog. The man said he's mixed with something else but they don't know what. "

"What's his name, Dad?" Dane asked.

"I don't know yet. Maybe Mom can pick one for him. Bring him here, son."

Jade was about to object but Dane thrust the puppy in her arms. It *did* look like he was smiling. She smiled back at him and Pierce knew it was all over. Jade was in love.

"Hi, little puppy. You're so cute and soft like a teddy bear," Jade cooed, holding him like a baby.

"That's it," Pierce declared. "We'll call him Teddy."

The kids clapped and cheered as their parents loaded them into the minivan and headed to the pet store. They got everything they needed to welcome the newest member of the Jamison family home.

"What's the matter, sweetheart?" Jade asked when she found Dane pouting on his bedroom floor.

"How come I'm not a bear?"

"What in the world are you talking about, baby?"

"You call Daddy Big Bear sometimes and then you say Pooh Bear, Sugar Bear, and now Teddy Bear. What about me?"

"Oh, sweetie, you're my baby bear."

"You never called me that before."

"Well, I didn't know it was important to you. But I call you baby all the time, right? So maybe we can just add bear," Jade said and pulled him into her arms. "Don't be upset, okay? You're very special to me and I love you *so* much. Look at me," Jade said, as she caressed his face. "You're my favorite little boy in the whole world and I love you dearly whether I call you by a nickname or not, okay?"

Dane nodded at her as she wiped his tears away. Then he wrapped his arms around Jade and squeezed her tightly. After the kids and Teddy were settled in the living room, Pierce joined Jade in the kitchen.

"You just can't catch a break can you, chick?"

"What do you mean?"

"I heard you talking to Dane and I was thinking that boy is just like me. We're some of the most emotional, possessive folks you ever wanna meet," he chuckled. "We all wanna be number one in your heart."

Jade was about to say something when she heard Teddy yelp and went running to the living room to see what was wrong with him. She spent the rest of the night checking on him. At midnight Pierce reached over for Jade. He got up to see where she was and shook his head when he found her on the floor in the hallway cuddling the puppy. Jade couldn't stand the idea of him sleeping in a cage so she fluffed a blanket and laid him on it. Teddy looked so lonely and pitiful that she couldn't leave so she held him in her arms until he fell asleep.

"Put that dog down and come to bed. He'll be fine," Pierce said, as he took the sleeping puppy and laid him on the blanket. "I'm not about to compete with you little dog," he whispered. "Now come back to bed, woman."

Jade could barely sleep worrying about Teddy Bear. Pierce basically had to pin her down to keep her from getting up every thirty minutes to check on him. She just didn't want him to feel alone, but Teddy Bear was perfectly content where he was. From his spot in the hallway he could keep watch over all of them.

Landon was standing in line at his favorite Chinese restaurant when someone tapped him on the shoulder.

"Hey, you," he smiled, nervously.

"Hey," his ex-wife smiled brightly. "How are you?"

"I'm good, how are you?"

"Yeah, you look good. But that's nothing new."

Is this chick flirting with me? Landon thought. It had been nearly two years since they'd seen each other. The two didn't exactly part on good terms and their divorce turned ugly. Even though Landon knew how desperately Gabrielle wanted children, he never told her he couldn't give her any because of a vasectomy he'd had years before. Then she, in turn, had an affair with a fellow colleague and ended up pregnant. Gabrielle had sincerely hoped they could move on and be a family again but Landon wasn't interested. And that's when things got nasty between them.

"So what are you doing here? As I recall this wasn't exactly your favorite place." Landon smiled.

"Yeah, I know," Gabrielle said, as she fidgeted and looked to the ground. "Uhm, I was hoping to run into you. As a matter of fact, this is the third day in a row I was hoping to run into you," she blushed.

"What are you talking about, Gabrielle?" he frowned. "You know where I live. You could've just come by the house if you needed to talk to me."

"It was supposed to look like a coincidence."

They both laughed.

"So what can I do for you?" Landon asked, after they had taken a seat. "Why does a beautiful, sexy young woman have to hang out in a Chinese Restaurant she hates looking for me?"

"Maybe because you're the only man that ever made me feel beautiful and sexy," she smiled. "I miss you."

"*Oh,*" Landon uttered, with his eyes wide with shock.

"I know that probably sounds odd considering how things ended between us, but I've been thinking about you quite a bit lately. I just wanted to know how you are, what you've been up to, if you've met anybody … you know, all that good stuff. More than anything I was hoping you and I could be friends again. I really do miss you, Landon."

"I miss you too, Gabrielle, and I'd love it if we could be cool again. It's not a nice feeling knowing you have enemies in the world."

"I'm not your enemy."

"Well, I'm glad to hear it."

They talked for nearly an hour over lunch catching up on each other's lives. And although Landon was enjoying himself, he couldn't let go of the feeling that Gabrielle wanted something from him and had yet to say what it was.

"So do you have any pictures of your son?"

"Yes, I do," she beamed. "You really want to see them?"

"Girl, let me see the pictures and quit tripping."

"Okay," she smiled then pulled out a small photo album from her purse.

"As a matter of fact," Landon said, as he reached in his back pocket for his wallet, "I've got pictures to show you too." They swapped photos and both smiled. "Oh my goodness, Gabrielle, this boy looks *just* like you!" he said of the bright skinned, big brown eyed toddler. "He's beautiful."

"Thank you. And look at these gorgeous kids here. I can't believe how big Dane is now. He's such a little man. I can totally tell how much he loves these angels. He looks very protective of them."

"Oh yeah, Dane will *kill* you if you mess with his girls. And they love him to death. It's sickening," Landon laughed.

"Check you out, the proud uncle whipping out pictures."

"What can I say? I love them to death. But that little one has some kind of power over me. She be having me jump through all kinds of hoops for her. All she has to do is bat those little hazel eyes at me and I turn into a big ole pile of mush."

"Just like her mom, huh?"

"What?" Landon frowned. "What do you mean?"

"I never told you but I used to be extremely jealous of Jade. She had your heart in a way I never could," Gabrielle admitted. "I always thought you had a thing for her."

"Are you serious?"

"Yep."

"Wow, I don't even know what to say to that."

"There's nothing *to* say. It was probably just my insecurities anyway. I mean, who wouldn't be jealous of Jade. She's exquisite."

"Oh, my, exquisite, huh? She'd love to hear that. Well, I'm sure she hears it everyday from that husband of hers. He's probably more in love with her now than when they first met. It's just the sweetest, most sugary mess you'll ever see in your life! Those two are nauseating," he laughed.

"I'm really happy for her, though. Jade went through a lot and I'm glad she found her prince ... a little jealous maybe, but glad."

"Girl please, I'm sure you've got the fellas lining up for you. You don't have to be jealous."

"Yeah right, they're kicking down my door."

Landon and Gabrielle stared at each other in silence for a few seconds before he spoke.

"So do you think you'll have more kids?"

"Oooh, I don't know. I mean, I love Da'rell and all but I don't know."

"You love *who*?" Landon asked, with his eyes wide as saucers.

"Oh, my son's name is Da'rell."

"I don't know whether to be flattered or scared."

"Why would you be scared?"

"Come on, Gabrielle, you have to admit that's kind of bizarre. Why would you choose my middle name to call your son?"

"It's not just your middle name."

"What do you mean?"

"My son's full name is Da'rell Landon Campbell."

Landon stared at her with his mouth opened. "I don't understand. We both know I'm not his father so why would you name him after me? I mean, I would think with the way things ended between us would make you not wanna *say* my name let alone give it to your son," Landon stated, still shocked. "What did you family have to say about that?"

"Nothing much. They just think he's named after his dad."

"*What*?" he shrieked. "So let me get this straight. Instead of telling your family that you screwed around and got pregnant by somebody else you let them believe that I divorced you and abandoned my own child? Is that what you're saying, Gabrielle? Your family thinks Da'rell is *my* son?"

"He is your son, Landon."

"What the hell are you talking about, Gabrielle? You know damn well it's not possible for him to be my son! What kind of game are you playing?"

Thankfully Landon and Gabrielle were the only two diners in the restaurant otherwise he would've caused a huge scene.

"Calm down, okay, and let me explain. See, Dr. Jacobs didn't believe he was the father and demanded a paternity test, and it turned out that he's *not* Da'rell's father. So that only leaves you, Landon. There are no other choices. Some of the other nurses and I did the research to find out if a man can become fertile again after having a vasectomy and it is possible. It's what they call recanalization. It's uncommon, but it does happen. And it looks like it happened with us."

"Is this some kind of sick joke?" Landon snarled.

Gabrielle stared at him sternly for a few moments. "Yes it is! April Fools," she declared, triumphantly and did a little dance. "Sucker! You always said I could never, *ever* get you for April Fools day but I got you this time," Gabrielle laughed, heartily.

"That's not funny, girl! I was about to go off on you for real," Landon stated then let out a sigh of relief. "You got me with that one. Oh, lord I thought I was about to have a stroke! You're wrong for that, Gabrielle," he said, as she continued to laugh. "So is your son really named Da'rell?"

"Of course not, his name is Gregory after my dad."

"Girl, you shouldn't do that kind of stuff. I almost pushed you out that chair," Landon chuckled. "Shoot, you got me scared now. I need to go to the damn doctor to get myself checked!"

Had anyone else played a joke like that Landon probably would have left her sitting in the restaurant. However, Gabrielle looked so beautiful smiling at him the way she had when he first fell in love with her. *Ms. Ventura*, he thought remembering how he'd fallen hard for the Italian, Mexican knockout. A short while later the two of them got up to leave.

"Well, this was nice, all but that cruel joke you played on me," Landon said, after walking Gabrielle to her Altima. "I don't think I'll ever forget that."

"I'm sorry, Landon, but I had to get you," she smiled. "To be honest, I'd like to get you in some other ways too."

"Oh my goodness, girl, you never used to be this forward! What's gotten into you?"

"Nothing's gotten into me and that's the problem. It's one I was hoping maybe you could help me with."

Landon stared at her wondering if she was playing another joke on him. When Gabrielle stood on her tip toes to kiss him, however, he realized just how serious she was.

"So my place or yours?" she asked, with a devilish little grin on her face.

Before Jade could stop him Dane popped up from doing his homework at the kitchen table to run to the door.

"Hey, Uncle Landon," Dane said, as he unlocked the screen door to allow him inside. "What's up?"

"What's up, little man?" Landon asked then hugged him. "Where are those girls of yours?"

"In the kitchen," Dane stated before hopping all the way back to his dreaded homework.

Pooh and Sugar were seated at the table eating watermelon while Jade prepped for dinner. They both giggled when Landon planted kisses all over their sticky little faces.

"Ugh, move, boy," Jade shouted after Landon kissed her cheek and got her sticky too.

After ten minutes of idle chit chat Jade could sense Landon needed to talk to her about something. So she helped Dane finish the last of his math problems and got the girls cleaned up. She put Sugar in her play pen and sent Dane and Pooh in the back yard to play with Teddy. A few minutes later Sugar was sound asleep.

"So what's up with you, dude?" Jade asked as she grabbed a skillet from the cabinet. "Is the publisher causing more drama?"

"Actually this time it's me." Landon took a deep breath. "I just went to bed with Gabrielle."

"Yeah right, Landon, if you wanna fool me you need to pick something more believable," Jade chuckled, as she began seasoning pork chops.

"I wish this was an April Fools joke. Speaking of which, Gabrielle got me good by making me think I had fathered her son," he said then told her everything that took place.

Jade stopped what she was doing and just stared at Landon. "So you're serious? You really just slept with your ex-wife?"

"Yeah, I did."

"Man, talk about coming out of left field," Jade said then went back to preparing dinner. "Last time I checked y'all couldn't stand each other and now this? And what about Chaundra? I thought you two had something good going."

"I knowwww," Landon groaned and placed his hands on top of his head. "I just got caught up. Gabrielle looked amazing and she started flirting and pushing all up on me."

"So is that really all it takes? A beautiful woman flirts a little bit and you just forget about the girl you love?"

"Well, Chaundra and I haven't known each other that long and it's not like we're serious or anything."

"Wow, Landon, you really gone go out like that? I mean, seriously?" Jade frowned. "When you came back from L.A. you were ready to marry the girl but now it's not that serious? So what, are you and Gabrielle reconciling?"

"See, that's the thing, Jade. I believe she might be thinking that even though I told her that wouldn't be the case before we even went back to my house. I mean, I obviously still have feelings for Gabrielle but we want very different things out of life. And I realize now that our marriage would've ended anyway because we just weren't on the same page. We never were and the only way our relationship could have lasted is if she gave up the only thing she ever wanted or if I did what I never wanted to do. And the bottom line is I don't want kids. Gabrielle already has a son and wants at least one more.

And she's somehow confused my love for your kids as me wanting that type of responsibility when it's not true. Hanging out with Dane and the girls every week or babysitting now and then is a far cry from the day to day grind of being a parent. I don't want the life that Gabrielle wants so there's really nowhere for us to go from here. I thought we both understood this was going to be a hit it and quit it type deal. But when Gabrielle left she kissed me and said she'd call me tomorrow. Why is she calling me tomorrow, Jade? Ugh, see I *knew* this would turn out to be a mistake."

"And you did it anyway."

"Give me a break, Jade," Landon huffed. "I was horny, okay? The woman I'm interested in won't sleep with me so I was weak and I gave in to it."

"Does that mean if Chaundra had slept with you a few weeks ago you wouldn't have gone to bed with Gabrielle today?" she snapped.

"No … I don't know, Jade. Damn, why are you taking this so personally? I made a mistake, okay? You act like I did something to *you*."

"Sorry," Jade uttered.

Oh geez, Landon thought, knowing Jade's feelings were hurt and she was about to shut down on him. He didn't know if he could handle her emotions and his but he would give it a try.

Chapter
EIGHT

BEFORE JADE SHUT DOWN completely, Landon decided to pick her brain and find out what she was so upset about. "Tell me what's wrong, baby girl."

"I just don't like hearing you blame Chaundra for a decision you made. You slept with Gabrielle because you wanted to and I don't believe today would've been any different if you and Chaundra had gone to bed. Do you?"

"You're right," Landon sighed. "But it's not that big of a deal. I won't sleep with Gabrielle again and hopefully things will move forward with Chaundra."

"So are you going to tell her?"

Landon looked at Jade like she was insane!

"I take it that's a no then," she stated then looked out at Teddy and the kids. She smiled. "So if Chaundra's ex-husband stopped by for a 'hit it and quit it' moment you'd be cool not knowing about it?"

"See, why you always gotta do that?"

"Do what, make you look at things from the other side?"

"Yeah," Landon barked. "I don't wanna be logical. I just wanna put this whole thing behind me and move on with my life. Chaundra's not my wife. Technically she's not even my girlfriend yet. I'm still a single man free to do what I want."

"You're absolutely right, Landon. But continuing in a relationship and not telling Chaundra about this makes everything you did to prove you're safe to sleep with null and void. Even using a condom doesn't, oh my god, Landon are you kidding me? You didn't use anything?" Jade asked when she saw the guilty look on his face.

"It just didn't seem right to use a condom with Gabrielle. We stopped using them after I proposed to her. Plus, she said she hasn't been with anybody since before she had her son and I believe her. I know her."

"Oh really? So you knew she was gonna cheat on you and get pregnant by another man? Come on, Landon, you know better than that. You haven't been celibate these last two years so what makes you think she has? Why wouldn't you protect yourself?"

"I honestly don't know, Jade," Landon admitted. "She was my wife and I, I don't know, I just got caught up, you know?"

"Yeah, I know. Remember Richard?" Jade softened her tone. "I haven't forgotten what it's like to get caught up. It's just that there are always consequences when you do. And not to be funny, but the reason your marriage ended with Gabrielle is because you didn't tell her the truth in the beginning. Do you really wanna make that same mistake with Chaundra?"

Landon knew there was absolutely nothing he could say. Jade was right. His reason for not wanting to tell Chaundra about sleeping with his ex was the same reason he didn't tell Gabrielle about having a vasectomy. He didn't want to lose the woman he loved. In the end, though, that's exactly what happened. Landon knew with certainty that if he didn't tell Chaundra the truth it would come back to bite him. And yet he didn't know if he could bring himself to do it.

"What the hell did I get myself into?" he groaned.

After placing the stuffed pork chops in the oven, Jade peeked out the window at the kids again as she washed her hands then went to hug her big brother.

"It'll be alright," she cooed, kissing the top of his head. "If Chaundra truly is the one then the two of you will find a way to work this out. But first you need to figure out if things are really over with Gabrielle. Are you still in love with her?" Jade asked, as she took a seat at the table.

"I don't know, baby girl. There's the logical side of me that already knows a relationship can't work between us. But then there's the emotional side of me that enjoyed being with her again, and not just in bed. I honestly had a good time at the restaurant talking and laughing like we used to. It was like coming back home after being away for a while."

"Well, are you sure Gabrielle wants to rekindle a relationship with you? Maybe it was a one time deal for her too. She says I'll call you to everybody so maybe it was just out of habit that she said it."

"Or maybe she took my pillow talk to heart."

"Why? What'd you say?" Jade panicked.

"Just regular stuff like I love you, I miss you so much, you're the best, oh, don't look at me like that. I told you I got caught up. It was nice to feel loved again in that way."

"I know, she said, remembering her mess of a relationship with Richard. "I'm not judging you, Landon. I honestly feel bad. I remember those feelings and I hate that you're going through it. I want you to be happy, bro. And from the way you've been since you met Chaundra, I think that's with her. So of course I was upset to hear about Gabrielle but it's not like I don't understand. I do. I know how much you loved her. And I know you feel guilty for hurting her. But don't make it worse by trying to rekindle something you both already know doesn't work. It's not fair to either of you," Jade said, as she squeezed his hand. "I can't tell you how many times I wished I'd just took off running that day I bumped into Richard. But hindsight is twenty, twenty, right?"

Landon leaned over to kiss Jade's cheek. Then Dane and Pooh, with Teddy in tow, came barreling through the door when they heard Pierce pulling into the garage. Sugar's little head popped up and she smiled.

"Oh, lord, she knows when he's home too? That's just sickening," Landon laughed.

"I know, huh?" Jade smiled. "Come on Sugar, Sugar. Let's go see Daddy."

Pierce hugged and kissed his family and tried to hide his annoyance at finding Landon there.

"Hey, Pierce, how are you?"

"I'm great, how are you?"

"Well, I've got myself into a little drama but I'll let your wife fill you in on all the details."

"Why don't you tell him yourself," Jade suggested. "Dinner won't be ready for another twenty minutes so you two can talk. Go ahead," she coaxed when they didn't budge.

They didn't want to talk but Jade put on the biggest, brightest smile that neither of them could resist and they headed to Pierce's man cave. Soon after, Jade heard Pierce gasp when Landon told him about Da'rell. Then he burst out laughing once he realized it was an April Fools joke. Jade knew how nosy her husband was and that he couldn't pass up the opportunity to hear something juicy. He was completely enthralled by Landon's tale. However, Pierce's advice shocked her.

Jade had called everyone in for dinner when Landon informed her that Pierce agreed with him about not telling Chaundra what happened.

"What?" Jade shrieked, as she frowned at Pierce.

"I just don't see the point."

"Oh, you don't? So you think it's cool for couples to keep secrets from each other? Well, what didn't you tell me while we were dating?"

"Oh my goodness, how did we get to *us*? This is a completely different situation, Jade," Pierce said, as he helped get the kids situated at the table. "First of all, I didn't keep any secrets."

Pierce and Jade soon realized it wasn't the wisest thing to be having that type of conversation in front of Dane. He was notorious for repeating bits and pieces of grown up conversations and getting the information wrong. They nearly had a blow up at Luisa's house over Dane repeating something out of context that Jade had said. Thankfully it didn't take much to get things straightened out but it could have turned out badly if Luisa hadn't convinced her daughter Veronica to approach Jade about it rather than taking Dane's word.

Pierce and Jade talked to Dane about eavesdropping and then repeating what other people say. But he was still a kid and didn't quite understand about what was private and what could be shared. Jade had always encouraged Dane to be open with his thoughts and feelings but she realized she also needed to teach him tact and decorum. However, he was only seven.

Landon decided not to stay for dinner. He knew how much Pierce loved having his family time after work and didn't want to intrude upon that. During their meal Pierce listened to Dane talk about his day at school as if it were the most fascinating thing he'd ever heard. Then it was Pooh's turn. Pierce was always so amazed at how well she could speak for her age. He figured it had to do with the fact that Jade never did the whole baby talk thing and carried on conversations with Pooh from the time she was born. He thought she was crazy sometimes when he'd come home thinking she was on the phone and find her gabbing away with the baby. And it seemed, from her constant babbling, that Sugar would be talking soon too.

They played a board game with Dane, ran around with Teddy in the backyard, and enjoyed some of Jade's homemade peach cobbler in the tree house. Pierce got the kids bathed and ready for bed while Jade cleaned the kitchen. Then she read one of her stories with the kids and Teddy surrounding her before putting them down for the night.

"So back to this whole don't tell Chaundra thing," Jade said, once they were comfortably in bed.

"Oh my goodness, Jade, are you serious? You've been thinking about that this whole time, haven't you?" Pierce chuckled and turned the volume down on the TV.

"Yeah, I wanna know why you think it's best for Landon to keep that a secret from her. It makes me wonder if you've kept stuff from me."

"Like I said before, I haven't kept *anything* from you. Our situation and theirs is completely different. Although Landon and Chaundra really like each other, they aren't in a committed relationship. I asked you to be in an exclusive relationship with me on our second date. We both knew where we stood with each other and where the relationship was going. None of that has been established between those two. So why should he go in there confessing stuff to someone he's not even officially involved with? I just don't see what good can come from that."

"So you think it's cool for Chaundra to sleep with him not knowing that he's recently slept, *unprotected,* with somebody else?"

"I do see your point on that, babe. But I still think it will mess things up for no reason. Landon knows he and Gabrielle aren't going anywhere with this so why ruin his future with Chaundra over a mistake? And who's to say she isn't off having some fun of her own? Landon isn't her man so she can do what she wants."

"Wow, Pierce, I'm really surprised to hear you say that. I thought you would …"

"Look, enough about Landon and *his* sex life. I'm trying to get mine going," Pierce said, as he planted kisses on her neck and ran his hand up her thigh.

"You're trying to manipulate me," Jade giggled.

"Uh huh," he uttered then made love to his wife.

The next day was definitely not one of Jade's best. She'd overslept and barely got Dane to school on time. Pooh didn't want him to go and cried the whole ride home. Sugar was teething so she was irritable and whiny and driving Jade insane!

Landon was surprised when he heard a knock at the front door and was tempted not to answer it. He didn't care much for uninvited guests. However, something was urging him to at least find out who it was. And Landon was *flabbergasted* when he opened the door!

"I take it you're looking for Jade, huh? Come in," he said and escorted his visitor into the living room. "Have a seat and I'll call her, okay? Wow, I can't believe this," Landon said, as he dialed her number. "She's gonna flip out when … hey, baby girl, you need to come to my house right now!"

"What is it, Landon? As you can hear, Sugar's still screaming her head off and Pooh is begging for more stuff to eat. I can't come right now. Maybe once Pierce comes home this evening I can come over."

"Trust me, Jade, you need to come now. I'll help you with the girls, okay? Just get over here *right* now. I can't explain it to you it's just one of those things you have to see with your own eyes. You know I wouldn't bother you if it wasn't important so just trust me and come now, alright?"

Jade, a bit nervous about what it could be, put the kids in the minivan and headed over to Landon's house. A few minutes later she was at his front door. "So what was so important that I had to, oh my *God!*" she shrieked.

"Come here, Sugar, Sugar," Landon cooed, as he took the baby from Jade's arms. "Come to Uncle. Hi, Pooh Bear," he smiled and carried his nieces into the living room.

"Justin?" Jade whispered, as tears fell down her cheek. Then she squeezed him so tight he could barely breathe. "It's really you."

Almost three years before she was born, Jade's parents had a son that was put up for adoption. And nearly thirty years later he was standing in front of her. There was no doubt whatsoever that he was her brother as they looked just alike! Both had Willa's eyes, honey-colored skin, and thick brown hair. Jade was an inch shorter than their mother at 5'8" and Justin was 6'5" like their dad. It was obvious he took good care of himself as his body was well toned and fit. Jade was proud to know her big brother was a heartthrob!

"I can't believe you're here," she said, gently touching his face. "I wanted to know you ever since I was seven when Mom first told me about you. After she did, you became my imaginary playmate. I didn't stop doing it until I was almost nine because it used to make her cry to hear me calling your name all the time. I always wanted to find you, Justin. I just didn't know where to begin. Mom swore she couldn't remember the name of the place where she had you and she didn't know your adoptive parents' name. We didn't even know for sure if they kept your name Justin or not and I …"

"It's okay, sis. I'm just happy to be here with you," he said and hugged her again. "I had no idea what you knew about me, if anything, and I was terrified of how you would react. I actually came out here about a month ago but no one came to the door. I told myself to let it go but I couldn't. I had to meet you and see if we could have a relationship. I didn't know for sure until a few years ago that I actually had a sister but in my heart I knew. It was just a part of me that was missing.

"And I hate to make it seem like I didn't have a good life because I did. My adoptive parents were wonderful to me and they worked hard to make sure I had the best of everything. And I've got an adoptive brother who I love dearly. But it's different knowing you have a real sibling. It took a few years but we were finally able to track you through your business. That's how I ended up with this address." Justin didn't mention it wasn't exactly legal the way he'd come across that information.

They both started crying and hugged each other again. Landon calling them into the living room was what made Jade and Justin finally let go of one another. His jealousy was getting the best of him and he felt protective of Jade. For nearly seventeen years *he* had been her big brother and was afraid of being replaced by the real one she'd always longed for. What Landon didn't realize was Justin was just as jealous of him. He could feel the closeness between Jade and Landon and it hurt to know he'd missed out on that.

"Come meet your uncle, Dana. Now you know it's a shame when your child doesn't know what her real name is," Jade said when her daughter didn't respond. "We've been calling her Pooh since before she was born and that's all she answers to. Dana," Jade said again then laughed when her daughter looked at her like she was crazy. "This little one here is Dina but we call her Sugar. She's teething now so be careful, she's cranky."

"She's fine. She just needed her uncle ain't that right, Sugar, Sugar," Landon said, planting kisses on her face. "You're Uncle's sweet girl, aren't you? Yeah, I know," he cooed in response to her squeals and giggles.

"Whatever," Jade laughed, rolling her eyes at Landon. "Aw, you like Uncle?" she said to Pooh who had her little arms wrapped around Justin's neck and her head on his shoulder.

"She's *so* beautiful, like a little porcelain doll," he said, as he gently stroked her long, jet black hair. "And Sugar's gorgeous just like you."

"Like *us* it would seem," Jade said, staring into her brother's eyes.

Landon couldn't stand the way she was standing there grinning at Justin like he was a god or something. *Bastard*, he thought, bitterly.

Pierce and Tripp stared with their mouths hanging open when Jade brought her brother into the store.

"Well, this *has* to be Justin! What's up, brother-in-law?" Pierce smiled, as he shook hands with him. "How did all of this come about? I know Jade's always wanted to know you," he said, taking Pooh out of Justin's arms and planting kisses on her cheek.

Jade introduced Tripp then she, Pierce, Justin, and the girls went to Pierce's office. They talked for over an hour asking her brother one question after another. Justin told them he lived in a small town in Arizona called Bitter Springs where he and his best friend Wesley owned a construction company. Jade excitedly told him that their father Miles owned one as well. She found that amazing and was even more curious about the details of Justin's life.

He was unmarried but lived with his girlfriend Shawn. He didn't have any children but said he'd like to have a few. Justin was college educated, well rounded, and seemed to have a good head on his shoulders. What Pierce found amazing was how alike he and Jade were. They had the same sick sense of humor and enjoyed a lot of the same things. If he didn't know any better he would've thought they'd always been in each other's lives.

Pierce was due for a huge delivery and had to cut their visit short. He kissed Jade, Pooh, and Sugar goodbye and told Justin he was looking forward to seeing him soon. Pierce knew his wife. And now that she had Justin in her life she'd want him to play a major role in it. Pierce could only hope she didn't end up disappointed. He couldn't put his finger on it, but something seemed off about Mr. Justin Randle.

"Oh my god, *Justin!*" Tamara screamed, when she opened the door for Jade. "There ain't no denying he your brother, is there? Lord, y'all look *just* a like! Ms. Willa left her stamp on y'all. Oooh, and he nice and strong too," she said, hugging him tight. "Girl, if I wasn't married ... umph, umph, umph!"

"Alright, Mrs. Addison, cut it out," Jade teased.

Tamara kept Justin entertained while Jade took Pooh to the bathroom and changed Sugar. Pooh sat at the table with Tamara's four-year-old son Terrell and had animal crackers and apple juice. Jade prepared Sugar's bottle then joined Tamara and Justin in the living room while she fed her. Sometimes it still bothered Jade that she had to stop nursing Sugar so abruptly when she got sick. However, with all the drugs they were pumping through her system there was no way she could continue to nurse her baby.

"So I bet Willa went crazy when she saw you, huh?" Tamara asked. "What did she say?"

"We haven't gone over there yet."

Justin was shaking his head no. "We don't have to go there. I came here for you, Jade, not her."

There was an awkward silence for a few moments before Tamara asked if they wanted anything to eat or drink. She would have used any excuse to get out of dodge at that moment. Justin was clearly upset by the idea of seeing his mother and Tamara hated that she was the one who'd brought it up.

"You really don't want to meet her, Justin? I thought you said you were trying to find out where you came from. Wouldn't meeting your parents be an important part of that process? I mean some questions only they can answer for you."

"I had parents, Jade. It's you and your family that I'm here to get to know. I don't think it's necessary to see Willa."

Jade felt like she was being put in a weird position. She wanted to respect Justin's feelings but it almost seemed wrong not to tell her mother about him. Jade felt like she would be betraying Willa by keeping Justin a secret.

"Maybe we can stop by for a little while," Justin conceded, not wanting to see that look on Jade's face.

Less than an hour later they pulled in front of Willa's house. It would be the first of many mistakes Jade made where Justin was concerned.

Chapter
NINE

Justin asked if they could just sit there for a few minutes so he could catch his breath. He was still unsure about meeting Willa. There were so many mixed emotions about her decision to put him up for adoption. Justin tried to understand the situation she was in getting pregnant at fourteen but still didn't get why she kept Jade and gave him away. From what he gathered all the same things were happening in Willa's life when she was pregnant with Jade as it was when she was pregnant with him and yet she'd chosen to keep one and not the other. Justin felt bitter, more so because he'd missed out on knowing Jade and growing up with someone who belonged to him.

Bill and Lillian Randle had loved Justin dearly and provided the best life they could for him. However, he still felt alone in a lot of ways. And he blamed Willa for that.

Jade reached across the driver's seat to squeeze Justin's hand. "We won't stay long, okay?"

"Okay," he smiled, before getting Pooh out of the car seat and carrying her to the front door. He knocked.

"I'll get it."

"Oh great," Jade mumbled, recognizing her mother's best friend's voice.

"Hey, Ms. Betty."

"Hey," the woman said dryly. "Who in the world is he?" Betty asked, rudely. "Willa, come here, girl. Who is this boy looking like you?"

"What?" she yelled from the kitchen. "What are you talking about?" Willa dropped the glass she was holding and it shattered all over the floor. "*Justin?*"

It seemed like an eternity passed with Willa and Justin just staring at each other, neither of them moving. Unsure of what to do or say, Betty went to get the broom and swept up the broken glass. Just then Daniel walked through the front door and couldn't hide the shock on his face when he saw Justin.

"Hello, I'm Daniel Wade," he said, extending his hand to Justin. "And you are?"

Justin was struck by the fact that everyone in Jade's life knew exactly who he was and no one in Willa's did, not even her husband. His bitterness for her grew. "I'm Justin Randle," he said simply, then shook Daniel's hand.

"Willa?" Daniel called, waiting for an explanation.

She ignored her husband and pulled Jade to the back. Willa closed the bedroom door then turned to face her daughter who was laying her sleeping baby on the bed.

"Why in the hell did you do this?" Willa snapped, as she came close to slapping her daughter. "Ugh, you just don't know what you've done."

"What *I've* done?" Jade frowned.

"Why would you just bring him over here like this? And where did you even find him?"

"I didn't find him, he found me."

"Well, that was really inconsiderate of you to bring him here. You have no idea what you've done."

"Look, Mom, I'm sorry for coming over unannounced like this, okay? I hate when people drop in on me too so I shouldn't have done it. I just thought it would be a wonderful surprise. You told me how much it hurt to be forced to give your baby up and how you wished you had the chance to tell Justin how much you loved him. I thought this would give you that chance. How in the world was I supposed to know you hadn't told anybody about him? I can see not telling Betty, but Daniel? Why wouldn't you tell *him*?"

"I didn't see the point. Why rehash all that old mess? It was over so I didn't see a reason to talk about Justin and Jamal."

"Daniel doesn't know about Jamal either?"

"For what?"

"What do you mean for what? Justin and Jamal are as much a part of you as I am!" Jade shouted, dumbfounded by her mother's attitude. "It's not that I don't get that there's a level of shame that comes with putting a child up for adoption but is it shameful to *bury* a child too? You didn't kill Jamal, Ma. The umbilical cord got wrapped around his neck and he died! What's shameful about that? I was there and I saw how much it almost destroyed you. Why couldn't you share that with the man you're supposed to be spending the rest of your life with?"

"Look, not everybody has what you have, Jade," Willa barked. "Besides, it wasn't relevant. Jamal is dead and I never expected to see Justin again in my life!" The two stared at each other for a few moments. "Look, baby girl, I know this isn't your fault," she said when Jade began to cry. "You just want everybody to be a big happy family and it's not like that. You don't know what bringing him here really means. There's a lot you don't know … that nobody knows and I can't deal with it right now."

"You don't *ever* have to deal with me," Justin yelled, after Daniel opened the door.

"Justin, please, you don't understand," Willa pled.

"I understand just fine. But what *you* need to understand is that I didn't come here for you! I came here for Jade. It's her that I've missed and it's her that I want in my life. So as far as I'm concerned you can go back to pretending like I never existed. You're obviously really good at it," Justin snorted. "I'll be outside, Jade."

"Justin wait," Willa called, but he ignored her and walked out of the house. She burst into tears.

Jade grabbed Sugar and Daniel took Pooh from Betty's arms and carried her to the minivan.

"I'm sorry, Daniel," Jade cried, once they got the girls loaded into their car seats. "I didn't mean to upset you."

"You don't have anything to be sorry for, baby girl. It's alright," he said, hugging her tight.

Jade couldn't even look at Justin and they drove in silence for a few minutes. He reached over and touched her shoulder when he saw tears continuing to pour down her face.

"I'm *so* sorry, Justin. I should've listened to you when you said you didn't want to go. I'm sorry," she sobbed.

"This wasn't your fault, Jade, so please stop crying. I can't handle it. You're breaking my heart, sis, so please," Justin said, wiping tears from his own eyes. "I'm here for you, so we can forget this whole mess as far as I'm concerned. I love you, Jade. I know that probably sounds crazy since I've only known you for a few hours but I feel connected to you and I don't want to waste time on useless junk. So let's go back to laughing and having a good time like we were before any of this happened. Okay?"

"Okay," Jade smiled, sadly.

A few minutes later she pulled in front of Ardenwood Elementary School to get Dane.

"This is your brother, huh, Mom?"

"Yes, it is."

"Hi, Uncle Justin, I'm Dane," he said, then wrapped his arms around Justin's neck. Then he climbed in the backseat and kissed his sisters. "Hey,

Mom, can you make me that grilled cheese again when we get home? I'm starving. That hamburger they served for lunch today was gross but I ate it anyway because I had to." He talked a mile a minute like it was just an ordinary day.

Justin loved him for it. Dane, like the rest of Jade's family and friends made him feel right at home. It was the first time in thirty years that Justin felt like he was exactly where he belonged. He smiled with tears in his eyes as he listened to his nephew go on about the woes of elementary school.

Once Jade got the kids situated and showed Justin to the guest room, she called her in-laws to share the news of her brother's arrival. As she expected, they all wanted to come over to meet him and made plans to bring side dishes to go along with Jade's famous enchiladas.

Justin was sitting at the kitchen table with Teddy resting at his feet when he witnessed the excitement of Pierce coming home from work. Sugar's little head popped up from the playpen when her brother and sister went running to the garage door. Justin was touched by the whole scene. It was obvious how much they all loved each other and it warmed his heart to see. He had no idea how much the "love fest" would increase when Pierce's family arrived.

They came by the carloads, all wanting Justin's attention and affection. He was slathered with kisses and hugs from people genuinely happy to meet him. Both sets of Pierce's parents, his sisters and brothers-in-law, and his nephews were all there to welcome Justin to their family. Landon and Tamara and her family joined them too. Tamara's husband Jamel and Pierce's brothers-in-law weren't too keen on how much their wives were swooning over the newest member of the family. It got even worse when Justin sang and had the women about ready to throw their panties at him! As much as the men couldn't stand it, they had to admit he really could sing. Roland, however, proved to be the most annoyed by Justin's presence--and for good reason.

"Girl, Justin is *phenomenal!* I swear if I wasn't married I would wear him out!" Hawn declared, as she did a few booty pops.

"Ewww!" Jade shrieked from her bedroom closet. Sugar had spit up on her shirt and she needed to change.

"Ewww nothing, Chicka. You be doing my brother how come I can't do yours? Shoot, I'd have Justin calling my name the way you have Juan calling yours! What you be doing to him anyway?" she laughed loudly, at the horrified look on Jade's face.

"Shut up," Jade laughed with her face red as a beet.

Since the next day was a work and school day they had to cut the night short. Luisa invited Justin over to her house before he left Monday afternoon. He accepted and hugged everybody before they left.

"Wow that was amazing!" Justin beamed. "I can't remember the last time

I had so much fun. And this food is incredible," he said, taking a bite of the enchiladas Jade had reheated for him. "You are truly blessed, sis. Your friends and family love you *so* much, especially that husband of yours. Anybody can see how in love he is with you. But what's up with your boy Landon?"

"What do you mean?" Jade frowned, as she fixed herself a bowl of ice cream.

"Well, for one thing Landon doesn't know anything about me but he couldn't seem to keep my name out of his mouth. Every time I turned around he was making some off the wall comment insinuating stuff instead of being a man and asking me about whatever has him so curious. And why is he so focused on me anyway? What he *needs* to be focused on is how to stop choking people to death with all that that damn cologne," Justin stated.

Jade laughed and that made Justin laugh too.

"Seriously, though, sis, Landon needs to back off. He doesn't wanna go there with me because I've got opinions too and I'm betting mine will be a lot more accurate. I doubt he'd appreciate it if I started questioning his intentions and asking him why he, well, never mind. Like I said before, Landon doesn't know jack so if there is ever anything you wanna know about me, just ask *me*, okay?"

"Okay," Jade said.

She was definitely curious as to what would make Justin question Landon's intentions. However, she chalked it up to him being upset about the silly comments that were made. Jade was frustrated with the way both Landon *and* Pierce had acted towards Justin. Even though there was no reason for Landon to be jealous, she did understand why he might be. Pierce feeling that way, however, made no sense.

"This is so good," Justin said, as he ate more of the enchiladas. "I probably should stop, though, since it has beans in it. The last time Shawn cooked chili those beans jacked me up. That gas was so strong I thought it was gone blow me up to the ceiling!"

Jade dropped to the floor laughing so hard that tears ran down her face! Justin loved the sound of her laugh and found himself doing or saying anything to hear it again, even a weird leprechaun sounding voice that she found hilarious. Though, Jade was as goofy as he was and she made him laugh just as much. For hours all Pierce heard was incessant cackling and it got on his nerves.

"I hate to break up your little comedy act, but the kids are waiting on their story," Pierce snapped.

"What's wrong with *you*?" Jade scowled at him.

"Nothing's wrong with me. I'm just letting you know your kids have been waiting for you. It's already later than their usual bedtime and they need to go to sleep."

As always, Jade's emotions registered all over her face and they both recognized how annoyed she was. That wasn't the first time since Justin arrived that Pierce had made it seem like she was neglecting her duties as a mother. And Jade was sick of it. The two of them would definitely have a conversation about it once they were alone.

Jade left to read one of her stories and tuck the kids in for the night. Teddy expected to be tucked in too so she fluffed his blanket and laid him in the hallway. It was all for show since most mornings Jade found him sleeping in the girls' room in front of Sugar's crib. Any other time he was in Dane's bed.

"Night, night, Teddy Bear," Jade cooed, as she dimmed the lights. "I'll see you in the morning."

Teddy still looked like he was smiling at her and it made Jade giggle.

"Well, we'll see you in the morning, brother-in-law," Pierce said, as he shook Justin's hand.

Jade sat back in her seat at the kitchen table and resumed eating the mint chocolate chip ice cream that was melting just like she liked it.

"Oh, it looks like *I'm* the only one going to bed, huh? Wow, okay then good night," he muttered, before tearing out of the kitchen like a spoiled child.

"Oooh, somebody's in trouble. You better get in there before you get a whooping," Justin teased.

"Shut up," Jade laughed, despite how enraged she felt on the inside. "So tell me about Shawn. You said you two live together, right? Are y'all getting married?"

It was almost midnight when Jade and Justin finally decided to call it a night. She threw the last load of clothes in the dryer before heading off to bed. Jade heard Justin on the phone and wondered who he was talking to at that time of day. She knew it was none of her business and went to wash her face and brush her teeth and hair. Pierce kept huffing waiting on Jade to ask him what was wrong. When she refused to acknowledge him he decided to say something to her.

"So do you think you can squeeze me in now that Justin's finished with you?"

"You know what? I can't believe you're in here acting stupid like this!" Jade snarled. "After twenty-seven years I finally got to meet my brother, Pierce ... my *brother!* The one I never thought I'd get the chance to know. He went through a lot to find me so of course I want to spend as much time with him as possible. And I would think you of all people would understand how important this is to me. You've always had your sisters and you still make time for them. I've *never* treated you like crap when you leave me to go running off to do stuff for them that their husbands could do because I know how much having time with them means to you. But you can't sacrifice a few hours so I can have that with my brother?" Jade frowned.

"And what have you had to give up because Justin's been here? Nothing! You still had a hot meal waiting on the table for you. Your house was clean and your kids were taken care of like they always are. *And* you still got laid! So what the hell are you mad about?" Jade snapped.

She snatched her pillow off the bed and headed for the living room. "I can't believe you're this selfish, Pierce. I would never have done this to you," she cried, then flung the door open. "Uh oh, Teddy Bear," Jade shrieked, as she stumbled to avoid stepping on the puppy.

He had started to scratch on the bedroom door trying to get to her. Jade scooped him up in her arms, grabbed a blanket from the hall closet, and got comfy on the couch.

"Ugh," Pierce groaned and covered his face with a pillow. He felt like the world's biggest jerk! All Pierce wanted to do was bring his wife back to bed and talk to her but he knew she needed a chance to calm down. Fifteen minutes was as long as he could wait, though, and he went to join her and Teddy on the couch.

"Hey," he said, tapping her foot so she'd move and allow him to sit down. "I'm really sorry, Jade. You *should* be able to enjoy your brother without your husband acting a damn fool. I didn't mean to hurt your feelings or make Justin feel unwelcomed and I'm truly sorry."

"Why did you act like that?"

"I don't know, babe," he said, dropping his head. "I just feel like I already have to share you with the kids, my family, *Landon,* and I didn't want to share you with anyone else. Yeah, I know," Pierce uttered when Jade shook her head at him, "I sound ridiculous right about now. I was jealous, babe, what can I say? This dude blows into town and you share stuff with him I never knew about you. Then when I make a comment about it he says, 'oh, it ain't nothing, man, she just needed her big brother to bring it out of her.' Like he has some kind of special power or something," Pierce huffed. "The bottom line is I feel excluded and I don't like it. I hate feeling like he can tap into some part of you I know nothing about."

Teddy barked at Pierce and Jade laughed. "See, even the puppy knows you sound crazy."

"Aw, that's just wrong, you little trader," Pierce said, when Teddy wouldn't come to him. "I saved you from a life at the pound and this is how you do me?"

he chuckled. "I don't blame you, though, Teddy Bear. I wouldn't wanna leave her arms either," Pierce stated, giving Jade his best puppy dog eyes.

"Don't even try it, dude. You know you're wrong."

"I know. And I'm sorry." Pierce leaned over to kiss her. "Shut up, dog. You ain't gone stop this," he said when the puppy barked at him again. Pierce took Teddy from Jade's arms and placed him on the floor. "Don't you make a sound, trader," he ordered, before kissing Jade again. "Come back to bed, okay? You know I can't sleep without you."

Pierce ran his fingers through Jade's hair as she snuggled up with him in their bed. "I love you," he whispered, as she dozed off in his arms.

Soon after, Pierce was asleep too. Justin, however, was still on the phone.

"So did you tell her the truth?"

"Please, don't start, okay? I told you …"

"Bye," the caller said before hanging up.

Chapter

TEN

THE NEXT DAY WAS fairly stressful for Jade. Landon showed up to discuss the time frame for releasing her next book and the tension between him and Justin was thick as fog. She thought it would make things better for them to talk about the comments that had been made the night before and clear the air. Unfortunately, it only made things worse and Jade felt trapped in the middle. Both of them were expecting her to defend him to the other. It was only when they saw how upset she was that they decided to let the matter drop. Whether they actually would or not was questionable.

After dinner Justin carried Sugar to the living room to watch Aladdin with Dane and Pooh. He left Pierce and Jade in the kitchen to continue their flirting. They were about to sneak off to the man cave for a quickie when Jade heard her father's panicked voice on the answering machine and went to pick up the phone.

Excited about meeting Justin, Jade called Miles from her cell phone and left him a message. However, after the horrible way her mother responded she was hoping he didn't get her message until after Justin had left. It figured that the one time she *didn't* want her father to call, he would.

"Hey, Dad, how are you?"

"I'm shocked! I had to go to Michigan City for business and I just got home and got your message. Are you serious? Justin's really there with you?"

"Yeah, he's really here. And there's no denying he's my brother. He looks just like Ma. It's been fun getting to know him."

"So what airport are you close to?" Miles interrupted.

"What airport ... *what*?" Jade stuttered, unable to believe her ears.

Pierce let out a deep breath knowing the drama was about to start. He had grown to hate Miles because every time he spoke to Jade she ended up devastated. Pierce wished she could cut the man out of her life altogether, but he was her father and she still loved him even though he hurt her over and over again.

Jade tried to control her emotions but tears were stinging at her eyes. She couldn't believe Miles was seriously considering coming to California to see Justin when he'd given her one excuse after another for why he couldn't come to visit her in the nine years she'd been living there.

"Let me speak to him right quick," Miles said.

Jade handed Justin the phone then rushed to the back. Pierce told Dane to keep an eye on his sisters then followed Jade to their bedroom. She was crying in a way he'd never heard and it broke Pierce's heart. He knew that pain was coming from a place deep inside her and he wanted nothing more than to take it away.

"Come here, babe," Pierce whispered, as he took Jade into his arms and held her close to him.

It felt like she was convulsing as her sobs jerked and shook her body uncontrollably. All Pierce could do was squeeze Jade tighter to reassure her he was there for her.

"What's so wrong with *me*?" she whimpered.

Pierce took a step back and grabbed her shoulders. "Don't you dare let him do this to you, Jade! Ain't a damn thing wrong with you! Your father's the one who is stupid as hell! He's the one missing out on the sweet, kindhearted, *amazing* woman you are," Pierce said, as he embraced her again. "We don't get to pick our family, babe. We're born into it and some of us luck up and get wonderful parents and some of us don't. And I'm sorry you got the short end of the stick with yours but *I* love you, Jade. Those three kids in there love you. My family adores you and treats you better than they treat me because of the wonderful person you are. Even Justin damn near went broke trying to find you because he could feel it deep inside that he needed you in his life. So don't you sit up here and let Miles and anything he do or say take that away from you. You're an incredible person and that's why all of us be acting jealous and possessive over you. We all want your love because we know what it is to have it."

Jade wiped her face with tissue and finally stopped with the hysterical crying. Pierce was grateful because he didn't know how much more he could take before breaking down himself. He couldn't stand to see Jade hurt and his instinct was to destroy the thing that was causing her pain. It didn't really matter to him that the thing was her father.

Pierce held Jade in his arms again until a knock at the door made him let her go. It was Justin wanting to know if she was okay. Jade felt bad because she didn't want her brother to think she was angry with him. What she was feeling towards Miles was from a lifetime of hurt and disappointment. He always made Jade feel like everybody else was more important. Time after time Miles chose to be absent from Jade's life but he was so eager to be a father to her half sister Jewel and now Justin. And as much as everyone told her not to take it personally, it was impossible for Jade not to. Miles was still her father and all she wanted him to do was love her.

"He's not coming here, sis," Justin said, as he embraced Jade. "I told him I was here to spend time with you and that he and I could meet at a later date. So after I go back home and check on everything with the business I'm gonna fly out to Indiana to meet him."

Jade was totally confused. She didn't understand why Justin had been so completely against meeting Willa but was willing to spend money to go meet Miles. His explanation was that from the information he received and the conversation he'd had with Miles, he believed their father had always wanted him and would never have given him up for adoption.

It was no secret how much Miles always wanted a son so Jade had no doubt he would have stopped the adoption if he'd had the power to do so. And Jade also knew she was being selfish not wanting Justin to meet Miles because of the way he'd been towards her. She had chosen to keep mum about her relationship with their parents as not to influence Justin negatively. Yet, there was still a part of Jade that felt betrayed.

Pierce was hoping Jade would tell Justin the truth about Miles and Willa but she suggested they get dessert instead. She was shutting herself down emotionally and there wasn't a whole lot Pierce could do to stop her.

Saturday, April 5th turned out to be a beautiful spring day and Jade decided to pack a picnic and take the kids and Teddy to the park. She needed a break from the men in her life and asked Tamara and her kids to join them. The two women ran around with their children and the puppy, pushed swings, and got on the sliding board a few dozen times before lunch. Afterwards, Dane and Tamara's three kids played on the jungle gym. Pooh and Sugar were napping in the double stroller with Teddy lying underneath. Jade and Tamara sat on a bench that was close enough for them to keep an eye on all the kids but far enough away that the two older ones weren't privy to their conversation. Then Jade told her best friend everything that happened with Pierce, Landon, Justin, and Miles.

"I know this probably ain't the right thing to say but I hate your father as much as I hate *my* sperm donor," Tamara confided then shared about her father for the first in eight years. "But the reason I brought up ole sorry ass

James Parker is because even with the trifling way he dumped us like trash, I still feel like he hurt us less than Miles hurts you. James wounded me deeply by leaving but it's a old wound. Miles keep popping up and each time he inflicts more damage on that same open wound. You know what I mean? Sometimes I wonder if it *would* be best for you to just cut him off. I mean what good do it do you to have him in your life?"

"I don't know, girl. I guess I'm always hoping he'll change. He's my dad, you know?"

"Yeah, but that's Willa's fault, not yours. You didn't have nothing to do with that so why should you have to keep suffering for it? Shoot, Jackie and Miguel have been more of a father to you in the three years you've known Captain America than Miles has your whole life. So love the people that love you and kick the rest of them to the curb. I hate to see you constantly hurt like this, beauty queen," Tamara said, as she squeezed Jade's hand. "You the best, girl, and you don't deserve to be treated like that."

"I just don't get it, Tamara," Jade said, wiping tears from her face. "Aren't your parents supposed to be the ones who love you the most? Even if nobody else in the whole world gives a damn shouldn't they? And sometimes it's hard for me to accept that other people really love me when my own parents don't. I mean how can …"

"Okay, you can stop that nonsense right there! Your parents are the screwed up ones, not you. But despite all the mess you went through with them and some of them jacked up relationships, you still managed to be one of the sweetest, most loving people I know and I love you to death, girl. And I know it hurt for Miles and Willa not to be what you want them to be but you lucked up and married into a wonderful family of people that adore you. See, you could've messed around and married somebody with a stupid, ghetto ass mama like I did."

"Girl, stop," Jade chuckled. "You need to quit talking about that woman like that."

"Yeah, that's easy for you to say since you ended up with Glenda the good witch for your mother-in-law and I got Evilene from the Wiz!"

They both laughed. Then Tamara gave her two cents on the situation with Justin and Landon as well as the way Pierce had behaved.

"Men just be tripping sometimes, girl. But all three of them love you, especially your husband. His spoiled butt just want you all to hisself," Tamara smiled. "I do have to give Captain America credit for one thing. He *always* open up to you about his feelings even if it's crazy. And I know that's why y'all so close. You talk and trust each other with everything. I wish Jamel was more like that. I have to beg him to share even the smallest things with me. That's why I be suspicious of him sometimes. It make me feel like he hiding something when he can't just open his mouth and talk. So you should be thankful your man share hisself so freely with you. Not everybody has that."

An hour later Jade and Tamara packed everything up and loaded their kids into the minivans.

"Thank you, Tamara, for coming and hanging out with me. I needed that," Jade said, as she squeezed the woman tight. "I love you, girl."

"I love you too, beauty queen. We all do."

"Are you ever gonna stop calling me that?"

"Not unless you suddenly turn ugly. But I don't think that's even possible, *beauty queen.*"

"Bye," Jade laughed, shaking her head.

They hugged one last time then headed off in separate directions for home. Once Jade made it back to the house she found it full of Pierce's friends. She was definitely surprised to find Landon and a few of his buddies there as well. It made her smile to know her husband was making an effort to include in his life the men that were important in hers. She would be sure to thank him later.

Hawn and Roland came over and Jade ordered pizza for everyone. At one point she noticed that Justin had become really quiet and withdrawn like something was bothering him. When she tried to talk to him about it he said nothing was wrong. The truth was, there was a lot wrong. Justin had quite a few things to tell Jade but was terrified of losing her if he did.

Chapter

ELEVEN

SUNDAY MORNING JADE COOKED a big breakfast for Pierce, Justin, and the kids and they lounged around talking and enjoying each other's company. Pooh definitely took to her Uncle Justin and was in his arms as often as he'd let her. Sugar loved for him to sing to her and she would stare at him all dream like when he did. Pierce had taken a dozen shots or more of them together. He loved taking pictures as was evident from the many family photo albums around their house.

Justin expressed sadness over having to leave the next day but promised to visit often. He didn't want to be a nuisance but now that he knew Jade, he couldn't imagine not having her in his life. Justin loved her very much. Jade loved him too but she couldn't help noticing how opposed he seemed to her coming to visit him. He said it was easier and less expensive for him to come to Union City than for the five of them to come to Bitter Springs. Jade wasn't buying it. Something was definitely up with Justin she just couldn't put her finger on it.

At around noon Jade got up to get herself and the girls bathed and dressed. The whole family was meeting at Luisa's at two o'clock and her mother-in-law couldn't stand for folks to be late. Jade didn't like it either so she always made sure her family was on time. By one-thirty Pierce and Justin were strapping Pooh and Sugar into their car seats while Dane put Teddy Bear in the back of the minivan. Jade was just about to get in the front seat when her mother pulled into the driveway.

"Can we please just go," Justin asked when he got a glimpse of Willa. "I don't want to deal with this."

Jade felt nervous and didn't quite know what to do. Her mom was obviously ready to talk and her brother wasn't the least bit interested. His eyes were pleading with Jade's to get rid of Willa. And as Willa approached, hers were pleading with Jade to help. *Oh god*, Jade thought, as she just stood there not knowing what to do next.

"Hey, baby girl," Willa uttered, nervously.

She spoke to Pierce and the kids and squealed with laughter when she saw Teddy Bear. He was so cute that Willa just wanted to squeeze him. However, that wasn't the reason she was there.

"Hi, Justin, I was wondering if I could talk to you for a few minutes."

"We're on our way out right now so maybe later," he said, coolly.

What Justin really wanted to say was nothing his nephew and nieces needed to hear so he chose that statement hoping Willa would get the hint. She didn't.

"Please, Justin, it will only take a minute. I just need to explain some things to you."

"Babe, why don't you guys go ahead and I'll meet you there," Jade interrupted.

She could see the rage building in Justin's face and wanted to stop it before things got out of control. Jade leaned across the passenger seat to kiss Pierce and gave Justin a look reassuring him everything would be okay. She blew kisses to the kids and waved at them as Pierce backed out of the garage. Then Jade and Willa went inside to talk.

"I'm sorry," Willa said, as she took a seat on the living room couch. "I thought if I just came over he might talk to me. Justin hates me, doesn't he?"

"I honestly don't know what he feels about you, Ma. I felt so bad after we left your house the other day that I didn't want to bring it up again. To tell the truth, I was prepared not to ever talk about it again when my dad called."

"*What!*" Willa yelled, with a look of horror on her face. "Why in the world would you call Miles?"

"Why do you think I called him," Jade snapped. "But after the way you acted I was seriously hoping he didn't call me back until Justin left."

"Oh my god," Willa mumbled, as she got up and started pacing the floor. "So what did Miles say?"

"Well, to my surprise, he was ready to hop on a plane and come out here to meet Justin. But they decided to meet later in Gary."

"Oh my god, Jade, why did you have to call him?"

"You know what? I'm gonna go," Jade said, as she stood from the lazy boy. "I'm not taking the blame …"

"Justin might not be Miles's son," Willa blurted.

Jade just stared at her mother as she plopped back down on the lazy boy.

"I met this nineteen-year-old boy named Louis on summer vacation in Alabama. The day before me and Mae had to go back home we went to the state fair and I ended up having sex with Louis in his father's truck. As you know, Mae was killed that night and my whole life was turned upside down. After her funeral the next week Miles took me back to his house and *we* had sex. When I found out I was pregnant I didn't know for sure who the father was. And I thought I'd be able to tell when I looked at Justin but he looked just like me. So I let another family take him and tried to put the whole thing behind me."

"Ma, are you *serious*?" Jade asked, still in disbelief. "And you never told anybody?"

"No. And I also never told anybody I was going to have an abortion that day I was late picking you up from school. So I always felt like it was my fault Jamal died. If I had never thought of killing him he would've lived."

"Oh, Ma," Jade cried, as she took her weeping mother in her arms. "I'm so sorry."

Jade understood that type of guilt. Throughout her pregnancies with Pooh and Sugar she was terrified of losing her babies. Jade always feared God would punish her for the abortion she'd had by taking one of the babies away.

Mother and daughter cried and held each other for a while before Jade asked Willa what she was planning to do. She could not believe her ears when Willa said she didn't see the point of telling Justin or Miles and warned Jade against doing so. It was supposed to remain their secret.

"Ma, you can't be for real," she frowned. "So I'm supposed to sit back and let Dad and Justin bond with each other knowing there's a possibility they aren't related? Justin's trying to find where he came from and how can he do that if he doesn't know the truth about who his parents are? You told me, so you have to tell them too. I'm not carrying that kind of secret around, Ma. You should've known I wouldn't."

The cuddly moment between them was over and Jade reclaimed her seat in the lazy boy across from her mother. Willa's blame game began by pointing out there wouldn't be a need for confessions if Jade hadn't brought Justin to her house. Normally she would hold her tongue to avoid a blow up with Willa. That day, however, Jade could no longer take it.

"You know what, Ma? I'm *sick* of you blaming me for everything wrong in your life! From as early as I can remember you've been blaming me for how hard your life was as a teenage mother when *you* were the one gapping your legs open and got pregnant! *You* chose to stay with Dad even though he was beating your brains in because you liked the big house and the cars and all the stuff he provided for you, not because of me. And when you left me to …"

"I didn't leave you, Jade. You know your dad and your granny kept you from me."

"Yeah that's right, *they* kept me from you. And you were so distraught that you took trips, and partied, and even met and got engaged to Mitchell and helped take care of his son!" Jade yelled. "It's always somebody else's fault, isn't it, Ma? Well let me ask you this. Whose fault is it that you live ten minutes away from me and I never see you? Who keeps you from calling just to see how I am or checking on your grandkids? Why is it so easy for you to live your life like I don't even exist? Why am I so unlovable?" Jade burst into tears.

"How could you say something like that, baby girl? I *do* love you," Willa cried. "I don't come around a lot because I feel like you don't really want me here. You seem to prefer Luisa and the rest of Pierce's family."

"Oh so it's Luisa's fault then?" Jade snorted. "See, that's what I'm talking about, Ma. Somebody else is always to blame when the truth is you're a woman that does exactly what she wants to do. So if you *wanted* to spend time with me, you would! If you wanted to be involved in our lives for more than just holidays and birthdays then you would be. I'm the stupid one for not recognizing that and accepting the fact that you love yourself more than you love anybody else," Jade said, as she grabbed her purse. "I need to go. My family is waiting on me."

"Oh, so I'm being dismissed?"

"It's whatever you wanna call it, Ma. I won't bother you with dinner invitations or pesky phone calls trying to include you in what's going on with us. I finally get the message."

"Fine," Willa huffed then walked through the door Jade was holding open for her.

Jade jumped into Pierce's Chevelle and tore out of their garage. She didn't notice that her mother was still parked in the driveway crying her eyes out.

The next day, after Justin and Jade said their tearful goodbye she put the girls down for a nap and was looking forward to spending some quiet time alone. Willa arrived and put that plan to rest. She let her mother in and they took the same seats they'd had the day before.

"Sometimes it's hard to show love when you've never really received it. But I do love you, baby girl. And I can't stand the thought of not having you in my life," Willa said, as tears ran down her cheek. "Please don't give up on me, okay? I guess I let my jealousy get the better of me. It just hurts to see you prefer Luisa and Pierce's family over me."

"Ma, I love Luisa very much but I don't *prefer* her over you. I want you here too. And I don't understand why I have to choose one over the other.

Why can't I have both of you? The kids need both of their grandmothers," Jade stated. "And I don't expect you to watch the kids like Luisa does. I just want them to spend time around you and get to know you. *I* want to spend time with you. I love you, Ma, and I have fun when we're together."

Willa squeezed her daughter tight and promised to do better. She loved Jade and didn't want to lose her.

A few days later Landon came over to discuss Jade's new book but somehow they got on the subject of Justin. He still didn't trust the guy and wanted to warn Jade not to trust him either.

"Look, baby girl, I know you love this dude and want him in your life, but you need to be careful. Something is off with him."

"You keep saying that but you never can tell me what that something is. Are you sure you're not just jealous?"

"Jealous for what? I know Justin's your biological brother but he can't take away all these years I've had with you," Landon stated. "I'm not jealous, Jade. I don't trust him. I mean who just walks away from his business and his life after knowing somebody for a few days?"

"Oh come on, Landon, you know Justin was *not* serious about moving here."

"Are you sure about that? Because he sounded pretty serious when he was talking to Shawn about it."

"What are you talking about? And when did you hear him talking to Shawn?"

"It was that day all of us guys went to the gym. Justin called her when we got back here."

"And you just happened to hear it, huh?"

"Can I help it that I got thirsty at that precise moment and needed to go to the kitchen?"

Jade chuckled as she shook her head. "So instead of taking your drink back to the man cave you had to stand outside of the guest room where Justin was, huh?"

"Yeah, the water tasted better from that spot," he smiled, guiltily. "Anyway, from what I gathered ole brother dear makes a lot of rash decisions and Shawn wasn't having it. But Justin told her to either get on board or get left behind. So he sounded serious to me and I think something's up with that. What grown man with a business, a woman, and a life can just pack up and go at a moment's notice? I'm telling you, Jade, something is off with this guy. He sounds like somebody running from something and I'm saying be careful. If he starts asking for money again then ..."

"What do you mean again?" Jade frowned.

"Well, what he asked was if he could take a few hundred of your books to sell."

"And you saw that as him asking for money?"

"Yeah," Landon said, shocked Jade didn't see it the same way. "It would've been like turning over a thousand dollars! So I gave him the opportunity to *buy* the books and sell them himself. He didn't take my offer but he's gonna check the ledger at his so called construction company then get back with me. Yeah, right," Landon snorted.

"Landon," Jade sighed.

"What? Look, my concern is for you. We don't know Justin and I'm saying be cautious. I don't want to see you get hurt, baby girl," Landon said, as he squeezed her hand. "I could be way off base, Jade, and I honestly hope I am. But until we know what Justin is all about don't be so quick to let him into your world. Make him earn your trust."

As much as Jade wanted to reassure Landon, she couldn't deny her own skepticism about Justin. It always seemed as though he was choosing his words carefully when she asked him questions about his life, especially when it came to his relationship with Shawn. And as petty as it seemed, Justin's hands bothered her too. Jade had spent most of her life around men who worked construction and she never saw any of them with hands as perfect and pretty as Justin's. Things just weren't adding up and she didn't know what to make of it.

"I love you, Landon, and I know you got my back."

"Damn right," he smiled then dove into the grilled steak and cheese sandwich Jade made for him. "Oooh, this is good. If you ever get sick of writing books you should open a restaurant. I'm serious."

"You and Pierce both can stop with that. I couldn't care less about running a restaurant. I don't love to cook. I cook because I love y'all. There's a big difference. I don't want to be in a hot kitchen all day long."

"The same way you only wanted to write children's books as a hobby? Now look at you, raking in the big bucks, Ms. Author."

"That's not the same thing!"

Landon knew that would get Jade all fired up and she argued with him about how writing books was a far cry from opening a restaurant. Truthfully, it was just a distraction. Neither of them wanted to keep talking about Justin. Only time would tell what and who he really was.

Chapter

TWELVE

June, 1998

IT WAS DANE'S LAST week of school before summer vacation and Jade was struggling to get everything ready for their trip to Universal Studios in L.A. The truth was she didn't really want to go. She found traveling with kids as young as Pooh and Sugar stressful. They couldn't sit in their car seats for more than an hour or two without getting cranky and whining nonstop. So a road trip that would normally take six hours took Pierce and Jade anywhere from ten to twelve because of the amount of times they had to stop to tend to the kids.

Planning the vacation with Pierce's entire family was another source of stress for Jade. Everyone wanted to do something different and it was causing unnecessary arguments. Jade suggested they all go to Universal Studios together and then let each individual family do what they wanted afterwards. Pierce and his family balked at that idea saying it defeated the whole purpose of going on vacation together. Still, no one could agree on which activities to participate in since each family's situation was different.

Dealing with Justin, however, was what Jade found to be most stressful. When he came back to visit for Mother's Day Luisa invited him on the family vacation without inquiring as to why Jade hadn't asked him herself. It was too late to explain why that wasn't the best idea since Justin agreed and was all excited to go. That was until he realized Willa would be coming then the drama began. He didn't want to be around her and tried repeatedly, and quite aggressively, to convince Jade to exclude Willa.

"Look, Justin, I get that this is an awkward situation for you to be in. It's awkward for all of us. So if you choose not to go I'll understand. But that's the only thing that's your choice. My mother is coming on this family vacation just like she went on the last one and will go on the ones to come. She's a part of my life, Justin, and you'll have to deal with it if you choose to be around me. My mom's gonna be at the kids' birthday parties and Christmas dinners and all the other family events we have. So you either need to find a way to work it out or be absent from my life like Miles.

"But I'll tell you what's *not* gonna happen. You're not gonna keep throwing these 'her or me' ultimatums up in my face every time something doesn't go your way," Jade had snapped. "I love you, Justin, and I want you in my life. But I'm not gonna put up with you threatening to leave when I don't do what you want. I can think for myself and I make my own choices. If I didn't, you and I wouldn't even be talking right now because not everybody thinks you're best for me. So like I said, if you don't wanna go on the trip, that's fine. But nothing you do or say is going to stop my mom from being there."

"Wow, little sis," Justin had uttered, as he took a step back. "You seem real pissed off at me when who you *should* be mad at is your mother! Why would you even want her on a family vacation after what she did?"

"Oh, so now *you* decide who I should be angry with or who can or can't go on a vacation with me?" Jade fumed. "Who the hell do you think you are?"

"Hold on, sis, I didn't mean it like that. I just don't understand why you're defending her after Miles and I had to take a paternity test because of her lies. But more than that, I don't think she treats you that great. I'm not stupid, Jade. I know your relationship isn't all you pretend it to be."

"I don't pretend it to be anything. The only reason I don't talk to you about my relationship with either of our parents is because I wanted you to get to know them for yourself. My experiences with them don't necessarily have to be yours," Jade had stated. "But if anybody's pretending it's you. I'm not stupid either, Justin. You do all that talking about how wonderful your adoptive parents are and how they gave you the best of everything. And yet they're noticeably missing from your life. Where are they, Justin? How come the last pictures you have with them are from your college graduation over eight years ago? Hmm?"

Jade felt bad when she saw Justin's eyes fill with tears. Whatever had taken place between her brother and his adoptive parents was obviously still very painful for him.

"I'm sorry, Justin. I shouldn't have said that."

"I'm sorry too. You've been considerate enough not to poison me with your feelings about Miles and Willa and I need to do the same. I apologize, okay?"

They hugged each other before Jade explained her thoughts about the paternity test. It wasn't that she didn't understand Justin's and Miles's feelings. She got why they were angry, especially her father. For over thirty years he'd carried the guilt and shame of having someone else raise his child only to find out it may not have been his after all. However, once the test results proved Justin was in fact his son Jade didn't understand why Miles couldn't move on and stop with all the nasty phone calls and threats. He and Justin were intent on punishing Willa for a decision she made as a scared fourteen-year-old girl. They made it seem as if the only reason Justin was given up for adoption was because Willa didn't know for certain who his father was. In truth, Justin would've been given up regardless, even if Willa had fought tooth and nail for him. Her mother had decided so. Dorothea didn't want to raise another child and she knew Willa and Miles were incapable of taking care of themselves let alone a baby.

Jade gave her mother credit for telling the truth after all those years. She could have not said anything and let Miles and Justin bond never knowing there was even the possibility that Miles wasn't his father.

"So are you going on the trip," Jade had asked.

"Yeah, I'm going. I'm looking forward to it."

"Good."

Despite the stressful drive and all the family drama, the first day of their vacation got off to a great start. They all had a delicious breakfast together before heading to Universal Studios. Landon, who'd flown down the day before, planned to meet them at the front gate. He was excited for the chance to introduce his two favorite girls to each other.

"It's so nice to finally meet you," Jade said, as she hugged Chaundra tight. "I've heard wonderful things about you. Landon came back all smitten after y'all first met."

Jade was trying hard to suppress her laughter. All she could think about was what Landon told her about Gonzo the Great! He knew it and was silently pleading with Jade not to start laughing like an idiot.

"I've heard wonderful things about you too. But Landon left out a vital piece of information that could have kept me from making a fool out of myself today."

"What are you talking about?" Landon frowned.

"He didn't tell me you were Ms. America, Jade! If he had I wouldn't have brought this makeup kit as a gift. I was gonna make you up for the date tonight but you *definitely* don't need it," Chaundra smiled, as she nudged Landon.

"Oh, girl, stop," Jade blushed. "I would love to get made up by a professional make up artist. I wanna get the smoky eye thing so I can entice that man of mine."

"Yeah right, like you really have to do all that," Landon teased. "Even when she's looking crazy Pierce can't keep his hands off her."

They laughed then Jade led them to where the rest of the family was waiting. Chaundra was overwhelmed by the amount of people in the group. She was relieved that Jade didn't try to introduce everyone by name. There was no way she would've remembered them all.

Landon tried not to show his irritation at the way Chaundra was grinning at Pierce like she'd never seen a man before! The only thing worse was the way she was gawking at Justin.

"Your mother is really beautiful, Jade. You and your brother are the spitting image of her, oh, and your baby too," Chaundra said, once she got a glimpse of Sugar. "You all are some of the most beautiful people I've ever seen in my life. I couldn't make *no* money off y'all," she laughed.

"Yes you will, girl," Hawn chimed in. "I saw that amazing kit you gave Jade and I'm gonna buy one for myself. That's unless my amazingly generous sister-in-law lets me have hers since she barely even wears makeup."

"Buy your own," Jade stated, trying hard not to show her annoyance.

Universal Studios was amazing and everyone genuinely had a good time. Justin's best friend Wesley joined them and he was so much fun to be around. He had a great sense of humor and an infectious laugh. Though, Jade couldn't help wondering why Justin's girlfriend hadn't come and when she asked her brother, he just said Shawn couldn't make it. Later, Wesley accidentally let it slip that Shawn hadn't been asked. However, before Jade could inquire further, their wonderful day took a turn for the worst.

The babysitting rotation that had been implemented so each couple could enjoy the park was ruined when certain couples came back two hours late then refused to take their shift. A huge argument ensued and everyone was just ready to leave at that point and packed up the kids to go. Jade called Landon to let him know they were heading to the hotel. She tried to reach Justin but his cell phone kept going straight to voicemail. She figured he was probably sleeping since he and Wesley had a long drive.

Back in their room things were tense, to say the least. Jade was still angry about the babysitting debacle and resented not having the time alone with her husband to watch the shows they'd waited all day to see. That annoyed Pierce because his oldest sister Eva and her husband Gerard had told them to go while they watched the kids but Jade refused. She didn't think it was fair for them to get saddled with all the children by themselves.

After Jade got Pooh and Sugar bathed, she told Pierce she was going down to the lobby for a little while to clear her head. With all the drama that took place at Universal Studios Jade didn't think they would be going on the group date and told Landon and Chaundra to go out and enjoy each other. They decided to go back to her house for dinner and, Landon hoped, dessert. He had no idea the dramatic evening that was in store for him. It would be enough to make Landon wonder if he and Chaundra in fact had a future together.

While Jade was waiting on the elevator she heard a group of people talking about the lounge on the fourteenth floor. So she decided to go up there instead to get a virgin strawberry daiquiri at the bar and relax. She got the drink and was making her way towards the back of the lounge when she spotted Justin and Wesley. Jade almost dropped her glass as she stood there with her mouth opened. It was quite clear the two of them were *much* more than friends!

"Oh, god, your sister," Wesley uttered.

Justin couldn't even turn to face her. He stared at the floor for what seemed like an eternity while Jade just stood there staring at him. Wesley actually got up and put his arms around Jade to guide her forward.

"I'll leave you two to talk," he said before heading downstairs to the room.

Jade put her drink on the table and sat next to her brother on the overstuffed leather loveseat. She held his hand in both of hers and told him to look at her.

"Why didn't you just tell me the truth?" Jade asked once Justin finally looked her in the eyes.

"I didn't think you'd accept me if you knew I was gay. Most people don't. My parents didn't. As soon as I told them the truth they told me not to ever come to their house again. Even friends that I'd known for years didn't want anything to do with me once they found out. Every time they saw me they'd shield their kids like I'm a pedophile or something. And I just couldn't handle you responding to me that way. I couldn't take seeing the look of disgust on your face, like the one you have now," Justin said then looked to the floor again.

"I'm not disgusted, Justin. I am shocked, though, I can't lie. I never would've guessed that in a million years," Jade acknowledged. "I guess I bought into the stereotype that all gay men are flamboyant and feminine just because all the ones I know act that way. But I wouldn't disown you, Justin. You're still my big brother and I love you. It just turns out we have a little more in common than I previously thought," she said in an attempt to ease some of the tension between them.

Justin smiled weakly as tears threatened to spill from his eyes. He wanted to believe things wouldn't change but his experience with being dumped once people found out made him doubtful.

"I'm sorry," he whispered. "I wanted to tell you the truth about everything, but I didn't think you'd understand. And then Shawn …"

"Oh my god, Shawn! How could you do this to her? Do you know how humiliating it is to think you're building a future with someone who has a whole other secret life? How can you say you love somebody and then …"

"So you just got all the answers right, Ms. Perfect?" Justin snarled. "Well, since you know everything there's really no point in us carrying on this conversation. You just keep sitting there on your little high horse, alright?"

"*Justin?*" Jade called after him.

He ignored her and kept walking.

Chapter
THIRTEEN

CHAUNDRA AND LANDON WERE sitting at the kitchen table both picking over the meatloaf and mashed potato dinner she had cooked. All he wanted to do was knock everything off the table and have his way with Chaundra. It had been months of them talking on the phone about what it would be like when they finally made love and Landon was sick of talking. He honestly thought they were going to be intimate the night before but Chaundra seemed content being held and she fell asleep on his chest as they watched TV on the couch. Landon couldn't take another night of cuddling.

"So tell me what's on your mind, Ms. Chaundra," Landon smiled, seductively.

She hesitated before answering. "I was just wondering why you never mentioned how insanely beautiful Jade is or that she's not actually your sister."

That definitely was not what Landon was expecting to hear. "Uh, I guess I didn't think it was that big of a deal. I'm her big brother and that's how it's always been."

"Did you ever wish it was more?" she asked, pushing her plate aside.

"Damn, Chaundra, you know how to kill a moment, don't you? I'm sitting here thinking of ways to get you out of those clothes and you wanna talk about Jade. And I bet that's gonna be your excuse for why you can't do it tonight either, right?" Landon huffed. "See, I'm starting to feel like you playing games with me and I don't like it. Or perhaps I'm just not your type. Maybe if Pierce came by you'd be more inclined to have sex."

"What is *that* supposed to mean?" Chaundra snapped.

"You tell me. You were the one grinning up in his face all damn day acting like you couldn't take your eyes off him! I guess it was the fascinating way he answered all your questions about owning a freakin' convenience store that turned you on, huh?" Landon snarled.

Chaundra fought the urge to smile. "I can't believe it. You're actually jealous, aren't you?"

"Well, I'm glad you find this whole thing amusing," Landon said, as he stood up from the table. He was sick of being played with. "I'm glad it makes you smile to see me upset."

Chaundra snatched Landon by his shirt and kissed him hard on the mouth. "I don't find you being upset amusing," she said, holding him tightly to her. "As immature as it sounds, it made me feel better to know something I did could make you jealous. I felt jealous and insecure once I learned Jade isn't really your sister. She's *so* beautiful and fun and I can't imagine a man not wanting her. Then I started wondering if you could have her if you'd still want me."

"Chaundra," Landon cooed, as he caressed her face. "I want *you*," he said then kissed her sweetly. "I love you."

"You do?" she beamed. "I love you too, Landon. And I want you *so* bad."

"I might be able to help you with that," he smiled then led her to the master bedroom.

Chaundra laughed when he pulled a box of condoms out of his overnight bag with her name written all over it. Then Landon overwhelmed her body with the most intense, the most rewarding pleasure she'd ever experienced! It was enough to make her do away with all her prudish ideas about sex and be free with the man she loved. And she was free, indeed.

"I must have been out of my mind to wait! You got skills, man, I can't even front. *Damn*, baby," Chaundra moaned then attacked Landon again.

He almost missed his flight on Sunday afternoon because she couldn't keep her hands off him. Monday evening Landon was annoyed by someone ringing his doorbell like a lunatic!

"You were right. You put it on me and now I'm sprung," Chaundra laughed then jumped into his arms.

They made love as many times as possible in the six hours before she had to fly back to L.A. for a job on a major motion picture. Landon was definitely flattered, but as the weeks went by he found her unexpected visits bothersome. There seemed to be little consideration for the fact that he had a job and a life of his own. Though, what upset Landon most was feeling less like a boyfriend and more like Chaundra's personal sex slave. There were other women he could call if that's all he was looking for.

It was Tuesday, July 14th, the day before Jade's twenty-seventh birthday and it was Landon's turn to celebrate with her. Instead of having a party, Jade said she wanted to have a birthday week. So on the days leading up to her birthday she had special dates with her family and friends. Tamara went first and took her best friend out for dinner and a movie. Willa was next and she and Jade spent a day being pampered at the spa and the night in a luxury hotel. After Sunday dinner where all of Jade's favorite foods were served, Luisa and her daughters took the birthday girl out for a few hours. They went to the home of one of Luisa's good friends who designed jewelry. She had made special necklaces for all of them with a square shaped pendant in their favorite colors. Even though Hawn's favorite color was royal blue, she chose yellow so she and Jade's necklace would be exactly the same. It was something Eva couldn't help commenting about and an argument nearly ensued. Jade was actually bugged by it too but she didn't want to ruin the special moment Luisa planned for her daughters.

Monday was Jade's day to spend alone with the kids. They went swimming in the backyard. She barbecued a few hot dogs and baked cupcakes. Then they climbed in the tree house along with Teddy Bear and read stories and sang songs. It was the perfect day.

Pierce was getting anxious for his time with Jade. He had her actual birthday and the four days after and planned to take her away so they could be alone. Jade knew they were catching a flight but to where she had no clue. She wasn't worried about it, though. Wherever Pierce was taking her would be wonderful simply because they were together.

"This was so good. Thank you, Landon," Jade said, after they'd finished lunch at Red Lobster. "So tell me what's up with you and Chaundra. You seem different now whenever you talk about her."

"Aw man, baby girl, that chick is driving me *nuts*. The first couple of times she showed up on my doorstep I thought it was cute. I was flattered, you know? But now she's out of control. If she's not dropping in unannounced, she's on the phone telling me all this stuff she wants to do to me. There's no, hi, baby, how are you, or hey, let's catch a movie. Everything is about sex."

"Well, that's what you get for putting it on her like that. What you be doing to these poor women," Jade teased. "But seriously, Landon, I thought that's what you wanted. I mean weren't you complaining about her holding out on you? Is it that you don't enjoy it?"

"No, it's not that. It's good … real good. I just wish there was some balance with Chaundra. It's always one extreme to the other with her. We went from not having sex at all to it being the only thing we do. At first she went overboard with all the talking and cuddling and now I can't pay her to do either one," Landon admitted. "I thought making love would enhance our relationship but it seems to have replaced it. I just want a normal, balanced, healthy relationship with a woman I love. I hate feeling under pressure."

"What do you mean?" Jade asked then took a bite of the banana cheesecake she'd ordered.

"Instead of just enjoying making love with me I feel like Chaundra goes into it waiting to be wowed. She expects each time to be explosive and I feel this pressure to perform. It really is a job and I don't like feeling that way. It's supposed to be fun," Landon said, taking a bite of her cheesecake.

"Did you talk to her about it? Because it sounds like something that could be easily fixed if you communicate how you feel," Jade said. "I can't speak for Chaundra but maybe she feels pressure to please you as well. You *did* make a big deal out of having sex, Landon. Maybe she thinks that's what's most important to you."

"Humph, you might be right. I hadn't thought about it like that. I'll have to bring it up tonight when I talk to her," Landon said then decided to change the subject. "So have you talked to Justin?" he asked, as he took another bite of her dessert.

"Nope, he still doesn't wanna talk to me. I called three or four times and left messages but he hasn't responded. So I guess that's it," Jade said, as she fought back tears. "I apologized and said I was wrong for saying anything when he just needed me to listen. I made a mistake, you know," Jade cried then grabbed a napkin to wipe her tears. "I guess when you do or say the wrong thing to Justin he cuts you off like my dad," she said then sobbed into her napkin.

"Hey, look, girl, you better stop that mess before I push you out this booth."

Jade burst out laughing like Landon hoped she would. He couldn't stand to see her cry and felt bad for bringing up the subject of Justin.

"Listen, why don't you let me get you another slice of cheesecake since I killed this one and then I'll tell you about my embarrassing moment at the bookstore this morning, okay?" Landon asked, as he signaled for their waitress. After placing the order he began his story. "Alright, so I went to Walden Books to replenish their shelves and I had a little pep in my step because I thought I was looking suave. I had on my new suit and shoes and I strutted on up to the counter where the cute little clerk was waiting for me. Well, apparently the damn shoes didn't have no kind of traction on 'em because when I leaned in to hand her the books, I slipped on the carpet and hit my head on the counter."

Jade fell over in the booth laughing so hard that her stomach began to cramp.

"And *then*, if that wasn't humiliating enough, the shock from the blunt force trauma to my forehead caused me to fart on my way down to the floor. I had to ice my head to get rid of the knot."

Jade was screaming by that point and her laughter made the waitress and some of the other diners laugh too. Landon loved the sound of her laugh and he would've gladly told a million of his embarrassing moments just to hear it.

Jade had no idea where her husband was taking her until it was time to board the plane. She had never been to Santa Barbara and was excited to go. It was beautiful there and the inn where Pierce booked their reservations was phenomenal. They were excited to try out the Jacuzzi in their room but as Jade changed for dinner Pierce became interested in something else. They made love within the first hour of being in Santa Barbara!

Everything was perfect and Jade enjoyed every second of her birthday. She and Pierce laughed all through an amazing seafood dinner and dessert. Some of the other diners thought the Jamisons were newlyweds because they seemed so blissfully happy together in the way a couple on their honeymoon would be.

"Happy birthday, babe," Pierce said, as he planted kisses on Jade's hand. "I love you so much."

"Aw, thanks, Butterscotch Thunder. I love you too," she laughed loudly.

He burst out laughing too. Before they were married Pierce told Jade about his fantasy of being her stripper. He had chosen the stage name Butterscotch Thunder and it became a private joke that they obviously still found amusing.

A little while after dinner Pierce suggested they go swimming. It was then that Jade experienced her first problem on their trip.

"Pierce, what in the world is this?"

"What do you mean? It's the swimsuit I packed for you to wear. Put it on so we can catch the sunset."

"This is *not* a swimsuit, Pierce. This is a few pieces of thread! I'm not going to the pool with my butt hanging out."

"Girl, quit tripping and put that thing on. We're on vacation. Besides, it's your birthday and you look *hot*."

"Where is my regular swimming suit," Jade said, as she rummaged through the suitcase. "You have lost your mind if you think I'm going outside with that thing on."

"Come on, babe, put it on for me. Don't make me cash in your I.O.U."

"What are you talking about? What I.O.U.?"

"Remember when you manipulated me into dressing up like Captain America for Dane's party?"

Jade closed her eyes and sighed. She did promise to do whatever he wanted whenever he wanted it. And even though they'd made the deal five months ago, Pierce would never let her live it down if she reneged. So Jade snatched the so called swimwear and took it to the bathroom.

"Come on, babe, we're gonna miss the sunset," Pierce called after she'd been in there for over five minutes. "Ooh, yeah, now that's what I'm talking about. Turn around, babe. Umm huh, look at that *booty*," he groaned.

Jade couldn't believe Pierce actually expected her to go outdoors with nothing but a few yellow strings barely covering her private parts. Then she burst out laughing when he removed the towel from around his waist to reveal a yellow Speedo. Jade let out a sigh of relief when Pierce grabbed her hand and led her to the Jacuzzi.

"You sit there and relax and I'll be right back. I've got a surprise for you."

A few minutes later Pierce came back with two tumblers. One, she assumed, was his favorite Crown and Coke but the other was something greenish she didn't recognize.

"I know you've never been drunk in your entire life so I figured we should try it tonight. I wanna see what you're like. I've been researching drinks for the last few months and I think I found one you'll actually enjoy. Hey, whoa, you have to sip it, babe. It might taste like juice but it'll sneak up on you and I don't want you to get sick. I want you to enjoy it and get loose."

"This is good. What is it?" Jade asked, as she took another sip.

"It's a Midori sour. I was hoping you'd like it."

Pierce joined her in the Jacuzzi and they talked and laughed for over an hour. At one point Jade asked if her chest was supposed to be burning and that made Pierce laugh. He'd barely put any alcohol in it because she wasn't a drinker and still it seemed potent to her. Before long, though, Jade ripped the yellow strings off and went wild! It was by far the best birthday she'd had in many, many years.

By Monday, July 20th, once all the birthday celebrating was officially over, Jade and the kids were back on their normal schedule. Dane, Pooh, and Teddy were in the girls' bedroom playing while Sugar scooted around the kitchen in her walker. She had discovered how powerful her little nine month old legs were and tore through their house like a madman! Jade was trying to keep from being run over while she finished cooking dinner when the doorbell rang.

"Hey, sis," Justin smiled.

"What are you doing here?"

"Well, I was hoping we could talk."

"Hi, Uncle Justin," Dane said, as he and Pooh came bouncing into the living room.

"Hi there, little man. How are you?" Justin asked and hugged his nephew. Then he grabbed Pooh and lifted her into the air. "You are just too pretty for words, little girl. Your dad's gonna have to carry a bat around to keep all the boys away from you. Hi Sugar, Sugar, how are … oww," he said when she hit his foot with her walker.

All three of the kids laughed when Justin fell to the floor dramatically as if he'd been hit by a car. Sugar was especially tickled and she laughed louder and harder each time she hit him.

"Somebody call nine-one-one and tell them a laughing little girl keeps running me over," Justin teased.

Eventually the kids stopped giggling and Justin got up from the floor. He was hoping to get his sister to at least crack a smile but Jade didn't seem amused by him at all.

"Do you think it's possible for us to talk?"

"I thought this last month and a half of silence meant you didn't wanna talk," Jade said, as she fought back tears.

Justin was close to tears himself once he recognized how hurt his sister was. Jade was all he had and he didn't want to lose her. Though, Justin feared he already had.

Chapter
FOURTEEN

Justin was about to say something to Jade when the frenzy of Pierce's arrival home from work began. He was struck by how genuinely happy Jade, the kids, and even the dog was to see Pierce. It brought tears to Justin's eyes as he desperately hoped to experience that type of love.

"Hey, brother-in-law, what's up?" Pierce asked then shook Justin's hand. "I didn't know you were coming."

Justin explained that he'd just shown up hoping for a chance to talk with Jade. She still didn't seem interested in him being there and went back to the kitchen to finish dinner. After Pierce had been run over a few times by Sugar, he followed his wife into the kitchen. He wrapped his arms around Jade's shoulders and planted a kiss on her cheek.

"Go ahead and talk to your brother, babe. I know it hurt your feelings for him not to call but he's here now wanting to talk to you. Every family fights but we have to make up and move on," Pierce said, as he rocked her from side to side. "I know you love him so gone and hash things out, okay? I've got the kids."

Everyone was starving so they ate the pot roast dinner Jade had prepared and then she and Justin headed to Marie Callender's to talk over dessert. They didn't say much on the ten minute ride to Fremont and ended up sitting in the parking lot instead of going inside. Justin shifted in his seat and pressed his back against the passenger door.

"First, I just wanna say I'm sorry. I shouldn't have let this much time go by without talking. And I know you were trying to fix things and I appreciate that. I was just hurt and angry and so much was happening at once that I couldn't handle it all. Down in L.A. Wesley gave me an ultimatum. I either need to move back to San Francisco and be in an openly gay relationship with him or part ways. And Shawn wants an exclusive, openly gay relationship or else. I guess they're both sick of feeling like my dirty little secret."

"So Shawn's a *guy*?" Jade asked.

"Yes, sis, I'm gay, remember?" he chuckled.

Jade finally understood why Justin always seemed to be choosing his words carefully whenever he talked about his relationship. He never used him or her, only Shawn's name.

"Oh my god," Jade gasped and put her hands up to her mouth. "No wonder you hated me," she stated, remembering what she'd said to him in L.A.

"I didn't hate you, Jade, I was just hurt. It broke my heart for you to think I would actually be in a relationship with a woman and then be cheating on her with a man. But then I realized I'd made you believe Shawn was a woman for months so what else were you supposed to think? I guess I assumed once you discovered I was gay you would automatically know Shawn was a man."

"Looks like we did a poor job of communicating, huh? I'm sorry, though. I shouldn't have assumed anything. And I shouldn't have been going off without knowing what I was talking about. I hate that and then turned around and did it to you. I'm sorry," she said, reaching out to hug him.

"So have you ever been with a woman?"

"No."

"Ugh, why you gotta look like that? It ain't that bad, is it?" Jade laughed. "I mean have you ever tried?"

"Do you really wanna know?"

"Yeah, tell me everything," Jade said.

She listened intently for nearly an hour as Justin divulged his experiences with the opposite sex. He had kissed and fondled girls but played the role of a Christian boy who believed in abstinence before marriage to get out of actually sleeping with them. People closest to Justin applauded him for being a faithful believer and the thought of him being gay never crossed anyone's mind. And he spent most of his life making sure it never did.

"I knew something was different about me from as early as seven. But contrary to what people assume I never wanted to be a girl. I'm not a cross dresser or anything like that. I like to take care of myself and look good but I'm not feminine. I'm a man who just happens to like guys."

"Well, you sound confident about yourself so why do you hide who you really are?"

"It's the rejection and hurt that comes when people find out that I can't take. So it just got easier to make folks think I'm a heterosexual while I had a whole other life behind closed doors. And both Wesley and Shawn are sick of it and forced me to make a choice. At first I thought it would be the hardest decision I've ever made because I love them both just in different ways. But once I took the time to really sit down and ask myself what I wanted from life, the choice wasn't hard at all. It just hurt to have to let go of someone who'd been such a huge part of my life."

"Okay, quit being all dramatic and just tell me," Jade laughed. "You trying to make it suspenseful and stuff."

Justin laughed too. "I chose to be with Shawn. When I think about growing old with someone he's who I picture sitting next to me on the porch swing. Wesley sort of represented my youth, you know? We met in college and he was always so much fun and full of life. I've always been pretty boring for the most part but he could convince me to do almost anything and it would turn into the best time ever. But as time went on, I wanted a more stable life. I didn't need to fly off to Jamaica on a whim or party until the sun came up. I liked talking over dinner about a movie we'd just seen or sipping coffee in the backyard and watching the sunset together. That's what Shawn's always given me. He truly is my best friend and I can't picture a life without him. But that's exactly what was gonna happen if I didn't cut all ties to Wesley. So he's buying me out of our businesses which, by the way is something I need to tell you about."

Jade looked at him nervously. Then Justin explained that he and Wesley were part owners in a construction company but it was their primary business which provided them with the money to invest.

"Wesley and I own a couple of clubs … *adult* clubs in San Francisco. People can come there to have dinner and drinks, dance and socialize, and have sex if they choose to."

"Alrighty then, so do you wanna go inside for dessert?" she asked.

Jade had heard of those types of clubs before and as curious as she was, she thought it was best to let that be a part of Justin's life he kept private. So they went inside where the two of them laughed and talked over strawberry cheesecake and coffee. Once they were done, Justin held Jade's hand as they walked to the minivan.

"I love you, sis."

"I love you too, Justin."

Pierce and Teddy Bear were waiting in the living room when the two of them returned. They were still giggling like kids and he knew everything had been resolved. Justin said goodnight then headed to the guest room to call Shawn. Jade carried Teddy to his spot in the hallway then looked in on the kids.

"So what happened?" Pierce asked once Jade climbed in to bed with him.

She told him about her conversation with Justin then asked if he'd ever go to a sex club. He looked at her like she was crazy!

"Do you *think* I'd go to a sex club? I know you want to be supportive of your brother but that's just taking things too far, Jade. There ain't no way in hell I could watch somebody else be with you."

"It's not a swinger's club, babe. You don't swap. You only engage with your own partner."

"I don't give a damn! I don't need to go to some orgy to have sex with my wife!"

"Okay, dude, calm down. Why are you getting so upset? You and I ask each other random questions like this all the time?"

"Yeah, that's true. And I know I've always said I'm down for whatever but I never meant anything like that. I just hope you're not actually considering it. It seems like you asked Justin quite a lot of questions about it."

"Actually, I didn't. Most of that stuff I already knew."

"Oh *really*, and how did you come about that knowledge?" Pierce asked, as he folded his arms across his chest and stared at her.

"Okay, look, I'm gonna tell you something but you can't repeat it. She made me swear I wouldn't tell you. So you can't be bringing it up casually when we're all together, you hear me?"

"Oh lord, please don't tell me one of my sisters have been to a place like that."

"No, actually it's your mom."

Pierce instantly starting coughing and gagging!

"I'm just playing, babe," Jade laughed hysterically. "I swear, Pierce," she said when he kept staring at her with a horrified look on his face. "It's Jamel and Tamara. I promise."

"Girl, I ought to push you out this bed! Why you do me like that?"

"I'm sorry, babe, I couldn't resist. You were getting all serious on me so I had to do something to make you laugh. But you should know better than to think I'd ask or want to go to a sex club or swinger's club or any place like that. You're all I need, Butter Scotch." They both laughed.

"So how long has Tamara and Jamel's freaky asses been going to the sex club?"

"She said they've only been a few times. I get the feeling that Tamara likes it a little more than Jamel does."

"So tell me this. What does Tamara know about me that she's not supposed to know?"

"Nothing," Jade said, with an innocent little girl look on her face.

"You need to stop lying," Pierce laughed. "I know y'all be talking about stuff. So what does Tamara know?"

"Well," Jade said, as she rolled on top of him. "She knows how much I love you."

"Uh huh," he groaned when she kissed his neck.

"And she knows I'll do *anything* to get you off."

"Is that right?" Pierce smiled, as she kissed him again.

"Umm huh, anything at all."

"I think you trying to manipulate me. But it's alright, I like it," he teased then let Jade have her way with him.

Chapter
FIFTEEN

DESPITE HER CLAIMS THAT Dane's party was the last house party she was throwing, Jade had Sugar's first birthday bash at their home on Saturday, October 4th. She transformed the sunroom into a beautiful butterfly garden because their baby girl absolutely loved butterflies. Pierce had stenciled them all over Sugar's side of the room and she smiled every time she saw them.

Unfortunately, as always was the case with Jade's parties, there was some form of drama. It started with Hawn and Luisa being upset at Jade's unwillingness to throw one big party since Sugar's actual birthday and Hawn and Roland's third anniversary was on October 7th. Jade hated combo parties and she knew her sister-in-law well enough to know she would've made it all about her. Sugar deserved her own special day and Jade made sure she had it.

When Jade learned that Justin had left Shawn at the hotel to keep from making a spectacle at the party, she urged him to go get his boyfriend. She appreciated their thoughtfulness but thought it was crazy for Shawn to be sitting alone in a hotel room when they were all there eating and having a good time. Twenty minutes later when Justin arrived with Shawn, Jade was surprised. She assumed he would be tall and fit like Wesley but Shawn was a teeny tiny, fragile looking thing who could have easily passed for a woman with his smooth brown skin and long, silky hair! He was 5'2" and barely 100 pounds with the longest eyelashes Jade had ever seen on a man or a woman.

"You're so cute," Jade said of her brother's Dominican lover. "But you wrong for those eyelashes. I'm about to get some scissors and glue and cut me a few of those things."

Shawn laughed then proceeded to making the first of his second plate of food. He definitely seemed to enjoy himself and had a good time mingling with everyone, particularly Willa. That seemed to bother Justin for Shawn to like her so much. The truth was he was starting to like her too despite his best efforts not to.

After they'd cut the cake and sang happy birthday to Sugar, she raised her arms to go back to Landon. Throughout the party she had rotated from one set of arms to the next but she always managed to end up back in his. They definitely had a special bond which Jade found endearing. Not surprising, Pierce did not. He was upset by it already when Marcus decided to speak and make matters worse.

"Dang, Sugar, Sugar, you act like *Landon's* your daddy. What's up with that?" he laughed.

"Damn it, Marcus," Jade snapped before she could stop herself. "Ugh," she huffed then stomped out of the sunroom.

As usual Marcus acted clueless as to what he could've possibly said to cause someone to be upset. Jade wanted to go off on him but chose not to cause a scene and upset the kids who were happily playing and running around.

"Don't be upset, beauty queen. Don't nobody pay him no mind. And we all know ain't no way in hell Landon is Sugar's father. So you need to stop tripping."

"No, what I *need* to stop doing is having these damn parties! Something crazy happens every time I do," Jade said, as she snatched and slung things around the kitchen in her attempt to clean. "Marcus knows as well as any of us how much tension there is between Pierce and Landon as it is. Why say something like that and make it worse? Because y'all might not pay him any mind but I promise you Pierce did and I'm the one who's gonna be stuck here dealing with all of his emotions behind it!"

"Aw, quit being dramatic, Chicka," Hawn said after listening to her sister-in-law's rant.

Tamara and Jade looked at each other in disbelief that Hawn, the most dramatic of them all, would tell someone else not to be. Before Jade could respond to her, however, Hawn made a comment that sparked a memory and Jade asked to speak to her alone.

"What's wrong with you, Chicka?" Hawn asked once Jade closed the door to the guest bedroom.

"Remember when I was planning your wedding and you kept trying to get me to meet Pierce?"

"Yeah?" she frowned.

"Well, you said that I shouldn't trip about dating your brother because you had dated one of his friends. Who were you talking about?"

"Ugh, Chicka, you and that damn memory. You *would* remember some junk I said a million years ago. It's just like that time you …"

"Don't even try it, Alejandra, you not about to change the subject on me. Who was it?"

"It's whoever I just made you think it was by whatever the hell I said to spark this memory of yours."

"Are you serious? You slept with Marcus?"

"Yeah," Hawn sighed. "He's actually the first person I ever slept with."

"Are you *serious*?" Jade shrieked. "Oh my goodness I never would've guessed that, *ever*! Well, I know for a fact Pierce doesn't know but did you tell anybody?"

"Just Roland. He knows all my dirt."

"And it doesn't bother him for Marcus to be around all the time?"

"Nah, he ain't tripping off that old mess. I was seventeen years old and had a crush on my brother's stupid ass friend. It only happened twice then he quickly moved on to the next girl. Marcus's only concern was making sure Juan didn't find out. He cared more about their friendship and knew a beating was in store for him if Juan ever found out. So I know it was fifteen years ago, but if you could not mention it to your man that would be great."

Jade and Hawn were about to leave the room when they were startled.

"Ugh, what the hell are you *doing*?" Hawn snapped and punched Pierce in his chest. "You scared the crap out of me!"

"I was looking for my wife. What *y'all* doing in here all tucked away from everybody else? What's going on?"

"Nothing," Hawn said as she tried to move past him. "Move, Juan, quit playing!"

"Nope, tell me what you was talking about."

"Your nosey ass don't have to know everything, now move!" Hawn yelled as she tried unsuccessfully to push him out of the doorway. "Fine, if you must know," she gave in.

Jade's eyes got wide thinking Hawn was actually about to tell Pierce the truth.

"I'm pregnant."

"Aw," Pierce cooed then hugged his sister. "Roland's little men finally worked, huh?"

"Shut up, stupid!" Hawn hit her baby brother before leaving the room.

Jade was about to leave the room too but Pierce blocked her exit. "So what were y'all really in here talking about? You looked as surprised as I did when

Hawn said she was pregnant so I know you was gossiping about something else. What was it?"

Thankfully, screams from the living room distracted Pierce enough for Jade to get around him. Hawn and Roland told the rest of the family about the baby and they shouted and clapped. Then Hawn, who was only four weeks along, started rubbing her stomach and waddling like she was about to give birth any moment.

Pierce shook his head at Roland after watching his sister's performance. "I feel sorry for you, bro."

Like she did after all of the parties, Luisa took the kids back to her house to have some quality time with them and give Pierce and Jade a chance to be alone.

Jade was hoping she and her man were about to have some grown up fun when she noticed the weird look on his face as he sat beside her on the couch. "What's wrong with you?" she asked.

"I need to talk to you about something," Pierce said, as he grabbed a card from the coffee table. He opened it and began to read. "Thanks for visiting. I hope to see you again soon. Richard," he said, waiting for an explanation.

Jade just stared at Pierce for a few moments before she rolled her eyes at him. Then she reached over to grab the envelope that card had come out of and thrust it at Pierce. He felt about two inches small when he saw the return address. It was from Richard Morgan, the owner of Speedee, where they took their vehicles to get the oil changed.

"So I'm assuming you thought this card was from my ex-boyfriend Richard the reason you sprung it on me like this."

"I didn't assume anything. I just wanted to know … okay, yeah, I thought it was from your ex," Pierce admitted when Jade stared at him with her don't even try it look.

"So if I know you as well as I think I do, I'm guessing that's what you thought Hawn and I were in the guest room talking about … Richard?"

The guilty look on Pierce's face said it all.

"Ugh, you get on my nerves with this junk," Jade huffed then got up from the couch.

"Look, I'm sorry, alright?" Pierce said, as he pulled Jade back down. "We promised each other we'd bring up whatever issues we had no matter how petty they might seem, remember? And if I hadn't brought it to your attention I would've assumed it was from your ex and that y'all have been in touch and all that. So don't be mad at me, okay? Just tell me what to do to make it better," he smiled before planting a kiss on her neck. "Is there anything I can do for you?"

Those intense eyes were working on Jade. "Yeah. Quit opening my mail," she laughed.

"Nah, you can forget about that," Pierce chuckled. "I still don't know why you don't open mine."

"Because it's yours and you should be able to open it yourself. And it doesn't have anything to do with having stuff to hide like you keep saying. I just don't like you rummaging through my mail *or* my purse."

"Well, you better find a way to get over it 'cause when you signed on the dotted line you gave up all rights to privacy, chick. So I suggest you start opening my mail and going through my wallet so we'll be even. That's the best deal I can make for you," he smiled. "You know I love you, though, don't you?"

"Do you?"

"Oh, so it's like that? I need to show you?" Pierce gave her that sly grin she could never resist.

"Yeah, show me something, Butterscotch," she smiled then enjoyed her trips to the moon!

Chapter
SIXTEEN

AFTER THE PARTY, SINCE Landon had consumed a few drinks, Chaundra drove his truck to the house. At each stop sign he noticed her staring at him.

"What's up?" he asked, once they'd pulled into his garage.

"Has anything ever happened between you and Jade?"

He frowned at her. "No, of course not, Chaundra. Why would you even think something like that?"

"It's the way you look at her, Landon. And it's how you act when she's around. You just seem so in to her. And I know you say you love Jade and you're proud of her but it's more than that. You're in love with her, aren't you?"

"Ugh, Chaundra, please, how many times must I tell you that I love *you*?"

"I know you love me, Landon, but you're *in* love with her, aren't you?"

"Oh my god, what else do I have to do, Chaundra? What can I do to prove to you once and for all that I'm in love with you?"

"Well, for one thing you can answer my question. Or maybe you are answering it by not just simply saying you aren't in love with her. You can't say it, can you? I don't know why I need to hear you say it anyway because it's written all over your face when she's around and even when you're just talking about her. I guess I should've gotten the hint when you blew off my birthday so you could be with Jade on hers. I should've …"

"See, that's what I'm talking about right there. You be telling your friends these bullshit stories about me blowing you off when you know that's not the truth! You and I made plans to celebrate your birthday on that Saturday but then *you* decided to fly out on Tuesday even though I told you I had plans to take Jade out. But you know what? It was three months ago. Get over it!" he snapped when she rolled her eyes at him. "Whatever, Chaundra, think what you want. I'm really tired of having this idiotic conversation with you," Landon said, as he hopped out of the truck and stormed into the house.

Chaundra lowered the garage door then went inside. She was waiting in the living room for Landon to come back downstairs to talk not realizing he was done talking for the night. He'd gotten undressed, turned off all the lights, and climbed into bed.

"Landon?" Chaundra called ten minutes later once she realized he wasn't coming back to apologize. She turned on the lamp on his nightstand. "Landon?"

"What?" he squinted.

"Can we finish talking? I don't want you to go to sleep angry with me."

"I don't have anything to say, Chaundra. And I honestly don't wanna hear nothing else about how insecure Jade makes you. If you don't trust how I feel about you by now then I don't know what to tell you. I just wanna go to sleep. It's been a long night and I'm tired. I've been drinking and I don't have the energy or desire to deal with all your emotions. I'll talk to you tomorrow," Landon said then turned over on his side. "Hit that light."

The Christmas season grew to be overwhelming for Jade. Not only did she have the stress of shopping for gifts for a huge family, but she was also planning Christmas dinner at their home. In the midst of it all, Jade's family and friends constantly came over or called to unload all of their problems on her. She wanted to be there for them but it had all just become too much.

"Welcome home, babe," Pierce said and gave Jade a kiss. He took off her coat and boots. "Now I want you to go enjoy the warm bubble bath I have waiting. After that you can slip into the pajamas I have on the bed for you. They look similar to these," he said, modeling the black, long- sleeved silk pajamas he was wearing. "Dinner will be ready in about an hour so take your time, relax, and enjoy yourself."

"Pierce, this is *wonderful*," Jade cooed as she looked at the living room he'd transformed into a romantic hideaway.

Candles were lit all over the room and soft music was playing. Jade quickly realized it was Joshua Redman, the album he was playing when they had their first date. On the floor were two of the biggest, plushiest pillows she'd ever seen in her life. It sort of reminded her of Aladdin with the shape, rich colors, and tassels on the ends of each square.

"I can't believe you did all this, babe. It's so beautiful and thoughtful and I really appreciate it. Thank you."

"Well, I know things have been a little stressful lately and you've been everybody's listening ear. So I wanted to give you the chance to talk your little heart out while I take care of you. Oh, look what else I have," Pierce said, as he reached inside a plastic bag.

Jade burst out laughing when she saw the video tape. It was Steel Magnolias, one of her absolute favorite movies, and she'd been trying to convince Pierce to watch it since they met. He thought of it as the ultimate chick flick and wasn't interested. They both knew it was because of how emotional he was. Jade had no doubt he'd be crying like a baby and Pierce knew it too. That's why he had avoided it for all that time. That night, though, he wanted to do something special for Jade and he was willing to look sappy in the process.

She assumed the kids were with Luisa and was shocked to learn Willa had them. Jade was curious how that came about and Pierce said he merely asked her.

"I think that's all your mom wanted was to be asked. It seemed to make her feel good to be needed. And the kids were excited to be there. So don't worry, they'll be fine. You know Dane will watch over those girls like he's their dad."

Jade was pleasantly surprised and it warmed her heart to see her mom really making an effort to be more involved in their lives.

"Ooh that smells wonderful, babe. Are you cooking what I think you're cooking?"

"Yes I am. It's the first meal I ever made for you. Do you remember what it's called?"

"Of course I remember. It was called chicken and rice," Jade laughed loudly. "No, seriously it's called uh, a rose can Apollo. Wait, its uhm …"

"Please, just stop butchering the poor dish's name," Pierce laughed. "For the one millionth time its called arroz con pollo."

"Yeah, that's what I said."

Jade laughed again then gave Pierce a kiss before she went to get into the bath. He brought her a virgin strawberry daiquiri with whipped cream and cherries and washed her back as she talked about one subject to the next. Forty-five minutes later Jade got dressed in her black silk pajamas and met Pierce in the living room. Once she got comfy on her pillow he presented her with a plate. It was a miracle they were able to digest any food from laughing so much during dinner. Then somehow they got on the subject of their attraction for one another.

"You're an incredibly attractive man, Pierce, and I'm drawn to you whether you're in a suit, a pair of jeans, or a towel. But I do think there are some times that I'm especially attracted to you that might surprise you."

"Like what?" Pierce asked with his interest piqued.

"For starters when you smile at me I just melt. I still think it's the most magical thing I've ever seen."

"Awww, that's so sweet," Pierce said, smiling at her.

"But the times I be ready to attack you are when you're running on the treadmill in a pair of shorts with no shirt and your dog tags on. And when you cut the grass in those jeans with your baseball cap on backwards. Good *lord* you should see me staring out the window like a crack addict waiting on that next fix! I be like when is he coming back *in*," Jade said, as she twitched and scratched.

Pierce laughed so hard that he nearly choked! "Girl, you are so crazy. But I know what you mean. I definitely have some crack addict moments when it comes to you. I never told you this before but I get turned on every time you put on your apron."

Jade burst out laughing. "Are you serious? What could possibly be sexy about that thing?"

"I don't know but it gets me going from the second you put it on. Oh, and your favorite pair of jeans, the Gloria Vanderbilt ones? Those are my favorite ones too. They display your butt perfectly. Every time you put them on I'm like *damnnn*, look at that booty!" Pierce groaned. "But it's like you said earlier, you could put on anything or nothing and I'd be attracted to you. You just sexy to me."

Pierce and Jade talked and laughed for another hour or so before he put the tape of Steel Magnolias into the VCR. Jade sat in-between Pierce on his pillow and he held her close to him while they enjoyed the movie. He was actually surprised at how funny it was. However, when they got to the cemetery scene Pierce fought hard not to cry. Jade could feel his chest trembling but he would cough or stretch to avoid breaking down. Jade was a blubbering mess as she always was during that part of the movie. Pierce eventually cried but he said it was because *she* was crying, not from the movie.

"You need to stop lying," Jade laughed, as she turned to face him. "Are you seriously trying to tell me that wasn't the most heartbreaking thing you've ever seen? Sally Field didn't just rip your gut out at the cemetery?"

"Nope, I'm cool," Pierce said with tear stained cheeks. "I wasn't affected at all," he laughed.

They talked over dessert, reminisced, and had a few slow dances before Pierce encouraged Jade to get some sleep. The two of them stretched out in bed watching TV as he held her and ran his fingers through her hair.

"I like you, you know that?" Pierce asked.

"I like you too," Jade smiled.

Soon after, she was sleeping soundly in his arms. Pierce kissed the top of her head and went to sleep as well. It was the perfect ending to the perfect date.

It was the second week of 1999 and Jade was excited for her and Pierce's first group date of the year. She enjoyed them very much and invited four other couples to dinner and a show. They all agreed to go to Cattleman's Steakhouse in Fremont followed by a night at the comedy club. As usual they got on the topic of relationships and went into their men versus women debates.

They were about to order dessert when Marcus's on-again, off-again woman Sheila made a statement that got things heated. "I hope you been paying attention, Marcus, 'cause you could use a few pointers on how to treat a lady."

"Well, when I'm actually *with* a lady I treat her just fine," he snapped.

"*Excuse* me?" Sheila frowned. "What is that supposed to mean? You think your philandering ways is how to treat a woman?"

"*Philandering*? Hold up!" he yelled.

"Hey, hey, guys this is supposed to be a fun night," Pierce said, as he tried to diffuse the bomb about to blow.

"Nah, man, the fun is over," Marcus said, as he glared at Sheila who was glaring back at him. "I wanna know how I get classified as a philanderer by someone who isn't my wife, girlfriend, *or* significant other! I'm a single, grown ass man and I'm free to do what or whoever I want. So don't sit there trying to make it seem like I'm doing you wrong when there's never been anything serious between us. You just my go-to girl when I ain't got nothing else to do."

Everyone at the table stared at them with their mouths opened not knowing what to say.

"Wow, Marcus," Sheila uttered, refusing to let a tear drop down her face, "so in these four years of us going back and forth with each other there's never been anything serious between us? Then why you keep coming back?"

"You let me," he said simply. "And since you worried about getting pointers won't you get some from Jade. If you were even *half* the woman she is you might have a ring by now!"

"Whoa, hey, don't do that, Marcus," Jade said.

"No, let him talk. I'm curious to hear what else he has to say," Pierce said, as he stared angrily at his friend.

"Don't trip, dude, you know what I mean. What man wouldn't want what you have … a beautiful woman and family that loves and cares for you? That's all I'm saying."

"Uh huh," Pierce muttered with a raised eyebrow.

It was no surprise to anyone when Marcus and Sheila chose to skip the comedy club. They all just hoped the two of them didn't kill each other on the way home. After dessert and more conversations about love and relationships, the remaining couples drove across the street hoping to laugh for the rest of the night. Jade chuckled when Pierce came back to the table with a Midori sour. He said he was curious to see if the Santa Barbara beast would re-emerge.

"Uh, oh what's this? Beauty queen is actually having a grown up drink?" Tamara teased.

"Yes she is," Pierce said with a huge smile.

"Aw, shoot, I guess we know who gone be leaving first, huh? I just hope y'all make it out the parking lot this time," Tamara laughed loudly.

"Girl, would you *shut up*?" Jade blushed, knowing her friend was referring to the time Pierce and Jade got busted in the backseat of his Chevelle outside of a nightclub.

Thankfully the show started before Tamara could fill everyone at the table in on the details of that night. The first comedian was horrible but the next two were funny and they all got a few good belly laughs from them. The headliner was a woman named Gracie Pays. She was a short, frumpy thirty-something year old who didn't seem to put much energy into trying to spruce up. They soon realized that was a big part of her act.

"Hello, everybody, my name is Gracie Pays for sex, uh, I mean Gracie Pays and I'm real happy y'all came out tonight. You can look at me and tell I don't get out much so it's nice to finally have some company."

The crowd of ninety erupted into laughter. After a few more self-deprecating jokes Gracie started messing with people in the audience.

"And see this table right here is, oh my heaven's, y'all see him? Hey, shine the light on him. No, not … yeah, yeah him! Umph, umph, *umph*! Sir, what's your name?"

"Pierce."

"He *would* have a sexy name too, wouldn't he? I thought you was gone say something jacked up like Ernest."

"Hey," a guy called from the crowd. They all assumed his name was Ernest and laughed.

"So anyway, back to you, Pierce. I'm gonna ask you a question and I really, really hope your answer is no."

"Okay," Pierce smiled.

"Oh, now wait you can't be smiling at me like that. My panties just fell off!" Gracie said, as she fanned herself with her hand. "Okay, so back to my question. Is this woman that's sitting all close to you like she ain't got a seat of her own with you?"

"Yes."

"Damn it, that's strike one! I told you the answer was supposed to be no, Pierce!"

"I'm sorry, I'm sorry," he laughed, throwing his hands up in mock surrender.

"Okay, well since you so fine I'm about to give you another chance. You better answer this one right, though. So are y'all casually seeing each other? Is this your first date? Would you have a problem ditching her in the parking lot to come hang with me?" Again the crowd erupted into thunderous laughter.

"She's my wife," Pierce said.

"Damn it, that's strike two, Pierce! You breaking my heart, man. Y'all wrong for that. See, two beautiful people like you and, what's your wife's name?"

"Jade."

"Ugh, whatever," Gracie rolled her eyes. "Of course she would have some exotic sounding name, right? Anyway, two beautiful people like you and *Jade* aren't supposed to be together. She was supposed to marry an old, ugly, raggedy man to balance things out. And you was supposed to hold out for a mediocre chick like me!"

Tamara nudged Jade and they both laughed along with the rest of the audience.

"Listen, I'm a failure in life, Pierce. I'm broke, out of shape, with no real hope for the future. But if you had waited for me like you was supposed to then at least people could say Gracie ain't worth a damn, but look at her man! But noooo, you had to run off and marry goddamn Ms. America and screw up *my* life! How could you be so selfish, Pierce? You were my one shot!" Gracie stated. "There's only one thing you can do now. You gone have to leave her, Pierce, there's no other way. I'm sorry, Jade, but go ahead and say your goodbyes 'cause it's over!" They all continued to laugh and applaud Gracie for being the funniest comic of the night. "Now see they got it right," she said, pointing to Landon and Chaundra. "This fine, milk chocolate man could've had any woman he wanted but he took one for the team and got a below average chick to keep things even!"

There was a collective gasp as everyone at the table looked at Chaundra. Tamara was pretty liquored up by then and she burst out laughing. Trish and Tony started laughing because Tamara was laughing so hard but Chaundra looked close to tears. Jade reached over to touch her hand but she snatched away and stormed out of the comedy club. For some reason Jade followed her. Landon actually said a few choice words to Gracie before he left. The rest of the table grabbed their things and headed out as well. They caught the tail end of Chaundra going off on Jade for patronizing her.

"You know what, Chaundra, I'm done. I've gone out of my way trying to befriend you but you obviously don't like me. I don't have a clue what I've done to you but at this point I don't even care," Jade said, as she waved her hand and walked away.

"Jade, wait ..."

"No, *you* wait," Tamara snapped. "Don't be talking to beauty queen like that! If you noticed, she was the only one that gave a damn your little feelings was even hurt. I felt like you needed to get some thicker skin and suck it up. Hell, we at a comedy club so why you gone sit there taking that mess seriously? Didn't you hear that hoe say me and Jamel didn't matter because we jacked up regardless? Did you see me get up and storm out like a little punk?"

"Okay, okay we got your point, baby," Jamel said, as he led his wife to their car. "Goodnight everybody. Drive home safe."

"I'll call you tomorrow, beauty queen. Don't even trip off Ms. Below Average she just jealous. Go home and let your inner hoe out, you understand me?" Tamara slurred.

"Barely," Jade teased. "Love you."

"Love you too," she shouted from across the parking lot. "I'll see you in the morning."

Pierce said goodnight to Trish then he and Tony made plans to stop by Marcus's house the next day. They wanted to make sure he was okay. Landon had said goodnight to everyone before whisking Chaundra off to his truck. He was so annoyed with her for treating Jade that way when she was only being concerned.

"What is your problem, Chaundra?" Landon yelled, as he slammed his door shut. "Why would you disrespect Jade like that?"

"You and your precious, Jade," she snorted. "She just can't do no wrong in your eyes, can she? All of y'all sat there marveling at her while she was at the head of the table dispensing advice like *nobody* else knows how to make a relationship work but her! And then after I'd already been humiliated, Ms. America reaches over and pats the below average chick on the head like she pitied me! But you don't see it that way, right? Instead of defending *me* you come running to the aid of your precious, perfect Jade!"

"I *did* defend you! And you would know that if you hadn't drawn even more attention to yourself by running out like a little kid! And as far as the whole dispensing advice thing goes I don't think you really paid attention. If anybody came across like a relationship consultant it was Pierce. But you couldn't stop grinning when *he* was talking. I thought you was about to pull out a pen and paper and start taking notes!" Landon snapped. "Jade shared what she learned from her mistakes in their marriage but you so determined to hate her that you twist everything she says.

"And you wanna know the truth, Chaundra? Jade's the reason you and

I even still have a relationship. When you started popping up unannounced and acting all crazy I was ready to leave. I'm for real. But Jade helped me to see ways I might have pushed you to acting that way and encouraged me to talk to you and make it work. She's always considering your feelings, even tonight, and you treat her like snot for it!"

Chaundra felt like a world class jerk! Though, she couldn't help being angry over Landon saying he was ready to dump her until Jade told him not to. She didn't quite know what to make of that.

Landon started his truck and backed out of the parking spot. He turned the radio up to discourage any more talking. Chaundra turned it down.

"So that's it, then? The conversation is over now that you've said what you wanted to say?"

Landon let out a deep breath. "What do you wanna say now, Chaundra?" he asked dryly.

"Wow, so that's how it is? Am I boring you?"

"I just don't wanna hear another word about how insecure Jade makes you. I'm tired of trying to convince you how I feel about you. And I'm tired of fighting. I don't wanna do it anymore so I'm done."

"You don't wanna do *what* anymore?"

"*This*, Chaundra," he said, pointing to her and then himself. "I really thought you were the one for me but clearly I was wrong. It shouldn't be this hard to get along."

She began to cry. "So it's over then, just like that? You can break it off with me and not even feel anything?"

"Who says I don't feel anything? I actually feel a lot about it, Chaundra, but I don't know what else to do. Back when I was in my teens this kind of fighting and making up kind of relationship was fun. But I'll be thirty-two this year and I don't have time for that kind of drama. I wanna get married again and travel and have a normal life with a woman I can get along with," Landon said, as he hit the garage door opener and drove in. He closed the door and shut off the engine. "I thought that woman was you. I really did. But I spend more time arguing with you than anything else and I don't want that. I'm not happy, Chaundra. And I can't imagine you are either."

She leaned forward with her elbows on her knees and sobbed. Landon rubbed her back and begged her to stop crying.

"Look, baby, I'm not trying to hurt you. I love you. But I can't keep doing this. Don't you feel the same?"

"Honestly, I think we're great together. It seems like things go wrong whenever Jade comes up. And I don't wanna lose you because of that. I love you, Landon," she said staring him in the face. "You're the best thing in my life and I don't wanna lose you. So please just tell me what I have to do to salvage what we have and I will. I can't lose you," Chaundra said and began to cry again.

Landon didn't know what to do. His mind was telling him to break things off and find a way to move on. His heart, though, was telling him to take Chaundra in his arms and never let her go. She did have a point about things going sour between them whenever Jade was present or spoken about. Landon didn't know what to do. Jade was his family and his best friend and she would always be in his life. Yet, women like Chaundra were rare and he didn't want to throw away his chance at happiness. For the first time Landon understood what Jade had been going through with him and Pierce. It was hard when the people you loved most couldn't get along.

"Come here," Landon said, as he took Chaundra into his arms. He just held her for a while, neither of them saying a word. "Let's go inside, okay?"

"Okay," she said, following him upstairs to the bedroom.

Chapter

SEVENTEEN

ON JUNE 26, 1999, two weeks after Hawn had given birth, Pierce and Jade hosted a barbecue to welcome Xavier Alan Powell to the family. None of them had a clue that would be the last time they all were together as one of their beloved would soon be lost.

Jade thought her heart was about to stop beating when Tripp called Sunday morning saying Quik Stop had just been robbed! The only thought going through her mind was why hadn't Pierce been the one to call her.

"Tripp … Tripp, where is Pierce? Is he okay?" she asked, interrupting the boy from talking a mile a minute.

"Oh, yeah, he's fine. He's outside talking to the police. I guess I should've said that at first, huh? I'm sorry, I didn't mean to scare you. I just wanted you to know what was going on. You want me to have him call … oh, here he comes now. Hold on a second."

Although Jade was relieved to hear Pierce's voice, she was still a nervous wreck and tried desperately to convince him to close the store and come home. She had a fit when Pierce refused saying he had to tend to things and couldn't run away from his responsibilities.

"I've got the Beretta if that makes you feel any better."

"No, it doesn't make me feel better, Pierce! Please, babe, just come home. It's nothing in that store worth losing you over. Please."

"I know you're upset, but … look, I gotta go. The officer needs to talk to me again. I love you, babe. Bye."

Scared and emotional, Jade called Marcus, Roland, and Landon and sent them to Quik Stop to make sure Pierce was safe. She knew he would be mad but it was the only way Jade could calm her nerves enough not to alarm the kids.

Soon after, Pierce called to let her know his bodyguards had arrived and that he'd be home within an hour to see Dane off. Tina was coming to get him so they could go to Myron's family reunion in San Diego.

"Pooh!"

"Sugah!"

"Hey, little girls, y'all can't do that. We're supposed to be playing hide and seek," Dane laughed as his little sisters did their daily routine of calling each other as they ran through the house.

He took his sisters and Teddy, who'd grown into a beautiful golden brown and black forty-pound dog, to his bedroom and told Pooh to close her eyes and count. She could only count to ten so he found it hilarious to hear her trying to count higher than that. Pooh squealed and clapped when she found the three of them all hiding under Dane's bed. Teddy's tail and Sugar's giggles may have had something to do with Pooh finding them so easily.

The next round Dane counted and let the girls run off to hide. Jade was in the kitchen making grilled cheese sandwiches when Teddy started barking like crazy! She took off running to her bedroom where he was scratching on the trunk at the foot of her bed. Jade heard Sugar's muffled screams and lifted the lid. It had snapped shut after the girl climbed inside to hide from Dane.

"It's okay, Sugar, Sugar, Mommy's got you," Jade cooed, as she held her daughter close.

Sugar was trembling and crying so Jade rubbed her back to try to calm her. Dane started crying feeling guilty and thinking Jade was angry with him. So she had to calm him down as well. Pooh was scared and cried because her siblings were crying.

"It's okay, babies, it was just an accident," she said to all of them, including Teddy.

Jade sat on the couch with Sugar continuing to rub her back and kiss her cheek. She rocked with her and tried to reassure her that everything was okay.

"What's wrong?" Pierce asked when he walked in from the garage.

"Sugar got stuck in the trunk," Dane answered.

"*What?*"

"It's okay, babe, everybody's fine. It was just an accident that lasted less than a minute. She's fine."

"She doesn't look fine, Jade! Look at her, she's drenched with sweat! Sugar had to be in there longer than a minute to be soaked like that!"

Pierce's raised voice startled Sugar and she started crying again. Teddy barked at him.

"Calm down alright, Pierce? You getting her all upset again," Jade said, barely above a whisper.

"Don't tell me to calm down when I come home and see that my baby damn near suffocated! And where the hell were you when all this was happening, on the phone talking about that stupid book?"

Dane and Pooh started crying. They couldn't take it when their parents yelled. Jade's eyes were filled with tears when she looked up at Pierce.

"Oh so now I'm the villain, right? My kid could've been killed but everybody wants to cry because I'm upset about it! Whatever. Shut up, Teddy," he screamed before storming out of the living room. Where was she ... never mind," Pierce said when he saw the open trunk. "I don't even know why you have these stupid things," he mumbled.

Pierce grabbed that trunk and the one from Dane's room and dragged them out to the garage. A few minutes later Jade and the kids heard banging and pounding as Pierce demolished the trunks with a sledgehammer!

"I'm sorry, Mommy. Dad wouldn't be mad at you if I had been watching her."

"Sh,sh,sh," Jade said, as she caressed his face. "It was just an accident, baby. It's not your fault, okay? Everything will be fine. Daddy's just upset and scared. Come here."

With Sugar dozing off on her shoulder, Jade hugged Dane and then Pooh. She took them to the kitchen to eat the sandwiches she made and put a brave smile on her face. As soon as Jade was out of their sight she began to cry. All she could think about was what would've happened if Teddy hadn't been there. Who knows how long Sugar would have been trapped in that trunk? The thought of her suffocating filled Jade's mind and tears poured down her face. Sugar lifted her head and looked Jade in the eyes. She wiped her mother's tears and that made Jade cry more. Her little hands felt so soft and the look on her face was adorably sweet.

"Mommy's sorry," Jade uttered, as she squeezed her little girl. "Are you okay? Do you wanna eat?"

Sugar nodded and smiled then Jade took her to the kitchen. She placed the toddler in her highchair and cut up the grilled cheese sandwich. Sugar wolfed it down and then drank a sippy cup of milk. Jade was about to take her out of the highchair when Pierce walked in with dust and wood chips all over him.

"Come here," he barked. Pierce took a deep breath. "Can I talk to you for a minute, please?" he said through gritted teeth when Jade looked at him like he was crazy.

She took the kids to the living room and put Aladdin on for them to watch. Jade put Sugar in her playpen knowing she'd be sleep within a few minutes. Dane and Pooh were snuggled up on the couch together.

"What do you want?" Jade asked, after she closed the door to their bedroom.

Pierce had undressed and was getting ready to shower to get all the dust off his body.

"What do you *think* I want, Jade?" he snapped. "I wanna know how our child that's not even two yet ended up in a locked trunk. What were you doing?"

"I was in the kitchen making sandwiches while the kids played hide and seek. I never would've dreamed Sugar would open the trunk and get inside of it. I feel sick thinking about what could've happened to her," Jade cried.

"You should," Pierce huffed. "Our baby girl could be gone right now!"

"I know, Pierce," she sniffed. "I guess you think I don't feel horrible enough already that you need to talk to me like this. You should know I would never do anything intentionally to hurt our kids and I feel awful that this happened. I'm *so* sorry," she wept. "I would've never forgiven myself if something had happened to her."

"Well, I made sure it'll never happen again," he said, coldly then went to the bathroom. Jade sat on the edge of the bed crying.

Pierce took a quick shower and had just enough time to talk to Dane before Tina and Myron showed up. Like always, Dane expressed his desire to stay home but for some reason he was even more emotional about it. Tina was seriously considering letting him stay since he was so upset. However, Pierce told Dane he had to go because his Mom and Myron loved him and wanted to spend time with him too. He walked them to the car, hugged and kissed his son, then watched Myron drive away. Jade and the girls waved and blew kisses until they couldn't see Dane anymore.

The next morning, after having a fight with Landon in which he hung up on her, Jade got up to get Pooh ready for her doctor's appointment.

"Wow, I never thought I'd see the day your boy actually got mad at *you*," Pierce chuckled.

"You need to stop it. Landon and I have argued plenty of times. He's just being emotional right now so I'll talk to him later. I need to get Pooh ready for her check up. Thanks for staying home with Sugar. It's easier when I don't have both of them to deal with," Jade said, as she planted a kiss on his lips. "Quit playing, dude, I gotta go," she giggled when Pierce grabbed her and started kissing her neck.

Jade managed to wiggle free and run off to get her daughter dressed. Afterwards Pooh asked Jade for a cookie and was told no.

"Dad-deee," Pooh called, with the most pitiful little look on her face.

"What is it, baby?" Pierce asked then picked her up.

"Can I have cookies?" she whispered.

"Mommy said no, Pooh Bear."

She looked at him with the sweetest puppy dog eyes before wrapping her arms around his neck and patting his back.

"Okay, you get one and that's it, you hear me? I mean it," Pierce said, as he handed the child an Oreo.

Sugar held her hand out when she saw her sister eating a cookie and Pierce gave her one as well.

Jade rolled her eyes and shook her head at him. "You big ole punk," she teased.

"She manipulated me. How was I supposed to resist those little sad eyes and her cute little hands patting me on the back? Plus, I know you not talking with the way Dane has you wrapped around his little finger."

"He does not!"

"Girl please, I live here and see it everyday. That boy can get you to do *anything*. So who's the punk now?" They laughed knowing their kids knew how to play them both.

"Okay, Pooh Bear, we need to go. We'll see you in a little bit," she said giving Pierce a kiss as well as Sugar who was in his arms. "Have fun with Daddy."

"We're gonna have a ball, huh, Sugar, Sugar? Jade, look at your daughter. What is she supposed to be doing, hypnotizing me?" he laughed.

Sugar put her hands on Pierce's cheek then leaned forward as if she was doing mind control on him. Then she burst out laughing like it was the funniest thing in the world.

"You are so crazy, little girl, but I love you," Pierce said, planting kisses all over Sugar's face. "Oh, where's her swimsuit, babe? I was thinking about getting in the pool for a while."

Sugar loved the sound of that and started clapping and bucking. She knew where her swimsuit was and ran to the room to get it. Pierce kissed Pooh and Jade and walked them to the garage door.

"Okay, I'll see y'all later. I'm being summoned," Pierce laughed when Sugar called him from her bedroom.

Even though it only took ten minutes to get to Kaiser in Union City, Jade left home thirty minutes before Pooh's appointment because parking was always a nightmare. She was pleasantly surprised to find a spot directly in front of the pediatric building. It was only when Jade was taking Pooh out of her car seat that she remembered she'd left the shot records at home. She debated whether to go back or not and decided against it. She would just have the nurse print out another copy. It was a decision that would haunt Jade for the rest of her life.

Pierce had just stepped into the pool holding Sugar when he heard the phone ring. He was planning to let the answering service get it so he could have time with his daughter doing her favorite thing. However, when it kept ringing over and over again he knew something was wrong.

Hawn was calling from St. Rose Hospital in Hayward. Luisa had been in a horrific car accident and was rushed to the operating room for emergency surgery! The doctors weren't giving the family any information so they didn't know how bad things really were. However, when Diana saw her mother's mangled car being towed off the highway she couldn't imagine anyone who'd been inside of it surviving!

Sugar tried to leap out of her father's arms and he turned in an awkward way to keep from dropping her. Pierce lost his footing and smacked his head on the pavement. Blood instantly seeped from the back of his head and everything went black!

"Your daughter is *darling*," said one of the moms in the waiting room. "I don't know how you can resist hugging and kissing her pretty little face all the time."

"Thank you," Jade smiled, as she watched Pooh play with the blocks at the toddler table.

A few other moms commented on how beautiful Pooh was and how sweet and happy she seemed. Jade told them she looked exactly like her father then pulled out a family photo from her wallet. They oohed and aahed about how beautiful her family was and said they looked like models.

"Mrs. Jamison," the nurse called.

"Yes," Jade replied.

"Dr. Rickman was called away on an emergency. The on-call doctor is on his way to replace her but it will be about twenty minutes before he gets here. Would you like to wait or do you want us to reschedule your appointment for later this afternoon?"

"Uh, I think I'll wait. I might as well just get it over with rather than having to come back and fight to find parking. I was lucky to get a spot right in front of the building this time."

The moms Jade had been chatting with chimed in about how horrible the parking was. Soon they were talking about childbirth, teething, and potty training.

"Dana Jamison," the nurse called thirty minutes later.

Jade gave Pooh a droplet full of Tylenol before they left the office. Her doctor had advised she do it to ward off any fever or pain Pooh may have had from the immunizations.

"You were such a brave girl, Pooh Bear. Mommy's proud of you," Jade cooed as she strapped her daughter into her car seat. "Let's go see if Daddy and Sugar want to get ice cream. You can get the bubble gum flavor you like."

Pooh clapped and cheered and chatted the whole ride home. Jade's heart dropped into her stomach when she turned onto their street and saw a fire truck, a station wagon, and two paramedics parked in front of their house.

"Mommy, fire truck," Pooh pointed, as they pulled into the garage.

Jade jumped out of the minivan and snatched Pooh out of her seat. Pierce's oldest sister Eva was standing in the living room crying with her arms wrapped tightly around herself when Jade walked in.

"Oh, honey, I'm *so* sorry," she sobbed. "No, Jade, wait, you don't wanna go out there."

Jade thrust Pooh in her sister-in-law's arms and went running towards the back yard. She bolted through the open sliding glass door and rounded the corner. The first thing Jade saw was Eva's husband Gerard wrapping Teddy in a blood soaked towel. Then she spotted Roland and three paramedics struggling to control Pierce. He was fighting to get off the lounge chair they were trying to make him lie on and became even more agitated when he saw Jade. Pierce was reaching for her even though the things he was saying made no sense.

Jade saw a pool of blood close to where the guys were standing and blood running down Pierce's back. She was trying to comprehend what was happening when her eyes went to the other side of the pool. Jade felt something break inside of her when a man she'd never seen before zipped up a black bag with her baby inside of it! She suddenly realized the station wagon parked out front belonged to the coroner. And that God had finally punished her for the decision she'd made years before.

Chapter

EIGHTEEN

ALL JADE WANTED TO do was scream at the top of her lungs and run to get her baby out of that bag. However, when she opened her mouth nothing came out and her legs wouldn't move. The pain she felt was indescribable and unlike anything she'd ever felt in her life. *Wake up, Jade. Wake up!* It had to be a nightmare, the worst one she'd ever had. Sugar couldn't actually be *dead*! Her baby girl couldn't really be gone!

Jade felt like she was having an out of body experience as she followed behind her husband and daughter being wheeled out on stretchers. Pierce had been mildly sedated so they could transport him to the hospital and tend to the open gash on the back of his head. Sugar was about to be loaded into a separate ambulance when Landon jumped out of his truck and ran to Jade.

"*JADE*! Who is that?" he pointed and screamed.

The look of terror in his eyes broke Jade's heart and tears began to stream down her face, although she didn't feel as if she was really crying. Jade didn't feel like she was even really alive.

"It's my baby," she whispered. "Sugar's dead."

"No, no, no, Jade, don't say that! Oh god *NO!*"

A crowd of neighbors had formed outside trying to figure out what happened. They were yelling out questions to Jade and trying to interrogate the paramedics. She didn't have the strength to deal with them. It was hard enough trying to get control of Landon who was on the ground screaming and crying. Roland and Gerard had to grab him and take him inside. Jade couldn't take it so she hopped in the minivan and followed the paramedics to Kaiser Hospital in Fremont. She needed to be with Pierce. She needed him to hold her and promise they would get through it and everything would be okay. Unfortunately, he was in no condition physically, emotionally, or mentally to do so.

"What's wrong with him?" Jade asked the emergency room doctor. "Why is he talking crazy like that? Wait, where are they taking him?"

Dr. Booker explained that Pierce was being taken to radiology for a CAT scan. They needed to run tests to determine whether a brain injury was causing his incoherent behavior. He explained that Pierce would be out of it for a while and suggested Jade go home and try to rest.

"I can't leave him."

"I understand, Mrs. Jamison, but he won't even know you're here. Go and let your family help you through this difficult time. I promise we'll take good care of your husband."

Jade clutched her purse and was about to leave the waiting room but took a seat instead. She had to see Pierce. She had to hold him and let him know how sorry she was.

"May I help you, sir?"

"Yes, I'm looking for my friend Pierce Jamison. He was brought in about an hour ago."

"Marcus," Jade called.

He and Tony hurried over to her.

"I'm *so* sorry, baby," Marcus cried, as he took Jade into his arms and held her tight.

She pushed away from him only to have Tony embrace her just as tight. Jade felt close to breaking down so she took a step back from both of them to explain what was going on with Pierce. Soon after, a nurse approached Jade with a clipboard full of papers to be filled out. Once she'd given all of their insurance information and paid the hundred dollar co-pay, Jade was told Pierce would be taken to room 316 when they were done with his tests. The three of them were on their way upstairs when Jackie, Daniel, and Willa came barreling through the emergency room. They'd run into each other in the parking lot and Jackie and Willa sobbed when they saw each other. They couldn't believe what was happening to their babies.

"Baby girl," Willa cried as she rushed to Jade.

The mother and daughter scene was unbearable and the men all broke down crying. Thankfully, Nurse Bennett came to inform them that Pierce was being moved to his room. Jade was grateful for the distraction as she didn't know how much more of everyone's sobbing she could withstand before shattering into a million pieces herself. It only got worse, however, when Pierce was wheeled into his room. No one was prepared to see him like that.

He looked so pale and broken that it made them all cry. Pierce was still restrained and babbling things which made no sense. Jade went over to the bed to talk to him and he became agitated to the point that the nursing staff had to ask her to leave. She was devastated! Even though the doctor explained that Pierce had a concussion, Jade was still heartbroken by his response. She didn't understand why he seemed so angry and hostile but only towards her.

"I know it's difficult but try not to take it personally," Dr. Webster said. He went on to explain the different side effects of a concussion and how they could last for days or even months. "Go home with your mother and try to rest, Mrs. Jamison. We'll take good care of your husband."

Jade didn't want to leave but she knew it was best.

"We'll be here for him so go ahead and be with your mama. Me and Marcus are staying the night so Pierce won't be alone, okay?" Tony assured her. He held Jade's and Willa's hand. "We're all gonna get through this together. I promise," he said, as tears streamed down his face.

Early the next morning Jade phoned the hospital again to check on Pierce. He wasn't doing any better and the doctor decided to keep him another night. And she was still advised not to visit. A few hours later Myron and Tina arrived with Dane. He knew something was terribly wrong but neither of them had the heart to tell him what happened.

"We couldn't," Tina uttered then turned her face into Myron's chest as she cried. Tears streamed down his face as he held his wife close to him.

"What happened, Mommy? Why does everybody keep crying?" Dane asked with tears in his eyes.

Jade led her son to the couch and held his hands as they sat beside one another. She opened her mouth to speak but nothing came out. Dane was looking at her with that sweet, innocent face and she couldn't bear to break his heart.

"Listen, sweetheart," Jade said, as her lips quivered. "Mommy has to tell you something really bad, okay?"

Dane nodded at her and his eyes were wide with fear.

"First, Grandma was in a terrible car accident. But she's gonna be okay. Her leg was broken really, really bad but the doctors fixed it. She won't be able to walk for a while but she's gonna be okay."

Dane frowned at Jade. He knew Tina and Myron weren't sobbing because of that.

"And then," Jade continued, "your dad and Sugar had an accident. Daddy slipped in the pool and hurt his head. And when he fell, Sugar hit her head on the hand railing and she," Jade swallowed hard as she squeezed Dane's hand. "She drowned, baby. Sugar died."

Dane recoiled as if he'd been shot! The shock of Jade's words caused a delayed reaction and he just sat there staring at her with his eyes wide and his mouth opened. A whole minute went by then Dane let out the sickest, most pitiful sound any of them had ever heard. Tina started jumping and screaming because she couldn't take seeing her little boy in so much pain.

"Come on, baby," Myron said, as he grabbed Tina and held her tight. "Come on now," he cried.

Jade dropped to her knees next to Dane and cradled him in her arms. He was inconsolable at that point and she didn't know what to do. If Jade had really allowed herself to go there with him she wouldn't have been able to get up. So she shut down, in a sense. She somehow managed to tuck her own pain away in order to focus on Dane's.

"I'm sorry, Mommy! Please don't hate me," Dane screamed. "I'm sorry. I'm sorry," he moaned, as he rocked back and forth. "I'm so sorry, Mommy, don't hate me!"

"Baby, what are you saying? I could *never* hate you," Jade said, as she squeezed him tighter. "Why would you say that, sweetheart? Mommy could never hate you."

"If I had been here I could've helped Daddy and Sugar wouldn't be dead! I would've helped her, Mommy," Dane screamed and cried. "I wouldn't have let my sister die! I wouldn't have let her die!"

Tina was hysterical by that point and Myron had to take her out. All she could think about was how much Dane didn't want to go and maybe if he *had* stayed Sugar would still be alive!

"You listen to me, Dane. Look at me," Jade said, as she caressed his face. "This was *not* your fault, you hear me? It was a horrible, horrible accident and there wasn't anything any of us could've done to prevent it," she said and nearly choked on her words.

Jade believed that if she'd just gone back home to get Pooh's shot records or rescheduled the appointment like she was offered her baby wouldn't be dead. There *was* something that could've been done to prevent it and she didn't do it. She blew it and her baby died because of it!

A few blocks away Landon was crying through his own guilt. All Chaundra could do was hold on to him as tight as she could and let him sob in her arms. She canceled her job and took the first flight out after she got Landon's call. Chaundra knew he was upset but was not prepared for how grief stricken he was. She'd always known Landon adored Jade's kids, particularly Sugar, but she didn't realize just how much he truly loved that little girl until she saw him. Landon was as hurt as if he'd lost *his* child.

"I could've saved her," he dissolved into tears.

"What are you talking about, baby? It was an accident. Nobody could've saved Sugar," Chaundra said, as she cradled him in his bed.

"I could have. I drove by there to apologize to Jade for how I acted on the phone. But then I had a little hissy fit and started thinking that *she* was the one who needed to apologize and I drove off like a punk! All I had to do was get my ass out the truck and Sugar would still be here! Something urged me to go over there at that precise moment and I let my stupid, hurt pride keep me from getting out the truck. All I had to do was get out, Chaundra. That's all I had to do," Landon wailed, as his body jerked from crying so violently.

"Baby," Chaundra cried hard, as she continued to squeeze him.

She didn't have a clue what to do or say to make things better. So she didn't say anything. Chaundra just cried with the man she loved knowing they'd get through it together.

What kind of man are you? What kind of father would just lay there while his baby fought for her life? You're not a man! You're nothing! That's why your wife hates you! Everybody hates you because you laid there and did nothing while your baby fought to live! You're not a man!

Those were the thoughts that greeted Pierce every time he awoke in his hospital bed. At one point during the night he became so emotional and combative that they had to sedate him and strap him back down to the bed. Pierce kept threatening to rip out the twelve stitches that had been placed in the back of his head and go to the safari! Marcus and Tony as well as the doctors and nurses were definitely alarmed. The concussion he had seemed to be causing slightly unusual behavior and they wondered if his grief was to blame.

Jackie and Gerard stayed the next night so Marcus and Tony could get a restful sleep. The rest of Pierce's family rotated between both hospitals to check on him and Luisa. Early the next day Jade awoke from a fitful sleep and went tearing out of her bedroom. "Oh my god," she cried.

"Sugah!" Pooh smiled as she ran through the house. "Sugah!"

Dane came running out of his room to help his mom catch Pooh who was really quick and agile for a little girl not even three yet.

"Tell Sugah to come out, Mommy," Pooh said after Jade scooped the child in her arms.

Pooh didn't understand Sugar's absence and assumed she was playing hide and seek. Jade had no clue how to make her understand. She didn't know how to explain that Sugar was never coming home again. *Lord help me,* Jade thought, as she and Dane sat on the living room floor trying to help Pooh grasp what had happened. More than ever she wished Pierce was there to help her--to comfort her.

By mid afternoon Jade felt overwhelmed by neighbors, friends, and relatives of Pierce she'd never met before. They'd all come with food and flowers to offer their condolences. And even though Jade appreciated their gestures, she wanted everyone to get out of her house. She was tired of telling the same story each time a new person showed up. They all wanted to know what happened and she felt obligated to repeat the coroner's unofficial findings for the umpteenth time. From what they could gather from the scene and Pierce's injuries, he'd slipped and fell backwards and on the way down Sugar's head banged into the railing and rendered her unconscious. She fell into the water and in a short amount of time, Sugar drowned. There was no evidence she ever regained consciousness or fought to live. She didn't suffer.

Along with having to repeat the story Jade was sick of doing the consoling when the people who were supposed to be there to comfort *her* fell to pieces. It was exhausting and she'd had enough.

"What can I do, beauty queen? Just tell me what you need," Tamara said, noticing the overwhelmed look on her best friend's face. "You want me to get these bastards outta here 'cause you know I'll do it. Just say the word."

"Actually if you could take Pooh and Dane to your house for a while that would be great. I think it would help them to be around other kids and play and not have to keep hearing people screaming and crying. Plus, I need to go get Teddy Bear. Gerard took him to the vet to get stitched up. My poor puppy almost broke his neck off trying to get to them. And the chain dug into his skin so hard that it cut him. So I need to get him."

"Baby, let somebody else do that. You need to eat something and try to get some sleep. I'll clear these folks out and take the kids so you ..."

"I need to do this, Tamara. *Please*," Jade's eyes watered.

"Okay, okay, I'm 'bout to get the kids and they can stay for as long as you need," Tamara said, not wanting to upset Jade. Just tell me what you want and I'll do it, okay?"

Once again Tamara tried to hug her friend and she pulled away. The only reason Jade was able to function and plan her daughter's funeral was because she'd tucked her emotions somewhere deep inside. And she feared that if someone she loved really held her she'd shatter like glass.

Tamara knew Willa was due to return soon and decided to wait for her. She needed her advice. "I don't know what to do," Tamara whispered so Dane wouldn't hear. "Miles left a message and I really wanna delete the stupid thing before Jade can hear it but I don't know if that's wrong. I mean is it worse for her to hear what he said or think he didn't call at all?"

"What did he say?" Willa frowned.

"The message is on the answering machine. Let me get the kids out of here so they don't hear it and you can decide what to do. Is that okay?"

Willa hugged Dane and Pooh before Tamara took them to her house. Then she hurried to Jade's bedroom to play the message. "You stupid son of a *bitch*!" Willa screamed.

She scrolled through the caller I.D. to find Miles's number then dialed it.

He answered on the second ring thinking it was Jade calling. Miles was not expecting the tongue lashing he got from his ex-wife.

"You are by far the sorriest bastard I ever met in my life! Our daughter is in the worst pain a parent can ever go through and you have the gall to call and say you can't come support her because *I'm* gonna be at the funeral? Who gives a damn, Miles? This ain't about us or Justin or none of that mess! Our baby lost her baby! You do remember what that feels like, don't you?" Willa snapped. "Even your crazy ass mama was able to put her hatred for me aside to be there when Jamal died. But you can't do that for your own daughter? You gone let some mess between us keep you from being there for Jade yet again?"

"Look, Willa, I don't know who you think ..."

"If you don't bring your ass here to be with Jade I'm gonna make your life a living hell! You might've thought I was a bitch before but don't come and you'll see how much of one I can *really* be," she threatened before slamming down the phone. Then she deleted his message.

Jade was putting Teddy in the back of the minivan when he jumped up and put his paws in her stomach. He stared her directly in the eyes and whimpered.

"I know you tried to help her, Teddy Bear," Jade cried, as she held him close to her. "I know you did."

The two of them sat in the van for a bit while Jade held Teddy and let him mourn.

Thursday evening Luisa was being released from the hospital so Miguel and their daughters got everything ready at the house that morning. She wouldn't be mobile for weeks so they wanted to make sure she was as comfortable as possible. More than anything they hoped being surrounded by her own things and family would help Luisa try harder to get better. She was riddled with guilt and would barely eat or drink anything. It broke Miguel's heart to hear his wife sob and say she wished it had been her that died and not her grandbaby.

Miguel didn't know the appropriate response so he just held Luisa and let her cry in his arms. Only when she was asleep did he sob. It broke his heart that Sugar was gone and he couldn't begin to imagine what Pierce and Jade were going through. However, the idea of losing Luisa was equally as devastating to him. It made Miguel feel horribly guilty to think of it in such a way but if it was a choice between the baby and his wife, he was grateful Luisa had survived. Every time that thought crossed his mind it made Miguel feel sick inside and tears streamed down his face.

Pierce also got to come home and Jade was truly hurt by how unresponsive he was to her. She had been waiting to hold him and finally mourn with him but he pulled away when she reached for him. Pierce was complaining of a major headache when Marcus and Tony walked him inside the house. He didn't even look at Jade when he mumbled a greeting and went to the kitchen to take two Vicodin. Later, when she asked Pierce if he wanted to eat for the second time he went off on her.

"Quit asking me if I wanna eat, alright? I'm a grown man so if I get hungry I can fix myself something!"

Seeing the devastated look on Jade's face, Tony reminded her that irritability was one of the symptoms of a concussion. He, Marcus, and Jackie had been dealing with it for the past few days. Pierce didn't seem to want anyone around him and he'd become mean and hostile. Jackie, who had arrived in time to see Pierce's outburst, wanted to say something to his son about the way he treated Jade but decided against it. He knew they both were hurting and trying to figure out how to deal with the worst thing to ever happen to them. Unfortunately, Pierce's way was to withdraw from everyone and he went to the guest room instead of joining Jade in their bedroom. She curled up in the fetal position and cried herself to sleep.

The next day the family planned to meet at Luisa's house to discuss the funeral arrangements. Jade didn't really know what was left to talk about. She had already chosen the funeral home, Sugar's casket, the burial plot, and the outfit in which her daughter would be laid to rest. Tamara volunteered her home as the place where everyone would come to eat after the funeral so there really were no other arrangements to be made. The last thing left to do was take Sugar's clothes to the funeral home. Most of the family wanted to accompany Pierce and Jade but she told them she'd rather it just be the two of them. Pierce didn't want to go at all and was dumbfounded when Jade told him she was going to dress their daughter herself.

"You can torture yourself if you want but leave me out of it," he barked then slammed the door to the minivan and walked into his mother's house.

"Daddy's mean," Pooh whimpered as little puddles filled her eyes.

"Yeah, why is Dad so mad at us, Mom?" Dane asked, irritated by his father's outbursts. "What did *we* do?"

Jade explained that Pierce's head injury was causing him to act differently although she wasn't a hundred percent convinced that was the reason.

"Come here, Juan," Luisa cried, as she held her arms out for him.

"No, Mama, I don't wanna disturb you."

"Boy, come here," she insisted.

Pierce reluctantly went into his mother's room and sat across from her on the bed. He didn't want to cause Luisa pain by hitting her cast but she motioned for him to come closer. All five of his sisters were in the room and they draped themselves around their baby brother and mother.

"I'm so, *so* sorry, baby," she said, as Pierce laid his head on her chest. "I would've gladly given up my life so your baby could've lived. I wish I had died."

"Mama, don't say that," Diana cried.

Hawn and Eva were bawling by that point as they held tightly to Pierce. Tamika and Veronica laid their head on his legs and they all sobbed together. The kids wanted to see their grandma so Jade went upstairs to make sure she was dressed and ready to receive them. Jealousy and hurt filled her heart when she cracked the bedroom door and saw Pierce allowing his mother and sisters to comfort him in a way he wouldn't let her. It was too much to take so Jade left. Nearly thirty minutes passed before Luisa asked to see her and the kids.

"They're not here," Hawn announced, after she'd gone downstairs looking for them. "I know Chicka ain't crazy enough to take those kids to the funeral home."

Eva, Diana, and Veronica stayed behind to take care of their mom while Hawn and Tamika drove to the funeral home. Their fathers followed them with Pierce in the backseat of Jackie's Lexus. He wasn't acting normally and they wanted to be sure he would be okay after seeing his daughter for the first time since that day in the pool. It would turn out to be more than any of them could take.

Chapter

NINETEEN

TAMARA MET JADE AT the funeral home and stayed up front with Dane and Pooh while she went to the back to put Sugar in her dress. Dane was holding the butterfly clip he had given his baby sister for her birthday. Jade promised he could put it in her hair like he'd done nearly everyday for the past nine months.

"Mrs. Jamison, I really think it would be best if we put Dina in her dress."

"We call her Sugar," Jade said, softly.

"Yes, ma'am," the funeral home director said. "I think it would be best if Colby puts Sugar in her dress and then we'll bring you in to do her hair and have some time alone with her," he said, gently holding her hands. "I know that you know an autopsy was performed but knowing it and seeing it are two very different things. I don't think you want that image burned in to your memory. So please, Mrs. Jamison, trust me. Let me take this beautiful dress to Colby and I'll be back in less than five minutes to get you, okay?"

Jade nodded then paced the floor as she waited for Mr. Bowers to return. The little black board with white letters stopped Jade in her tracks.

Viewing for Dina Jamison:
Monday, July 5, 1999 from 5pm-8pm
Funeral service:
Tuesday, July 6, 1999 11am
Burial immediately following

"Mrs. Jamison?" Mr. Bowers called, startling Jade. "You can come back now."

Jade wrapped her arms around herself and followed him into a small parlor. Mr. Bowers told her to take as long as she needed then closed the theater-like curtains behind him. Jade couldn't move. She just stood there staring at the white casket that held her precious baby girl.

"Come on, Jade," she prodded herself.

Then she moved forward and got the first glimpse of her sweet baby. A sad smile spread across her lips.

"You look so pretty, Sugar, Sugar," Jade whispered, as she touched her daughter's hair. "You're like a sweet little angel."

Jade hadn't known what to expect but she was grateful Sugar looked as though she was sleeping. There were no signs of the traumatic last moments of her life. She was beautiful and perfect just like she'd always been. That somehow gave Jade comfort and she talked to Sugar like she'd done a million times before. After twisting her daughter's curls and making sure her pink butterfly dress was straightened, Jade called for Dane to join her.

She thought he would be hysterical once he actually saw his sister but Dane was very brave. He cried but didn't let his emotions stop him from talking to Sugar like it was just an ordinary day. Dane told her how pretty she was before placing the butterfly clip in her hair.

"You be good in heaven, Sugar, Sugar. Big brother loves you," Dane said, as tears streamed down his face. "I'll love you forever."

He kissed Sugar's cheek then flung his arms around Jade's waist as he cried. She held Dane until he felt strong enough to let go. Then Jade told him to tell Tamara she'd be out shortly. Once she was alone again Jade stood beside the small casket just staring at Sugar. Memories of their short time together filled Jade's mind as she laid her face next to Sugar's like she did every night to put her to sleep.

"I love you, Sugar, Sugar. And I'm so happy I got to have you in my life even if it was just for a little while," she whispered. "I'll miss you."

Jade could feel those emotions she'd fought so hard to suppress rolling up inside of her. So she kissed her baby's cheek and all but ran out of the parlor. *Just make it outside. Just get outside,* Jade thought, as she made her way through the corridor.

"Beauty queen, you okay? You need me to …"

Jade ran full speed to get out of the funeral home. She was trying to make it to the minivan but as soon as she got outside the doors a horrific scream left her body and she fell to her knees.

"Oh my god!" Tamika screamed, as she jumped out of Hawn's SUV before it had come to a complete stop.

"WHYYYYY! God, whyyyy!" Jade wailed.

Tamika and Hawn sobbed as they dropped to their knees and held their sister-in-law as tightly as they could.

Jackie, who had pulled into the parking lot right behind his daughters, jumped out quickly to deal with Pierce. He had bolted out of the backseat trying to run across the parking lot to get away from the sound of Jade's pain.

"Come here, son," Jackie cried, as he grabbed the back of Pierce's shirt to keep him from getting away. "Come on now, boy, I got you. I got you, son," he said, holding him close. "It's alright, son, I got you."

Jackie and Miguel basically had to hold Pierce up as he was overcome with grief. Each of Jade's screams felt like a dagger to his heart. The woman he loved was in the worst pain of her life because of him. Pierce couldn't bear to even look at Jade for fear he would see the hatred he'd convinced himself she felt for him in her eyes. He knew it would only be a matter of time before she left him.

Miguel drove Jade's minivan to her house as Tamika held her in the backseat. Hawn threw a fit because Tamika wouldn't drive her SUV so *she* could be in the back holding Jade! "She was my friend first!" Hawn had screamed until Jackie told her to shut up and drive the damn truck!

Tamara took Dane and Pooh home with her and Jackie drove Pierce back to his mom's house. Luisa needed to be close to him and asked for her son to be brought to her. Willa obviously had the same feeling and she was waiting when Tamika and Miguel brought Jade inside.

"Daddy," Jade uttered and ran into her father's arms.

Despite everything that had happened with Miles, Jade was glad he was there and she cried hysterically as he held her close to him. Then Miles picked her up like he'd done when she was a little girl and carried Jade to her bedroom. She had been so focused on her father that she didn't realize Justin and her sister Jewel were there as well.

Still crying herself, Willa told Jade's in-laws that she would tend to her daughter and went to climb in bed with her. She held Jade in her arms and rocked with her.

"I know, baby," Willa sobbed, as Jade trembled in her arms. "Just let it go, baby girl. Just let it all out."

Jade cried so long and hard that her head started pounding. Miles had Justin bring her a ginger ale and two Tylenol. When she sat up to take the capsules, her brother kissed her cheek and said he loved her. Jade nodded at him as she was still crying too hard to talk. Then Miles and Willa stayed with their daughter, stroking her hair and back until she eventually cried herself to sleep.

Bower's and Evan's Funeral Home was filled to capacity with hundreds of mourners there to pay their final respects. After the reverend from Luisa's church did the welcome and opening prayer, Justin played the piano and sang an amazingly beautiful song. It was one he had written called Butterfly Kisses that he sang to Sugar every time he visited. She loved the song and it hurt his heart to know he'd never get to sing it to her again. Justin broke down halfway through and played the piano until he regained his composure and could finish singing. There wasn't a dry eye in the entire place.

When Justin finished, Jade squeezed him tight and thanked him for honoring her baby with such a lovely song. Miles hugged him too and Willa touched his hand when he walked by her. Jade's in-laws thanked and hugged him too. Even Pierce shook his hand and said thank you.

Jade requested a fairly short service as she didn't want it to be dragged out. So after an hour, mourners were doing the final viewing and loading up to go to the cemetery. Jade, her closest family and friends, and Pierce's family and friends were the last ones in the funeral home. Mr. Bowers came to close the casket and load Sugar into the hearse when Pooh went wild!

"No, she hates the box!" Pooh screamed and flailed, as Jade tried to hold on to her. "Mommy, no, Sugah hates the box! Don't close her in there!"

Pooh knocked Jade's sunglasses off the top of her head and hit her in the nose as she lunged for Mr. Bowers.

"Come on, baby," Pierce said, as he grabbed Pooh from Jade and walked out of the room.

"NO, Daddy … Sugah!" Pooh screamed at the top of her lungs. "She hates the box!"

Miles sped out of the funeral home. He couldn't take it. Landon and Justin stood on either side of Jade and escorted her to the limo. They all were crying as Pooh continued to scream. Pierce tried to console her but it was Dane who finally got her calmed. Pooh sat in his lap with her arms wrapped around his neck while he rocked her and rubbed her hair. Justin got into the limo behind Jade and Landon joined Chaundra who had driven his truck.

The burial service was heart wrenching and there wasn't a dry eye on the lawn. Nearly everyone left before they lowered Sugar's casket into the ground because they couldn't bear to watch. Both Willa and Hawn collapsed and had to be carried to the car. Tamara, who'd been fairly composed for the most part, lost it when the reverend started with "ashes to ashes" and Jamel took her to their minivan.

Pierce was being comforted by his family as they led him and Pooh back to the limo. Myron and Tina took care of Dane and before long it was just Jade and Justin. He stood behind her and wrapped his arms around her shoulders. Justin wanted to say something, *anything* to help but he had no idea what that could possibly be. So he just held his sister until she was ready to leave.

Jade and Justin climbed into the limo where Pierce was waiting with Pooh in his arms. As they pulled away, Jade stared out the window not believing what had just happened. It seemed so unreal that she'd actually buried her baby girl. Then she glanced at the obituary that was on the seat next to her. Right there in bold letters underneath her sweet baby's smiling face: **Dina Elisha Jamison, October 7, 1997- June 29, 1999.**

"It's over," she whispered to herself, then closed her eyes for the duration of the ride. Justin held her hand struck by the coldness and distance between her and Pierce. They had always been so close and loving with each other and it worried him that at a time when they needed each other most, the two of them were acting like strangers.

As much as Jade wanted it, she felt it was pointless to keep expecting comfort from Pierce. He had made it abundantly clear that he wanted nothing to do with her. At the funeral home he'd made sure to keep space between them and sat as far away from her as possible in the limo. Jade never imagined burying her child or that she'd have to get through it without the man she loved.

Jade really wanted to go home and skip the gathering at Tamara's. She didn't want to hug or talk anymore about what happened to Sugar. Jade just wanted to be left alone. However, she feared a crowd of people showing up at her house if she didn't show at Tamara's. So she went with the intentions of only staying for a short while.

Instead of eating the plate of food Eva had given him, Pierce chose to drink. No one knew he'd already taken three Vicodin for his headache or that there was mostly rum in the three glasses of soda he had downed. Before long, though, it was obvious that Pierce had been drinking something a lot stronger than Coke. He kept talking about safaris and race cars and a bunch of other things that seemed to make no sense. Eventually Marcus and Tony told Jade they were taking him home and that they'd stay there with him. After he fell asleep, Tony took the photo album out of Pierce's hand and finally understood what he'd been talking about. It was a little carnival that came to town every year that Sugar loved to go to. One of the rides was called Safari and her favorite was the race cars. Pierce had been thinking about his baby when everybody thought he was going crazy.

"Come on, beauty queen, you need to eat something," Tamara said, as she handed her friend a plate.

Jade never took it as her attention quickly switched to something else. Jewel had come into the living room and sat across from her sister.

"You know, Jade, I'm really sorry. I can't even imagine how I would feel if something like this happened to me. But I was wondering how come your husband, uh what's his name, Piers or Pierson or something? How come he didn't just put some of those floaty things on your baby's arms? I mean that's what they for, right? She probably wouldn't be dead if he had."

Jade had jumped up and punched Jewel in her mouth two times before anyone could grasp what was happening! "Shut up, you ignorant bitch!" Jade screamed, as she continued to pummel her. "Why are you even here? Get out!" Landon grabbed Jade around the waist and pulled her off Jewel. She was still swinging and screaming. "You don't give a damn about my baby! You didn't even know her so why are you here? Get the hell out!" Jade yelled, as Landon carried her to Tamara's bedroom. "I hate you! Get out!"

Chaundra was caught off guard by the violent way Jade responded and annoyed by Landon's need to rescue her. He had thrown his plate on Chaundra's lap in order to get up to tend to Jade. *Great,* she thought before getting up to clean herself off.

"Didn't you hear her?" Tamara barked at Jewel. "What you still sitting there for? Get out!"

Jewel was in shock. She hadn't expected Jade to get upset, especially not to the point of attacking her! However, when Miles snatched her up and took her outside, Jewel thought about how she'd feel if she had just buried her child and someone said something like that to her. Suddenly those blows she endured didn't seem so undeserved. She wanted to apologize but Miles said it was time to go and led her to the rental car so they could return to the hotel.

"Now ain't the time for this, Daniel," Willa said, as they stood in front of his BMW. "I already told you there's nothing to worry about."

"Don't talk to me like I'm stupid, Willa! You think I can't see what's going on here? You and Miles can't keep your hands off each other but you trying to tell me nothing's going on? How big of a fool do you think I am?"

"Humph. Well, let me put it to you like this. I was doing with Miles whatever you and Sharon were doing on your last few business trips!"

"Uh, what ... who, uh, what'd you say?"

"Oh, so you can't hear now?"

"Look, this isn't the time or place for this. We need to support Jade."

"*Now* we need to be here for Jade? Funny how you weren't thinking about that when you came out here going off about Miles. But I guess you need a few minutes to get your lies together, huh?" Willa snorted. "But know this. I'm a firm believer in what's good for the goose is good for the gander. You might wanna remember that," she rolled her eyes and headed back towards the house.

Daniel and Willa weren't the only couple having issues. Things were more than a little tense between Jamel and Tamara too. He was upset that she volunteered their home without asking him and that she'd taken on the cost of all the food and drinks. Jamel knew Pierce's family had money and Jade was doing well with her books. There was no reason his and Tamara's bank account should have been close to empty for feeding people they didn't even know. Jamel loved Pierce and Jade and he was heartbroken over what had happened. However, Tamara's little boutique was barely breaking even and business had slowed at the garage where he worked as a mechanic.

"You a asshole, you know that?" Tamara snapped. "My best friend is going through the worst thing anybody could ever go through and you worried about money! Well I hope this make you feel as stupid as you look," she said, pulling a check out of her pocket.

Jamel did feel stupid when he saw the fifteen hundred dollar check Jade had written out to both him and Tamara. It was a thousand dollars more than they'd spent and Tamara tried to tell Jade that but she wouldn't listen. Jade truly appreciated how much her friend had helped her with the kids and just getting through the funeral planning stage. Tamara and Jamel didn't have to open their home and she was grateful they did that for her family.

"Baby, I'm so sorry. I shouldn't have …"

"Just shut up talking to me," Tamara huffed, as she rolled her eyes and walked away.

Jade was ready to go and was about to ask Gerard and Eva to take her and the kids home when Hawn asked to speak to her. Tina was with her and they took Jade to Tamara's bedroom and closed the door.

"Chicka, we were thinking that maybe somebody should take the kids for a while. We think your grief is causing you to make unwise decisions," Hawn stated.

"What are you talking about?" Jade frowned.

Tina frowned too. She didn't know why Hawn had asked her to join them or why she was saying "we".

"Why in the world would you take Dane with you to help dress Sugar?"

Jade glared at her sister-in-law for a moment. Then she turned her attention to Tina.

"Jade, I'm sorry, I had no idea this is what she was coming back here to talk about. All Hawn said is that she needed to talk about Dane and I was involved," Tina said then cut her eyes at Hawn. "I know you would never do anything to hurt him. And even if I had a problem with it I wouldn't see the point to bringing it up, *especially* not now. It's done and I know how much that butterfly clip meant to Dane and why he would've wanted to put it on his sister for the last time. So I'm sorry you even got approached with something this ridiculous."

"Well, I think it was wrong for you to take him and I'm not scared to say you were wrong," Hawn said, refusing to back down. "I mean would there have ever been a good time to bring it up?"

The rage Jade felt on the inside was all over her face and Tina feared she was going to beat Hawn the same way she had Jewel. Though, what she said to her sister-in-law was more painful than any hit would've been.

"You are the most selfish and petty person I've ever met and I *hate* you!" Jade said, as tears ran down her face. "You'll use any excuse to make yourself the center of attention. But it would've been nice if you had waited until my baby was in the ground just a *little* bit longer before you forgot about her and made it all about you!"

"Chicka?" Hawn gasped then sobbed hysterically.

Jade pushed past her and Tina followed. Once Eva got wind of what Hawn had said she went ballistic on her baby sister! She screamed at the top of her lungs and even pushed Hawn a few times. When Roland came in the room his wife looked to him to defend her.

"You're on your own. I'm taking Xavier home," he said, not believing Hawn had actually approached Jade with such nonsense.

Everyone seemed more interested in their own drama than the fact that Jade had buried her daughter just a few hours before. She was hurt and extremely bitter about it. Then Jade shut down so she didn't have to feel anything.

Chapter
TWENTY

FOR THE FIRST FEW weeks after the funeral Pierce and Jade were on autopilot. They did things out of habit like feeding and caring for Dane and Pooh and working at the store. However, there wasn't much life behind their actions. Jade slept as much as possible because she hated how she felt when she was awake. Her twenty-eighth birthday came and went without her realizing it. She and Pierce were also supposed to attend her ten-year high school class reunion in Gary but she forgot all about it. Jade just didn't care about much of anything.

Gone were the days when Dane and Pooh went running to greet their dad after work. For one thing he barely came home. If Pierce wasn't at Quik Stop then he was at the gym. Working out had always been a stress reliever for him but after Sugar's death it became an obsession. Though, no one was really complaining about him being gone all the time because when he *was* home, Pierce was a nightmare!

Everything and everyone, including Jade and the kids, seemed to get on his nerves. Pierce was irritable and just flat out mean to his family and employees. They all tried to be patient with him but it was getting harder to do.

By the end of August Jade began to come out of her fog and felt ready to start putting her life back together. Naturally she could never forget about Sugar but she just didn't want to be sad and miserable anymore. Jade was hoping Pierce would be ready to do the same so early one morning she turned over in bed to touch him. She thought maybe if they made love it would draw them close together again. It was the first time since Sugar's death that she actually felt like having sex and was hoping he did too. Jade wrapped her arms around Pierce as she planted kisses on the back of his neck. She thought he was responding but he grabbed her hand to stop her from touching him.

"I'm sorry, Jade, I can't," Pierce said, as he got out of bed. "I can't."

"I need you, Pierce … *please*. I don't wanna be alone anymore. Please don't keep ignoring me," she cried.

He could barely look at her. The devastated expression on Jade's face broke his heart. "I'm sorry," Pierce said then left their bedroom. He ran for miles on the treadmill.

Jade fell back on her pillow and cried. She felt so hurt and rejected. However, after a few minutes she began to wonder if something was wrong with her. Was she a horrible person for even thinking about sex when it had only been a few months since burying her child? Did it mean she hadn't loved Sugar as much as Pierce because she wanted to move on with her life? Those thoughts and many more like them filled Jade with guilt until she eventually cried herself to sleep.

Perhaps a glutton for punishment, Jade took lunch to the store a few days later in an attempt to talk to Pierce and encourage him to open up to her like he used to. He acted completely disinterested in her and what she was saying.

"You know what, Pierce? I think the kids and I are gonna go stay at my mom's for a while. That way you don't have to work as hard to ignore us," Jade said, as she threw her half eaten sandwich in the trash.

Pierce looked at Jade with panic all over his face. Ever since Sugar died he feared she would leave him. He was convinced she hated him and would never forgive him for letting their daughter die, especially after the way he'd treated her over the trunk incident. Pierce didn't seem to realize it was the hurtful, hateful way he'd been treating her and the kids that made Jade hate him. And it was something which could have been cleared up if Pierce had just been willing to talk about his feelings. He wasn't.

"What are you saying, Jade? You're gonna take my kids away because I'm not in as big of a rush to forget our daughter as you seem to be?"

Jade burst into tears then ran out of his office. Pierce called to her but never made a move to go after her. He couldn't bear to see the hatred in Jade's eyes.

Instead of going to Eva's to get Dane and Pooh, Jade headed over to Landon's. She needed to talk and figure out what to do about her marriage.

"Hey, you," Landon said, as he allowed her inside. "What's wrong?"

Jade was reaching out to hug him when Chaundra walked out from the kitchen.

"Oh, guys, I'm sorry. I shouldn't have just dropped by like this. I'm sorry

I didn't know you were here, Chaundra. I didn't mean to interrupt your plans. I'm sorry," Jade said, as she grabbed her purse and opened the front door.

"It's okay, Jade."

"Baby girl, come here," Landon said, as he reached for her. "Tell me what's wrong."

"Nothing, it's just one of those days. I'll call you tomorrow, okay? You two enjoy your time together. It was good to see you, Chaundra. I'm digging those shoes," Jade smiled, weakly.

"Baby girl …"

"I'll see you," Jade stated, trying to hide her tears.

She closed the door and ran to the minivan hoping to get away before Landon could catch her.

"So are you ready to eat? I made your favorite, uh, what are you doing?" Chaundra asked when Landon grabbed his wallet and keys.

"I'm going over to Jade's. Something was really wrong and I need to talk to her about it."

"And you just gonna leave me here even though I flew in to be with you? Wow, Landon, that's, wow!"

"Well, if you hadn't just *shown* up I would've been here helping Jade. I know it's over for you but some of us still miss Sugar. Some of us are having a hard time dealing with the fact that she's gone! If you can't understand that then I don't know what to tell you."

"I'm sorry," Chaundra cried, as she wiped away the tears that began to roll down Landon's cheek. "That was really selfish and inconsiderate of me and I'm so sorry, baby. I'll be here when you get back, okay?" She hugged him tight. "I love you."

"I'll see you," he said, not returning her affection.

Chaundra plopped down on the couch and cried knowing she had hurt Landon. It was something she seemed to do a lot. Ever since Sugar died he was much more emotional and things hadn't been the same between them. And it wasn't that Chaundra expected him to forget about Sugar. She just thought Landon would be ready to move forward after a few months of mourning. Some days he was as devastated as the day it happened.

After fixing a plate of the roast beef dinner she'd prepared, Chaundra realized she didn't have much of an appetite. She pushed the button to open the microwave and chipped her nail. A few curse words later Chaundra was in the bathroom looking through drawers for a nail clipper. She went to Landon's bedroom next and found something much more interesting.

"What the …" Chaundra mumbled.

A yellow envelope caught her attention and she pulled it out of his sock drawer. Seeing Gabrielle Campbell's name on the return address upset

Chaundra but not nearly as much as the date on the postmark. *Don't jump to conclusions,* she thought trying to decide whether to open the envelope.

Chaundra knew she had no business reading Landon's mail but she couldn't resist. Unfortunately, the conclusions she'd warned herself not to jump to were exactly right. Gabrielle had sent a card thanking Landon for an incredible afternoon. She also told him he was still the best, most selfless lover and she thought of him often. Gabrielle apologized for the way things ended between them and promised to always love him.

Chaundra felt enraged! At that time she thought of Landon as her man and it hurt to know he was still fooling around with his beautiful, petite ex-wife. It made her wonder who else he'd been sleeping with. "Ugh," Chaundra groaned. She felt like a fool for trusting Landon. Apparently he was no different than every other man she'd known.

Nearly an hour later Landon returned and found Chaundra's overnight bag by the front door. He assumed she was upset about him leaving to go to Jade's until he found her on the couch holding the yellow envelope. Initially Landon was aggravated by Chaundra rifling through his things. Then he wondered why he'd kept the card or why he didn't just come clean like Jade had urged him to.

"So how long was all this going on?" she asked, holding up the card.

"It only happened once."

Landon sat on the loveseat across from Chaundra knowing he didn't have a leg to stand on in the way of defending himself. She looked at him with an expression that seemed to say I know you don't expect me to believe that.

"I'm really sorry, Chaundra. I definitely didn't plan for anything like that to happen. Up until that day I thought she still hated me."

"How did it happen then?"

Landon explained the whole situation as well as how incredibly guilty he felt about it. He admitted being too scared of losing her to confess. "I swear to you it was only once. And there hasn't been anyone else, Chaundra," Landon said, hoping she'd forgive him. "I know my credibility is shot right now but I'm begging you to believe me. I got caught up in a bad situation and made the wrong choice. Please forgive me, baby. I'm really sorry."

Chaundra snorted and rolled her eyes at Landon. She was turned off by how little effort he put into trying to win her over. There were no tears, no pleas, no *nothing* that a man scared of losing his girlfriend would do. When Landon thought he was going to lose Jade to Priscilla's publishing company he was beside himself. He was willing to do or say anything to keep her from leaving him but his woman, the one he supposedly couldn't live without, had her bag at the front door and all he could say was "I'm really sorry".

"I gotta go," Chaundra said, as she rose and threw the card on the couch.

"Okay," Landon sighed.

"*Okay?*" she snapped. "Really, Landon, I tell you I'm leaving and all you have to say is okay? Wow! You really don't give a damn about me, do you?"

"What are you talking about?" he frowned. "I'm trying to give you your space, Chaundra. I know I screwed up and there's nothing I can say to excuse what I did. If the shoe were on the other foot I'd want to be alone to think things through. I get it. But don't think I don't care about you. I love you, Chaundra, and I feel horrible right now. I *want* you to stay but I understand why you need to leave. I just hope the relationship we've built will be enough for you not to leave me for good. I don't want to lose you, baby."

Chaundra stood there staring at Landon not knowing what to do. She felt hurt and confused. And it only got worse when he wrapped his arms around her and whispered how much he loved her. Chaundra wanted to believe him but there was a part of her that didn't.

"I don't wanna be your consolation prize, Landon."

"What does *that* mean?"

"It means I don't want to be the woman you settle for because you can't be with the one you really want."

Landon stressed again that what he and Gabrielle did was a mistake which only happened once. Then it registered with him that she wasn't talking about his ex-wife. Landon let out a long, frustrated deep breath then plopped back down on the loveseat. He was sick of defending his relationship with Jade to someone who was determined not to believe him. At that point he was hoping Chaundra *would* leave!

Instead of going home Pierce decided to visit with his mom. She'd been leaving messages asking to see him for the past week. Luisa was still having trouble getting around but Pierce knew if he kept ignoring her she would find a way to get to him. The problem he had with Luisa and the rest of his family was that they always wanted to talk about how he was doing. They wanted to talk about Sugar and their feelings and guilt and Pierce didn't want to hear it. He was barely making it through the day as it was.

As expected, Pierce was greeted with looks of pity from Luisa, Miguel, and Jackie who was there visiting as well. He couldn't take it for more than thirty minutes and got up to leave. Luisa called after Pierce but he kept walking towards the door.

"Hey, boy, your mama's calling you," Jackie said, as he followed his son. "Oh, so you don't hear me talking to you either?"

"I need to go, Dad."

Jackie grabbed Pierce by the shoulder and turned him around. "Look, son, I know you going through it right now but you better watch how you treat us. As a matter of fact, you better watch yourself altogether before you lose everything you got."

"What is that supposed to mean?"

"It means if you don't straighten up your act and find a better way to deal with your emotions, you ain't gone have a wife and family to go home to. Even the best woman will get fed up with being mistreated and rejected. Jade's a beautiful girl with quite a few arms open and waiting for her. You better open your eyes, boy."

Pierce actually wanted to punch his father! "Not everybody cheats like you do," he said, instead.

"You better watch your mouth, *fool*! I'm trying to help you! But you just keep right on doing what you doing. You'll see," Jackie huffed before leaving Pierce standing in the kitchen.

Luisa and Jackie had words about the way he spoke to Pierce. She felt he'd been insensitive and needed to apologize to their son. Although Miguel didn't agree with the way Jackie had done it, he did think someone needed to talk to Pierce about his attitude. Once he expressed his opinion Luisa was upset with both men and told them to leave her alone.

Pierce drove home feeling overwhelmed by fear. He knew his dad had a point and if he kept treating his family the way he had been he'd lose them. And Pierce definitely didn't want that. Despite the way he'd been acting, he truly did love them all. It was the guilt he felt for Sugar's death that was eating him alive. However, Pierce felt ready to talk to Jade and was planning to until he arrived home and went ballistic over what he saw!

"Get out of there!" Pierce yelled.

"But, Dad, Mom said we could."

"I don't give a damn *what* she said! Get out now!"

"Pierce, stop!" Jade screamed, as she jumped up from her seat at the patio table.

Teddy growled and barked at Pierce when he yanked Pooh out of the pool. Thankfully he was chained or he just may have attacked Pierce.

"Shut up, Teddy!" Pierce snapped.

Dane and Pooh were crying when they ran past Jade.

"Ugh, I *hate* him," Dane mumbled.

"What is your problem?" Jade demanded.

"What the hell is *your* problem? Why would you ever let them get in that pool?"

"There's no reason they shouldn't get in it."

"There's no *reason*?" Pierce asked, incredulously. He couldn't believe what he was hearing. "Are you serious?"

"What happened to Sugar was a tragic accident, Pierce. It was an *accident*," she stressed when he shook his head at her. "Things happen that are beyond our control but that's no reason to raise fearful, paranoid kids. They don't have to be afraid. Dane and Pooh are excellent swimmers and they love the water. And I'm not gonna take that away from them because you're scared. They don't deserve that. And they *definitely* don't deserve being screamed at and bullied and neither do I. If you don't want to be here then you don't have to be. You're free to go."

"What?" Pierce said, as tears filled his eyes.

"You're not the only one who lost Sugar, Pierce. We *all* did. We're all hurt and trying to learn how to live without her. But the point is we have to *live*. Nobody's trying to forget about Sugar as you seem to think but we can't be miserable for the rest of our lives over something we can't change. I want our home to be happy again. I want us to be a family again and I wish you wanted that too."

Once again Jade reached out for her husband. And once again he walked away from her. Pierce changed his clothes and ran on the treadmill for hours. The next day he brought a contractor to the house while Jade was out running errands. She got home sooner than he was expecting.

"What is going on?" Jade asked, as she stepped through the sliding door.

"I'm having the pool filled in," Pierce informed her then turned his attention back to the contractor.

"No, you're not!" Jade yelled. "I told you before you're not taking something my kids love away from them. They *will* have a pool either here in this house or the one you force me to move them to! Take your pick," Jade stated before storming back inside the house.

Pierce let the contractor out through the gate then went inside to find Jade. She was in their bedroom crying.

"Jade, I'm sorry," he said from the doorway.

"I can't take this anymore. I can't keep living like this, Pierce. If you don't want to be with me then go."

"I do wanna be with you, babe. I'm just having a hard time. But I don't want to lose you, Jade. I don't want to lose my family. Please, don't give up on me."

Pierce agreed to look into some sort of grief counseling. And even though he couldn't promise things would just go back to normal, he did promise to try. Pierce's first effort was to apologize to Dane and Pooh. He knew he had hurt them and wanted to make things right. Fortunately, as was the case with children, they forgave easily. Pierce told them how sorry he was and the three of them hugged and cried in each other's arms. Sadly, it wasn't so simple for him and Jade. There was a wall between them that Jade just couldn't break through. And it was breaking her heart more and more every day.

As the month of September went by they tried to put their lives back together. Pierce came home every night for dinner and they spent time with their families. Intimacy was still an issue for them, though. Pierce was stand offish when it came to being close to Jade and she grew tired of the rejection. Then it seemed as if Jackie's words were coming to pass. Pierce came home for lunch one afternoon to spend time with Jade. When he pulled up she was hugging Landon at the front door. He spoke to Pierce and let him know he'd come to drop off the proofs for Jade's new book.

"Wow, Jade, it seems like every time I turn around you and your boy are all hugged up. Isn't that interesting?"

"Well, maybe he's the only one who considers I might actually need a hug. Isn't *that* interesting?" Jade sneered before walking away from Pierce.

After that exchange he made more of an attempt to be affectionate towards Jade. Pierce hugged and kissed her but still couldn't make love. He tried but things just didn't work out. Jade felt embarrassed that she couldn't turn her husband on and eventually stopped trying. That was a problem she and Pierce *never* had before and she didn't know how to handle it.

One night Jade caught him off guard and asked if he was having an affair. It was the only thing that made sense to her. Pierce was hurt and offended Jade could even suggest something like that. He tried to reassure her it had nothing to do with another woman but she wasn't convinced. However, what should have been Sugar's second birthday was a few weeks away and Jade was more concerned about that.

Pierce pled with her not to throw a party to honor their daughter. He thought it was too soon and that it would only bring back the pain they were all trying so hard to get over. Jade felt Pierce had disregarded her feelings for months so she wasn't particularly interested in his, especially on that subject. Besides, everyone else thought it was a wonderful idea and tried to convince Pierce it was a good thing for all of them to be together to celebrate Sugar. If only he'd joined his family that day. Perhaps Pierce wouldn't have ruined his life!

Chapter

TWENTY ONE

ON THURSDAY, OCTOBER 7ᵀᴴ at six o'clock in the evening Pierce and Jade's house was full of their friends and family. The only person missing was Pierce. He and Jade had fought earlier because he still thought having a birthday party for Sugar was ridiculous. She called Pierce at around four to see if he would come home. Jade begged him to but he refused saying it was too much to deal with. Not long after she'd slammed the phone down on him, Pierce began drinking at his desk. He didn't want to think or feel anything and by the end of his second bottle of Hennessey and two Vicodin he'd accomplished just that.

Back at the house, after dinner, everyone gathered around the living room to watch the video Gerard made. Hawn and Eva sat on either side of Jade holding her hands as Sugar's smiling face popped up on the screen. It was a mixture of still shots and video clips of her with Butterfly Kisses playing in the background. There were pictures of Sugar when she was born and when they brought her home from the hospital. Everyone laughed at the shot of her taking her first bath as she clearly didn't like it.

There were pictures of Sugar with nearly everyone in the room and it made them all smile and cry. Jade's favorite was the shot Marcus took of Dane and Sugar when he gave her the hair clip. She seemed so happy and so in love with her big brother. Jade looked over at the huge smile on her son's face as tears ran down his cheek.

After a few more photos of Sugar and Pierce showed up, Marcus decided to go to Quik Stop to get him. He thought it was crazy for him not to be there. Truthfully, Marcus was having a hard time keeping his emotions under control and wanted to leave before everyone could see him sob. Tony volunteered to ride with him as did Roland. They came back ten minutes later asking Jade for the key to the store. Pierce's car was parked out front but the place was completely dark and he wasn't answering their knocks or their phone calls. The three of them tried to keep the panic out of their voices as not to upset Jade but she could see how scared they were and it made her scared too. If only she hadn't pushed having the party against Pierce's wishes.

Jade's hands were trembling when she gave Marcus the keys. He held them steady and told her everything was going to be okay. A few minutes later Roland called to let Jade know they hadn't found Pierce. He wasn't inside the store and they had no idea where he could have gone. Even though Jade was worried, she breathed a sigh of relief that they hadn't found Pierce dead inside his office like she'd feared they would.

The rest of the men met at Quik Stop so they could split up and search the area for Pierce. Two hours passed and there was still no sign of him. Luisa and all the women prayed together begging God to send her son home safely. They were planning to stay with Jade but she sent them all home. She knew Dane and Pooh were upset by all the emotions in the house and she needed to talk with them and try to reassure them everything would be okay. *Please, God, let everything be okay.*

The next morning, with still no word from Pierce, Jade took Dane to school and dropped Pooh off at Willa's. She was beside herself with worry when the phone rang at nearly nine o'clock. Jade assumed it was Luisa again but was delighted that it was Pierce.

"Hey, babe," he said, with a groggy voice.

"Pierce," Jade gasped and began to cry. "Babe, where are you? I was *so* scared. Are you okay?"

"Yeah, I'm okay. I'm about to get in my car and I'll be there in a few minutes."

Jade called Luisa and Willa to let them know Pierce was okay and on his way home. She asked them to call everyone else so they wouldn't continue to worry. When Pierce walked in from the garage Jade jumped in to his arms. She cried so hard that her body jerked and he held tightly to her. Jade was about to kiss Pierce's neck when she pushed away from him and stared angrily in his face.

"Where have you been?"

"I woke up in a hotel room but I don't really recall how I got there. The last thing I remember was drinking in my office. I vaguely remember talking to Tripp and I think he took me there."

"So you're telling me that the boy who calls here every other day just to say hi took you to a hotel instead of bringing you home. And then he was so inconsiderate that he wouldn't even bother to call and let me know where you were? Is that what you want me to believe?"

"I told you I don't really remember, Jade."

"And I bet you don't know why your skin and clothes smell like soap and detergent we don't use. Since when do hotels use Zest or wash their guests' clothes in Gain?"

"So what are you, the soap police?" Pierce snapped. "What exactly are you saying, Jade?"

"I'm saying don't talk to me like I'm stupid, Pierce! You and I both know you weren't at a hotel. So where were you that you couldn't call me to come pick you up?"

"What exactly are you accusing me of, Jade?" he frowned. "Do you really think I was out screwing around?"

"Just tell me the truth, Pierce, because what you've said so far doesn't add up. Please, just be honest with me."

"No, I want you to look me in my face and tell me you really believe I was with someone else last night. Tell me to my face that you think on what should've been my baby's second birthday, on what *would've* been her second birthday if it weren't for me, I was boning somebody else! You actually think that little of me?"

"Things just aren't adding up, Pierce."

"I know they're not! I told you the last thing I remember is drinking in my office. I'm trying to figure this out too but I would expect you to know better than to think I would do something like that! That hurts, Jade. It almost hurts more than the reason I drank myself into oblivion in the first place. I just wanted to drown out that voice in my head. I didn't want to think about my baby fighting for her life anymore," Pierce said, as tears began pouring down his face. "She must have been *so* scared, Jade," Pierce sobbed then crumpled in her arms. "She had to be wondering where her daddy was to just let her struggle like that! I was right there, Jade. Everybody else keeps talking about if they had just gotten out of the truck or come home from the doctor's but I was right there! I was just laying there while my baby died!" he screamed.

Jade felt like her heart was being ripped out as she held on to Pierce as tight as she could.

"It wasn't your fault, babe. It wasn't your fault," she said, continuing to rock him in her arms. "Sugar wasn't fighting for her life, Pierce. She wasn't gasping for air or trying to survive. Sugar didn't struggle, babe. So please stop punishing yourself like this. What happened was a terrible accident. It was just a horrible accident."

Pierce and Jade held on to each other and cried together for the first time since their daughter died. An hour passed before they got up from the floor.

"I know things seem suspicious, Jade, but I'm begging you to trust me. You know I would never hurt you like that. I just couldn't handle the party last night and I'm sorry I made you worry unnecessarily. I wish I had been strong enough to be here with you but I wasn't. I'm sorry."

Jade decided to ignore her instincts and trust her husband. They agreed to put the whole thing behind them. And for a few weeks it actually seemed like they had.

Jade had just walked in from the garage with her hands full of grocery bags when she heard the phone ringing. She put them down quickly and ran to answer just in case Dane's school was calling.

"Hello?"

"Hey, Laila. How you doing, baby?"

"*Hey*, stranger," Jade beamed.

"I know it's been a while but I was wondering if I could come see you this evening. I miss you."

"I miss you too," she said, as her eyes filled with tears. "I love you, Pierce."

His eyes watered as well. "I love you *so* much, Jade. And I'm sorry I haven't been much of a husband to you lately but I promise that's about to change, starting right now. I want us to be happy again, babe. So be ready, you hear me? We've got some serious making up to do."

"Okay," Jade smiled.

"I really do love you, girl. I always have." Pierce could hear Jade crying. "Alright, cut that out now 'cause you know I can't take it," he said, trying desperately to keep his own emotions in check. "You don't have to cry anymore, Jade. Everything's gonna be all right, okay? I promise. We'll be happy again. So go ahead and take some vitamins to build up your stamina because I'm a wear you out, chick!"

They both laughed. Then Jade made arrangements for the kids to be taken care of so she and Pierce could have the house to themselves. And their time together was every bit as magical and amazing as she thought it would be. They tore the house apart because Jade attacked Pierce the moment he walked through the garage door and they went at each other like nobody's business!

"Damn, baby, you were like a lioness or something! That was *incredible* but we can't ever let that much time go by without you getting what you need. Shoot, you almost paralyzed me," he teased.

"You hung in, though, Captain America. I love how strong you are and that you can lift and fling and toss me wherever you want. It turns me on," she moaned.

"Dang, girl, why you say it like that ... flinging and tossing?" Pierce laughed loudly. "You make it sound like I'm abusing you."

"You know what I mean, dude. When you want me somewhere you put me there. I love that junk!"

"Do you really?" he smiled then put her where he wanted her.

Three days later Jade was in the kitchen finishing dinner when Teddy ran to the front door. Dane popped up to follow him.

"Don't even try it," Jade said, as she motioned for her son to sit back down. "Finish that homework, little boy. You'll use any excuse to get up," she smiled then opened the door to retrieve the mail. "Hello, Johnny, how are you?"

"I'm fine now that I see your beautiful smile. It's been missing for a while but I'm glad to see it back."

"Thank you," Jade said, as she smiled even brighter. "You be careful out there."

"Yeah, it would be a lot easier if all dogs were as sweet as yours. Isn't that right, Teddy Bear?" Johnny laughed, as the dog looked like he was smiling too.

Jade still had a smile on her face as she went through the mail until one particular letter caused her to frown. It was addressed to Pierce but the sinking feeling in Jade's gut let her know it concerned her as well. So she tore it open.

"What's the matter, Mom?" Dane asked after he saw Jade wiping tears from her eyes.

Teddy Bear sat in front of her with his paws on her feet as though he was waiting on an answer too.

"Nothing, baby," she lied. "Listen, why don't you put your homework away and you and Pooh go wash up for dinner, okay?"

"We're not waiting for Dad?" he frowned.

"He'll eat later, okay? Now take your sister to get cleaned up while I fix your plates."

Dane knew something was wrong and was scared things would be bad again. He wanted to talk to his mom but figured it was best to just obey her and stay out of the way. So he took Pooh to the bathroom to wash their hands.

Jade could barely make her kids' plates her hands were trembling so badly. The rage she felt was difficult to contain and she was close to exploding. Once she got the kids seated at the table Jade went to her bedroom to use the phone. She left an urgent message for Hawn to pick up the kids as soon as she possibly could. Jade was hoping her sister-in-law made it there before Pierce did but he arrived a little earlier than she was expecting.

"Where's your mom," Pierce asked, after showering Dane, Pooh, and

Teddy with affection. He picked up the gift-wrapped lingerie he'd brought for his wife and called out to her. "Hey, beautiful lady, how are you? What's wrong?"

"Dane, take Pooh and Teddy Bear out to the backyard. Y'all can play in the tree house for a little bit. Don't forget your jackets, okay?"

Pierce knew something was seriously wrong and he began to panic. Once the kids were outside he moved towards Jade and she backed away.

"Babe, what's wrong? Why are you so upset?"

"You got a real interesting piece of mail today. And since I have permission to go through your things, I decided to go ahead and open it. Maybe you can explain it to me," she sneered then slammed the envelope in to his chest!

"Jade, what's wrong with you?" Pierce turned the envelope over and his mouth went dry. He didn't need to open it to know what was inside.

"So explain it to me, Pierce. Tell me why a faithfully married man needed to get tested for STDs!"

Tears streamed down his face as he stood there staring at Jade unable to speak.

"You can skip the dramatics, alright? You played me before with all that stuff about how scared Sugar must have been and how she was wondering where her daddy was but it's not gonna work this time around! So tell me who you were with, Pierce. And try not to lie this time, okay, because unless there's something I don't know about you I'm pretty certain you weren't with Tripp," Jade snarled at him. "So tell me, Pierce. Who made it necessary for you to go running to the doctor?"

"Jade, please, I can explain."

"Who were you with, Pierce?" she demanded.

He swallowed hard and took a deep breath. More tears streamed down Pierce's face as he opened his mouth to speak. Nothing came out at first. "Regina," he murmured.

It was as if everything went black for a few moments as Jade stared at him in complete and total shock! Even though she hated the stupid jokes Pierce played on her, she was praying that that's all it was, just a stupid joke. Jade knew it wasn't. And the pain seizing her heart felt similar to that day she watched a stranger zip her baby in a black bag!

"I swear it's not what you think, babe."

That was the last thing Jade heard before memories from her past started flooding her mind. She began recalling all the times she'd heard a man in her life utter those very words. Her childhood sweetheart Alonzo said it every time he paraded another girl in front of her face. Then there was Damien, her high school boyfriend who'd slept with his ex-girlfriend and when busted cried his eyes out and claimed, "I swear, it's not what you think". All the times Richard left Jade high and dry he promised it wasn't what she thought. Worst of all was Levi. He proposed to Jade then swore it wasn't what she thought when she found out about the wife and child he failed to mention. However, all of those situations put together didn't hurt nearly as much as Pierce's betrayal. She never thought she'd hear him say, "it's not what you think".

"You know I would never hurt you intentionally," Pierce was saying when Jade snapped out of her reverie. "I was drunk off my ass and I don't even remember *talking* to her let alone going home with her, Jade, please," he called when she started walking away from him. "Baby, wait. Jade, *please*. I'm *so* sorry. Please, just listen to me."

Pierce grabbed Jade and held her close to him begging for a chance to explain. He was expecting her to fight and scream or cry but Jade didn't do anything. And even though he was holding her tightly, it was like he couldn't feel her. She seemed lifeless in his arms.

"Jade, please, don't shut down on me. I need you to understand that I never meant to hurt you. I swear."

"Hi, Auntie Hawn," Dane and Pooh sang from the tree house. A few minutes later they, with Teddy in tow, came barreling through the sliding glass door to open the front door for her.

"Y'all act like you love me or something," Hawn laughed, as the three of them lavished her with affection.

"Where's Xavier?" Dane asked.

"He's at home with your uncle Roland. Xavier is getting so big and," Hawn paused when she got a glimpse of Pierce and Jade and knew something was terribly wrong. "Hey, why don't you guys go watch TV for a little bit and then Auntie will join you in a few minutes, okay?"

"Why everybody keep sending me away?" Dane shouted. "I'm not a little baby. I know something's wrong!"

"Come with me, sweetheart," Jade said as she grabbed Dane's and Pooh's hand."

"Jade, wait, let me talk to you."

"Let's go finish your homework," she said, ignoring Pierce. "And then we can have some of that banana pudding I made. It's still your favorite, right?"

"Juan, what's going on?" Hawn demanded, once Jade and the kids were out of the living room.

"Look, I need to talk to Jade right now, okay? Please, can you just take the kids for now so I can talk to my wife? Please."

"It don't seem like your wife wants to talk to you. Now what the hell happened, Juan?"

Pierce didn't want to discuss anything with his sister but he knew she wouldn't let up until he told her. He groaned loudly and put his hands on top of his head. Hawn's heart felt like it was going to beat out of her chest when tears started flowing down her brother's face.

"Please, just tell me what's wrong," Hawn cried.

"I made a horrible mistake."

"What does that mean?" she frowned.

Pierce explained the situation and, to his surprise, received two vicious slaps across his face! Hawn was crying and going off on him as if he'd cheated on *her*.

"None of this would've even happened if you'd just brought your stupid ass home!"

"I know," Pierce cried. "I know."

Hawn was scared by how cold and detached Jade seemed. It was how she was right after Sugar died. She was functioning but didn't seem really there. Hawn tried to take Dane and Pooh with her so Pierce and Jade could work things out but Jade wouldn't let her. And Hawn knew well enough not to push the issue so she left.

Pierce made it clear he wasn't going to leave Jade alone even if he had to talk to her in front of the kids. So she sent Dane and Pooh to their rooms to get pajamas to put on after their baths and stood at the kitchen counter just staring at Pierce. He didn't know how to act because Jade was looking right at him without seeing him. She seemed so empty and emotionless and he didn't know how to reach her. Pierce still tried, though.

"I'm so sorry, babe. But you have to know I would never do anything purposely to hurt you. I was drunk."

"I really don't care. I just want you to get your stuff and go," Jade stated, matter of fact.

"*Go*? What do you mean? I'm not going anywhere, Jade. I need to make you understand what …"

"Then I'll go," she said, before heading to their bedroom.

Pierce followed her still pleading for a chance to talk. He closed their bedroom door and tried to prevent her from packing the duffel bag she pulled out of the closet.

"Don't do this, Jade, *please*. Just let me explain, okay? If I could just tell you what really happened then you'll know that I never meant to hurt you. We can work this out, Jade, just give me a chance. Please, babe. Okay, okay, I'll go," he conceded when Jade wouldn't stop packing her clothes.

"What's wrong with Daddy, Dane?" Pooh asked, as tears sprang to her little eyes. They could hear his muffled cries and pleas.

"I don't know, baby girl. He did something bad and Mommy doesn't like him anymore," Dane answered, holding his baby sister close to him. They sat in the middle of his bed crying in each other's arms.

Pierce, finally accepting that his wife wasn't going to talk to him, packed a bag and told her he'd be at Marcus's. He went to Dane's room to talk to him and Pooh. Pierce explained that he'd hurt Mommy's heart really bad and was going to Uncle Marcus's house for the night. He told them to stop crying and not to worry because he was going to fix everything. Pierce hugged and kissed them both and promised to see them in the morning. He looked at Jade one last time when she walked past him to get to the kids. Teddy barked the entire time he followed Pierce to the garage. *Even the dog hates me,* he thought as he drove to his best friend's apartment across town.

Chapter

TWENTY TWO

MARCUS WAS IN THE middle of enjoying the company of one of his lady friends when he heard a knock at the door. Normally he would have ignored it, but it was the special knock he and his boys had been doing since junior high. Marcus knew it was either Pierce or Tony and that something was wrong since neither of them ever just popped over unannounced.

"Hey, Marcus, I'm sorry to drop in on you like this but I was wondering if I could crash here for the night."

"Boy, get in here. You know you don't have to ask nothing like that. Just give me a minute, alright?"

"Oh, no, dude, I'll go. I didn't know you had a guest."

"Pierce, stop," Marcus said, as he grabbed the duffel bag from his friend's hand. "You know ain't no tramp taking precedence over my dawg. So fix yourself a drink and I'll be right back."

If only he knew. The last thing on earth Pierce wanted was a drink. Marcus's lady friend, whose name he couldn't recall, was upset and very annoyed by the way she was being thrown out of the apartment.

"It was nice to meet you and I had a good time but my boy needs me right now. Maybe I'll give you a call some other time."

"Don't bother," she said and got dressed in a huff.

"That's cool too," he chuckled then escorted her to the door. "See ya." Marcus closed the door behind her then joined Pierce in the living room. "Sorry about that, bro. So tell me what's going on."

Pierce explained the whole situation.

"So where did this tramp even come from? Y'all hooked up before or something?"

Pierce looked at Marcus like he had two heads! "*No,* I've never hooked up with her before, are you crazy? You know that ain't me, dude. Jade is everything to me and I never even thought about screwing around on her. I love that woman, Marcus, and I can't lose her over some stupid mess like this. I can't man," he said, as tears ran down his face.

"If I had just went home that night none of this would even be happening. And I hate to sound like a punk but I can't stand Regina! She had to know I wasn't right. Plus I never once flirted or did *anything* to give her the impression I was interested. I gave her another chance after that little incident with Jade because I felt sorry for the girl and didn't want her to lose her job. But I barely saw her after that. I have no clue what she was even doing up at the store that night. But when I woke up naked in her bed she was smiling and talking like we were a couple or something. She seemed so hurt and confused when I didn't remember anything."

"Damn, dawg, I don't know what to say. How the hell did Jade even find out? Did you tell her?"

"No, that's the kicker. I took a round of STD testing to make sure I didn't bring no mess home and I left specific instructions for Kaiser to call the store with the results. And they did. I just didn't know they were also gonna mail a copy to the house."

"Aw, damnnn, you lying," Marcus exclaimed, as he placed his hands on top of his head. "Damnnn! I know Jade went ballistic, didn't she?"

Pierce explained how shut down Jade was and that he didn't know how to reach her. Marcus reminded him that that's how she was when Sugar died. It was like the pain was too much to deal with so she tucked it somewhere deep inside of herself just to be able to function.

"Man, what are you gonna do to get your woman back? Y'all can't let that raggedy ass Regina win. As a matter of fact, I think I might grab Tamara and do a little RECON to find out where that tramp lives. She need her ass beat for this! I'm serious, dude," Marcus said when Pierce shook his head. "I've seen you drunk and there ain't *no way* she didn't know. She took advantage of the situation and she gone pay for it."

"I don't give a damn about her, Marcus! I just want my wife. Jade is the only woman I've ever loved and I can't go back to a life without her. I can't."

"Alright, well just give it a little time and we'll figure something out. In the meantime you know you can stay here as long as you need to. And if there's anything you need me to do to help just name it. You know I got your back."

"Thanks," Pierce said, as he stood to hug his friend. He grabbed his duffel bag and went to the guest room. Pierce plopped down on the bed and lay on his back. He covered his face with his hands unable to believe what had come of his life. Tears streamed down Pierce's face as he thought about Jade and wished they could go back to having a happy marriage and three kids in a home full of love. Pierce's tears turned to sobs.

Eventually he stopped crying and reached for his duffel bag. Pierce had packed a pair of pajamas and a change of clothes but what had filled the bag was the private tapes and pictures he'd taken of Jade. She had been somewhat reluctant to let him film her when he first asked afraid someone else would see them. Pierce reassured her that would never happen and bought a lock box to which only the two of them had a key. As he was packing to leave the house he imagined Jade destroying both the pictures and the videotapes in a rage and he didn't want that to happen.

After pulling the box out of his duffel bag, Pierce unlocked it and pulled out a stack of pictures. They were provocative shots of Jade in various stages of undress smiling at Pierce, trusting him in a way she'd never done another. She was so beautiful and so sweet and his heart ached for her. Pierce could not *believe* he'd hurt Jade in the way he vowed never to. Worst still was the thought of losing the love of his life over someone he had never desired or even considered. Pierce's sobs returned as he held the stack of pictures next to his heart and cradled them.

Then he got up to make sure the bedroom door was locked before putting one of their love tapes in the VCR. It was pure torture but he couldn't stop himself from watching. Pierce needed to feel close to Jade and, for the moment, the tapes and pictures was the only way he could be. He watched for over an hour trying to resist the urge to call her. Eventually he gave in and dialed their number. Pierce was silently praying Jade would answer even though he knew she wouldn't. The voice mail system they'd ordered through Pacific Bell picked up and he poured his heart out. He called back so many times that it could no longer record messages. Then, at nearly three o'clock in the morning, Pierce fell asleep with him and Jade making love being the last thing he saw.

"Damn it," Pierce yelled.

It was almost eight o'clock and he promised Dane he would be there to take him to school. Pierce grabbed his things, threw them in the duffel bag, and ran for the front door. He was in such a rush that he forgot about the tape still in the VCR.

"Thanks, Marcus, I'll holler at you later," he said before running out the door.

Marcus showered, dressed, and ate a bowl of cereal before heading out to work. He was the director of physical fitness at Logan High School as well as the football team's coach. Marcus was like a cool big brother to all the kids and they loved him dearly. So when he arrived that morning they knew something was wrong.

"You alright, Mr. Moala?"

"Hmm? Yeah, I'm okay, Keenan," he said to his star running back. "I guess I'm just distracted. One of my boys is having a hard time and I wish I could help him."

Then Marcus got an idea and decided to take an early lunch. He drove by Pierce's house and caught Jade as she was backing out of the garage. He blew the horn to get her attention then jumped out of his black Jeep Grand Cherokee.

"Hey, Jade, how are you?"

"I'm fine, but I'm kind of in a rush, Marcus."

"Okay, I won't hold you long I just wanted you to know ain't nothing there with Pierce and that tramp Regina. That's my boy and I know he would never intentionally mess up what he has with you, Jade. He loves you so much and that hoe Regina gone get dealt with for what she did!"

Marcus went on for a few minutes before Jade was finally able to get a word in. "Look, Marcus, I really don't wanna hear about Pierce's other woman," she stated after listening to him say Regina's name repeatedly. "I gotta go."

"Jade, wait, I'm sorry. I wasn't trying ... damn it," he yelled once she backed out of the driveway and drove off.

Marcus was making his way down Monterey Court when Pierce rounded the corner like a bat out of hell. He turned around to follow his friend back to the house.

"Damn it, Marcus," Pierce snapped. "Who told you to say *anything* to her?"

"I'm sorry, man, I was just trying to help. I thought if I told Jade what really happened she would be willing to talk to you and work things out. But it backfired and I made things worse," Marcus acknowledged. "I'm so sorry."

Pierce was beyond frustrated. Once he'd arrived home and found the minivan gone he assumed Jade took Dane to school. He wanted to wait for her but Tripp kept calling saying he needed Pierce at the store. So he rushed to get done at Quik Stop hoping for the chance to talk to Jade only to have his best friend show up and make her even angrier! Pierce banged his fists on top of the Chevelle to keep from pounding on Marcus. Without another word, they parted company.

Marcus went back to work and Pierce went inside to wait for his wife. Something just felt wrong when he walked through the house and it took him a few minutes to figure out what it was. A piece of Jade's luggage was missing as well as Pooh and Dane's overnight and sleeping bags. Pierce grabbed the phone to call Hawn but she hung up on him and wouldn't answer when he called back. He was leaving to go to her house when Tripp called for the third time.

"Boss, where *are* you? The reps from …"

"Look, you're the manager, right? So manage the damn store and leave me alone! I'm trying to find my wife," Pierce barked then hung up.

If Tripp didn't love Pierce so much he would have quit right then and there! The fact that Pierce paid him incredibly well also played a part in his decision to stay.

"Open this damn door, Alejandra!"

"It's Daddy, Auntie Hawn," Pooh frowned, not understanding why her aunt wasn't letting him in.

Teddy obviously didn't understand either and he barked at her. Even Xavier was crying so Hawn opened the door for Pierce but wouldn't look at him or answer any of his questions. It wasn't until Roland came home for lunch that Pierce learned Jade had made arrangements for them to take care of Dane, Pooh, and Teddy for a few days.

"Where did she go, Roland?"

"I don't know, man. She wouldn't say."

Pierce hugged his daughter and nephew goodbye then took off to Landon's house and then Tamara's. Neither of them had a clue where Jade went. According to Tamara, after their visit last night, she was no longer speaking to them. Jade was furious that her best friends would take Pierce's side and she threw them out!

"I'm *sick* of everybody acting like Pierce is the only one who lost Sugar!" Jade had screamed. "He treated me like crap for months and all any of you could say was 'Be patient with him, Jade, he's going through a lot,' or 'It's different for him because he was there.' It's almost like my grief didn't count. Everything was about Pierce and how *he* was feeling. And now this bastard has gone out and boned somebody else … boned *Regina* on what should've been my baby's second birthday and you excuse him for that too! Well, to hell with both of y'all! Get out!"

"Baby girl, we're not taking sides," Landon insisted. "I just know first hand that a person can do something under the influence that he would *never* do sober. And we've all witnessed how bonkers Pierce is when he's liquored up. Remember how he was after the funeral? I've never heard him talking crazy like that before. That dude was out of his mind! Just think about that before you throw your marriage away, Jade."

Tamara had nodded in agreement before sharing her opinion. They both kept stressing how out of it Pierce was after the funeral.

"You're absolutely right. I've never seen Pierce like that in my life," Jade had said. "But y'all wanna know what I remember most about that day? I remember how Marcus, Jackie, Roland *and* Tony had to manhandle Pierce to get him in the car. The men he trusts the most damn near had to choke him out because he didn't wanna go. But y'all sitting here trying to convince me that Regina, who's five foot two and *maybe* a hundred and ten pounds was able to get Pierce's big strong ass to go somewhere with her against his will!" she snapped.

Landon and Tamara looked at each other knowing there was nothing they could say. So they left through the door she was holding open. Neither of them had heard from her since and Tamara was worried.

"Why didn't you just come home?" she cried.

"You don't know how much I wish I had," Pierce said then hugged her goodbye.

He sat in the car for a few minutes trying to get his emotions under control. In one regard Pierce was grateful for Tamara, and particularly Landon, sticking up for him. They knew how much he loved Jade and would never have done anything to purposely hurt her. Both of them had been willing to say so even to the point of angering Jade. And it was a relief to know she was feeling *something*. Jade had been so cold and emotionless the night before that it actually scared him. The fact that she had taken off without a word, however, terrified Pierce more. Then he realized Jade would never leave and not tell somebody where to reach her. *Willa*, he thought then took off for his mother-in-law's house. He sat out front for nearly an hour waiting for Willa to come home. Pierce was positive she knew where Jade was and he prayed he could convince her to tell him. He never got the chance, though. Even when he came back later that evening, Willa still wasn't home. She was off trying to persuade her daughter not to make a decision she would regret.

It was almost ten o'clock when Marcus got back to his apartment. He'd taken his team out for pizza to lift their spirits after the one point defeat. Once inside, Marcus called out to Pierce. He'd given his friend a key just in case he needed to crash a little longer.

"Yo, Pierce, you here?" Marcus asked, as he opened the door to the guest room.

It was empty and Marcus was about to leave the room when he noticed the VCR was still on. He had meant to hit the power button to turn it off but instead he hit eject.

"Ooh, what do we have here?" Marcus asked, as he put the tape back in and took a seat on the bed. "W*hoa!*" he shouted when Jade appeared on the screen in nothing but a pair of stilettos! "Good *lord* that woman is fine!" he groaned. "*Damn!*"

Marcus watched every second of the two-hour video and was tempted to rewind it and watch it again. Jade excited and surprised him and he went to sleep wondering what it would feel like to have her for himself.

Pierce felt like he was in a living nightmare! He still had no idea where Jade was and he'd had a huge fight with his sister over the kids. Hawn thought she could prevent him from taking Dane, Pooh, and Teddy home because Jade had asked *her* to keep them. Roland intervened by reminding his wife they were Pierce's kids too and he had just as much right to them as Jade did. When she called that night to speak to Dane and Pooh Jade wasn't upset like Hawn thought she would be. No matter what she may have felt towards Pierce, he was their father and she would never try to keep him from them.

"Chicka, are you okay? You don't sound good at all," Hawn said, as she listened to the hoarseness in Jade's voice.

"I've had better days but I'll be okay. Thanks for taking care of the kids for me. I'll talk to you soon," Jade said then hung up quickly.

Hawn heard a man's voice in the background and wondered where in the world her sister-in-law was. Pierce wondered the same thing when Jade called home to speak to Dane and Pooh. She had no interest in talking to Pierce and hung up when he kept trying to explain what happened the night of Sugar's party instead of putting Dane on the phone. A few minutes later Jade's cell phone rang and her son was on the line. She talked to him and Pooh for over twenty minutes telling them she'd be home in three days on Monday, October 25th. Jade knew Dane would mark it on the kitchen calendar and keep track until she arrived.

Pierce was beside himself with fear that he'd actually lost his wife. She called the kids every night but refused to even say hello to him. He thought after the shock of his confession wore off Jade would at least be willing to talk. She wasn't and it tore Pierce up inside. He felt so helpless and found himself checking the calendar more than Dane and Pooh did. He couldn't wait for the 25th thinking a face to face talk with his wife would do the trick. Pierce soon learned just how wrong he was.

Chapter

TWENTY THREE

JADE WASN'T THE LEAST bit interested in having a face to face or any other type of conversation with Pierce. A whole week went by without her uttering a word to him. Then when she finally did speak it was about the kids. Jade had registered Pooh at the same preschool Dane attended. She couldn't start until her third birthday which was still two weeks away. However, there was an upcoming orientation and Jade gave Pierce the time and date. He suggested they go together and she agreed reluctantly before heading off to the grocery store.

Jade returned to find Marcus's truck parked in the driveway. She was instantly annoyed by him being there and that he was blocking her entry to the garage. Jade honked the horn and Marcus came from the side of the house in shorts and a tank top exposing his muscular body. He was holding a rake and a garbage bag. She frowned wondering why he was in fifty degree weather dressed like that or why he was at her house at all.

Marcus smiled and continued to hum as he approached the minivan. Jade thought it was odd for him to hum *that* song and her mind instantly went back to the night she dressed as Cat Woman and performed a strip tease for Pierce. For a brief moment Jade wondered if he had told Marcus about it but she knew better. Pierce would never tell his friends or anybody about what the two of them did in their bedroom.

Jade asked Marcus what he was doing there and he said he'd dropped by to help with the yard work. He assumed from the absence of leaves on the lawn that Pierce had taken care of it already.

"Yeah, he still takes care of all of that," Jade stated. "So can you move your truck? I've got work to do."

Marcus threw the rake and garbage bag in the back of his truck then moved out of Jade's way. She wondered why he even had garden tools since he lived in an apartment complex. Something was definitely up with Marcus but Jade didn't have time to worry about it. She lowered the garage door and was unloading the groceries when he knocked on the front door.

"What is it?" Jade's annoyance was evident.

"I didn't know if you'd seen this," Marcus said, as he held a package out to her. "It was on the front door step. Oh, let me help you with those."

"No, it's okay," Jade sighed when he moved around her to grab the bags. He carried them to the kitchen and started unpacking one when she stopped him. "Marcus, it's fine. I've got it, alright? I'm not trying to be rude but I really do have a lot to do. So if you don't mind," she said, holding the front door open for him.

"Oh, it's no problem. I'll get out of your hair," Marcus said then surprised Jade by engulfing her in a bear hug. She felt his lips brush against her neck and pulled away from him. "Let me know if there's anything at all I can do for you, okay? You've got my number," he said then walked out the door. "I'll see you, Laila."

"*What?*"

"I said I'll see you later," Marcus smirked. "What's wrong with you?"

"Nothing, I guess I'm hearing things. I'll see you."

Jade put away the groceries then turned her attention to the package Priscilla had sent to her. She had no doubt it was a third draft of her latest book with even more changes to be made. Deciding to sign on with Priscilla had definitely been a humbling experience for Jade. She was used to everyone telling her how great of a writer she was and how perfect everything she did was but that was not the case with Priscilla and her team. They knick picked her to death. Sometimes Jade wondered if it had been a mistake to join a publishing house. Deep inside she knew it was the best choice. And even though Landon was upset at first, Jade knew he was relieved to have Priscilla take over. She just had access to things and people he didn't and they both knew she'd take Jade to a much higher level.

Being worldwide was not something that appealed to Jade at first. She was quite content being a "neighborhood celebrity" as her friends and family referred to her. However, with the way things had changed so dramatically in her life, Jade needed to be able to take care of her kids and herself. She didn't want to need Pierce for anything and in order to do that she'd have to work harder than she ever had before. Remembering how she'd ignored so many opportunities out of respect for Pierce's feelings only made Jade bitter.

If she had done what Landon had asked of her in the beginning she may have already been nationwide.

"Ugh," Jade groaned when she heard Pierce pull into the garage. "Are y'all double teaming me?" she barked once he entered the house.

He was thrown off guard by her ferocious tone and just stared at her momentarily wondering what she meant by being double teamed.

"Whatever," she huffed then turned her attention back to the red marked papers in front of her.

"Uh, I was wondering why you didn't pay the mortgage," Pierce finally said.

"What are you talking about? The mortgage *is* paid."

"Are you sure because it hasn't come out of the account?" Pierce frowned.

"I didn't pay it from your account."

"*My* account? Oh, I didn't realize we had separate ones," he said, sincerely hurt by that information.

"Yeah, well things change. So is there anything else? I need to work."

"Yeah, there's one more thing," Pierce said, as he snatched the pencil out of her hand. "How long are you gonna keep this going, Jade? How long are you gonna punish me?"

Jade let out a deep breath. "Look, I don't have time for this right now. I'm under a deadline and I *have* to work."

"Well when *will* you have time? Every time I try to talk to you I get the big blow off!"

"There's nothing to talk about, Pierce."

"There's a lot to talk about! Like how long are you gonna punish me and keep me from my family?"

"I've never kept you from your kids and you know it. They love you and I would never do that to them."

"You know that's not what I mean. *You're* my family, Jade. I wanna come home. I want *you*."

"Yeah, well, you had me but I wasn't enough. So as far as I'm concerned you can go be with Regina. Y'all can get your own place or whatever you wanna do. Just leave me alone."

"Why would you say something like that?" Pierce glared at her. It was the only thing he could do to keep from crying. "You just wanna hurt me, don't you?"

"No, I don't want anything to do with you. And I honestly don't get what the problem is. You didn't want anything to do with me for months. I guess you *can* resist me after all. At least now I know why."

"Wait, what are you saying, Jade? You think I was having an *affair*?"

"It makes sense to me," she said, hunching her shoulders. "You barely came home and when you did you were mean and didn't wanna be bothered. You didn't even look at me let alone touch me so I figure Regina must have been keeping you really busy. You let me humiliate myself trying to turn you on but you could get it up for her. I was the idiot for believing that whole story about you being too grief stricken to be with me."

"I *was*, Jade! Why can't you understand that? If Sugar had died in that chest would you have been able to get over the guilt? Could you have been happy and made love and just moved on with your life knowing your baby had died on your watch?" he asked. "I hated myself and I couldn't imagine you didn't hate me too. How could you not? That day Sugar got locked in the chest I was *so* mad at you. Even after I knew she was okay I still resented you for not paying better attention to our baby. And then I let her drown!" Pierce yelled, as tears poured out of his eyes. "She died on *my* watch and I just couldn't move on from it. But it never had anything to do with not being attracted or wanting to be with you. My body just wasn't responsive because of what was going on in my head and heart."

"Well, apparently you didn't have that problem with Regina. I guess she's got what you need. Why else would you have kept rejecting me? Oh, well I suppose you were waiting on your test results, huh? I probably should thank you for being so considerate," she snorted then rolled her eyes at him. "Now can I have my pencil back? I really do need to get to work."

To Jade's surprise Pierce started screaming at her about how unreasonable she was being. He said she was forcing herself to believe something that wasn't true because she didn't want to forgive him. After a few minutes of that Jade got up from the kitchen table and started walking away. Pierce grabbed her and snatched the papers out of her hand.

"I'm talking to you, Jade! Quit ignoring me and acting like I don't mean anything to you! Please, baby, talk to me so we can work this out. Just talk to me."

"What could you possibly think I'd have to say to you, Pierce?"

"I'm hoping you'll say you still love me … that you forgive me. And you want me to come home."

"Yeah, well good luck with that," Jade said, as she held her hands out for him to give her papers back. "I need to get to work. The bills aren't gonna pay themselves."

Pierce just stood there staring at Jade. He couldn't believe how cold and heartless she seemed. It was like she'd changed into a completely different person and Pierce knew he was to blame.

"I never had an affair, Jade. I swear."

"It doesn't really matter at this point, Pierce."

"It *does* matter! You're suggesting I made a conscious decision to deceive you and carry on a sexual relationship with another woman when that's not at *all* what happened! I never even thought about being with someone else, Jade. I don't know why she was at the store that night because I promise you I didn't call her."

"Oh, so you remember now? Every other time you swore you couldn't recall a thing from that night but now you know what you *didn't* do? I thought you were so drunk, drunk off your ass I think you said that you couldn't recall even talking to Regina let alone going home with her. Right?"

"I don't remember that night, babe. I'm just trying to explain that I couldn't have called her because I don't have her number. And I'm also trying to get you to understand that she had to know I wasn't all there."

"Wait, let me guess, she manipulated you, right?"

"I know you're trying to be funny but yes, she did."

"You know what, Pierce, we can go back and forth over who knew what but it doesn't matter. If it was really what you say then you wouldn't have lied to me when I begged you to tell me the truth."

"But, Jade, I was just scared and …"

"And even if I did believe you," Jade talked over him, "I'm not willing to deal with the possibilities of what could come from your night of passion."

"There's nothing to deal with, Jade, I promise."

"Really, Pierce, so you can swear to me right now that Regina's not gonna walk in your store with two lines on her pregnancy test? You can promise me that?"

He looked sick! The thought of a pregnancy never crossed his mind and he felt completely defeated that it was on Jade's.

"So can you promise me that?" she asked again.

"No," he mumbled. "But I believe in my heart that nothing happened. I can't imagine that I would've done something like this to you."

"Wow that sounds familiar. It sounds just like the story you shared with me on our first date. Only then I admired you for being so open and honest about your drunken one night stand with Tina with me. This time, not so much," Jade sneered. "No matter how drunk you claim you were or how much you couldn't imagine yourself being with another woman, you were. And you lied to me when I gave you the chance to tell the truth. I *begged* you to be honest with me and you chose not to because you thought you were gonna get away with it. Now that you've been busted here comes this story."

Pierce tried to speak but Jade held her hand up for him to be quiet. She wasn't interested in any more of his excuses or declarations of love. Jade just wanted to be left alone so she could finally get her revisions done.

"So for the last time can I *please* have my papers back? I really do need to work."

Knowing there was nothing else he could say, Pierce gave Jade her pencil and papers and then he left.

Monday, November 21st, Luisa called to ask Jade to come over. After she dropped Dane off at school Jade and Pooh got breakfast and took it to her mother-in-law's house.

"I'm really sorry, Jade. I know how much it hurts to have the man you love betray you and I'm heartbroken my son has done this. Even though it's different from what I went through with Jackie, I know it doesn't hurt any less."

"It's nothing for you to apologize for, Mom."

"I just feel so bad. Y'all have gone through so much and I feel like I haven't really been there to help you through it. And I normally wouldn't get in the middle of this because it's between you and Juan. But my grandbabies are being affected by it and I can't have that. They aren't the same happy-go-lucky kids they used to be. And I know some of it has to do with losing Sugar. It's only been four months and everybody's still learning how to deal with it. I've been wrestling a lot with God on this one, baby. I know we don't have the right to question Him but I just don't get why my sweet baby girl got taken and I was left. That never should've happened and I feel so guilty that it did."

"Uh uh, Mom, don't you do that. We all wish it didn't happen at all, not that one should have been saved over the other. So don't you waste another minute letting stuff like that go through your mind, you hear me? I love you and I'm so grateful you're here. You've been wonderful to me and I would've been devastated to lose you," Jade said, as she hugged Luisa tight. They both were crying. "Don't let me hear you say that again or else I'm gonna have to beat you." They both laughed.

"But listen, Jade, I'm not trying to rush your decision about Juan. I know you need time to figure out what to do. I'm just asking that you find a way to make sure Dane and Pooh are okay. Alright?"

"Okay."

Jade left Pooh with Luisa and Miguel for a few hours so she could have some time alone with Dane once she picked him up from school. Before that she decided to go to Lake Elizabeth for a little quiet time to think. It was a bit chilly so Jade fastened her coat and tied a scarf around her neck. Then she walked the path around the lake trying to figure out what to do next. Thirty minutes later Jade decided to go to Quik Stop and at least attempt to talk to

Pierce. She felt like a fool when she saw him outside with Regina and made a hasty retreat before anyone saw her.

After Pierce stormed back in from telling Regina to stay out of his life, Tripp wanted to tell him he'd seen Jade pull into the parking lot. However, he thought better of it. He figured nothing good could come from it. Plus his boss had warned him about getting involved in other people's personal business. Though, that was one time Pierce could have used a little meddling.

Chapter

TWENTY FOUR

JADE HAD TEN MINUTES before school was dismissed. So she made herself stop crying and cleaned her face with the wipes she kept in the van for the kids. There were no words to adequately express how stupid she felt at that moment. Jade had allowed other people's opinions to influence her and she nearly made a fool out of herself by attempting to reconcile with the man who had betrayed her, the one who obviously couldn't let go of his other woman! As far as Jade was concerned, her marriage was over. She checked her face in the rearview mirror one last time before Dane hopped in the van.

"Hey, Mom, how was your day?" Dane asked, as he fastened his seat belt. "Are you okay?"

"I'm fine, baby. It's you that I'm worried about. So I took Pooh over to Grandma's so you and I could hang out for a while. I want to talk to you about something, okay?"

"Okay," Dane said, sadly.

They went to one of his favorite places to eat, Pizza Hut, and Jade asked Dane about school and his friends but he seemed distracted.

"Am I in trouble, Mom?"

"No, of course not, baby, why would you be in trouble?"

Dane tossed his cheese pizza on the plate as tears fell down his face. "So are you and Dad getting a divorce? That's what you wanna talk to me about?"

Jade got up from her side of the booth to sit next to Dane. She wrapped her arms around him and kissed the top of his wild curls. "What I want to talk to you about is all this worrying you're doing about me and your dad.

I don't want you to stress out about this, okay? No matter what, Dad and I will *always* love you and Pooh and we'll always be here for you. Nothing will ever change that," she said, wiping tears from her son's face. "You want me and your dad to fix it and go back to being a family, right?"

"Yeah," Dane whimpered.

"I know you do, baby. It's just sometimes things aren't so easy to fix. Even when you try really hard you can't always do it. And I know you and Pooh and everybody else want me to make things all right but in some cases you can't do stuff just because other people want you to. Do you understand what I mean?"

"You can't forgive people because someone else tells you to. It has to come from your own heart, right?"

"Right, and even when you forgive it doesn't mean everything will go back to the way it was. It's sort of like when Ramone blabbed your secret in front of the whole class. At first you were furious and never wanted to talk to him again, remember? But after his apology and a little time you forgave him. And y'all even played together again. But will you ever tell him another secret?"

"No way!" Dane said, as he took a bite of his pizza.

"Well, it's kind of like that with me and your dad. Even when I'm not mad anymore I don't know if things can ever be the same. But that's for me and Pierce to worry about, not you. I know you love us but we have to figure this mess out on our own. I just want you to be my happy, funny, sweet little boy again. I want you to eat and laugh and play with your friends. Can you do that for me?"

"Yeah," Dane mumbled while devouring another slice of pizza.

Jade picked up a slice and spent the next hour talking and laughing with her son. She knew Pierce would be at Luisa's and she dropped Dane off so he could spend time with his dad. Pierce was hoping Jade would stay for a while but she came in just to ask what time he'd be bringing Dane and Pooh home so she'd be there. She decided to call Tamara to see if it was okay to stop by.

"Hey, beauty queen," Tamara said, as she hugged her friend tight. "Come on in. I finally decided to give your meatball recipe a try but they don't taste like yours. Maybe you can tell me what I did wrong."

Jade followed Tamara to the kitchen where she was greeted with big hugs and kisses from the kids. Then she tasted Tamara's meatballs to figure out what was missing. In typical Tamara fashion, she didn't have any cumin so she replaced it with paprika!

"Girl, you do some crazy stuff!" Jade laughed loudly. "How are cumin and paprika remotely similar?"

"Shoot, I don't know. I just didn't feel like going all the way back to the store for half a teaspoon of cumin."

The two of them talked and laughed like old times. It was nice to Jade to feel normal again even if it was just for an hour. Unfortunately, it only lasted about that long. When Jamel got home Tamara fixed their plates then took Jade to the bedroom to talk privately.

"So what's really going on with you, beauty queen? I know you was trying to act like nothing's wrong but it's written all over your face. What happened?"

Jade hadn't intended on talking about what she'd seen at Quik Stop but decided to do so anyway. She described how incredibly stupid she felt for even going up there to talk to him when he obviously wants to be with Regina.

"You can't really believe that, do you?"

"Oh, here we go," Jade snapped. "I saw him wrapped up with another woman and you still defending him! I guess I'm just confused then. All this time I thought you were *my* friend but your loyalty is obviously with Captain America! I don't even know why I came over here," she mumbled and she made her way to the bedroom door.

Tamara blocked her path. "Sit your ass down, Jade! I'm sick of you running off and throwing people out every time somebody try to talk some sense in to you!"

"Who the hell do you think you talking to?"

"I'm talking to *you!*" Tamara yelled, as she walked right up on her. "Ain't nobody scared of you, Jade, so you can stand there scowling with your fist balled up all you want to. If that's the way you wanna handle things we can go for it! I ain't like Jewel that just sit there and take it. I'll knock you upside that pretty little head of yours and hopefully beat some sense in to it!"

"You go ahead and knock me upside my pretty little head and see what happens to you!"

Neither Jade nor Tamara was willing to back down and they stood in each other's faces daring the other one to swing first!

"Listen to me, beauty queen," Tamara said, after backing up a little. "I *am* your friend and I'm not afraid to tell you that you being real stupid right now. You can't stand here and tell me you honestly think that after all the begging and crying Pierce been doing he would really be hugged up with that tramp in the front of his store! Do that even make sense to you?"

"I know what I saw."

"Do you? How do you know that fool didn't just run up and grab him? Think about it, Jade. How many times has Richard snuck up and wrapped his arms around you? If somebody didn't stick around long enough to watch your reaction they could've easily thought he was your man. And you said yourself that you turned the van around and sped off. He could've punched her for all you know! So why don't you get all the facts first before you start talking about divorce!"

"And who exactly am I supposed to be getting these facts from, Tamara ... the one who cheated on me and then lied to my face about it? Is that the person I'm supposed to trust for the truth?"

"Hell, ask Tripp! He had to be in the store if Pierce was outside, right?"

"So it's no end to the humiliation you want me to put myself through, huh? You want me to go ask this boy if my husband was cuddled up with another woman or not. And then I'm supposed to wait around for the announcement that he's having a baby with some other chick!" Jade yelled. "Well, I ain't doing it. I'm not asking somebody else to vouch for Pierce and I'm not raising another one of his kids. It was different with Dane because he was here before I was even in the picture but I'll be damned if I accept a child he made while he was married to me!"

"Whoa, whoa, what are you talking about? Regina's *pregnant?*"

"She could be for all I know. And I'm not about to sit around worrying and waiting to find out if another woman is pregnant by my husband. I can't do it. I *refuse* to do it!"

"So you gone throw away your marriage over something that probably ain't even gonna happen? Come on, beauty queen, don't do this."

"Move," Jade demanded, as she reached for the doorknob. "Get out of the way, Tamara. It's pointless to continue talking. I never should've come here. Move!"

"Nobody's perfect," Tamara said, as she moved out of the way. "He made a mistake, Jade. You know better than all of us Captain America would never hurt you on purpose. He love you more than anything in this world. But I guess since your knight in shining armor turned out not to be perfect, he ain't good enough for you now, right?"

Jade took her hand off the doorknob and turned to face her friend. "Shut up, Tamara! I'm sick of you making it sound like I just woke up one day and decided I didn't want my marriage! I loved Pierce and gave him every part of me. I didn't deny him *anything* and it still wasn't enough. He left me! He left me to deal with the worst thing to ever happen to me on my own!" Jade began to cry despite her efforts not to. "He took his grief, his heart, and his body and shared it with somebody else!"

"Beauty queen ..."

"*Beauty* queen," Jade spat. "That's all anybody ever talks about! 'Oh, Jade, you're so pretty. Jade, you're so beautiful.' Well, what good does it do me? Being beautiful didn't keep me from having to put my baby in the ground!

171

And it didn't stop *every* man I've ever known from cheating on me!" she cried. "Whatever, I gotta go," Jade said then left the bedroom.

Thankfully the television was so loud that Jamel and the kids didn't hear what had taken place in the room. Jade grabbed her purse, waved goodbye to them, and took off for home.

"What's wrong, baby?" Jamel asked when he saw his wife crying.

"I just screwed up," she said then went back to her room. "Damn it!"

Tamara lay across her bed and cried. She realized what she did was the last thing Jade needed. It had only been a few months since she'd buried her daughter. And whether it was intentional or not, Pierce *had* betrayed her and hurt Jade tremendously. Then her idiot friend had tried to fight her! Jade needed someone to listen and understand not attack and insult. The more Tamara thought about her actions, the more she cried. She knew Jade wouldn't want to talk to her and she couldn't blame her. When Jamel came to the room to find out what happened, Tamara hoped he would say what she'd done wasn't that bad.

"You need your ass kicked!" Jamel snapped. "You don't have the first clue what that woman is going through! I hope she never talks to you again. *Then* maybe you'll finally learn to keep your mouth shut when you don't know what the hell you talking about!" He slammed the bedroom door behind him. "Idiot!"

When Jade got home after her fight with Tamara, Pierce and the kids were already there. They had eaten at Luisa's and he got them both bathed and helped Dane with his homework. Jade gave her kids hugs and kisses before heading to her bedroom. Pierce, recognizing she was terribly upset, asked what was wrong but Jade ignored him.

"You can get it," Pierce said to Dane when the phone rang. He knew how much his son loved answering it. "Great," Pierce mumbled.

"Mom, Uncle Landon's on the phone," Dane called.

Pierce couldn't make out what Jade was saying but it infuriated him that she was confiding in Landon and refused to talk to him. Something had happened to upset her and he was desperate to know what it was. Pierce almost snapped at the kids when they kept talking and making noise because he was trying to hear what Jade was saying.

Pooh had started coughing earlier that evening so Luisa gave her a little cough syrup. Pierce decided to use that as an excuse for why he couldn't leave the house. He knocked on the bedroom door to inform Jade of his decision. When he told her Pooh was sick she got off the phone to go check on her. It was clear that her daughter was fine but Pierce was acting like the girl was on her death bed!

"Daddy wants to stay and take care of you but Mommy won't let me,"

Pierce said, as he held Pooh in his arms. "Don't you want Daddy to stay with you?"

Naturally Pooh said yes and looked at her mother with the saddest little eyes in the world. Jade was enraged that Pierce would stoop so low as to use their kid to manipulate her. However, she managed to control herself enough to speak without screaming.

"Daddy's gonna stay in *here* okay, sweetheart? Love you and I'll see you in the morning," Jade said, as she kissed her daughter's face.

"Give Daddy kisses," Pooh ordered, as she smiled and clapped. She was used to seeing her parents be affectionate with each other.

"No, sweetie, that's …"

Before Jade could finish her sentence Pierce leaned down to kiss the side of her mouth. Then he ran his fingers through her hair and kissed her lips. He knew Jade was turned on despite how angry she was acting. Pooh smiled and cheered having no idea how much her mother wanted to slap her father! Jade composed herself knowing there was another way to fix Pierce for playing games. So she kissed Pooh good night again, tucked Dane in and made sure Teddy Bear was comfortable. Then when she was sure the three of them were sleeping soundly, Jade got on the phone.

Pierce was only able to catch bits and pieces of what she was saying but he could feel himself getting angry. He went to the kitchen where he eased the phone off the receiver to find out who his wife was finding so amusing. He was surprised to hear a dial tone and realized she was talking on her cell phone. Then Pierce tiptoed to the bedroom and listened outside the door.

"Yeah, he's here. He made a big deal out of staying because Pooh coughed and I guess it's the end of the world," Jade laughed. "No, it's not like that. He's just here in the house. No, you don't have to worry I *promise* you nothing like that is happening." Pierce turned the handle then kicked the door and told Jade to open it. "Let me call you back. No, this won't take long. I'll call you back in a few minutes, okay?" Jade opened the bedroom door. "What the hell is wrong with you? Why are you kicking on the door like you ain't got no damn sense?"

"Who you on the phone with?" Pierce asked, as he shut the door behind him.

"None of your business! And why are you in here anyway? What do you want?"

"I wanna know who's so important for you to be on the phone with when you should be taking care of your sick daughter!"

"First of all, Pooh had a *cough*! She's obviously fine and sleeping soundly. But you're here to take care of her, right? Wasn't that the reason you manipulated your way into staying in the house? So why aren't you in there with her instead of worrying about what I'm doing? I'm no longer you're concern."

"You'll *always* be my concern!" Pierce stated, as he snatched the cell phone out of her hand.

"What are you doing? Give me my damn phone," she screamed and tried to snatch it back. "Ugh, why don't you just get out and leave me *alone!*"

"I'll never leave you alone, Jade. You're my wife and you promised to love me for better or worse."

"Yeah, and you promised to forsake all others but you didn't! As far as I'm concerned all that for better or worse junk went out the window when you decided to screw Regina! So go be with her since that's obviously who you want and leave me alone!"

Teddy was barking up a storm and Pierce opened the door to tell him to be quiet. He was shocked to find Dane standing there with tears in his eyes.

"Don't fight," he cried.

"Come here, baby," Jade said, as she pushed past Pierce to kneel in front of Dane. "Mommy and Daddy were just talking, okay? I'm sorry we scared you by being so loud. Everything is fine. Come on let's go back to bed."

Pierce followed Jade and they both reassured him everything was okay. She laid her face against Dane's and ran her fingers through his hair until he fell asleep. Jade and Pierce went into the living room to talk. Teddy lay across Jade's feet with his eyes locked on Pierce.

"I'm not gonna hurt her, Teddy Bear.

The dog barked once then rested his head on top of his front paws. It was only when Jade rubbed him and told him it was okay that Teddy relaxed enough to take his eyes off Pierce.

"We need to," both Pierce and Jade started.

"Ladies first," he said, giving her the floor.

Jade started off by saying they couldn't keep putting their children in the middle of the mess going on between them. Pierce was seconds away from smiling thinking she was going to tell him to move back home. He was shocked when Jade asked for his keys so he would stop coming in whenever he wanted. She felt like it would be less confusing for the kids and for her if he called before he came and stuck to whatever schedule they decided on.

"Are you *serious?*"

"Yes, I am. I think it'll help avoid situations like the one that happened tonight. And I need some boundaries, Pierce. Having you here all the time makes things harder and I know it confuses Dane and Pooh. Until we can figure out what to do I think it'll be best for you to stay at your mom's or wherever and spend time with the kids on the schedule we come up with."

"I disagree with that. This is my house and my kids and I shouldn't have to be away from either of them. And how are we supposed to work things out if you want even more distance between us, Jade? How is what you're suggesting gonna fix anything?"

"Fixing things with you is not my priority right now, making sure our kids are okay is."

Jade's words were like a dagger to Pierce's heart and his eyes filled with tears. He couldn't even look at her so he grabbed his keys and left. It was six o'clock in the morning when he returned. Pierce made a pot of coffee and invited Jade to join him in the kitchen.

"If setting up boundaries is what will help me get you back then I'll do it. I don't want to, but I will. I won't turn over my keys but I will call you if I need to come here outside of our schedule. I just want you to understand that in no way am I giving up on us. I love you, Jade, and I believe we can get through this."

Jade thanked Pierce for respecting her wishes and then attempted a conversation with him. "Humph," she grunted in response to his answer to her question. Then Jade left to get Dane up for school.

Chapter

TWENTY FIVE

Thanksgiving morning Pierce, Hawn, Diana, and Eva were at Luisa's getting everything cleaned and organized for dinner. Pierce turned on music to discourage his sisters from asking him about Jade or if he thought she was going to change her mind about staying for the family dinner. Then the first song they'd ever slow danced to began to play and Pierce was on the verge of tears. He left the living room and went to grab the extra table and chairs his mom asked him to set up. He just wanted to work and keep his hands busy so his mind wouldn't focus on the fact that it was the first Thanksgiving without his daughter and his wife. It was impossible to do since their pictures were all over the house and they were all anybody wanted to talk about. Pierce felt like he was losing his mind and had no idea how he'd make it through the day. Every place he looked was a memory of him and Jade making love and it was killing him.

Things only got worse when Jade came to drop the kids off. They had spent the early part of the day at Willa's and Pierce assumed she would be spending the evening with Landon. He didn't know Justin would be in from Arizona in a few hours to stay with Jade.

"Baby, please don't leave," Luisa cried, as she squeezed Jade's hand. "You belong here with us. We just as much your family as we are Juan's. You don't need to be alone, Jade. Please stay here and have dinner."

Miguel and Jackie surrounded Jade both begging her to stay. Then Diana and Eva joined in their pleas.

"We need to be together, Jade," Luisa said.

"I'm sorry," Jade said with her heart breaking into a million pieces. "You know I love all of you and I miss you. But it hurts too much to be here. Memories are all over this house and I just can't take it. Last year I had three children and a wonderful marriage. Now I don't. So please, I need to go," she said and took off for the door before she fell apart.

Jade kissed Dane and Pooh quickly before grabbing her purse and heading outside.

"*Do* something," Hawn urged Pierce.

He had already grabbed his coat to follow Jade. Pierce called to her but she ignored him and kept going towards the minivan. Jade just wanted to get as far away from there as possible.

"Babe, you don't have to leave. We can be in the same house without it turning into a problem. Please, don't go. It's Thanksgiving. It's the first one without our ..."

"I don't want to be here," Jade said, coolly. She opened the door and climbed into the van.

"Well maybe it's not about what *you* want!" Pierce snapped, as he prevented her from closing the door. "Did you ever stop to think that perhaps our kids need you here? Do you even give a damn how they might feel about you running off on Thanksgiving? For once why don't you think about someone other than yourself?"

Pierce was desperate. Jade had become distant and cold towards him again and he was willing to do anything to get a rise out of her. Pierce didn't want her to be angry but at least she'd be feeling something for him. Unfortunately it didn't work. Jade was even more frosty and emotionless than she'd been before.

"Look, I know you hate me but that's no reason to make our babies suffer. It's not about you and me right now so why don't you grow up. Come back inside and be with your family who put a lot of effort into making sure you'd be comfortable."

"Are you done?" Jade asked, dryly.

Since making her angry wasn't working Pierce decided to plead with her instead. That didn't work either and he was forced to close her door and watch Jade drive away. Pierce sat out in the cold on the porch letting tears roll down his face. His sister came and sat beside him.

"She really hates me, Hawn. I did my best to get some kind of reaction from her and she wouldn't even look at me. And you know Jade. She wears her emotions all over her and there was *nothing*. Her expression was just blank. She doesn't care about me anymore and I don't know what the hell to do. I wish I had just brought my stupid ass home that night and my family wouldn't be destroyed!"

Hawn didn't know what to say so she wrapped her arms around Pierce and let him cry.

"Oooh, you stupid son of a … *oooh!*" Jade screamed once she'd turned the corner. "Who the hell does he think he is trying to make it seem like I don't care about my own babies? Whose fault is it that our family is split apart? Huh? Whose fault is it, you ignorant bastard," she ranted the entire ride home.

Jade's anger grew once she got inside the house and realized she had no one to talk to. Landon and Tamara would have been the first people she called to vent but they both thought she was wrong for her unwillingness to forgive Pierce. And after the fight with Tamara, Jade didn't know if they would even have a friendship. Tamara had left a message crying and apologizing but Jade wasn't ready to deal with her. She was still too hurt. Justin knocked on the door and forced Jade to stop rehashing the horrible fight.

"Happy Thanksgiving, sis," Justin beamed.

Jade tried to smile back but she fell into her brother's arms and sobbed.

"Oh, baby girl, I'm so sorry," he whispered, holding her tightly to him. "I know this has to be hard."

Justin let Jade cry in his arms until she felt ready to stop. Ten minutes passed before she pulled away.

"I'm sorry, Justin. That's some kind of greeting, huh? I didn't mean to depress you," Jade said, as she wiped her tears. "I'm sorry. Let me fix you something to eat."

"Stop, sis, you don't have to wait on me. And you definitely don't have to apologize. I'm here because I want to support you, in whatever way you need. So if you need to cry then we'll cry. If you want to laugh and just hang out then we'll do that. Just tell me what you need, okay? I'm here to take care of you for a change," Justin stated, as he hugged her again. "So are you hungry? I actually brought a Thanksgiving meal with me. I just need to heat it and we'll eat and talk and whatever else you wanna do."

Justin brought a cooler full of the most amazing food! Jade kept teasing him saying he was lying about cooking everything himself.

"Oh so you can cook but I can't, right?" he laughed. "We got the same blood pumping through our veins so I can do everything you can do, all but have babies. What," Justin asked when Jade started to say something then stopped.

"Nothing, I was about to ask you to tell me what's going on with you. The last time we talked you were making some big decisions. What's going on?"

Justin explained that he had decided to give his lifelong dream of being a serious singer a shot. Jade was very impressed by the demo he played for her.

His voice was beautiful and it gave her goose bumps every time she heard him. He had such a soulful sound and the things he sang about were touching.

"You should sing with me on a couple of tracks."

"Plggh!" Jade sputtered. "You must not wanna sell anything," she laughed then took another bite of Justin's delicious turkey and dressing.

"I'm serious, sis. You've got a great voice … when you talk," he laughed loudly.

"Shut up," she giggled. Shoot, I'm not worried about trying to sing. I'm having a hard enough time getting these revisions done on my book. Priscilla just won't let up. She keeps saying I need to write with more emotion."

"What?" Justin frowned. "Why do you need more emotion for the kind of stories you write? I thought they were *supposed* to be lighthearted and funny."

"Normally they are, but this one is different. I wanted to write a story to help kids deal with death. This one is about a family of butterflies that lose their youngest one and they all have to learn how to deal with it."

Justin reached across the table and touched his sister's hand. She grabbed a napkin to wipe her tears and continued to talk to him about the story.

"Would you like to read it? I mean, it still has to be tweaked a little here and there."

"I would love to read it, sis."

Jade got up to clean her face and get the proofs from her bedroom. She watched Justin's facial expressions as he read to see if he was grasping what she wanted to convey. He smiled and then cried.

"This is absolutely beautiful, Jade. I don't know what Priscilla is tripping on because it's perfect just like it is. I wouldn't change a thing. And I know I'm a little biased but I think this is wonderful. I believe it will help a lot of people, including *your* family."

That opened the door for a conversation about Pierce and how they were doing in their marriage. Jade told Justin about seeing him with Regina at the store and the fight she had with Tamara behind it. He acknowledged that her friend had gone about it all wrong but he understood her point. It seemed unlikely Pierce would flaunt a relationship nobody but Jade believed he wanted. Justin also understood why his brother-in-law didn't volunteer information about whatever happened at the store that day. He could see how agitated Jade was becoming and decided to let it go.

"How are things going with you and Shawn? He wasn't mad about you coming here, was he?"

"Oh, no, he totally understood. That's what I love about him is his big heart. So to answer your question, things are going really well. I'm happy."

"Yeah, I can tell," Jade smiled. Her eyes were still sad, though.

Justin reached across the kitchen table and touched her hand. "I'm worried about you, sis. I wish there was something I could do to help you through this."

"You're doing it. Coming here and spending this time with me is a huge help. I just couldn't handle a big family dinner or all the memories that come flooding back the second I step into my in-law's houses."

"What?" Justin asked when she blushed.

"A lot of those memories are of me and Pierce. I guess we were the horniest folks in the world. Every place I look, I remember being all over each other." Jade's eyes filled with tears. "What are you doing?" she asked when Justin pushed his plate aside and sniffed the table.

"Oh, I'm just making sure nobody's ass was right here where I've been eating!"

Jade burst out in hysterical laughter like he hoped she would. "Thank you, Justin," she said once they finally stopped laughing. "I love you and I'm glad you came."

"I love you too, sis. And I want you to know I'm here for you the same way you were for me. You provided me with a place where I could be open about any and every thing and I'd like to return the favor. So go ahead and tell me whatever it is you've been holding back."

"What?" Jade frowned.

"You were about to tell me something earlier but you stopped yourself. So what was it?"

Jade dropped her head trying to hide the tears about to fall. "Well, let's just say I learned that alcohol isn't the only thing to make a person do something they regret. Sometimes hurt and anger can too."

Justin didn't know what that meant but it was obvious his sister wasn't planning to elaborate. He decided not to push her. If Jade wanted to tell him what she'd done, she would.

"Are you up for a walk around the block?"

"Is that your polite way of telling me to get my fat butt up from the table?" Jade laughed loudly.

"You know I wouldn't say that."

"Yeah, but you were thinking it."

Jade had put on about ten pounds. For the first two weeks after Sugar died she could barely keep anything down. Then, as a way of dealing with her sadness, she ate constantly and slept as much as she could. Jade had started to shed the extra pounds but when she found out about Pierce and Regina, food became her best friend again. She had always had a ravenous appetite but once Jade stopped exercising, the weight crept up on her.

"Believe it or not, I *have* started working out again. When I had to put on a pair of my maternity pants to feel comfortable, I knew my weight had gotten out of control. So don't worry. I'm not about to pack on forty pounds like I did when I was pregnant. That was not cute," she laughed.

Justin reassured Jade she would be beautiful at any size. He just wanted her to be happy and could tell she was embarrassed by the extra weight. She admitted thinking that was the reason Pierce hadn't wanted to be with her.

"I hope you don't still believe that, do you? I wasn't here during your pregnancies but I heard plenty of stories from Tamara and your in-laws about how Pierce couldn't keep his hands off you because he thought you were so beautiful and sexy. I can't imagine him not being attracted to you because of a few extra pounds."

"Yeah, well I know now why he didn't want to be with me."

"Jade, don't do that."

"Come on, let's go for that walk," she said, not wanting to talk about Pierce or Regina.

Later that night, Pierce asked his sisters to keep an eye on Dane and Pooh. He wanted to talk to Jade and decided to drive home to see her. Pierce was instantly upset when he saw a strange car parked in front of his house. And even though he wasn't supposed to be there until the next morning, Pierce burst through the front door thinking he was going to catch Jade with another man.

"What's up, brother-in-law?" Justin asked, as he and Jade sat on the couch watching movies.

He saw the crazed look on Pierce's face and knew exactly what he'd been thinking. He didn't know Justin had bought a new car. Jade knew what Pierce thought too and almost laughed. She was glad he was going crazy. In fact, she had been doing things to make him that way. The night Pierce nearly kicked her bedroom door in, Jade wasn't talking to anyone on the phone! She just wanted to hurt him. Unfortunately, a lot of Jade's recent decisions were made to punish Pierce for breaking her heart.

Chapter

TWENTY SIX

ON MONDAY, NOVEMBER 30ᵀᴴ, Pierce arrived at the house bright and early for Pooh's first day of preschool. He got teary eyed when his little princess came out of her room to give him a look at her.

"Do you like my dress, Daddy?"

"I love it, sweetie! You look *so* pretty," Pierce said, as he knelt with his arms outstretched.

Pooh ran to him with a smile that lit up her entire face. Pierce held her tight then planted kisses all over her cheeks as he stood. Pooh looked like a living doll in her pink and white polka dot dress and white tights. Her shoes were pink and shiny as was the headband atop her head. Dane had given it to Pooh for her birthday and she couldn't wait to wear it on her first day of school. Jade finally gave in and let the girl wear her hair hanging down her back instead of the two ponytails she wore nearly everyday.

"Get your butt in there and do what I told you," Jade snapped. "Hey, boy, don't act crazy. You better straighten up your face before I straighten it for you. Now get in there. And hurry up," she fussed.

Pierce put Pooh down to see what was going on with his son. Dane was mad because he assumed he was going with his parents to take Pooh to school. He felt like *he* had to meet her teacher and make sure everything was up to par. When Jade told Dane he'd be going to his own school, he threw a fit. She popped him across his butt a few times to help him come back to his senses.

"Come here, boy," Pierce said, as he snatched him by the back of his t-shirt. He closed the door to Dane's room. "Do I need to take off my belt?"

"No," he mumbled.

"What?"

"No, sir," Dane said more clearly.

"Don't you ever treat your mama like that again, you hear me?" Pierce asked, directly in his son's face. "You don't make decisions around here. You're a kid and you do what we tell you. Now get dressed and get your stuff ready for school. And let me hear something slam in here and I'm coming back with my belt. You got it?"

"But why can't I go, Dad? This is Pooh's big day and I wanna be there with her. I wanna see her little seat and meet her teacher too. I'm her brother, Dad."

Pierce chuckled. "I know who you are, boy. And I know you want to be there with your sister but you have to go to school. We aren't trying to be mean to you, okay? I know there's a good reason Mom won't let you miss the first part of your day and you just have to accept it. We don't always get to do what we wanna do, son. Now get dressed so you can eat breakfast."

Jade was in the kitchen making bacon, eggs, and toast when Pierce joined her. He whispered to her asking why she wouldn't let Dane go with them. Jade reminded him about Dane's test. All the students would be taking state exams to measure how well they were doing as a school. Their teachers had been sending notices home for weeks stressing how important it was for the kids to be at school on time. If it weren't for that, Jade would have let him go. She knew how much Dane adored Pooh and wanted to be there for all the important things in her life. And apparently he wasn't the only one.

About ten minutes before Pierce was planning to drop Dane off, a posse showed up on their doorstep! Miguel, Luisa, Jackie, Eva, and Hawn arrived with balloons, flowers, and a backpack full of goodies.

"Oh, lord, y'all act like this child is graduating high school," Jade giggled.

They all smothered Pooh with affection and told her how absolutely beautiful she was. Luisa had bought her a gold bracelet and fastened it on her little wrist. Jade just shook her head and smiled. She loved that they all loved Dane and Pooh so much and appreciated them always being there for them. Pierce took a few more pictures before he had to get Dane to school. His grandparents and aunts wished Dane luck on his tests and smothered him with hugs and kisses too. Within fifteen minutes of Pierce's return, he, Jade, and Pooh were in the minivan heading for Preston Preschool.

Jade tried not to be annoyed by Pierce continuously staring at her while she drove, but she couldn't help it. However, she wanted to focus her attention on Pooh and not get sidetracked by the tension between the two of them. The day wasn't about their issues. It was about their sweet baby girl who hadn't stopped smiling since she awoke.

They arrived twenty minutes early to meet Pooh's teacher, Mrs. Wheaton. Pierce and Jade were pleasantly surprised when they walked into room seven and learned that Mrs. Wheaton was the former Ms. Mathis who'd been Dane's preschool teacher!

"It's so good to see you," Mrs. Wheaton said, as she hugged Jade and Pierce. "And who do we have here? Are you Dana?" she asked, kneeling in front of her.

Pooh nodded with a smile as bright as the sun.

"Oh, you are just *too* precious, sweetheart. Is it okay if I give you a hug?"

Pooh wrapped her arms around Mrs. Wheaton's neck and patted her back. The teacher all but melted. She thought Pooh was adorable and fell in love with her instantly.

"Dana's such a sweetheart. And she looks exactly like her father," she laughed.

Pierce and Jade laughed too. Then Mrs. Wheaton congratulated them on getting married. When she was Dane's teacher they were dating. Jade forced a smile even though she wanted to slap Pierce's hand away from the small of her back. She was glad when he left her side to walk around the classroom with Pooh.

"And how is Dane? I bet I wouldn't even recognize him now," she said. "I know teachers aren't supposed to have favorite students but he was definitely one of mine. And I think the same will be true of his little sister."

Jade took a picture out of her wallet and handed it to Mrs. Wheaton.

"Oh my goodness, look at him! He's such a protector. I can totally tell how much he loves these girls. And this little one looks just like you, Jade. How old is she?"

Again her smile was strained. "She would have been two. She passed away this summer."

Mrs. Wheaton gasped and placed her hand over her heart. "Oh my god, I'm so sorry. I didn't know."

"It's okay. There's no way you could've known."

There were a few moments of awkward silence before Mrs. Wheaton turned her attention back to Pooh who was sitting in her seat. Instead of individual desks there were tables and chairs set up around the room for the kids to sit. Mrs. Wheaton took Pooh by the hand and showed her where the toys were located.

"*Stop* it," Jade mumbled through gritted teeth.

Pierce kept touching her and it was getting on her nerves. It was hard enough being there together without him pretending like they were a happy couple. Jade was trying hard to keep her composure after telling Mrs. Wheaton about Sugar. Having Pierce touching her back and shoulders and wrapping his arm around her waist was just too much.

Thankfully, Mrs. Wheaton dismissed all the parents so she and her students could begin their day. Jade raced to the minivan. She wanted to drop Pierce off and get him away from her.

"What's the hurry?"

"I've got things to do," Jade said. "What are you doing? Stop playing games, Pierce! Give me the keys," she snapped when he snatched them out of the ignition.

"We need to talk, Jade."

"I don't have anything to say."

"Well, maybe you can listen to me. I just need for you to know how sorry I am, babe. I truly am."

"I know you're sorry, Pierce. It just doesn't matter."

"Why would you say that to me, Jade? How can ... hey, where's your ring?" he frowned.

"It's in the garbage along with our marriage."

Pierce stared at her with a wounded look on his face. "You just wanna hurt me, don't you?"

"You keep asking me that and I keep telling you I don't want anything to do with you. We have kids together so I have to deal with you but that's the only reason. Believe me if it weren't for them I would never see you again."

Tears began welling up in his eyes.

"Just stop," she said, rolling her eyes. "I don't feel like going through this with you. Give me the keys so we can go. I just wanna go home."

"I know I hurt you, Jade. And I'm truly sorry. But what about all the good years we had? What about the times when we were happy and in love? They don't matter at all?"

"Did they matter to you, Pierce?" Jade asked, as she turned to face him. She pressed her back against the door and crossed her arms. "When you left me to be with another woman, did those times matter? Were you thinking about how wonderful our life was when you had your wedding ring touching all over Regina's body? Hmm? No, I didn't think you did. So why should it matter to me now?"

"It should matter because what happened that night wasn't intentional. I *never* would have knowingly betrayed you, Jade. I love you."

"Really, Pierce? So if I told you I was *so* distraught after your confession that I unintentionally had one too many Midori sours and ended up in bed with Landon, you'd understand? You'd know in your heart that I never 'knowingly betrayed' you?"

Jade could see the rage building in Pierce's body! He was biting down so hard that she thought he'd break his teeth. And he kept clenching and unclenching his fist.

"Why what's wrong, dear? You seem upset," she said sarcastically.

"So was that an example or a confession?"

"Whatever, Pierce, just give me my keys."

"Why can't you answer me?" he asked, growing more enraged. "I know you were with Landon that night and y'all had drinks. So did you sleep with him?"

"Could you forgive me if I did? For years you've been convinced Landon has feelings for me. And for years I've told you there's absolutely nothing but a sibling relationship between us. So if after all that convincing and reassuring I ended up in bed with him would you excuse it just because I was drunk off my ass?"

Pierce knew what Jade was getting at and there was nothing he could say. She, Tamara, and Tripp had warned him about Regina. They all recognized that the woman had feelings for him but Pierce reassured them, particularly Jade, there was absolutely nothing to worry about. Even when he let Regina remain as his Lay's representative, Pierce was adamant about her being meaningless to him. For him to sleep with her after swearing he never had those types of feelings was an insult to Jade's intelligence.

"It would be hard to forgive something like that but I know I would try. I couldn't just stop loving you because I was hurt. I wouldn't throw away everything we've built together over a mistake."

"Well, I guess you a better person than me. Can I have my keys now?" Jade asked, as she held out her hand.

"Do you still love me?" Pierce asked, his eyes pleading. "Do you?" he asked again when she didn't answer.

"Are you gonna give me the keys or do I need to call Landon to come take me home? Fine," Jade said then opened the door to get out of the minivan.

"Jade, wait, here," Pierce said, as he handed her the keys.

They were silent during the five minute drive back to the house. Pierce closed his eyes and let tears run down his face. He was heartbroken and terrified his wife would never forgive him.

"Are you gonna leave me?" Pierce asked once Jade had pulled into the garage.

She climbed out of the van and went inside. Pierce sat in the garage for a few minutes unable to move. Eventually he climbed out of the minivan and got into his own car. He lowered the garage door and sat staring at the house for over twenty minutes.

"What the …?" Pierce grumbled then hopped out of his car. "What the hell are you doing here?"

"Oh, I told Jade I would come by to clean out the gutters for her so she didn't have to worry about it," Marcus said, as he opened the trunk to retrieve his tools.

Pierce slammed the trunk shut and walked right up in Marcus's face. His heart was beating wildly as rage pulsed through his veins! "So this how we doing things now? You supposed to be my boy but you here tiptoeing and sniffing around my woman?"

"Oh, so now I'm *supposed* to be your boy? What you saying, dude?" Marcus asked as he muscled up to Pierce.

"I guess you think I'm a damn fool, huh?"

"I don't know what you are but you better back up before you get hurt!" he threatened. "I can't believe you coming at me like this. We've been boys since elementary school so you should know me better than that. I mean damn, man, you honestly think I'm here trying to move in on your wife? That's really what you think I'm about?"

Pierce didn't know what to think. He wanted to believe his best friend wouldn't betray him but his instincts were telling him otherwise.

"Just don't do this again, you hear me? You have no reason to be here if I'm not here," Pierce stated.

"Whatever," Marcus huffed before speeding off. He was nervous from just having been busted.

Pierce didn't have time to worry about his friend. He was more focused on getting his wife back. Then he took off to talk to the one person he thought could help him do it. Tamara invited him in and Pierce asked for advice on what he could do to reach his wife. He also told her about their little chat in the minivan.

"I wanna help but beauty queen probably hate me more than she hate you. After the fight we had she won't even talk to me."

"What fight?" Pierce frowned.

"Oh, I guess she didn't tell you, of course she didn't, sorry. Anyway, after she saw you with Regina at the store she ..."

"Wait, what, she was at, oh my god *please* tell me you lying, Tamara! Jade was at Quik Stop? Damn it! I just can't catch a break!" Pierce shouted. Then he felt sick to his stomach. "Aw, *damn,* Jade gave me the chance to tell her about it and I didn't thinking it would make everything worse! Now she'll never believe me but I was trying to get rid of that psychopath!"

Pierce realized Regina had to have seen Jade. It explained why she was smiling and suddenly hugged him when he was telling her never to set foot in his store again. At the time he thought she was insane but Regina was clearly manipulating things. And Pierce was certain she'd done the very same thing that fateful night. The problem was convincing Jade. Pierce lost all credibility with her the moment he chose to lie.

"*Ugh*," he groaned, throwing his hands on top of his head. Pierce was upset by the fact that Jade had at least been willing to talk to him and he blew it again by not telling her the truth. Another stupid decision might have cost him his chance at reconciling with the only woman he ever loved.

Pierce excused himself and nearly ran out of Tamara's house. He needed to hit something and decided the gym was the safest place to do it. Pounding and kicking the punching bag only made Pierce bitter. He had a perfectly good bag that wasn't being used because he was exiled from his own house. Little did he know, on the other side of town, Jade was getting plenty use out of it. She figured it would benefit her more to use the punching bag to deal with her emotions than a knife and fork. And after a few weeks those extra pounds were nowhere to be found.

Pierce was shocked when he came to get Dane and Pooh for the night and Jade came out of their room in a little black dress. She looked amazing and it was torturous for him not to be able to touch Jade or kiss that special spot on her neck that always made her laugh. Once again tears welled up in his eyes. It was unbearable to feel irrelevant and invisible to the love of his life.

For as sad as Pierce felt when he picked his kids up, he was enraged when he dropped them off! Jade had just pulled into the garage when he arrived wearing the same little black dress. Her hair was a mess and when she walked by Pierce to hug Dane and Pooh he got a whiff of cologne!

The kids were barely out of earshot when Pierce snapped at her. "You got quite the little social life, don't you? Every time I come get the kids you running off somewhere. So I guess you think I'm your personal babysitter, huh?"

"Dane and Pooh are your kids so that's not considered babysitting, Pierce. Besides, I don't ask what or who you do when they're here with me so why are you worried about what or who I do when they're not? I'm free to do what I want."

Actually, no you're not! You're my wife!"

"Stop yelling before you upset the kids."

Pierce was beside himself. The thought of Jade being with another man filled him with fury! It took every ounce of self control he had not to punch a hole through the living room wall!

After he stood staring at Jade for a while, Pierce finally left. He drove straight to the gym and beat the punching bag mercilessly. Though, no matter how hard he hit it Pierce couldn't rid his mind of one thought. The only man he knew who wore that particular type of cologne he'd smelled all over Jade was Landon!

Chapter

TWENTY SEVEN

IT WAS THE WEEK before Christmas and Pierce had reached his breaking point. Even after two months of being separated, Jade didn't seem any closer to forgiving him and he was at his wit's end. She still threw Regina up in his face no matter how many times he tried to convince her nothing was going on between them. Jade didn't believe him and apparently never would again. Pierce was heartbroken and didn't know what else to do to reach his wife.

He heard Luisa say Hawn was at his house watching the kids and he drove there to find out why Jade hadn't asked him to keep Dane and Pooh. Pierce was greeted by the sound of Jade's laughter and it made him smile. He hadn't heard her laugh that hard since Sugar died. However, Pierce grew angry the more he listened. He couldn't understand what she found so damn funny when he was miserable and barely hanging on to his sanity! And he wanted to know who was able to amuse his wife to the point of hysterical laughter.

"Okay, I'll see you in a few minutes," Jade giggled as she exited the bedroom. "Alright, bye."

"You look pretty, Mom," Dane said.

Pooh smiled and clapped as she echoed her brother.

"Chicka, make sure you take care of that outfit 'cause I'm wearing that bad boy next!" Hawn said of the burnt orange, long sleeved jumpsuit her sister-in-law was sporting. "And I'll be taking those heels and the jewelry too. Yep, just gone and leave it on the bed when you get home and I'll take it to Mama's cleaner in the morning. Girl, you laughing but I'm dead serious. I'm gonna arrive for Christmas dinner with it on, watch!"

"You look beautiful, babe," Pierce stated, as he stared at her lovingly. Jade

189

looked *so* pretty to him and it tore his heart out that he wasn't accompanying her like he normally would've been. "Where you off to?"

"Thanks," Jade smiled.

Then she gave Dane, Pooh, and Xavier kisses and hugged Hawn goodbye before they went to watch movies.

"So you don't hear me talking to you? I asked you a question, Jade. Where are you going?"

"Don't start, Pierce," she snapped then grabbed her new coat from the closet. "Why are you even here? Never mind, it doesn't matter. I have to go."

"Oh, so it's like that? You just gone walk out when I'm trying to talk to you? Jade, wait."

She left and closed the garage door behind her.

"Juan, what the hell are you *doing*?" Hawn screeched when she went to get popcorn and saw her brother walk out of the bedroom with his gun! "Juan! Juan, stop," she said, trying to prevent him from leaving.

"Move," Pierce muttered before pushing her off him. He hopped in his car and took off. The only place that served the cheddar cheese biscuits Jade had joked about on the phone was Red Lobster. Pierce spotted her minivan immediately and went charging towards the front door. Through the window he was able to see a tall, handsome young man stand up from the table to greet Jade. He embraced her warmly and kissed her cheek.

"Excuse me, sir, you have to wait to be seated. Sir, wait," the hostess called as she trotted behind Pierce.

"My party's already here," he snapped and kept moving towards the spot where he'd seen his wife.

Jade was definitely startled when Pierce came barreling up to their table. "What are you doing here?"

"Oh, no reason, I just wanted this dude to know he's out on a date with my *wife*! I wasn't sure if you mentioned that or not. It was hard to tell with all the hugging and kissing y'all were doing."

Pierce drew the attention of some of the other diners and wait staff. The hostess had sent word for the manager and he was on his way to their table. Jade was about to tell Pierce to leave when she saw the imprint of his gun and knew she had pushed him too far.

"Pierce, I'm not here on a date," Jade said, as she caressed his hand. Her touch instantly calmed him. "Jeffrey is my new publicist and he came here to meet with me ... see here's Landon now. And Priscilla should be here any minute. It's just a business dinner, okay?"

"What's going on?" Landon asked.

"Is there a problem here?" the manager frowned.

Jade smiled and reassured everyone things were fine. She put her coat on then gave Landon her purse to hold. As she led Pierce outside, Jade realized the whole embarrassing scene could have been avoided if she had just answered him back at the house. Her game playing had gone too far and she felt guilty knowing someone could've actually gotten hurt. Jade had never seen Pierce like that and it scared her.

"So you came here to take me out?" she asked, motioning towards the gun tucked in the front of his jeans.

"No, of *course* not, Jade! You know I would never hurt you … well, not like that," he said in response to her raised eyebrow. "It's not even loaded. I just wanted to scare that dude away. When I saw you with him I thought," Pierce trailed off as he dropped his head and cried. "Jade, I can't take this anymore. I can't," he choked. "I'm lost without you and I wanna come home. *Please*, I'll do whatever you say just please let me come home. *Please!*"

A group of guys heading inside for dinner heard Pierce's pleas and decided to tease him about it.

"Maybe we should talk later," Jade stated, embarrassed by the attention they were drawing to themselves. "I need to get back inside anyway."

"Jade, please stay with me. We can go wherever you want. I just wanna talk to you. There's gotta be a way for us to work this out. Please."

"I'm sorry, Pierce, I can't. Like I said this is a business dinner and I need to go back."

He planted kisses on her hand then held it next to his heart as more tears streamed down his face. It actually made Jade sad to see him like that. Pierce seemed so broken, so desperate, so completely different from the man she'd fallen in love with. Yet, every time Jade began to soften, an image of him and Regina would flash through her mind and harden her all over again.

"Pierce, please," Jade said, as she tried to remove her hand from his chest.

He held tightly to it. "Just tell me what to do to fix this and I'll do it."

"I don't know that it *can* be fixed. But if it could be, you'd have to start with the truth." Jade removed her hand then hugged the coat around her to block the bone chilling wind. "You would have to stop trying to convince me you're not attracted to Regina the same way I had to stop making myself believe I was never afraid of her. That's why I responded to her the way I did. She's beautiful, smart, ambitious, all the things you used to love about me. And I always feared she could take you from me. I wanted to believe what we had was strong enough to keep that from happening but," Jade sighed and looked to the ground to keep from crying.

"*Nobody* could ever take me from you, Jade. You're the love of my life and no one can compete with that," Pierce said sincerely. "I'm *so* sorry I hurt you, babe. I swear I didn't mean to. It was a horrible, horrible mistake that I've regretted every second since. And I know it's a cowardly thing to say but I lied because I was so scared of losing you. I didn't trust the truth and it's cost me the only thing that matters. It's put doubt in your heart which I've never wanted you to have. But I *am* being honest with myself and you when I say that I'm not, nor have I ever been, attracted to her. You're all that I've ever wanted and I'm begging you to forgive me and let me come home."

Landon tried to focus his attention on what Priscilla was saying but he couldn't stop looking out the window at Jade. He wanted to believe Pierce would never hurt her but couldn't be sure by the crazed way he had behaved. So Landon watched for any sign that Jade was in distress. All he saw, though, was a heartbroken man desperate for his wife's love. And Landon couldn't blame him for that.

"Do you still love me, Jade? Do you miss me at all?"

She kept staring at the ground trying hard to blink away the tears forming in her eyes.

"Jade," Pierce whispered, as he gently touched her face. "Look at me."

Jade closed her eyes wanting so much to collapse in his arms. Even as cold as it was outside his hands felt so warm and comforting. She did miss Pierce and wanted nothing more than to have their relationship back the way it used to be. She just didn't think it was possible. Jade didn't know if she could ever offer him her heart again. She opened her eyes and stepped away from Pierce.

"I need to go back inside, okay? Pierce, please," she said, and took another step back when he tried to touch her again. "I'm sorry but I need to go."

"Is it that hard to say whether you love me or not?"

Jade stared at him momentarily. "I'll always love you, Pierce," she finally admitted. "I just don't trust you anymore. I'm sorry, okay, I gotta go," Jade said and took off before he could see the tears rolling down her face.

Pierce called after her but there was no use. So he sat in his car for a few minutes with the heat blasting. He hadn't realized how cold it was until then. His adrenaline had been pumping so hard that it kept him warm. Though, with the hope of being back with his wife dashed, Pierce felt cold as ice. He finally pulled out of the parking lot and headed back to his house. Pierce knew Hawn was worried sick and he wanted to let her know everything was okay.

It was obvious how much Jade was struggling through Christmas dinner at Luisa's. Every place she looked was a memory of Pierce or Sugar and it was almost too much to bear. The only reason she'd even bothered to come was because Dane asked her to. And her in-laws tried so hard to make Jade happy but they could see in her face how sad she was. Pierce was just as pitiful and the fact that they didn't have each other to lean on made things worse. Jade all but ran out of the house the moment the gift exchange was over.

"Go get her," Hawn encouraged.

"She doesn't want me," Pierce said then busied himself with putting the tables and chairs away. Alone in the garage, he cried out to his daughter since God didn't seem to be paying him any attention. "Help me, Sugar. Help Daddy fix this mess. *Please*," Pierce sobbed.

A few days later Jade asked him if he'd be willing to join her therapy session at the beginning of the year. She'd started seeing Dr. Rosin again and he suggested marriage counseling. At first Jade was resistive towards it. His office was the only place she didn't have to hear someone telling her how ridiculous she was being for not forgiving Pierce. Jade hadn't been willing to let that go. However, the next time Dr. Rosin mentioned it she was more open to the idea.

"I'll do whatever you want me to do," Pierce smiled.

Unfortunately things didn't work out the way either of them had hoped.

Chapter TWENTY EIGHT

On Tuesday, January 4, 2000, Pierce pulled into the parking lot of Union City Kaiser. He was meeting Jade for their two o'clock session with Dr. Rosin. She actually giggled when he walked into the waiting room wearing a three piece suit. Pierce laughed too when he got a look at Jade in a pair of jeans and a sweater.

"I didn't know what I was supposed to wear."

"I see," she smiled.

Thirty minutes into their hour session things went wrong. It was obvious to both Jade and Dr. Rosin that Pierce was only there to appease his wife. Every time he was asked a question his response was whatever he thought Jade wanted to hear. That made her angry. After they left the session Jade told him it defeated the purpose of them being there if he wasn't going to be honest. The following Tuesday at their second session Pierce was very candid and expressed his resentment over Jade's unwillingness to forgive him and move forward. That made her angry too.

"See, Dr. Rosin, I can't win. No matter what I do it's wrong," Pierce said, as he threw his hands up in frustration. "I don't even know why we're here because it's clear she doesn't wanna be in a relationship with me."

"Why do you think Jade doesn't want to be in a relationship with you?"

Pierce looked at the psychologist as if he'd just asked the stupidest question in the world. "Have you been listening to her?" he snapped.

"Have *you* been listening to me?" Jade sneered. "No, I guess not since all you can do is talk about how you would have forgiven me if the situation were reversed. It's easy to sit there and say what you *think* you'd do but you don't know what it feels like to be betrayed by the one person you trusted most!"

"Are you sure about that, Jade?"

"What does that mean?"

"You're not innocent like you claim to be, Jade. Why don't you tell Dr. Rosin about your new social life? You constantly throw Regina up in my face but there's never any mention of all your late night meetings and phone calls. Maybe that's the reason you're so opposed to letting me stay in the house because you don't wanna give up your other man!"

"If that's what you really think then why are we even wasting our time here?"

"Unlike you, I'm willing to forgive and try to rebuild our marriage. But you won't meet me half way. Everything is about you and how *you* want things to be. It's like you don't care what this ridiculous schedule you have us on is doing to our kids! Nobody's happy, Jade! But who gives a damn as long as it's convenient for you, right?" Pierce snapped. "You don't care how unfair it is that you got me twisting in the wind waiting on you to decide whether you wanna be with me or not."

"Well, let me make it fair. I don't wanna be with you," Jade said before snatching her purse and coat to leave. "I'm done!" she shouted then slammed the door behind her.

Both Pierce and Dr. Rosin called after her but she kept walking. They waited for the remaining twenty minutes of the session hoping Jade would return but she didn't. Instead, Jade called Landon to see if he was free then picked up Chinese food from his favorite spot.

"So how long are you gonna keep punishing Pierce? You know he's losing it, about to shoot folks and stuff. Why won't you stop this mess and gone and work it out? Despite your dramatic exit from the therapy session I know you still love him."

"Sometimes love isn't enough," Jade said. "I know everybody thinks I'm wrong for not taking Pierce back. But every time I think I can put it behind me I get these mental pictures of him being with Regina and it breaks my heart all over again. I can't honestly say I forgive him. I wish I could. But until then, I think it's wrong to invite Pierce back into my life only to send him away again when I can't deal with the fact that he slept with someone else," she said, sadly. "To be honest, some days I look at him and wonder what the hell I'm doing. Then other times I can't stand the sight of him."

"Are you gonna see Dr. Rosin again?"

"I doubt it. I just don't wanna hear somebody else who doesn't understand what I'm feeling tell me I'm wrong."

"I wanna understand, Jade. And I'm sorry if I made you feel like I'm not on your side. You know I am. I just know what it feels like to make a horrible mistake and lose everything that matters to you. I did it with Gabrielle and almost with Chaundra. If she hadn't been willing to forgive me I'd be alone again," Landon admitted. "I know Pierce broke your heart but I still don't believe he meant to. And I don't believe he'd ever let something like that happen again, do you? I'm serious, Jade, do you?" he asked again when she huffed and put her fork down.

"I never thought he would do it in the first place so it's hard to answer that."

Landon was frustrated with Jade but decided to change the subject before they got into it again. He asked if she'd spoken to Tamara.

"Yeah, I wished her a happy Thanksgiving and dropped off some Christmas gifts for the kids. I'll probably go over there again soon."

"Alright now, don't y'all be over there kickboxing."

"You need to stop," she laughed. "So what's going on with you and Chaundra?"

"Actually everything's cool. I asked her to move out here with me. That long distance thing is starting to take its toll. Sometimes I just wanna catch a movie spur of the moment or go to a local festival or something and I hate not being able to do that with her. Everything has to be planned. Plus all those flights and long drives are getting expensive. We wanna be together so it seems silly to keep doing all this. So the last time Chaundra was here she started looking into some jobs. Everywhere she applied called her back instantly. Someone of her caliber will have no problems working."

"Aw, check you out, bragging on your woman. You're proud of her, huh? That's so cute."

"Cute," he chuckled.

Before Jade left Landon's house she decided to call Tamara. She apologized profusely thinking Jade was still mad at her. Once Jade reassured her she wasn't angry, Tamara asked if they could hang out on Saturday.

"I miss you, beauty queen. You my girl and I love you. I'm so sorry I hurt you," she began to cry. "You know Jamel cussed my ass out telling me what a damn fool I was. He was absolutely right, though, and I'm sorry."

"I'm sorry too. I love you, Tamara, and I'd love to hang out on Saturday. If I can just make one request."

"You ain't even gotta say it. I won't mention you know who," she laughed.

On Sunday, January 30th, Jade and Landon were on the phone laughing and talking when he got another call.

"Baby girl, let me call you back. This is Chaundra on the other line. I'll call you later, okay?"

"Okay, tell her I said hi, or better yet, don't. I know I'm not her favorite person so it would be best not to mention me. I'll talk to you later."

Landon clicked back over to find out what was wrong with Chaundra. She sounded upset. As he listened to her talk for ten minutes straight it was obvious her insecurities had kicked in again. Landon couldn't even count the number of times she'd said Jade's name.

"So what do I have to do to prove that I love *you*, Chaundra? What else do you need?"

"Move down here with me."

"What?" Landon definitely wasn't expecting that. "I thought you were planning to move up here with me."

"I was, but I think it would be better if we started our lives here. Or we could start over fresh in a place neither of us has been. I just want it to be you and me, Landon."

"It *is* you and me, Chaundra," he said, frustrated. "I don't know why you've convinced yourself that there's something sinister between me and Jade. She's my family and I love her but it's not the way you make it seem. I love you, Chaundra. I really do. But I'm sick of being put back in this position that I have to defend myself to you. I don't know what's happened but I think what you're asking me to do is completely unfair. Every place you inquired about up here was ready to hire you on the spot. What am I supposed to do for work down there?"

"Oh come on, Landon, you are *not* hurting for money. And it's not like I'm asking you to come down here and take care of me. I've been taking care of myself for a long time just like you have. So you could take some time off until you figure out what you wanna do next. It's the land of opportunity out here so you'll have no trouble finding something you wanna do. Maybe it'll be good for you to finally have a career that doesn't revolve around Jade."

"Ooh, you know what? I think it would be best if I hang up now because you really starting to piss me off! I don't know how many times I have to ... never mind. I'll talk to you later, Chaundra," Landon spat and was about to hang up. "Wait, you know what? You're the one with the problem, Chaundra. You're jealous of Jade and instead of just owning up to that you try to make it seem like I've done something wrong. Hell, you say Jade's name more than you say mine so maybe *you* the one that's obsessed with her!"

"I can admit she makes me feel insecure. To you Jade is this beautiful, perfect woman and I feel inferior to her. So yes, I'm jealous, insecure, and probably a little irrational sometimes too. But it doesn't change the fact that the man I'm in love with would choose another woman if he had a chance with her. And it pisses me off that you keep denying it when I can *see* it! I'm not stupid, Landon. I know you're in love with Jade no matter how many times you talk in circles and refuse to admit it."

"So you really don't believe that it's you I love?"

"I know you love me, Landon, just not in the same way you love Jade. And the fact that you won't even consider moving away from her only proves it. Why can't you let go of her and come build a life with me?"

"Jade and the kids are my family, Chaundra. Why does being happy with you mean I have to leave them? Why do Dane and Pooh have to grow up without me in order for you to be pleased? I would never ask you to give up your family for me. And you know I don't particularly care for all of them but they matter to you. So why do I have to give up everything to be with you?"

"Isn't that what you're asking me to do? I'd have to give up my house, my family, and a job I've worked really hard to keep. But I was willing to do it because I love you just that much. I was willing to do it not knowing if you'll ever marry me. I was willing to risk it all for you but you won't even *consider* doing it for me."

They were silent for a few moments.

"So what now?" Chaundra asked.

"I still want you to come here like we talked about. But I guess that's not gonna happen now, is it?"

"No, I guess not."

"Chaundra, please don't do this. I really do love you. I wanna be with you and build a life together."

"I love you too," she said and began to cry. "I just can't be second in your life. I won't be your conciliation prize, Landon. I don't deserve that and I won't accept it."

"Chaundra …"

"I have to go. Bye, Landon," she said then hung up the phone. "How come I'm never good enough?" Chaundra shouted, as she crawled into bed and cried herself to sleep.

Landon couldn't believe what had just happened. He definitely wasn't expecting to break up. It hurt but he didn't feel like it was anything that could be fixed. Landon wasn't willing to give up the only real family he had.

"Well, I guess we can scratch the whole moving in thing off the list since I no longer have a girlfriend." Landon announced when he called Jade back.

She fixed herself a cup of coffee and sat on the couch listening to Landon recount his conversation with Chaundra. Normally Jade would have jumped in with her opinion but she realized how irritating that is when no one's asking for it. So she just listened and let Landon vent his feelings. She had no idea that her own relationship was about to have a dramatic ending.

Chapter

TWENTY NINE

MONDAY MORNING PIERCE ARRIVED at the house and followed the sound of blaring music to his makeshift gym. Jade was working out using the punching bag and he was instantly turned on by the aggressive way she was hitting it. And her body looked *amazing* in the black form fitting workout Capri pants and sports bra she was wearing.

When the music changed Jade alternated between punching the bag and dancing. For some reason Pierce thought she knew he was there and was dancing provocatively for him. The way Jade screamed bloody murder after spotting him put that notion to rest.

"You scared me to death!" she shouted after turning off the stereo.

"I'm sorry," Pierce said, eying her seductively. "I didn't want to disturb you since you seemed so in to your workout. I was in to it too," he smiled.

"How long have you been here?" she asked, ignoring his attempts at flirting.

"Just a few minutes … long enough to see you beat the mess out of that punching bag. I've never seen you work out so aggressively before. I think I like it."

"Oh yeah? Well you can fill in for the bag since you like it so much. I'd love to beat the mess out of you."

Even though Pierce knew she was being serious, he laughed. Then he walked over and stood in front of it. Pierce looked Jade up and down as he gave her that sly grin.

"What do you want?" she huffed and rolled her eyes.

Pierce kept smiling at her with a raised eyebrow.

"Oh geez, do you have something to say to me the reason you dropped by unannounced again?"

"I did call. Maybe if the music hadn't been blasting you would've heard the phone ringing."

"Sorry," Jade mumbled. "So what is it?"

"I wanted to talk to you about February 5th."

"What about it?"

"Well, it's our anniversary and I was wondering if you'd have dinner with me. We can go wherever you want."

Jade looked at him like he was insane then she walked out to grab a water bottle from the fridge.

"So, I'm guessing that's a no then," Pierce said, following her into the kitchen. Babe, you look good," he moaned, staring at her body, "delicious, in fact."

Jade grabbed her t-shirt that was draped across the chair and put it on. Then she opened the bottle of water and nearly drank it all.

"Will you at least consider having dinner with me?"

"I'm not much for role playing these days, Pierce. Trying to act like a happy couple out celebrating their anniversary is too much of a stretch for me. I don't think I could pull it off."

"Ouch," Pierce said, as he stared at her with those intense eyes.

"And stop looking at me like that!"

"Like what?"

"You know like what. Just stop," Jade stated, as she tried to fight off her growing arousal.

"You look *so* good, babe."

Jade left the kitchen hoping Pierce would leave her alone but he was right behind her.

"Why you running, Jade? You don't trust yourself? Scared something might happen if you get too close to me?"

"Stop playing games with me, Pierce," she said when he snatched the bottom of her shirt and pulled her to him. "Please just stop, okay, this isn't gonna fix anything."

"It might," Pierce smiled, as he removed the rubber band from her ponytail.

"Stop!" she yelled, pushing his hand away.

Pierce grabbed her by the waist and they just stared at each other for a few moments before Jade pushed him away. At least she tried to push him away but he didn't budge. And that only turned her on more.

"Move," she sneered.

"Make me," he challenged.

Jade tried to push him and again he didn't budge.

"Look, I need to finish my workout," she said and nearly ran back into the gym.

"That's cool. I need to work out too."

Pierce removed his sweat suit to reveal a form fitting pair of shorts and the dog tags Jade had given him against his bare chest. He got on the treadmill and started walking to warm up. Before long, he was running. Jade went back to punching the bag trying desperately to ignore Pierce.

"Oh, *shoot*," he shouted after losing his balance. "I almost broke my damn neck looking at that booty!"

Jade tried hard not to smile.

"So?" he asked, continuing to run.

"So what?" Jade frowned.

"Don't my booty look good too? I see you looking at it," Pierce smiled at her. "Oh come on, you know you wanna laugh. That was funny."

That time Jade did smile and it gave him confidence to bring up their anniversary again. Pierce soon regretted doing so.

"What would be the point, Pierce? Do you really think it would be fun to talk about how wonderful things were before Sugar died and you decided to bone somebody else?" Jade snapped. "Are we supposed to remember back to the good old days when we used to love each other?"

"I still love you, Jade," Pierce said despite how much her words hurt him. "I've always loved you and only you."

"Yeah, well you've got a real funny way of showing it," she said then left the room.

Pierce chose not to follow her that time.

Jade went to her room to shower. Afterwards she was sitting at the vanity table brushing her hair when Pierce walked in with nothing but a towel wrapped around his waist. He had taken a shower in the guest bathroom and walked in whistling as he put on deodorant and cologne like it was just an ordinary day. Jade stared at him not knowing what to think. Then she began to wonder if it was really as simple as that. Could they just go back to their lives as though nothing happened? Could they actually be happy again? Jade continued to stare at him as if she was waiting for an answer. Then she stood up to leave when he grabbed her by the arm. The towel she had on fell off.

"I want you *so* bad," Pierce whispered, as he ran his hands around her waist and backed her against the wall. "Don't you want me? Don't you wanna feel me all over you … *in* you?" he asked then kissed the side of her mouth.

Jade all but melted! He felt and smelled so good. And when Pierce took her face in both his hands and stared deep into her eyes, Jade wanted to tell him she still loved him. She wanted him to make love to her and take all the hurt away. She wanted back what they once had but didn't know if it was possible to get.

"It's still me, Jade," Pierce said, caressing her face. "I'm still the guy from Quik Stop, the one you fell in love with and married … the man you started a family and built a life with. I'm still the man who loves you most."

Jade wanted to kiss him and she was about to but hesitated.

"What is it? Tell me, babe," he said, continuing to rub her hair and face. Please talk to me."

"Have you been with her?" she finally asked.

"*No*, Jade … *hell* no!" Pierce exclaimed, shocked she would even think such a thing. "I never wanted to in the first place so I sure as *hell* wouldn't do it again! Believe me, Jade, *please*," he cried. "Baby, I'm so sorry I hurt you. I'm so, *so* sorry. But I swear if you give me another chance I'll never hurt you like this again. I promise to take better care of your heart, Jade. I'll never break it again. Please trust me and give me another chance."

That time she did kiss him. And it was with all the passion and love she'd always had for him. She removed his towel and held him close to her. Then Pierce picked Jade up and she wrapped her legs around his waist as he carried her to their bed. For the first time in months they made love. It was different, though. Jade kept her eyes closed through most of it and he could sense she wasn't fully there. And for the first time ever, he couldn't get her to the moon.

"What do you want from me, Pierce?" she asked when he expressed his frustration.

"I want you to make love to me, Jade."

"And what exactly do you think I've been doing?"

"You've been letting me have sex with you but I want your heart too, Jade, not just your body. I want you to …"

Something sticking out of her nightstand caught Pierce's attention. He reached for it and a rage like no other pulsed through his body!

"Wait, Pierce, it's not what you think," Jade explained when she saw the look on his face.

"So you really *have* been screwing somebody?"

Despite his suspicions, Pierce never really believed she was sleeping with anyone. Finding condoms, however, made him realize just how wrong he'd been to think she could never actually cheat on him.

"Who the hell is it, Jade?"

"Nobody, Pierce, I …"

"So I'm stupid now? You and I have *never* used condoms but you got a drawer full of them! But you not screwing nobody, right? I guess they just in here for decoration, huh? Tell me the truth, Jade!" he yelled, pinning her down on the bed with his body.

"Get off me!"

"Why? Apparently you like having men on top of you, right?" he sneered before rolling off her.

Jade got up and grabbed a robe from her closet to put on. He jumped out of bed and snatched a pair of jogging pants and a t-shirt out of the closet. Pierce mumbled the whole time he was putting his clothes on and when Jade tried to leave the room he jumped in front of her.

"So I guess that's why you couldn't cum for me, huh? Mr. Condom's been knocking it out for you? So who is it, Landon, or do you have other dudes I don't know about?" Pierce scowled. "Oh, so you don't hear me talking to you? You just gone stand there looking at me like I'm crazy? You brought some dude up in my house, in my bed and *I'm* the one that's crazy? I asked you a question, Jade, and you better answer me *now!*" Pierce yelled, as he snatched her by the belt of her robe.

"Get your hands off me, Pierce!"

"Who the hell have you been screwing in my bed?"

"I haven't screwed anybody! *You're* the only liar and cheat in this relationship!"

He just stared at her for a few moments. "So I guess you think I'm boo-boo the fool, huh?" he snarled.

Pierce didn't think he could ever hate Jade but that's exactly what he was feeling as he stood there trying to resist the urge to slam her into the wall! What happened with Regina was a horrible mistake but what Jade had done was deliberate and malicious.

"You know what? *Fuck* you, Jade!" he yelled. "I've been kissing your ass for months trying to prove how sorry I am and how I never deliberately hurt you but you don't give a damn! You just wanna keep hurting me! Even now you standing here all cold and emotionless like it doesn't bother you that you killing me! I've been miserable everyday without you while you been in here screwing other dudes! I guess that's why you always been so sensitive to being called a whore because you are one!"

Jade was stunned by his words and began to cry.

"Oh so *now* you got emotions? I've been crying and begging and going crazy over losing you and you didn't feel jack. But I call you a whore and you wanna cry! Ain't that 'bout a bitch?" he sneered.

"Just get out, Pierce," she continued to cry.

"I ain't going no damn where! If you don't wanna be here then *you* go! I'm not being banished from my own house anymore!" Pierce snapped. "But before you go you *are* gonna answer my question. Who have you been using condoms with, Jade? I think I have a right to know. You are my wife, after all."

"Move, Pierce!" Jade shouted when he wouldn't let her get by him.

"So you don't wanna tell me, huh? Well I guess I'm gonna have to find out the hard way," Pierce said, as he grabbed the cordless phone off the charger. He hit redial. "Let's see who you been talking to last. Maybe he can tell me what I need to know."

Jade tried to snatch the phone away from Pierce but he put his hand on her chest and held her against the wall. She started screaming and swinging at him. One of those swings connected and Jade hit Pierce in his face.

"*Oooh*, girl," he groaned through gritted teeth.

It took all the self control he could muster not to hit her back. They tousled with each other and continued to argue. Pierce told her she wasn't going anywhere until she answered his question. They were still screaming at each other when the front door opened.

"Jade!"

"What the … I *know* this son of a bitch didn't just walk up in my house! So it's like that, Jade? He's got a goddamn key?" Pierce shouted as he made his way to the living room.

"Jade!" Landon screamed.

He was the last person Jade had talked to and he heard them fighting over the phone after Pierce hit redial.

"You must have lost your damn mind! You don't just walk your ass up in my house like it's yours! *Nothing* in here belongs to you!"

"Jade, are you okay?" Landon asked, as he looked past Pierce like he hadn't spoken.

"Yeah, I'm okay. I just … Pierce, what are you *doing*?" she screamed, when he lunged at Landon and punched him dead in his face! "Oh my god, stop! Landon, Pierce, stop this!"

Neither man was listening to her as they were intent on doing damage to one another. Landon cracked Pierce in his jaw and stomach then took another hit to the face. They were exchanging blows at lightening speed and all Jade could do was watch in horror thinking they were going to kill each other!

Pierce swung Landon around and slammed him into the entertainment unit. The TV and stereo system came crashing down and it sounded like an explosion. Picture frames and vases were broken as well as the mugs and other souvenirs The Jamisons had collected from their travels. Landon rammed Pierce into the wall and their family portraits fell and shattered. Jade felt as if she was watching her life be destroyed right in front of her.

Pierce kicked Landon in his stomach which such force that it sent him flying back onto the couch. And just when Jade thought they couldn't do any more damage, Landon tackled Pierce then lifted him in the air and slammed him on top of the coffee table. It shattered into a million pieces beneath him.

"Please, stop! Landon, Landon, *stop*," she screamed and jumped in the way when he picked up one of the speakers to slam on top of Pierce. "Why are y'all doing this? Please just stop," Jade sobbed.

Both breathing hard and bleeding, Pierce and Landon finally stopped attacking each other. Pierce grimaced as he sat up slowly trying not to cut himself on the broken glass. Landon used the bottom of his shirt to wipe blood from his nose and limped over to the lazy boy. He put a protective hand over his ribs and lowered himself into the seat. Pierce managed to get off the floor but not without groaning in pain. He wondered if some of his ribs were broken from the sharp pain shooting through them as he lowered himself on the couch.

Jade looked around her demolished living room not believing what had just happened. All she could do was cry and the only sound in the house was her sobbing. Pierce leaned forward with his elbows on his knees and let tears drop from his face. Landon cried too.

"I'm sorry, Landon," Jade sniffed. "I never meant for you to get caught in the middle of this."

"It isn't your fault, baby girl. This was a long time coming. Your husband hates me."

"Your boyfriend hates me too," Pierce snapped. "Why do you think he was fighting me?"

"Because you attacked him, Pierce! What was he supposed to do just stand there and let you hit him?"

"That wasn't the reason, sweetheart. Landon was fighting for the woman he loves just like I was," he stated, looking across the room at him.

Jade was waiting for Landon to defend himself but he lowered his head and didn't say a word. Pierce grimaced as he stood up from the couch and walked by Jade towards the front door.

"Oh, you might wanna wait a while before you go in, Mr. Condom. Right now she's full of my DNA," he snorted.

"I *hate* you, Pierce! Get the hell out of here!"

"Man, I didn't sleep with your wife and you know it."

Pierce stared at Landon for a few moments. "But you want to and that's just as bad. It's just as disrespectful. So why don't you do me a favor and tell her the truth. Maybe then I'll stop looking like the jealous asshole that doesn't know what the hell he's talking about?"

Again Jade was waiting for Landon to defend himself and he said absolutely nothing. After Pierce left she stood staring at him, confused.

"Why didn't you tell Pierce he was wrong, Landon?"

"Why didn't *you* tell him the nurse at Kaiser gave you those condoms when you went to get tested? Maybe if you had I wouldn't have gotten my ass handed to me," Landon said, and winced as he stood up.

"I'm sorry. I swear I never meant for that to happen. I tried to tell Pierce the truth but he was too busy calling me a whore to listen. Like an idiot, I thought we were about to put our lives back together. He swore he would never hurt me again and then that's exactly what he did. I guess Pierce figured if he could bone somebody else then I could too."

"Yeah, well you might have a little something to do with why he thinks that," Landon said, as he slowly walked to the kitchen.

Jade had confessed playing head games with Pierce to torture and drive him crazy. Landon warned her to stop because things could turn out badly. He had no idea they'd turn out badly for him.

"Whatever," she said, following him, "so why didn't you tell Pierce the truth when he accused you of wanting to be with me? Why didn't you tell him he was wrong?"

After Landon used a wet paper towel to wipe dried blood from his face, he stood in front of Jade and stared into her eyes. "Because he's not."

"*What?*" she frowned. "What do you mean he's not? Of course he's wrong, Landon, I'm your sister."

"No, Jade, I'm your brother. There's a difference. If I thought for one second I had a chance to make you see me in a different way I swear I'd take it." Tears sprang to his eyes. "I *am* in love with you, baby girl. I have been since the moment I laid eyes on you. I never had a crush on Willa. It was always you. And I obviously did a poor job of hiding my feelings. Pierce saw it. Gabrielle saw it and so did Chaundra. *That's* why she left me."

Jade closed her eyes and shook her head as tears streamed down her face. "Get out," she whispered.

"What?"

"Get out!"

"So you're mad? I tell you I love you and you're *mad* at me? Baby girl, please, just let me ..."

"I can't handle this, Landon. Please, just go, I can't handle this right now," she said and began walking away.

Landon grabbed Jade and turned her towards him. And despite the pain shooting through various parts of his body, he kissed her. Touching her soft, sweet lips for the first time made Landon's heart skip a beat and he wanted nothing more than to hear Jade say she was in love with him too. He wanted her to take him in her arms and promise never to let go. Landon wanted Jade to make love with him and connect in the one way they hadn't. Though, what he wanted most at that moment was for Jade to kiss him back.

She didn't. Jade put both of her hands on Landon's chest and gently pushed him away. Her head was swimming and she didn't know what to think.

"Please love me, Jade," he whispered. "I love you *so* much and I can give you all the things you need. I promise I'll never hurt you, baby girl. I love you in a way I've never loved anyone else," he cried. "Maybe the reason our relationships never work out with other people is because you and I should be together. I know you best, Jade, and I can love you better than he can. Just give me a chance."

"Landon …"

"Don't you love me at all, Jade?"

"I love you *death*, Landon, just not like that. I'm sorry," she said when his head dropped and shoulders slumped. "I don't wanna hurt you, Landon. But you're asking me to feel something for you that I just don't."

He looked devastated and brokenhearted.

"Look at me. Look at me, Landon," Jade said again when he tried to turn away from her. "You've been one of the most important people in my life and I cherish what we have. I've been counting on you and confiding in you since I was a little girl. You've been my big brother, my best friend, my business partner, and the man I trusted most. And I don't wanna lose you over some fantasy you've built up in your mind about me. So we're gonna forget this conversation ever happened. And then you're gonna move to Santa Monica with the woman you really love and build a life together."

"Oh, so that's what we gonna do? You not gone even *try* to love me, Jade? You just discount my feelings like I'm too stupid to know what's in my own heart!"

"I don't think you're stupid, Landon."

"Do you think a fantasy would last for damn near twenty years?" he snapped. "I *know* you, Jade … the good, the bad, and the ugly and I'm still in love with you. And it hurts so bad to hear you blow off my feelings and try to send me away," Landon admitted. "You really want me to leave?"

"I don't *want* you to leave, Landon, but I think you should. Chaundra loves you in the way you want and deserve to be loved. Don't throw that away," she said, gently touching his cheek. "I love you, Landon, but I can't be what you want me to be. I'm sorry, but I can't. And you don't want someone who has to *try* to love you. You want the woman that just does. And that's Chaundra. So be with her, Landon. Love her the way she deserves, you hear me? You need to go live your life with her and let me figure out what to do with mine."

Landon kissed the palm of her hand then held it close to his heart. He closed his eyes and softly stroked her hand as tears ran down his face. Jade cried too knowing things between them would never be the same.

"I wish you could see what's in my heart," he said, kissing her hand again. "I love you so much, baby girl, and I'll do anything for you. Even leave you," Landon whispered, as more tears ran down his face. "I love you, Jade Jamison. And I always will." Then for the second time, Landon kissed her lips. "Bye, baby girl."

"Bye."

Landon wasn't quite out of the house when Jade broke down sobbing. He stood outside her front door doing the same.

Chapter
THIRTY

A WEEK AND A half went by without Jade and Pierce speaking. She either dropped the kids off at Luisa's or he had his sister pick them up and bring them home. Pierce didn't even look at her when they had Dane's ninth birthday party at McDonald's and their fourth anniversary went by unacknowledged. So as painful as it was to do, Jade made a decision about her marriage.

At nine in the morning on Wednesday, February 9th, Jade heard a knock on the door. It was a messenger sent by Priscilla with the preview copy of Jade's new book. She ripped the package open and smiled brightly when she saw the cover. It was amazing. The butterflies were so beautiful and vibrant. And Jade loved the way they gave each of the five butterflies a personality. It was easy to tell which one was the mommy and daddy butterflies and which ones were the girls and boy. The smallest of the group was flying away from the rest of them towards the sun. The book was entitled "Where Do Butterflies Go?" and Jade hoped it really would help children deal with death. Before she could finish reading it there was another knock on the door.

"Hey," Pierce said with a faint smile on his face.

"Hey," Jade replied, allowing him inside.

She closed the front door then they both stared at each other silently for a few moments. Pierce was about to take something out of his back pocket when he saw what Jade was holding.

"Wow, is that your new book?"

"Yeah, it just came. I didn't get a chance to finish reading it yet but it looks good."

"Do you mind?" he asked, holding his hand out for the book.

"No, not at all," she said, relinquishing it.

A huge smile spread across Pierce's face as he ran his hand across the butterflies on the cover. Tears quickly filled his eyes but he opened it and began to read. Jade had to turn away because it broke her heart to see him cry.

"This is beautiful, Jade," Pierce said, as he wiped his eyes with the cuff of his sleeve. "It's really beautiful and I think it will help a lot of people. I'm proud of you."

"Thank you." They both were silent again. "So, you wanted to talk to me?"

"Yeah," he said, handing her the book. Then Pierce removed a folded envelope from his back pocket. "I wanted to know why you sent this to the store. Do you really wanna divorce me?"

"I thought that's what you wanted. I mean why would you wanna stay married to a whore?"

Pierce closed his eyes and let out a deep sigh. "Jade, I don't ..."

"Besides, you made arrangements for nearly two weeks to see the kids without seeing or talking to me so I figured there was nothing else to do but go our separate ways."

"Babe, I didn't stay away because I don't wanna be with you. I stayed away because I couldn't face you. After the fight with Landon I stood outside the front door debating whether to get my gun and come back or not. And what I heard destroyed me inside."

Jade's heart dropped to her stomach.

"When he asked why you didn't tell me about the nurse giving you those condoms I literally got sick to my stomach. I can only imagine how humiliating that was. And then look how I acted. I did exactly what I had been mad at you for doing. I jumped to conclusions, wouldn't listen, or give you the benefit of the doubt. I realize now that if the shoe had been on the other foot I would have felt and acted the same way you did. It hurts to feel betrayed and that's all I was going off was my hurt feelings. I called the woman I love a whore and mistreated you because I was terrified someone else had taken my place. That's all it was, though, Jade. I swear I've never thought of you that way and I had no business talking to you or snatching on you like that," Pierce said with his eyes full of pain.

"I wanted to call you every single day but I had no idea what I could possibly say. I've said sorry so many times that I didn't think it would even mean anything. And to think, I had done all that promising I would never hurt you again and as soon I felt betrayed, that's exactly what I did. I know it sounds weak but I *am* sorry, Jade. I've screwed up everything and I don't know how to fix it. But I do know one thing. I can't spend the rest of my life without you. I can't and I'm not gone even try. I just need to know if you can really live the rest of your life without me. Do you honestly wanna divorce me?"

Jade started crying, but it was that gut wrenching, heart breaking sob coming from deep within her. Pierce hadn't heard her sound like that since Sugar died. And then all at once it hit him. He finally understood what Jade meant when she said it wasn't just one thing he had done wrong.

"Oh my god, baby, I'm *so* sorry," Pierce cried as he squeezed her as tightly as he could. "We went through the worst thing that could ever happen to parents and I made you suffer alone. I was supposed to be there to hold you and comfort you and I refused because of my own guilt. I promised you that no matter what happened in our lives we'd always get through it together and I left you when you needed me most. Jade, I'm so sorry. Please forgive me," he wept. "I've hurt you so much and I'm sorry."

Jade was crying so hard that she nearly threw up. She ran to the bathroom and Pierce was right there with her. He held her hair back as she dry heaved over the toilet. And he rubbed her back while she put a cold, wet towel on her face to reduce the puffiness.

"Thank you," Jade said once she was composed. "I know we have a lot to talk about but I really do need to go. I have to meet Priscilla in less than fifteen minutes. But maybe you can come back at around eleven. Is that okay?"

"Yes," Pierce smiled, feeling hopeful for the first time since their lives were turned upside down. "Yes!"

Jade felt hopeful too. On the ride to the coffee shop where she was meeting Priscilla, she daydreamed about being a family again. When she arrived her boss could sense something had changed. She was thrilled to hear what had taken place despite her own heartache. A month earlier, Priscilla's husband wrote a letter informing her that he was ending their twelve-year marriage to be with another woman! She was devastated and felt hopeless for what the future had in store for a Black, single, overweight, forty-one-year old with nothing but her business and a cat.

"So what in the world are you doing up in here? Go get your man, girl. This can wait. That can not."

Jade hugged Priscilla then left the coffee shop. She still had an hour and a half before Pierce was meeting her back at the house and she decided to go by Tamara's.

"So are you gone let him come back home, beauty queen? You forgive him?"

"Yes, I forgive him," she said, wiping tears from her face. "I miss him *so* much, Tamara. I love him."

Tamara was crying too. "Then go get your man, girl. And don't waste all that time talking either. Get naked and bang it out! That's all the talking y'all need to do. Keep all that old mess out your head and take your ass to the moon!"

Jade hugged her friend and kissed her cheek then drove home with the biggest smile on her face. She had just enough time to change into Pierce's favorite lingerie, light the fireplace, and arrange for Hawn to get the kids from school. Jade smiled when she heard a knock and ran to open the door. It most definitely was not who she was expecting!

"Jesus," Jade uttered, as she closed her silk robe to cover the yellow lace panties and bra she was wearing. It was the story of her life. Every time Jade thought things were going to work out, someone or something popped up and proved her wrong.

"Mrs. Jamison, wait, please don't close the door. I really need to talk to you," Regina pled.

Thirty minutes later there was another knock on the door and Jade opened it to a huge bouquet of yellow roses. Pierce was confused by the look on her face. He knew they still needed to work through some things but he seriously thought she was ready to reconcile. Then he saw what had caused Jade to change her mind.

"Get the hell out of here!" Pierce barked, as he pulled Regina up from the couch. "What part of stay out of our lives don't you understand?"

"Pierce, please, I'm sorry, okay? I just wanted ..."

"Get out and don't you *ever* come here again!" he shouted and slammed the door behind her. "Well, I guess that's it for me, isn't it?" Pierce asked then he sat the vase of flowers on the table and pulled the envelope out of his back pocket again. "I just can't catch a damn break!"

He searched for an ink pen and found one on the new entertainment center. Pierce unfolded the divorce papers and scribbled his signature on it.

"There you go."

"Thank you," Jade said then ripped the papers in half. She tossed the shreds into the fireplace. Pierce looked bewildered when she walked over to him and caressed his face. "I still love you. I forgive you. And I want you to come home," Jade smiled sweetly, repeating the words he'd asked her to say months before.

Despite being incredibly confused, Pierce swept her up in his arms and carried her to their bedroom. That time he had no problems getting Jade to the moon!

"Hi, Daddy!" Pooh beamed then pounced on her father's chest.

"Oooh!" Pierce grunted, holding her with one arm while tucking the sheet around him with the other.

"Did you have a sleep over with Mommy?" she asked, running her little fingers through his wild hair.

"Umm huh," he uttered.

"Dane, Pooh, come get your breakfast," Jade called.

Breakfast? Pierce thought.

"Bye, Daddy, see you later," Pooh sang then kissed his face before running out of the room.

Pierce was about to get up then pulled the sheet back over his naked body when Dane came to the door.

"Hey, Dad, what's up? You good?"

"Yeah, I'm good," Pierce smiled at his handsome little man. "Let me get up and get dressed and I'll come out to talk to you, okay?"

"Okay," Dane smiled. He was happy to see Pierce back in his own bed. "Love you, Dad."

"I love you too, son," he grinned. "I'll see you in a few minutes, okay?"

When Pierce looked at the digital clock on his nightstand he thought it was seven thirty at night. He couldn't believe he'd been asleep for nearly sixteen hours! He took a quick shower, brushed his teeth, and joined his family in the kitchen.

"Hey there sleepy head, are you hungry?"

"I'm starving, believe it or not," Pierce said.

He stood behind his wife and wrapped his arms around her waist. He planted kisses on Jade's neck and told her he loved her.

Dane and Pooh giggled at the sight. They loved seeing their parents happy again.

"So why didn't you wake me, babe?"

"You were sleeping so peacefully I didn't wanna disturb you."

"I *was* at peace just being home. Thank you. It's the first time I've really slept in months."

The four of them talked over breakfast before Jade took Dane and Pooh to school. Pierce was waiting in front of the fireplace when she returned.

"I was hoping maybe we could have a confessional. Let's put everything out on the table so they'll be no secrets, no questions, no nothing to get in the way of our marriage moving forward. Is that cool?"

"Yeah, that's cool. Just let me get a cup of coffee. You want one?" she asked then fixed them both a cup.

The first thing Pierce wanted to know was what happened with Regina. He thought for sure their marriage was over when he found her in the house. Jade explained to him what happened. That was actually the second time Regina had tried to talk to her. However, it was what she blurted before Jade closed the door that made her finally decide to hear the woman out.

"We didn't have sex," Regina had shouted.

Jade stared at her for a moment making sure she'd heard correctly. Then she allowed Regina inside. Jade offered her a seat on the couch before taking a seat in the lazy boy. Then she stared at the woman waiting on her to say something. Regina swallowed hard and fidgeted before anything came out of her mouth.

"I can imagine this is as uncomfortable for you as it is for me but I need to be candid with you. I just can't take the guilt anymore and I know it's the reason everything is so messed up in my life. I lost my job and I'm about to be evicted from my apartment. My hair is falling out by the clumps," Regina said, as she touched her knit cap self-consciously, "and my stomach hurts all the time. I was just gonna move and start over somewhere else, but I don't think anything will ever go right in my life until I come clean."

Jade took a deep breath trying to prepare herself for what Regina was about to say.

"The night of your daughter's party I was parked at the gas station directly across from Quik Stop. I did that quite a bit since it was the only way I could see him," Regina admitted. "But that night I could tell something was wrong with Pierce. He was stumbling and dropped his keys a few times trying to lock the store. I couldn't believe he was actually about to drive so I pulled up next to his car and got out. Pierce recognized me but he was talking so crazy that it was hard to understand what he was trying to say. So I told him to give me his keys and I'd take him home." Regina dropped her head and began to fidget again.

"I helped him get into my car and I, uh, I kissed him when I leaned over to fasten his seat belt."

Jade could feel her blood start to boil but she managed to keep her composure so Regina would finish talking.

"I was driving in the direction of your home but I decided to turn around and go to mine instead. I was leading Pierce up to my apartment when he started *screaming* your name! The only way I could get him to shut up was by promising you were on your way to get him. Once we got inside he was stumbling all over the place trying to find you. Even as drunk as he was Pierce knew he didn't belong there. All he wanted to do was to get to you. And I'm embarrassed to say it but that made me mad. I wanted him to pay attention to me for once but all he wanted was you."

Tears filled Jade's eyes as she recalled how Pierce had tried so hard to tell her he would never intentionally hurt her. He and everyone else tried desperately to convince her that Regina was not who he wanted. And Jade refused to even consider his innocence. She refused to listen or try to get to the truth. Those tears ran down her face as she gave her attention back to Regina.

Tears ran down Regina's cheeks. "He never wanted me, Jade, not sober *or* drunk. Even in the delirious state Pierce was in he only wanted you. And like a jealous fool, I hated you for that. So when Pierce woke up I put on this big act and made him think we had spent the night making wild, passionate love to each other. I honestly thought if he believed he'd done it once he would do it again, especially after you two broke up. I felt so desperate that I was even tempted to invent a pregnancy just to get some attention from him. But once I got over being angry, the guilt started to eat me alive," Regina whimpered, as she wiped tears from her face. "I'm so sorry. All Pierce ever did was befriend me and I messed up his life because I wanted something that didn't belong to me. I saw how much he adores you and I wanted some of his love for myself. I'm so sorry. I know you hate me and I don't blame you. I just couldn't leave without telling you the truth."

Before Jade had the chance to respond to Regina, Pierce showed up and threw her out.

"What are you thinking?" Jade asked after she'd finished telling him what happened.

"Wow, I'm shocked she would do something like that. But I'm also relieved to know the truth. I believed in my heart I hadn't done anything but the evidence said otherwise. I am curious about one thing, though. Is she the reason I'm sitting here right now?"

"No, she's not the reason, Pierce. I had already forgiven you and decided to be a family again. You can call Tamara right now and ask her if you need to. I went to her house after I left Priscilla."

"I don't need to call Tamara. I believe you," Pierce said then kissed her tenderly. "Thank you," he smiled and kissed her again. "Now it's time to put all cards on the table. Do you have anything to confess to me?"

Jade let out a deep breath. "Yes. And I can only hope you'll be more forgiving than I was."

Pierce's heart started beating wildly wondering if their reconciliation was going to be short lived.

Chapter

THIRTY ONE

JADE TOLD PIERCE HOW stupid she felt when she opened the door in her underwear expecting to see him and found Regina. "I guess that's what I get for all the games I played with you?"

"What did you do?" Pierce frowned.

"Well, remember that night I came out wearing the little black dress?"

"Yeah?"

"I didn't go to any party. After you left with the kids I went to get something to eat and I had Landon drop me back off at home. I parked my van in his garage because I *knew* you were gonna pop back in to see when I got home. I was actually in our room when you opened the garage. I turned the TV off so you wouldn't see any lights on just in case you came inside. But you closed the garage back once you didn't see the minivan. Then the next day I walked over to Landon's to get it. He didn't realize it but I actually sprayed some of his cologne on my dress and in my hair."

"Are you *kidding* me?"

"Nope, I'm dead serious. Then I waited in the garage with the door open to make you think I was just getting in. I walked by you on purpose just to make sure you smelled the cologne. I never considered that doing something like that would contribute to you and Landon beating the hell out of each other! All I was thinking about was hurting you and making you feel as bad as I did."

"Damn, Jade, you must have really hated me."

"Actually it was the opposite. I still loved you but I was mad and wanted to punish you. Who would go through all that trouble for somebody they

216

really hated? Who would pretend to be talking to some man on the phone just to watch you go wild?"

"So that night our son was crying and all upset because his father had lost control you weren't even talking to anybody?"

"No," Jade said and dropped her head.

Once again she had been so focused on her own hurt that she didn't think about how her actions were hurting other people. Pierce and Landon probably wouldn't have beaten each other and Dane and Pooh wouldn't have been as upset as they were if Jade had chosen not to play games.

"I'm sorry," she uttered. "I really wasn't thinking about anything other than hurting you. I didn't realize other people were getting hurt in the process. I'm sorry, Pierce."

"That's jacked up, Jade," Pierce said. "But I'm kind of turned on knowing you still loved me enough to do all that crazy mess. I was definitely losing my mind behind it, though, I can't lie. I probably owe 24 Hour Fitness a new punching bag because I beat the stuffing out the one they got! "Why you do me like that, girl?"

Jade confessed all the other things she had done to torture him including intentionally leaving a corner of the condoms sticking out of her nightstand for him to find. However, Jade forgot about it. When Pierce actually did see the condoms it was the last thing in the world she wanted to happen! They were in the process of reconciling and Jade was done with the games. Unfortunately, that one backfired and nearly cost her everything she wanted.

"That's just *evil*, Jade. You know that, don't you?"

"Yeah, I know and I'm not proud of it. I was hurt and lost and I made a lot of decisions that I regret."

"What haven't you told me?" Pierce asked when Jade's eyes filled with tears. His heart dropped. "It's gonna hurt me, isn't it?"

"Yeah," Jade uttered.

"Alright, just tell me," Pierce said, nervously.

"Yesterday before you went to sleep you talked about us having another baby but I can't."

"Oh, babe, I wasn't talking about right now. I meant later on like in a year or two."

"Pierce, listen to me. I'm trying to tell you I can't have more children."

He rolled his eyes at her and folded his arms across his chest. "So you went ahead and got your tubes tied, huh?" he huffed then stared at her for a while.

"No, I didn't. I had a hysterectomy, Pierce."

"Wooow," he said, still unable to believe what he'd heard. "That's some kind of hatred you got there, Jade."

"Don't think that, Pierce."

"What am I supposed to think then? *Love* didn't make you do something this drastic!" he snapped. "You hate me."

"Okay, before you go and make this all about *you,* consider a few facts. First of all, no one can just walk up in a doctor's office and say hey, give me a hysterectomy! There has to be some medical reason for it. As you well know, my uterus was full of big, painful fibroids that had me nearly hemorrhaging every month. Remember The Menace? So I did the hormone therapy and other treatments to try to shrink the fibroids and control the bleeding. Having a hysterectomy was the last resort but it *was* an option."

"So you're trying to tell me what happened with us had *nothing* to do with your decision?"

"It had a lot to do with it. And I felt guilty afterwards because I shouldn't have made the decision out of anger. *But,* I know I would have made the same choice at some point."

"I guess that's what's so hurtful. You made the choice without me," Pierce said. "So you went through it all by yourself?" he asked and held her hand.

"No, my mom was there and she took care of me for those days I was gone. She tried to convince me to wait at least until things between you and I were worked out. But at the time I didn't think that was possible."

"So what made you feel guilty because you sound pretty happy with your decision?"

"I felt guilty because my doctor presented me with one other option to have another baby and *then* do the surgery. And a month or two after Sugar died I did think about it. But after I got those tests results in the mail I never wanted to have kids with you again."

"So do you wish we could have a baby now?"

"Honestly, no, I don't. I think it was grief that made me even consider it. As I said before when I talked to you about getting my tubes tied, I don't wanna be pregnant again. And it's not like having another child will replace Sugar. I want the child I had back, not a new one. I'm sorry," Jade said, as she squeezed Pierce's hand. "I wasn't trying to hurt you by saying that. I just meant in my grief I thought having a baby to hold again would somehow take away the pain. But I miss Sugar and nothing can stop that. I'll always miss her."

Pierce took Jade into his arms and they cuddled up on the couch together. Neither of them said a word, they just held each other. And there the decision was made to leave the past behind and move forward in their marriage and life.

Saturday, February 12ᵗʰ turned into a celebration at Luisa's house. The family got together for dinner and tears and hugs were in abundance as everyone welcomed Jade home. And it wasn't long before they all realized what the house had been missing . It was her laughter. She filled whatever room she was in with it and it was infectious. Jade danced, talked smack with her father-in-law during a few games of spades, and just enjoyed being with her family again. She really had missed them and was glad to be back where she belonged.

It was a little after nine when everyone left Luisa's house. Pierce and Jade took eight-month-old Xavier home with them so Roland and Hawn could have some alone time. They were working to give him a little brother or sister!

"Alright, little boy, get off my wife," Pierce teased.

Jade was in their bed cradling Xavier while she gave him a bottle. Dane and Pooh were next to her watching TV and Teddy was on the floor watching them. The next thing they knew Pierce was snapping pictures. It was pointless to complain because he was just going to keep taking them. Pooh loved it and she smiled and posed until her father finally put the camera away.

After Jade had burped and changed the baby, Pierce and the kids played with him on the bed. Xavier loved them and found everything they did funny. His laughter was so sweet and it made Jade laugh too. Then her eyes filled with tears as she looked at her husband, the kids, and Teddy too. Seven months before, she didn't think it was possible to feel happy again. Jade thought she'd be sad and miserable forever and it felt wonderful to have laughter and joy in her home again--in her heart again.

Chapter
THIRTY TWO

JADE WAS EXCITED TO have one of her infamous group dates and invited a few couples over for Valentine's Day. Everyone was shocked when Marcus arrived with Sheila on his arm. After the last date no one thought they'd ever see each other again. They would've been surprised to learn Marcus was actually considering marrying her because he'd given up hope of ever finding his one true love.

During dinner and drinks, they all laughed and enjoyed each other's company. It wasn't until Marcus made one of his usual unnecessary comments that the mood changed.

"Man, I know you glad you didn't do old girl or you would've missed out on all this great food. Cinderelly can cook," Marcus laughed.

"Give me this," Tamara said, as she took his glass. "You don't need nothing else to drink."

Everybody seemed to accept the fact that Marcus was drunk and resumed their conversations—everyone but the hosts. Pierce and Jade were upset but for very different reasons. It was quite clear from Marcus calling Jade Cinderelly that he had knowledge of her and Pierce's private life. Jade assumed her husband had told him about her glass stilettos and the joke she'd made about the little mice singing in the movie. They called Cinderella Cinderelly and that's what Pierce called Jade anytime she wore the glass shoes. There was no way someone could've guessed that.

Pierce knew Marcus hadn't guessed it either and felt sick once he remembered leaving the tape at his apartment. Jade went to the kitchen to get the cheesecake she'd made for dessert and asked Pierce to join her.

"I swear it's not what you think, babe," he whispered as soon as they were alone.

Jade dropped the serving utensils she was holding and covered her face when Pierce told her about the tape. She was so embarrassed that she didn't want to go back into the dining room. She knew *exactly* what was on that tape and the thought of Marcus seeing her in that way made Jade cringe!

"Why in the hell did you have it at his house in the first place?" Jade snapped.

"I'm so sorry, babe," he said, with a disgusted look on his face. "I took the tapes and the pictures so you wouldn't destroy them. I needed to feel close to you and that's all I had. I'm sorry, Jade, but I'll get the tape back."

"Plggh! What good is that gonna do now? He's already seen it who knows how many times so it's not like taking the tape is gonna erase his memory. Ugh," she cringed as another memory of what she'd done on it filled her mind. "I could *kill* you!" Jade said before she realized Dane had come into the kitchen for dessert. The look on his face was heartbreaking. "Oh, baby, don't worry. We're not breaking up again. I'm just upset but it's nothing to worry about, okay? I promise," she said then kissed his face.

Pierce hugged Dane and reassured him everything was fine. Then he helped his son serve dessert to the kids in the sunroom. Jade served the adults and was thrilled when Sheila announced she was taking Marcus home. Without making eye contact, Jade said goodbye and hightailed it to the kitchen to load the dishwasher.

"Beauty queen, what's wrong with you?"

Hawn came in carrying the dirty glasses and was curious to know what was wrong with Jade too. She'd assumed it was the mention of Regina that had her sister-in-law upset and nearly peed herself from laughing when she found out about the tape.

"What the hell is funny about that?" Jade asked when both Hawn and Tamara laughed hysterically.

"Oh, come on, beauty queen, you know damn well you'd be laughing if I told you somebody watched me and Jamel doing something freaky," Tamara said, as she nudged Jade. "Yeah, it's embarrassing but we all do it, so quit tripping. Marcus watched the tape like any one of us would've did in the same situation. I know I would've watched just to see what y'all be doing. And you can stand there and act all appalled if you want to but I know you would've watched if you had found a tape of one of us. Admit it."

Hawn didn't want to see her brother in action but said she would've watched everybody else. Jade didn't verbally agree but the look on her face was enough for them to know she would've spied on them too. Eventually she laughed at some of their jokes about the kind of stuff they imagined her doing on the tape. They were talking and laughing so much that Jade didn't realize Pierce had left.

"Is something wrong, Pierce? What are you doing here?" Sheila asked, as he walked by her.

"He knows why I'm here," Pierce said to his drunken friend who was sprawled out on the couch. "Where is it?"

Marcus stared at his friend through half opened, red eyes and pointed to the guest room. Pierce stormed out of the living room to retrieve the tape from the VCR.

"This is the only copy, right?"

"Yeah."

Pierce stood there staring at Marcus debating whether to pummel him or not. "I don't ever wanna see you again," he stated then headed for the door.

"Pierce, wait, I'm sorry. I didn't mean …"

"What's going on?" Sheila asked after Pierce slammed the door shut.

"Just go home," Marcus sneered then turned over to hide his tears.

Jade had talked Pierce into having a party for his thirty-second birthday. Luisa volunteered to cook dinner at her house and then Jade was planning to steal the birthday boy away for one of her infamous private shows.

"Here you go," she said, handing him an invitation. "I thought you could drop this one off personally."

"I hope this is a joke," Pierce said, handing the invitation back. "I told Marcus I never wanted to see him again and I meant it."

"So you really gone throw away a twenty-five year friendship over that?"

"Oh, so now *I'm* the one tripping? A week ago you were all bent out of shape about it but now everything's cool? What, you like knowing he saw you?" Pierce frowned at her.

"See, now you going way out in left field somewhere. *No,* I don't like knowing Marcus saw me. It's embarrassing as hell. That was supposed to be something private between you and me. But it's over, Pierce, and I don't think you should throw away a friendship, especially knowing that if the situation were reversed you would've watched the tape too. Don't even try it, dude," she said when he started to object. "Are you really trying to tell me that as nosey as you are, if a tape of Marcus getting down with one of his women popped on you wouldn't watch it?"

"Nope! Why in the world would I wanna see him have sex? I mean, he's my boy and everything but I don't need to know him like that."

"But, babe …"

"Look, I'll be for real with you. If that tape had been of me and some random chick I probably would've watched it with him. But you're my *wife*, Jade, and that's a line that never should have been crossed. I don't care if it was my fault for leaving it there. Marcus never should've watched it out of respect for me."

"When you and I were going through our junk you asked me if one mistake could undo everything we had."

"Oh, geez, why you always do this? I wanna be mad right now. I don't wanna be forgiving," Pierce pouted.

"It's hurts when someone you love won't forgive you, doesn't it?"

"Okay, okay, shut up!" Pierce kissed her then snatched the invitation out of her hand. "The things I do for your love," he chuckled. "Before I go, I just want it acknowledged that you manipulated me and …"

"Get your butt out of here," Jade giggled.

"Why you looking at my butt?" he asked and stuck it out at her provocatively.

"You so stupid," Jade laughed loudly.

Pierce laughed as he put on his coat. "I'll be back in a little bit. Then I'll let you touch it." After a quick kiss he drove to Logan High School.

"Mr. Moala, you have a visitor," the office clerk said.

Marcus turned around and was shocked to see Pierce.

"I didn't know what time you took lunch but I was hoping maybe we could grab something right quick."

The two of them made idle chit chat during the three minute drive to Subway. Before they got out, though, Pierce told Marcus what was on his mind.

"Look, man, I don't wanna get into a long, drawn out scene about what happened. I'm upset that you watched the tape but it's pointless to keep harping on it. You're my boy and I love you and I don't wanna lose you over no mess like that. So I say let's put it behind us and move forward, cool?"

"Cool," Marcus said and shook Pierce's outstretched hand. "I'm so sorry, dawg."

"I know. So come on let's get some of these sandwiches 'cause I'm starving."

February 25th was Pierce's thirty-second birthday. And as planned, after the big family dinner, Jade stole him away for a private celebration back at their house. Once again Pierce was mesmerized and couldn't wait to get his hands on Jade.

"I love you so much," Pierce whispered, as he and Jade lay entangled in their bed. "And I've been trying to think of a way to express that to you."

"Oh, you expressed it *very* well, Butterscotch," Jade smiled, "very well indeed."

"Yeah, but I think I can do better." He rolled over to retrieve something out of his nightstand. Then Pierce knelt beside their bed. "I love you and I wanna spend the rest of my life showing you just how much. So I need to ask you something," he said, opening the lid on the ring box. "Jade Elise Jamison, will you marry me ... again?"

Just like the first time he proposed, Jade was too stunned to speak. She didn't think there was anything more beautiful than the ring he'd given her five years ago. However, the huge five-carat diamond sparkler Pierce was holding out in front of her changed her mind.

"Are you serious, babe?" Jade smiled with tears in her eyes. "You really wanna marry me again?"

"Of course I do, he said removing her original ring and replacing it with the new one. Pierce kissed her hand then climbed back in bed with her. "And we're gonna do it up big this time. I want all that stuff ... bridesmaids, veils, flowers—the whole nine."

"*Seriously?*"

"Yes! And don't worry about the expense of it either. Laila can pay for it," he chuckled.

"Oh, she can, huh?" Jade laughed. "Well, we do have a year to plan."

"No we don't."

"Oh, we don't? And why is that?"

"I want you to have your dream wedding, babe, the beautiful summer one you described to Hawn. Your birthday falls on a Saturday so I think that's when we should have it. Then from now on we'll have two anniversaries to celebrate each year. So what do you say? Are you game?"

"Are you sure you really wanna do this because planning weddings ain't no joke?"

"I'm positive. I want you to get on my nerves talking about color patterns and flowers and junk. And then you can complain about how I'm not helping and you feel like you're planning the wedding by yourself. That's part of the experience we missed out on the first time around when you manipulated me into eloping," he teased.

Jade just shook her head and laughed. "You ain't got it all, you know that?"

"Yeah, well you married me and you about to do it again," Pierce said and kissed that spot on her neck. "I only have one request as far as the wedding goes. I wanna choose the song you walk down the aisle on. Actually I've already chosen it."

"What is it?"

"You'll see when you walk down the aisle."

"Pierce, that's not right."

He kissed her before she could fuss about it. "Okay, let's play honeymoon. Let me practice."

"*Trust* me, babe, you don't need practice. You got it like that," she smiled and fully participated in playing honeymoon.

With only five months to plan, Jade jumped into it with both feet. She and Pierce chose The Fremont Golf and Country Club to have the wedding and reception. They also chose to keep their wedding party small and the guest count at two hundred. Jade knew there would be hurt feelings but she wanted to alleviate as much stress for her and Pierce as possible. Unfortunately, she couldn't get rid of it all. Jade didn't expect to have drama over who would walk her down the aisle, but she did.

"Babe, what's wrong?" Pierce asked when he came home for lunch and found her near tears on the couch.

"I think I should just walk down the aisle by myself."

"Why?"

"Because somebody's gonna be hurt no matter who I choose. My dad just called saying he got the save the date card and how happy he is to finally get to walk me down the aisle. And that came after both Justin and your dad assumed they'd be doing it. I don't know what to do, babe. I don't wanna hurt either one of them."

"Who do you want to walk you down the aisle?"

Jade stared at him momentarily before answering. "Landon."

"Then that's who should be doing it. Don't you let these folks upset you, you hear me? This is our day and it's gonna be exactly the way we want it to be," Pierce said, as he sat next to Jade and held her hand. "I personally don't think your father deserves that honor. And I don't know what my dad is even talking about. He'll be with me anyway so forget about him. I know Justin would love to do it but he's just gonna have to get over it. Besides, he has a special role in the wedding so he'll be fine. Now come on and eat lunch with me and quit worrying about these grown men."

Pierce laughed and talked over a big bowl of chili not letting on how anxious the idea of seeing Landon again made him. They hadn't seen or spoken to each other since the fight and he wasn't exactly sure what to say. One thing was for sure, though. Pierce wanted to resolve whatever remaining tension there was between them before the big day. He didn't want anything to get in the way of giving Jade her dream wedding. So if he had to apologize for giving Landon a beating he still believed he deserved then he would do it, for the love of Jade.

Chapter

THIRTY THREE

It was the second week in March when Jade went to choose her dress. Willa, Luisa, Hawn, Tamara, and Eva met her at Belle's Bridal in Fremont. With all of the emotions in the room a person would assume Jade was getting married for the first time. When she came out of the dressing room Willa and Luisa were already crying.

"Y'all need to stop," Jade said, trying to fight back her own tears.

Jade's bridal consultant Anjalise helped her up on the platform and fluffed the dress. "This one is a strapless taffeta gown with a sweetheart neckline and trumpet bottom skirt. The bodice is decorated with hand made flowers with a lace up back and ..."

"Why is she saying all that?" Tamara leaned over to whisper to Hawn.

"Girl, I don't know," Hawn whispered back.

Then the two of them giggled about how little the consultant was. She was barely five feet and probably a size two. The wedding dresses looked like they were going to swallow her whole when she pulled them from the racks.

"So what do you guys think?" Jade asked once Anjalise had finished her description.

The women looked one to the other.

"It's pretty," Eva said.

"I like the shape of the dress but, I don't know," Tamara said. "This one just don't seem like the *one*."

"I agree. But it's a good start," Hawn stated.

Jade went back to the dressing room to try on a second dress when she heard a commotion out front.

"What are you doing here?" Luisa snapped. "This is no place for you!"

"Hold on, ladies, don't beat me," Marcus said, holding his hands up in surrender. "I'm just the messenger. My boy wanted me to bring this to his bride."

He handed an envelope to Willa and was about to leave when Anjalise stopped him dead in his tracks! Jade had sent her out to see what all the noise was about not expecting the woman to have a love at first sight moment.

"Uh, what's this child's name?" Luisa asked. "Little wedding girl, you need to help Jade with her dress."

"Oh my god, I'm sorry," Anjalise said once she finally came back from la la land. "Let me go help her."

"I'm Marcus Moala," he said.

"Anjalise Moala," she winked and shook his outstretched hand.

"What? They *related*?" Hawn shrieked.

"No, fool, she being funny. She saying they gone get married," Tamara explained. "Girl, you be slow sometimes."

"Well, I guess I'm slow too 'cause I didn't get it either," Eva laughed.

After accepting Marcus's business card and saying goodbye, Anjalise finally went back to the dressing room to help Jade then they came out and stood on the platform.

"Okay, ladies, this is a strapless …"

"Nope," Tamara interrupted. "We don't even need to waste time with this one. It's not it."

The rest of the women agreed, including Jade, and she went back to the dressing room. When she came out the third time, however, it was no question she'd found her dress. All of them were crying, even Anjalise.

"That's the *one*, beauty queen!"

Jade smiled at herself in the mirror as she turned and swayed in the dress. It was a diamond white, strapless A-line gown with a trumpet bottom and sweetheart neckline. It had a lace up back and 72" train. Soutache and hand embroidered flowers decorated the dress that fit Jade's body perfectly. There was no need for alterations.

"How much is it?" she asked.

"Don't worry about it," Willa interjected before Anjalise could answer. "My son-in-law sent over a blank check for you to get whatever you want. So gone and take that tag off, Anjalise, and hand it here."

Willa knew her daughter would have put the dress back despite how perfect it was for her if she saw the thirty-two hundred dollar price tag on it. So they all ignored her rants about not wanting to spend too much and helped her find the perfect veil. The one they agreed on was a 30"x36" diamond white veil with bugle bead, sequin, and pearl edge. When Anjalise showed

Jade the headpiece she thought would be perfect, tears instantly sprang to all of their eyes. It was silver with yellow highlights and the design was in the shape of a butterfly. It was subtle, delicate, and the most beautiful thing Jade had ever seen. She stopped fussing about the money or anything else as she stood staring at herself in the perfect dress and veil. She couldn't wait for Pierce to see her in it.

The months seemed to fly by and the planning, for the most part, was stress free. The hardest part was probably when Pierce and Jade had to decide how to acknowledge Sugar at their wedding. At the Mothers' Day brunch Miguel had arranged, Luisa suggested putting a picture of Sugar at the altar. Then her daughters chimed in with suggestions of their own. Jade felt overwhelmed and Pierce told his family that he and his wife would decide what to do. Later that evening, Jade admitted how she was feeling.

"I hope it doesn't sound horrible but I don't want pictures of our baby at the wedding. I just feel like it will be more like a funeral if we put a big picture of Sugar at the altar. Everybody's gonna start remembering her death and that's not what I want on that day. Do you know what I mean?" Jade asked. "Obviously we're never gonna forget Sugar. I just don't think it's necessary to have a picture or reserve a chair or anything like that. I have my own special way of having her with me that day and I'd like to keep it that way if you don't mind."

"I don't mind at all. I totally agree," he said, pulling Jade into his arms.

June 29, 2000 marked the one year anniversary of Sugar's death. Pierce and Jade went to her gravesite and mourned together in a way they hadn't the year before. It was heart wrenching but bearable because they had each other to lean on. Everyone was a mess at the dinner Luisa had put together as they all remembered Sugar and wept over the fact that it had been a whole year without her. Later in the evening Pierce and Jade along with their family and friends released pink balloons into the sky and watched until they were no longer visible. It was definitely a sad day and their hearts were heavy with grief. Before departing, however, Pierce reminded everyone that the wedding would be a day of joy and celebration and only happy tears were allowed.

"So get all your sadness out now," he said and wiped tears from his face, "because we're gonna party that day."

The week before the wedding Jade made a request that Pierce wouldn't even consider.

"Girl, you must be out your mind!" Pierce said, as he stared at her in disbelief.

"Ah, come on, babe, you said you wanted the whole experience, right? You can do it."

"It's not an issue of whether I *can* do it, I don't want to! Shoot, now that The Menace is gone I get loving every night and you want me to hold out for a *week*? Uh, uh," he shook his head. "I was planning to do it in the limo on the way *to* the wedding so that whole abstinence thing ain't gonna happen. Sorry, but that's one experience I can do without repeating. I couldn't get none for six months the first time around when you made me marry you before you gave it up. I ain't doing it again. As a matter of fact," Pierce said and threw her over his shoulder.

Jade screamed and laughed as he carried her to their bedroom and had his way with her. The same thing happened each night leading up to their special day. They even made love right before Pierce was supposed to leave to get ready with his boys.

"Juan, get your ass out of here," Hawn fussed when she, Eva, and Tamara arrived to help Jade get ready.

"I'll see you at the altar," Pierce kissed her tenderly. "I love you, Mrs. Jamison."

"I love you too."

Pierce and Dane left for Luisa's house where his groomsmen; Marcus, Tony, and Roland were having breakfast. Jackie and Justin were there as well since Jade had all of the tuxes and accessories set up the night before so no one forgot anything. All of Pierce's groomsmen and the ushers had black tuxes, white shirts, and yellow vests and bowties. The groom had the same accessories but his tux was white.

"Damn, dawg, you crying already?" Marcus teased after Pierce opened the gift and card Jade had left for him.

"No, dude, you ain't never seen somebody sweat before?" Pierce laughed, as he wiped tears from his face. "I wouldn't be laughing too much. Your turn is coming. September will be here before you know it," he said referring to Marcus and Anjalise's wedding.

"You okay, Dad?"

"I couldn't be better, little man. Now come on, let's get ready. I've got a beautiful woman waiting for me," Pierce said, as he fastened the diamond watch Jade had given him around his wrist.

The contrast between the men and women was comical. Pierce and his groomsmen were laughing and toasting to the future while Jade and her bridesmaids were bawling their eyes out! Willa and Luisa each presented her with a sentimental gift and said the sweetest things to her. Then Hawn gave Jade the gift from Pierce. Strangely enough, it was a diamond watch with the same inscription she'd had engraved on his, "For the love of my life". When

Jade told the women about it they cried even more. Thankfully they were able to pull it together by the time the make-up artists arrived.

"You all look so beautiful," Jade said as she handed out the white rose bouquets.

Her matron of honor Tamara and bridesmaids Hawn and Eva each wore a yellow strapless, floor length gown with a sweetheart neckline. Tamara's eight-year-old daughter Jamara was the junior bridesmaid and she wore a similar, shorter version of the dress with spaghetti straps. Pooh looked like a living doll in her big, poofy white flower girl's dress that she'd been twirling in for hours. And Willa and Luisa both wore long, yellow gowns that accentuated their school-girl figures.

"Look at them. That don't make no sense," Tamara teased the two mothers for looking sexier than the rest of them.

By eleven o'clock the photographer was snapping the last pictures of them as they climbed into the limo. Some of Jade's neighbors came out to wish her well and tell her how beautiful she looked. Then they were off to the country club. Jade hired a planner named Shay to manage everything for the day of the ceremony and had stressed how important it was for things to start on time. At one o'clock whoever wasn't seated would be waiting outside until Jade took her stroll down the aisle.

"Oooh, *ba*-by," Tamara groaned. "You looking kind of fine, Mr. Campbell. Chaundra better watch out," she said then embraced Landon. "I like this little beard and goatee thing you got going. You look hot!"

"Well, you know," Landon said then struck his best Ebony Man pose. They all laughed. "For real, though, thank you. All of you look stunning. I bet your men …"

Jade came out of the powder room and stopped Landon's heart! Her eyes instantly filled with tears as they stared at each other.

"Wow, baby girl, you look *so* beautiful," Landon said, as he tried to blink back tears.

"You look good, Landon, like a grown up," she giggled and fanned her face to keep from crying.

"Uncle Landon," Pooh sang when she and Willa walked in from getting a snack.

"Oh, Pooh bear look at you," he said before picking the girl up in his arms and squeezing her tight. "You look *so* pretty. Too bad I'm gonna have to kiss your face off," Landon teased as he planted kisses all over her face.

Pooh laughed loudly then gave him a big hug. "I miss you, Uncle Landon. How come you don't come play with me anymore?"

The look on her face broke Landon's heart and he was glad when Shay came to let them know it was time to start. He kissed Pooh once more then put her down so she could go line up for her big entrance. Willa gave Landon a hug and kiss then left to be escorted into the ceremony.

"So, you're ready?" Landon asked when he and Jade were alone.

"I'm nervous and I don't know why. It's not like we're getting married for the first time."

"Well, it's a new beginning, right? You and Pierce have been through a lot and you deserve to be happy. So I want you to enjoy every moment of this day. Isn't that what we used to tell our brides?" he smiled.

They stared at each other for a few moments and the tears began forming in their eyes again. Jade reached for her bouquet and a sad smile spread across Landon's face. It had beautiful crystal butterflies that looked like they were kissing the yellow roses.

"Are you okay with all of this?"

"Girl, quit tripping. I would've beat you down if you had somebody else walk you down the aisle," Landon laughed, as they made their way to the ceremony.

Jade laughed too. "Are you happy?"

"Yes, I'm happy," he smiled brightly.

Shay closed the door behind Pooh and motioned for Landon and Jade to take their places. One of the songs from Aladdin was playing but all Jade could hear were people saying how absolutely adorable Pooh looked. She walked down the aisle with the biggest, most infectious smile on her face and flashes were going off everywhere as many of their guest snapped pictures of her.

"Hi, Daddy. Do you like my dress?"

Laughter filled the room as Pooh ignored her flower girl duties and ran to her father's outstretched arms.

"You look beautiful, baby girl," Pierce knelt then gave her a hug and kiss. "I love you."

Pooh was beaming. "Mommy's dress is better than mine but that's 'cause she's the bride and I'm her little helper."

The entire room burst out laughing. Pierce kissed Pooh again then sent her to Luisa in the front row. She gave Dane a hug and kiss too before running to her grandma. Then the song Pierce had chosen for his bride began and he started bawling.

"Oh, lord," Willa said and began fanning her face. She swore she wasn't going to cry anymore but seeing Pierce break down was too much.

Tears instantly began to spill out of Jade's eyes when she heard her brother singing "The Love of My Life" by Brian McKnight. She knew Pierce had selected it because that's how he felt about her.

"Look, girl, don't make me push you down in this floor," Landon said when Jade wouldn't stop crying.

As expected, she laughed. Shay dabbed Jade's eyes with tissue and asked if she was ready for the doors to be opened.

"Here we go," Landon said as he lowered the blusher on her veil. He linked his arm with hers and for a brief moment wished he was the one standing at the other end of the aisle waiting for her. He pushed the thought from his mind knowing Jade was with the person she was meant to love and so was he.

"Everyone please rise," Luisa's minister instructed.

"Oh my god," Pierce said when he saw Jade for the first time. He was nearly inconsolable at that point.

Their entire wedding party was a blubbering mess by then, including the bride. Her heart was overflowing as she walked towards the love of her life. He smiled at her and Jade remembered the first time she'd ever laid eyes on him. She had known right then and there he was the one for her and she felt truly blessed to be sharing a life with him.

Just when Willa thought she couldn't cry anymore, Justin took a seat next to her and caressed her hand in both of his. He looked at her with tears rolling down his cheek and Willa mouthed I love you. He squeezed her hand then they turned their attention to Pierce and Jade.

"Who gives this woman to be married?"

Landon looked at Jade and smiled. "Her big brother does." He shook Pierce's hand then placed Jade's inside of it. "Take good care of her," he whispered.

With all eyes on the bride and groom, Landon left. He flew back to Santa Monica where Chaundra was waiting for him. He was anxious to give her the engagement ring he'd purchased the week before.

"I now pronounce you man and wife. You may kiss your bride."

Loud claps and cheers filled the room as Pierce caressed Jade's face and kissed her with all the passion he could muster.

"Okay, y'all, it's kids up in here," Hawn teased.

"Everyone please rise and help me welcome the new and improved, Mr. and Mrs. Pierce and Jade Jamison."

The bride and groom danced their way down the aisle with their guests dancing and cheering along with them. After an emotional ceremony, everyone was ready to eat, drink, and celebrate. The reception was everything Pierce and Jade dreamed it would be and they all had a ball. The guests were enjoying themselves so much that they didn't realize the bride and groom had left. It was only when Roland and his pregnant wife spotted Pierce and Jade on the lawn that a group of them watched through the picture windows wondering what on earth they were doing.

"So are you ready?" Pierce asked.

"Are *you* ready? You're the one about to get smoked," Jade laughed.

Both barefoot, the bride and groom got into a racing stance. When Pierce said go, they took off hand in hand across the lush, green lawn leaving the past behind and racing towards a future full of love, happiness, and many trips to the moon!